That Autumn in Edinburgh

CIJI WARE

THAT AUTUMN IN EDINBURGH. Copyright 2013 by Ciji Ware. All rights reserved under International and Pan-American Copyright Conventions. By payment of the required fees, you have been granted the non-exclusive, non-transferable right to access and read the text of this book, whether on screen or in print. No part of this text may be reproduced, transmitted, down-loaded, decompiled, reverse engineered, or stored in or introduced into any information storage and retrieval system, in any form or by any means, whether electronic or mechanical, now known or hereinafter invented, without the express written permission of Lion's Paw Publishing, a division of Life Events Media LLC.

The characters and events, real locations and real persons portrayed in this book are fictitious or are used fictitiously. Any similarity is not intended.

Cover design 2013 by **The Killion Group, Inc.**
Cover and colophon design by **Kim Killion.**
Photo credit of Abercromby Place, Edinburgh: **Tony Cook**
Formatting & copyediting **AThirstyMind.com**
ISBN: 978-0-9889408-3-3

Additional Library of Congress Cataloging-in-Publication Data available upon request.
1. Women's fiction 2. Scottish Woolen and Textile Industries – Scotland, U.K. 3. American Home Furnishing Design and Designers 4. Ancestors research 5. Scottish – American Genealogy. 6. Genetic Memory. 7. 21st century—Fiction. 8. Romantic Fiction

EBook Edition © November, 2013
Print Edition © December 2013

Published by Lion's Paw Publishing, a division of Life Events Media LLC, 1001 Bridgeway, Ste. 224, Sausalito, CA 94965.

Life Events Library and the Lion's Paw Publishing colophon are registered trademarks of Life Events Media LLC. All rights reserved. No part of this book may be reproduced in any form or by any electronic or mechanical means including information storage and retrieval systems—except in the case of brief quotations embodied in critical articles or reviews—without express permission in writing from its publisher, Lion's Paw Publishing / Life Events Library / Life Events Media LLC. Please respect this intellectual property of the author, cover artist, and photographer.

For information contact: **www.cijiware.com**

Praise for Ciji Ware's Contemporary and Historical Fiction

"A fascinating portrayal...with characters convincingly drawn...Ware again proves she can intertwine fact and fiction to create an entertaining and harmonious whole."
— PUBLISHERS WEEKLY

"...Fiction at its finest...beautifully written...a master storyteller.."
— LIBBY'S LIBRARY NEWS

"A mesmerizing blend of sizzling romance...love and honor...Ciji Ware has written an unforgettable tale."
— THE BURTON REVIEW

"A novel so lively and intriguing, you don't realize you've learned anything till after you close the book. Exciting, entertaining, and enlightening."
— LITERARY TIMES

"Ware gives readers a...novel that is hard to put down once started. This story can't be recommended enough."
— MAUDEEN WACHSMITH

"...A story so fascinating that it should come with a warning—do not start unless you want to be up all night!"
— ROMANTIC TIMES

"A well-researched and entertaining novel...excellent."
— LIBRARY JOURNAL

"...Intriguing characters, exciting dialogue, and a highly interesting woman at the center of it all...a must read."
— NIGHT OWL ROMANCE REVIEWER TOP PICK

"Ciji Ware has created a gorgeous tapestry...this is a"...A deep, complex novel exploring love, betrayal, healing, and renewal in the human heart."
— AFFAIRE DE COEUR

By CIJI WARE

Historical Novels

Island of the Swans
Wicked Company
A Race to Splendor

"Time-Slip" Historical Novels

A Cottage by the Sea
Midnight on Julia Street
A Light on the Veranda

Contemporary Novels

The Four Seasons Series

That Summer in Cornwall
That Autumn in Edinburgh

Nonfiction

Rightsizing Your Life
Joint Custody After Divorce

Coming Soon:

That Winter in Venice
That Spring in Paris

This novel is dedicated to:

The stalwart regulars—along with our occasional "drop-in" members—of the Women's Dog Walking Group whose friendship and camaraderie make this writer's life a lot less lonely on Tuesdays, Thursdays, and Saturdays…and a lot more fun!

FIONA MAXWELL FRASER

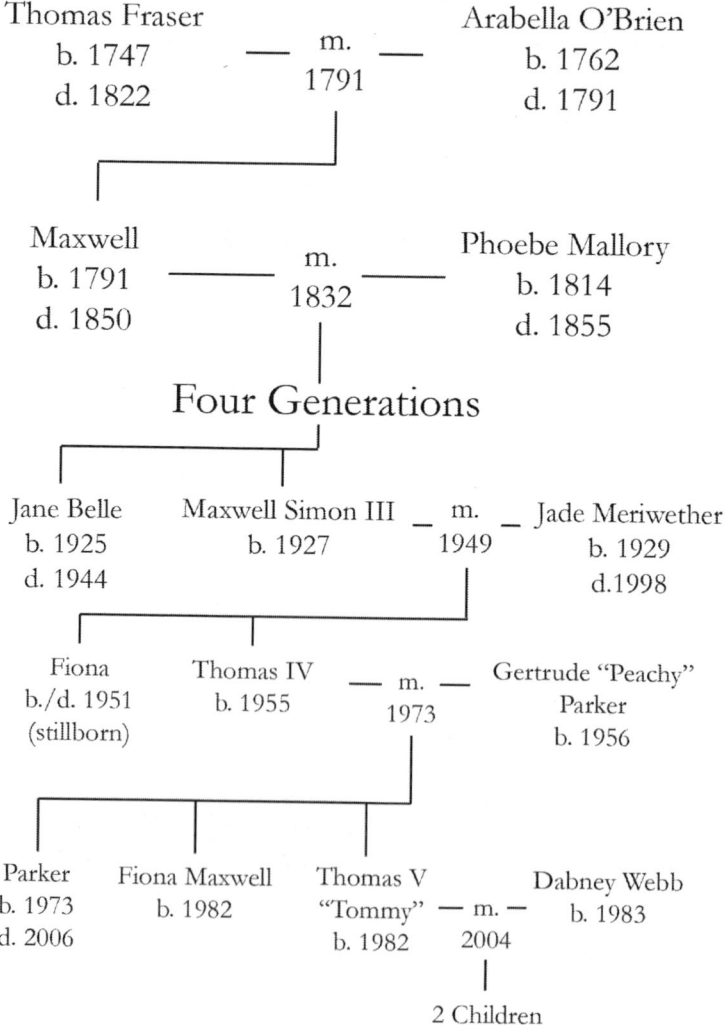

ALEXANDER MAXWELL

Descendants of the brother of Jane Maxwell, 4th Duchess of Gordon

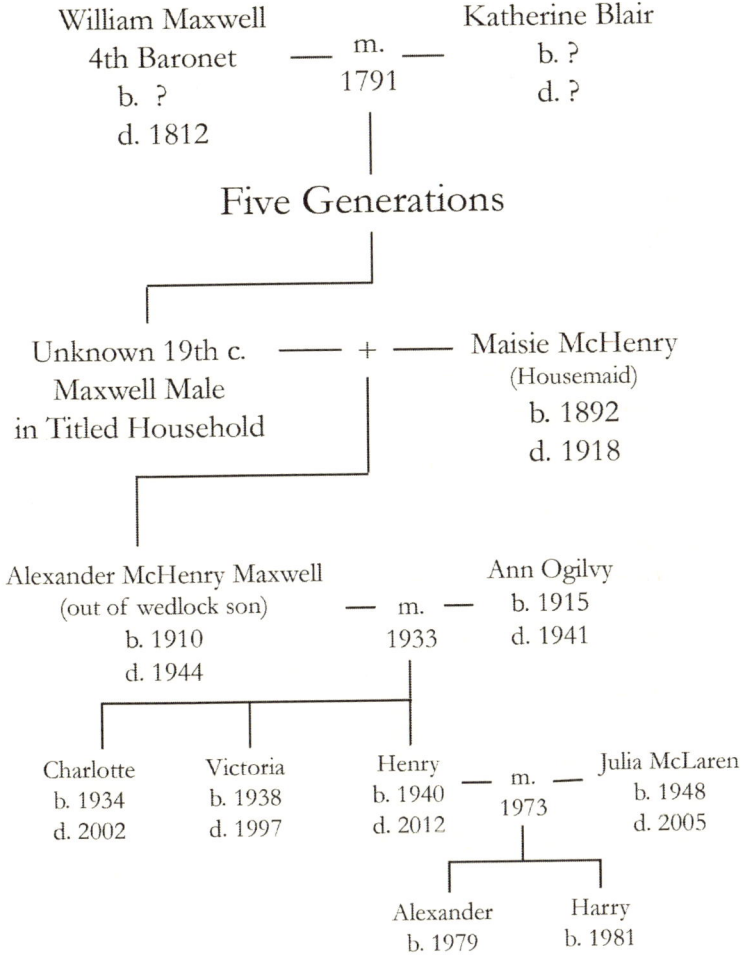

William Maxwell
4th Baronet
b. ?
d. 1812

— m. —
1791

Katherine Blair
b. ?
d. ?

Five Generations

Unknown 19th c.
Maxwell Male
in Titled Household

— + —

Maisie McHenry
(Housemaid)
b. 1892
d. 1918

Alexander McHenry Maxwell
(out of wedlock son)
b. 1910
d. 1944

— m. —
1933

Ann Ogilvy
b. 1915
d. 1941

Charlotte
b. 1934
d. 2002

Victoria
b. 1938
d. 1997

Henry
b. 1940
d. 2012

— m. —
1973

Julia McLaren
b. 1948
d. 2005

Alexander
b. 1979

Harry
b. 1981

The Gordons boldly did advance...
The Frasers fought with sword and lance.
— Anonymous

I Flourish Again...
— Clan Maxwell Motto

I Am Ready...
— Clan Fraser Motto

PROLOGUE

July 2009

"Jared, do you hear that?" exclaimed Fiona Fraser to her booth mate. "*Listen!*"

She craned her neck to see if she could spot the source of the earsplitting sounds suddenly filling the Jacob K. Javits Convention Center in mid-Manhattan.

Jared Finnegan clamped his hands over his ears and screwed up his face as if he were in pain.

"What in the *world?*" he shouted.

Fiona knew full well that the piercing whine of Scottish bagpipes either tended to send the heart soaring—or seriously set a person's teeth on edge. But as far as she was concerned, holding down the Bernard Sterling information counter at the annual Textiles Expo, her reaction to hearing the skirl of the pipes in such an unlikely place was one of pure joy—and amazement.

She strained to see if the building's security agents were in hot pursuit of whoever had burst into this professional gathering on a muggy, miserable, you-bet-there's-such-a-thing-as-Climate-Change, mid-summer New York day. In fact, she would have bet her brand-new degree from Parsons School of Design that there would be an instantaneous—to say nothing of a loud—howl of protest from the hundreds of fabric and furniture exhibitors whose booths lined row after row in the mammoth hall. She could imagine how these verbal objections would rival the intense, melancholy sounds of *The Skye Boat Song* that blared from an aisle some fifty yards from where Fiona stood passing out the Sterling firm's glossy brochures about their latest home furnishing lines to any attendees who would take them.

The great exhibition hall, with its dramatic glass-and-steel entrance and two-story ceiling, crisscrossed with black metal girders, only served to amplify the wailing sounds reverberating off the industrial light fixtures overhead.

As the source of the high-pitched music grew closer, Fiona had a sudden stab of childhood memory. In her mind's eye, she saw her father, decked out in his Clan Fraser kilt and swinging tartan sash affixed to the left shoulder of his trim, waist-length jacket by a silver and topaz broach that had been handed down in the family for generations. He'd seized her hand and guided his five-year-old, flame-haired daughter through the crowds milling on the grass at the annual Scottish Gathering at MacRae Meadows in Linville, North Carolina, a few hours' drive from her family home in High Point.

An artist to his un-callused fingertips, Thomas Fraser the Fourth couldn't be bothered to come to work at the Fraser Furniture Mill in High Point most days, but he had been steeped in Scottish-American lore all his life—as had she—and always remembered the lyrics to *The Skye Boat Song*. His loud baritone had lustily blended with her reedy soprano as the two of them had sung along with one hundred pipers marching past them on that long-ago afternoon. It was one of the few times she'd ever felt she'd had her father's full attention.

> *Speed, bonnie boat, like a bird on the wing,*
> *Onward, the sailors cry.*
> *Carry the lad that's born to be King*
> *Over the sea to Skye...*

The familiar sounds of the lilting tune echoed throughout the Convention Center, and Fiona's heart noticeably speeded up as she stared at the multitudes of furniture manufacturers, home furnishing designers, interior decorators, and architects—not to mention swarms of fabric reps hawking their cotton, knit, leather, linen, silk, synthetics, vinyl, and wool fabrics in hundreds of booths within the vast pavilion. Tall as she was at five-feet-eight-inches, she stood on tiptoe in an attempt to catch a glimpse of the madman playing that plaintiff dirge about the tragic failure of Bonnie Prince Charlie to regain the throne from the English usurpers after the military disaster at Culloden Moor in 1746. What American-born Fraser worth her salt didn't know about that battle of lost causes, or couldn't identify *that* tune?

"Holy crap!" exclaimed her fellow Parsons classmate, leaning his skinny frame across the counter they'd been manning all morning while peddling their wares and answering questions. Jared and she had applied for work at Bernard Sterling the same week and had both been hired a few months previously in identical entry-level positions.

"What do you mean?" demanded Fiona. "I *love* this sound!"

"Bagpipes?" he asked rhetorically. "Really? I *hate* bagpipes! Reminds me too much of marching eight miles in the Saint Ann's parade with my Sunday School class from Saint Augustine's on Mardi Gras morning! *Spare* me," he shouted over the rising din. To emphasize his distaste, he again put his fingers in his ears, but this time, he stuck out his tongue like a five-year-old.

"I see they don't call you Finicky Finnegan for nothing," Fiona shouted back, laughing at her companion's reaction to a sound she'd always treasured.

She peered down Center Aisle H's premier location from the vantage point of her company's booth and watched with incredulity as exhibitors and attendees alike—in contrast to her booth mate—smiled and nudged each other excitedly, as if they expected a flash mob of kilted pipers suddenly to appear. Fiona was astounded to see the crowd around her virtually freeze in place, fixated on the apparition that had just turned a corner into their aisle and was marching in their direction in purposeful, stately rhythm.

Jared uncovered his ears and said on a long breath, "Well...hel-*lo* there, handsome!"

Jared was definitely not looking at the short, squat man in a rumpled kilt squeezing a cloth-covered bladder on a set of pipes under his arm about a hundred feet from the Sterling booth. Rather, his attention was focused, laser like, on someone a head-and-a-half taller, also in full Scottish attire, who was clearly the object of Jared's rapt attention.

Hello, there, handsome, indeed...

Fiona's eyes were also riveted on the figure at the head of the mini-parade who was wearing a formal, black, Prince Charlie Coatee of a style that Fiona's father had worn for years. However, the visitor marching down the aisle had the broad shoulders of a champion hammer thrower. In fact, the crisp, swinging pleats of his crimson and forest-green kilt hugged his hips and flat stomach in a fashion to make Liam Neeson or Sean Connery green with envy. The front of his jacket sparkled with polished silver buttons and layers of lace frothed at his collar and cuffs. On his left shoulder, an enormous, bejeweled broach set in sterling silver held a swag of matching tartan that could have doubled as a stadium blanket. The fabric flowed down his back like a wedding train, one corner kissing the floor, and at his waist on his right side, the other edge of the plaid material was fastened with a smaller silver pin, creating a cape-like effect.

Stunned by the sheer magnificence of this dark-haired paragon, Fiona was startled when a faint buzzing rang in her ears and strange ripples began radiating throughout her chest.

All right already! So he's wickedly good-looking in that getup. Put blue jeans on the guy and he'd probably look like any other Joe.

And besides, even if he was a pretty dishy specimen, she'd sworn to avoid all handsome men for at least a year—and for very good reason.

As the music continued to drone, and the vision of perfect Celtic manhood drew closer, she wondered if some woolen manufacturer had hired a top-flight male model—or a jock from the NFL, perhaps—to advertise this rather old-fashioned textile—the Scottish tartan. It was perfectly natural with a name like Fiona Fraser that her pulse sped up at the sight that had suddenly appeared before her, for she had been raised in the Mid-Atlantic States where many families traced their origins back to the United Kingdom. Her father and grandfather had schooled her to admire all things Scottish and over her twenty-seven years, she had read Sir Walter Scott's *Ivanhoe, Rob Roy,* and the *Waverley* novels, and each and every volume of Diana

Gabaldon's *Outlander* series. As far as she was concerned, this gorgeous hunk striding down Aisle H could have been a movie stand-in for any one of those heroes—and was as great an advertisement for wearing wool in July as she'd ever seen in a lifetime of attending Scottish cultural events.

"Whoa, there," Jared said, his elbows on the booth's counter. "I might just change my mind about hating hairy men in kilts."

"Jared, trust me," she murmured, "the tall guy is definitely *not* gay."

A split second later, Fiona grabbed a pile of company leaflets and stepped out from behind the booth to get a better view of the extraordinary sights and sounds unfolding before her. She swiftly began handing out the Bernard Sterling fliers to a semi-circle of people carrying tote bags already laden with information about the goods for sale at the expo.

Not to be outdone, Jared immediately followed suit, figuring, she supposed, that he, too, could get a better bead on the good-looking visitor while simultaneously taking advantage of the crowd that had gathered near Sterling's booth where the company's line of drapes, cushions, and upholstered furniture and fabrics were on display. The fewer the brochures left in their booth, the better for both of them, junior hires that they were.

Both Fiona and Jared knew only too well that the recession of 2008 had hit full-force just a few months before they had finished their courses at Parsons, and though both graduates were fully qualified to design anything in the home and fashion field that their employer might throw their way, their short time at Bernard Sterling had mostly consisted of tasks any lowly intern could do. Nevertheless, given the current state of the economy, Fiona and Jared were grateful just to have jobs.

Any minute now, Sterling was due to appear at the booth where he had impetuously decided to spend a bundle on room settings featuring various samples of his lifestyle home-furnishing collections. Based on their employer's fabled, Gatsby-like advertising photo shoots in the Bahamas or Bali, the croquet fields in England, or the yacht harbors in the Florida Keys, Fiona had learned in her five months working for the fashion design czar to accept that her boss was both a genius designer and marketer, and…well, she shrugged mentally…reckless, neurotic, and pretty damned narcissistic. And his temperament had only gotten worse as more red ink showed up on the company books these past few months.

Noting that the two men dressed in their alluring Scottish attire had paused at competitor Ralph Lauren's booth some fifty feet away from her, Fiona was reminded once again that she'd been cautioned never, *ever* even to whisper RL's name in Bernard Sterling's presence.

To be fair to her mercurial boss, famous for his rages whenever RL got more press than he did, who *wouldn't* be under financial pressure with hundreds of employees on his payroll, huge stored inventories of expensive props from every era imaginable, and apparently a less-than-heads-up personal money manager?

Fiona repressed a shudder at the memory of their leader— red faced under his perpetual tan—screaming at all of them in the meeting preparatory to moving into the booth.

"It'll be *your* fault if we don't at least get a slot on the *Today Show* or *Good Morning, America* during the expo! You people gotta make this *work*!" he exhorted his PR team, his desperation showing when he'd seen the final budget for the textile show.

By now, a TV crew with a steady-cam circled the two Scotsmen bowing to the staff in the Ralph Lauren booth and then resuming their parade down Aisle H. It was a pity that Sterling wasn't holding forth in *his* booth right now. Her boss would definitely clap his hands with glee at the deafening approach of the extremely tall, raven-hair James Bond-looking character with shapely calves and well-turned ankles clad in heavy, woolen, cable-knit knee socks.

*Forget James Bond. Long live Mel Gibson in his glory days…*she thought.

The giant of a man in the kilt probably epitomized everything Bernard Sterling wished he could be: tall, dark, handsome, and with a full head of hair. An obvious thoroughbred.

Mesmerized by the sight of the six-foot-plus figure, now only yards away, Fiona felt her own heart skip a beat as she absorbed a close-up view of the kilted interloper whom she would guess was in his early thirties. By contrast, his red-faced, rotund piper's balding, gray head signaled he was decades older and was dressed in a kilt that looked to have seen many a previous parade.

By this time, the unlikely pair was mere feet away from the Sterling booth and still being followed by the camera crew as their music continued to blare forth. Fiona recognized instantly that the taller man was wearing the distinctive red and green Maxwell tartan, which only served to cause another quake in her solar plexus. After all, with a name like Fiona *Maxwell* Fraser, a wayward Southern belle who'd attended her sixteenth birthday ball in a long, white gown and elbow-length kid gloves, she'd happily annoyed her mother by punctuating her costume that night with a splashy green-and-red Maxwell tartan sash. Gertrude "Peachy" Parker Fraser thought any daughter of hers should have been clad in the subtler Clan Fraser pattern, "and in *taffeta*, darlin', not that scratchy wool. You looked as if you're about to ski off a cliff!"

Pipe music soaring ever nearer, scores more textile expo attendees had lined the length of Aisle H from all directions, waving excitedly as the television camera passed them by. Meanwhile, the two kilted gentlemen arrived opposite the Sterling booth. Fiona impulsively slapped her brochures on the nearby counter, raised her arms in an oval above her head, and pointed the Prada-clad toe of a pair of shoes she'd bought wholesale—but had still cost her half a week's salary. Before she knew it, she'd begun to execute the classic, gliding steps of a Highland Strathspey—sometimes also called a 'slow air,' she remembered from dancing classes she took throughout her childhood. *The Skye Boat Song* was a Scottish country dance performed in stately, steady rhythm. Her waltzing movements in the direction of the tall man dressed as an up-market *Braveheart* brought his forward progress to an immediate halt, causing his tubby piper to step to one side, barely avoiding a collision with the cameraman following closely behind the duo.

The stunning stranger's dark brown eyes lit up at the sight of her dance pose, and his mouth quirked into a welcoming, but rather bemused smile in response to her impetuous intervention. He offered her a faint bow and the two began to dance.

Alexander Maxwell was startled to see a slender young woman with wine-red hair tucked neatly into the sleek chignon of an up-and-coming New York careerist suddenly appear before him, blocking his path. She was dressed in an exquisitely cut, longish black skirt with a discreet split at the back, matching black tailored jacket, crisp white shirt with turned-back cuffs at her wrists and an equally crisp stand-way collar. Expensive leather pumps shod her aristocratic-looking feet, and small, simple gold earrings completed her stylish attire. He marveled at the way she executed a very fine dance pattern mere steps from where she'd made her unexpected appearance, and thus brought his long march through the Javits Exhibition Hall to a complete standstill.

He could see immediately that the young woman knew what she was about and as they mirrored each other's movements in the age-old dance, he wondered what a professional Scottish country dancer was doing in a hellhole like New York City in July? She must be as mad as he was to have come all this way to attend such a lackluster convocation of people in the textile trades. He'd been equally barmy to think he could attract investors in this sputtering economic climate, even with a camera crew from some unknown TV station following along behind, and a hired piper in a moth-eaten kilt blaring out *The Skye Boat Song* in the world's financial and rag trade capital.

In desperation, he'd played his one, last card, which was the only reason he'd flown the Atlantic and donned a heavy, woolen kilt in the doldrums of July. He was in hot, frantic pursuit—here in the heart of American capitalism—to secure funding to stave off the increasing financial threats to the hundred-and-fifty-year-old Maxwell Mills where his dubious branch of Clan Maxwell produced tartan fabric in the Scottish Border town of Selkirk. His family enterprise had clothed untold Scottish regiments, dance troops, wedding parties, pipe bands, as well as tourists from around the world, seeking tangible proof of their family roots.

If his brother Harry refused to pull his oar in the family business, Alex would do it all—even, at the risk of appearing utterly ridiculous.

His plan for an online start-up selling Scottish goods to the world's Celtic and Gaelic diaspora might sound crazy to some, but if he could only get a couple hundred thousand quid, it might actually save the family business, long term. The problem was, he didn't have a British pound to spare for this project *and*, at the same time, continue to keep the mill running, the latter enterprise having taken a terrible beating during the recession and the rise of brutal competition from the slave textile factories in the Far East.

While the piper's music had continued to resound across the exhibition hall, Alex was acutely aware that the redheaded beauty had now drawn even closer. She was tall, nearly to the shoulder of his six-foot-four frame, and willowy as the reeds that grew along the banks of the River Tweed. Her lovely peaches-and-cream complexion didn't sport a single freckle that he could see, though he noted her eyes held a diffident, questioning look, and a faint sheen of perspiration glistened on cheekbones that gave her the profile of a classic beauty in some eighteenth century painting.

From these observations, he'd wager that she was a bit nervous about her unrehearsed performance in front of the TV crew who had suddenly broken away from interviewing a canvas manufacturer when he'd entered the convention hall—and he admired the young woman's courage all the more.

The co-owner and General Manager of Maxwell Mills could feel a grin begin to spread across his face as he continued to execute the gliding steps and turns with his arms raised above his head like his partner's. To him, if felt as if they'd long performed

The Skye Boat Song together, one of the most popular dances at any *ceilidh*—a Scottish party requiring participants to sing a bit, dance a step, and recite a line or two of poetry.

From the sidelines, a cheer went up from the swelling crowd in response to their spontaneous dancing, and then rhythmic clapping began, accompanying their graceful dipping and weaving movements as Alex and his impromptu partner kept cadence in perfect harmony. Out of the corner of his eye, he saw the camera operator rack focus and come in for close-up shots of the pair of them dancing together.

It's as if we're in a Hollywood film…a fantasy of old world romance.

Alex was shocked by the visceral response coursing through his body, prompted by the sight of this swan-like, absolutely stunning young woman. She obviously had some connection to Scotland and the textile field…but what? They were a perfectly matched couple for this particular dance—as close to a waltz as Scottish country dancing had in its repertoire—and he was certain as anything ever before in his life that neither one of them could put a foot wrong.

It's as if I know her…as if I've always known her.

Alex quickly glanced at his charming dance partner's left hand, bare of any gold band or engagement ring.

Some lucky lad will claim her soon, he mused, and then—as if he'd been stabbed in his gut with a claymore—added silently, *and how unlucky for me is that?*

Fiona leaned against the railing of the Circle Line ferry, now nearing its second hour of a two-and-a-half hour circumnavigation of the entire island of Manhattan. Her shoulder was inches away from the Scotsman who had appeared in Aisle H and then asked her to show him Manhattan in the short time he had remaining in New York.

With her hand grasping a paper cup filled with an indifferent brand of iced tea, she pointed off the ferry's port side in the direction of the Statue of Liberty standing sentinel at the mouth of the Hudson River.

It was nearly seven o'clock and the heat had diminished a jot as the first puffs of a balmy breeze rippled the collar of her starched, white blouse. It had been a magical few hours since the moment she'd laid eyes on Alexander Maxwell and then, somehow, persuaded Jared to close up the booth so she could accept Alex's request to provide a brief look at New York City. Her dancing partner had immediately embraced her suggestion that the fastest, *coolest* way to see Manhattan was to hop on the tourist ferry at Pier 83, just a few blocks from the Javits Convention Center, and observe the thirteen-and-a-half mile long island from the deck of a boat.

"Look…there she is!" cried Fiona as the Statue of Liberty hove into view.

"Aye…" murmured her kilted fellow passenger who'd garnered startled but admiring glances all afternoon, "She's quite a sight, just as you said she would be."

"Well, at least we finally lost that camera crew by sneaking onto the ferry," Fiona said, then added with a laugh, "It takes an out-of-towner to get me onto one of these tours. It's my first time, too, to see Miss Liberty at such close range."

"Who *were* those fellows chasing after us?" he asked.

"Bloomberg TV guys. They report on business, but I guess they thought you provided pretty good visuals at a boring textile show."

"As did you, my excellent dancing partner," he complimented her, and Fiona felt her cheeks grow warm.

"Well, be sure to watch the news later," she advised, and hoped that her boss would be pleased since she figured the Sterling booth in the background was good publicity, even if it wasn't the *Today Show*.

She felt Alex's sideways glance studying her. Then he said, "You must tell me about that strange but charming accent of yours. Surely, you're not a born and bred New Yorker?"

"Y'all guessed that, huh?" she replied, poker faced. Then she smiled at him, perfectly aware she was pouring on the southern charm when, normally, she would attempt to keep her southern inflections under better control. "I'm a transplant, sure enough," she replied. "I left North Carolina to come here to go to design school and just never went home."

There was far more to the story than that, but time was precious.

"Well, native New Yorker or not, I'm awfully glad you suggested we do this tour. Thanks to the breeze on deck, this is the first moment I've felt comfortable in this kit since I arrived at JFK."

"Kit?" she asked with a puzzled look.

"My kilt—and everything one wears with it. Knee socks. Sporran. All that. My kit," he repeated.

"Ah…yes…I see. It wouldn't be too rude to ask why in the world you're wearing a wool costume in this weather?"

"To garner attention from the wool merchants and their bankers," he readily replied. He gently nudged her shoulder, an action that sent a shiver down her spine along with cooling wafts of river air blowing past them. "And I must hasten to remind you, Fiona, the kilt is not a 'costume.' I wear mine at least four times a month at home. And donning it today worked wonders! Between the time we ended our Strathspey and the exhibition closed for the day—to say nothing of being followed around by that camera crew—everyone, it seems, wanted to talk to me…including some bankers specializing in textiles. Thanks to wearing this kilt, I have four appointments tomorrow to discuss raising some much-needed funds before I have to head for the airport."

"I'd say you had some help from your piper, wouldn't you agree?" she replied with a teasing smile.

"Yes, the laddie did his job well, considering I recruited him just this morning from the St. Andrews Society when I heard him practicing in St. Thomas's church basement on Fifth Avenue. Bringing a piper along to the Expo turned out to be rather an inspired, attention-getting ploy, don't you think?"

"I'd say so," Fiona nodded, taking another sip of her lukewarm tea. "Do you mind my asking what you need to raise money for if your family already owns a tartan mill?"

Alex paused, as if he were deciding whether he should

confide in someone he'd just met. Then he said soberly, "Up until fifteen years ago, our firm was doing very well, thank you very much. But these days, we're getting buried by the competition from the Far East. Cheaper goods, even if poorly made, outsell the quality tartans Maxwell Mills produces. And besides," he added, "we desperately need to modernize the plant and. I want to launch selling all sorts of Scottish goods on the Internet."

Fiona was silent for a moment, and then asked, "Do you really think people will buy fabric, sight unseen, over the web?"

His expression brightened and she knew he was repeating to her what he'd probably pitched to the bankers with whom he'd just wangled appointments.

"My best friend from Edinburgh University, Lachlan MacNeil, is a tech fellow who works on contract for me now. He's figured out a way to present true-to-life colors on our website's widget that indexes all the tartan patterns we produce. You type in your family name in our search box and up comes a very close rendering of the pattern, if we have it on file."

"Wow…you mean I can just type in the word 'Fraser' on your site and see what my tartan looks like and how much it costs per yard—and then order it and you'll send it to me in America?"

"Absolutely," Alex confirmed. "We're one of the few mills that will do small runs of a particular tartan. And in the case of Clan Fraser, there are a number of choices: dress, hunting, ancient…all versions of the same basic pattern, but in different colors of yarn."

"That's fantastic!" Fiona replied, impressed.

"There's already some online competition out there, but we're not just going to sell woolen goods over the Internet," he said, his voice betraying his excitement. "We plan to offer everything from party napkins in whatever tartan the customer wants, to flags and bunting, stadium blankets, made-to-measure kilts, daggers, sporrans, knee socks, the *best* Scottish shortbread …and even custom hand-knit sweaters," he said, nearly out of breath from his recitation. "Whatever we make in the land of the

Celts and the Gaels I want to sell to Scots living throughout the world! And non-Scots, too."

"You'll be the Amazon dot com of all things Scottish," she said, smiling. "A pretty clever idea, I must say."

"Well, thank you! There are five million Scots living in my country. When I told several investment bankers this afternoon there were five times more Scottish descendants living *outside* Scotland than living *in*, they started paying attention."

"That's a nice, niche market," Fiona agreed.

"Once I'd explained my startup scheme to sell—as you've just named it—'all things Scottish' to this loyal, specialized audience on the web with just a small infusion of American cash, they were amazingly willing to arrange a meeting."

Fiona shaded her eyes as the ferry made a turn directly into the setting sun that glistened on the Hudson's sluggish waters.

"How small an infusion of cash?" Fiona asked doubtfully. "We're truly in a deepening recession over here right now, Alex. The moneymen whom I know generally won't part with a penny these days, and the rare ones that will...well...I'm warning you, they are a greedy bunch and pretty much play hardball and tend to take over the companies they put money into."

Curt Vandervort would eat this nice man for breakfast, Fiona thought glumly, her thoughts unwillingly drawn to a man she would rather forget.

"Oh, I just need a couple of hundred thousand," Alex said with a shrug of his shoulders as he stared at Lady Liberty receding in the distance. "Pounds, that is. And I have no intention of giving anyone a majority stake in either Maxwell Mills or AllThingsScottish.co.uk," he added with a lopsided grin. "By the way, I *like* the name you gave it. May I use it?"

Fiona grinned back, nodding her permission.

"It's all yours. Just send me a Fraser lap rug when you do the deal."

"Splendid!" he exclaimed. "As soon as we land, I'm immediately going online to see if anyone has nabbed that domain."

"Fingers crossed," she said, slightly giddy at how easily they exchanged creative ideas. "And I must say, I like the notion of being able to buy a tartan sash or a cashmere scarf online." Then she sobered. "But honestly, Alex, I'd watch out for American investment banker types. They're sharks."

Alex glanced down and caught her gaze.

"It sounds as if you speak from experience."

Fiona took a last, deep draught from her paper cup.

"I do. I *did*, I mean. Know about these Wall Street characters. I lived with one for a while. He had been selling mortgage derivatives until the crash last fall."

"Is that why you ended it? The crash caused a...rupture between you?"

It was a very personal question and brought Fiona up short.

"You mean I missed Curt Vandervort's million dollar monthly income?" she asked sharply. "No. While he was busy creating the global financial meltdown, he was also doing a little Strathspey of his own with his cube mate at his firm. I found out, of course, just before Christmas. He was genuinely shocked that I felt his behavior was a betrayal," she added with a short laugh. "He actually said to me that the affair meant nothing to him *or* to Christiane. Christiane Amsler was her name...the little Swiss Miss in his division. Given that, he said, he couldn't really understand why I was upset. 'No harm, no foul' I think his exact words were."

"Bloody hell!" Alex responded. "He sounds like a complete blighter."

Fiona nodded. "I assume you mean he was a total jerk, and in many ways, you would be correct." She felt color flooding her cheeks again. "Why am I telling you all this? Too much information, for sure."

Alex sought her gaze. "That must have...hurt quite a bit. Finding out about his involvement with his colleague, I mean. What happened after that?"

"I had just gotten my job in January with Bernard Sterling, thank heavens, so I moved out and a month later he married Christiane." Alex reacted by slowly shaking his head. Fiona shrugged. "Soon after that, they both just...disappeared."

"Really? From New York? Where'd they go?"

"I have no idea where they went after their marriage. Curt sent me a note, with no return address, containing a cashier's check for some money he owed me, saying he needed to 'clear his head,' but forgetting to mention he'd married Christiane." Fiona blew a small puff of air through her lips. "I found out from a friend a week later. Then I got a phone call from some investigator. When I told the agent Curt had dumped me and married his co-worker, they left me alone. I guess the gumshoe was teed off because, in his next breath, he revealed his theory that Curt and his bride skipped town to avoid talking to the Grand Jury about those derivatives their company was selling. Seems they probably got married so they couldn't testify against each other...who knows?"

"Good heavens! Do you have any idea where this Curt character is now?"

"Oh, yes. Things apparently cooled down with the Feds after a couple of months. I just heard recently that he's started his own company, selling God-knows-what to unsuspecting investors. Drives a very cool BMW and recently bought a place in the Hamptons with his first profits," she added, and instantly regretted how caustic her last words must sound.

"It would seem as if you're well clear of the lad, but I'm very sorry you had to go through such a thing."

Fiona merely nodded.

Curt Vandervort and Chip Reynolds—both *out of my life now—and I haven't even hit thirty.*

But despite these dark thoughts, Fiona found Alex's expressions of sympathy soothed her sore heart. She never had thought Curt was the *one,* but he'd been an interesting, high-energy companion and taught her the ways of Manhattanites—and a few other useful things.

Alex Maxwell placed a well-muscled forearm on the railing beside hers and Fiona had the strangest yearning to lean against his shoulder, clad, now, in a fine cambric shirt that he'd wore under the heavy Prince Charlie Coatee which he'd long since hung on the back of a deck chair.

She heaved a small sigh. "You know, I *am w*ell clear of Mr. Curt Vandervort. I think his abrupt departure embarrassed me, more than broke my heart. Thank you for reminding me."

"It's good to know you feel that way."

And as they had when they'd danced together in Aisle H, their glances locked and to Fiona, the Circle Liner seemed to stop all forward motion. A kind of magnetic force field seemed to be at work, she thought, pulling her mind, body, and spirit toward this man that she had only met five hours previously. She was certain that Alex could feel it too, for he continued to gaze at her, lips slightly parted, as if in the next moment he would take her in his arms and kiss her senseless.

"By the way," she said, suddenly feeling unaccountably shy, "m-my middle name is Maxwell, too. I've been meaning to tell you that all afternoon." She felt her glance pulled into the depths of his eyes, dark as a starless night. "You and I might be cousins, you know," she added, as if that information would somehow interrupt the electric current she sensed was flowing between them.

"You're joking," he said with an amazed expression. "Did your Frasers marry into some American Maxwells somewhere down the line?"

Fiona finally was able to look away and was surprised to see that the ferry was making its approach to Pier 83. She stared over the railing at the water churned up by their boat reversing its props as deckhands prepared to make fast at the dock.

Their tour was over.

To answer Alex's question about her middle name, she quickly explained how, since the early eighteen hundreds, in every succeeding generation of her family in North Carolina, the first male was always named either Thomas or Maxwell— "or both, if there were two sons. And believe it or not, every female Fraser in subsequent generations had the middle name of Maxwell bestowed on her, no matter what."

"Really?" Alex said. "The same names in each generation? And why was that?"

"No one knows why anymore," she replied with a shrug.

"Just that it's a *must* any time someone in the family produces a child. All boys named Thomas or Maxwell," she repeated, "and Maxwell as a middle name for all the girls. All I've ever heard was that there was a Thomas Fraser who arrived in Maryland—way back when—and his descendants eventually came to North Carolina for some reason or another. The first Thomas must have had a Maxwell in his family line somewhere, but who knows?"

Alex gave her the strangest look, as if he wanted to tell her something, but instead, he gave her shoulder a gentle squeeze and said, "I must say, I rather like thinking that perhaps we *are* distant cousins, back in the mists of time."

Fiona was highly conscious of the sensation of his hand having touched her shoulder and of other tourists beginning to line up near where the gangway was being attached to the boat's deck. She crumpled the paper teacup she'd been holding and tossed it in a nearby bin.

"So tell me, Cousin Alex, before we jump this ship...what lassies' hearts have *you* broken recently?"

Fiona expected Alex to laugh and make light of the women he'd undoubtedly been with in the past, but his expression grew grave.

"I've not broken a heart in many a moon, for you see..." He paused and inhaled deeply. "I'm a well and truly married man, Fiona. Have been for eight years, now...since I was twenty-two."

She had never been one able to mask her emotions, what with a complexion that blushed as red as her hair when she was excited or upset.

"Married?" she repeated, and felt as dumb as a post.

"Yes."

"I-I didn't think...well, you had no ring on, or—oh, what a stupid thing for me to say!" She knew she was babbling and flushing scarlet by this time. She was furious with herself for allowing even a scintilla of romantic interest for a total stranger to have surfaced after the vows she'd made when she walked out on Curt.

A man not wearing a ring means nothing! *You've always known that, Fiona.*

She remembered how her father had snidely lectured his two sons that it simply wasn't a tradition for any true Scot to wear a wedding ring—blah, blah, blah. Whether that was true or not, Thomas the Fourth had often posed as an *un*married man, hadn't he now—as Peachy Parker Fraser would frostily attest.

Fiona gripped the railing to steady herself, hugely embarrassed that her emotions had so obviously hijacked her composure. Why was she feeling such a sense of crushing disappointment, she raged silently? She had no right to *assume* anything about a man she'd known for mere hours! Alex Maxwell had not made one inappropriate gesture or taken any action other than being a curious visitor to Manhattan. In the friendliest manner imaginable, he'd asked if she'd be willing to show him the city. He'd done nothing, whatsoever, to misled her, other than to agree to dance with her when she accosted him in Aisle H.

A voice inside her head sharply reminded her that there could be no denying that sparks *had* been flying between them from the moment they'd met, but then her complete mortification gained the upper hand and all she wanted to do was dash down the gangplank and out of Alex's sight.

She'd obviously and foolishly presumed the way they'd danced so perfectly together, the way they fell easily into conversation, the way Alex eagerly proposed she show him something of New York after the textile show closed for the day—that the electric current she'd felt so strongly right from the start had gone in two directions.

He's married, Fiona, and at least he had the decency to tell you before—

Before *what*, she demanded of herself? She knew virtually nothing about the man. He was here to charm the bankers and he was no doubt merely practicing on *her*. He and his Scottish *shtick* would weave their magic on the moneymen tomorrow and then, like a character in *Brigadoon*, he'd disappear into the land of her ancestors.

No harm. No foul.

That's the way most men thought about these things, she supposed, and felt a measure of her self-possession return. She had *not* made a fool of herself, she insisted silently. She had behaved just as he had, with friendly, perfectly proper decorum.

Just then the ferry bumped hard against the dock and Fiona grabbed onto the railing again with both hands, this time, to keep her balance. Alex immediately threw a protective arm around her to steady her as she fell against his chest.

"Whoa there!" He smiled down at her and, again, their glances held. After a long moment, he said softly, "Well…isn't this nice?"

Fiona allowed the shelter of his embrace to last for a few seconds longer and then righted herself and took a step away.

"Kinsman or not, Alex, I'm afraid I must go." Her southern manners kicked in. "It was lovely meeting you and I wish you all the best in your efforts to raise funds for All Things Scottish dot UK dot com," she added, hearing a faintly mocking tone in her voice that she assumed she'd summoned in self-defense. "And thanks for the Strathspey."

"But I thought we'd…I thought perhaps I could thank you for showing me the city by taking you to dinner somewhere? Your choice."

Fiona paused only a second before she replied. "No, Alex. Thank you, but no. I wish you tremendous good luck with your interviews tomorrow." Then she added with a bit too much emphasis, she thought, after she'd said it, "And a safe journey *home.*"

Alex's expression was troubled. "May I at least have your business card?"

Fiona gave a slight lift to her shoulders as if to say, "Why bother?" but all she replied was, "I have to be an employee at Bernard Sterling for eight months before they issue personal cards. I'm keeping my fingers crossed that they give me mine with the title 'Designer' sometime next month."

"Well at least, let me give you mine," he hastened to say.

He swiftly dug into the sporran that hung around his trim

waist and fished out his own business card from the manly "purse" that was covered in ermine. The back of his card was embossed with the same red and green pattern of the Maxwell tartan. Fiona examined the printing on the front that said, "Maxwell Mills, Selkirk, Scotland, Alexander Maxwell, Co-owner & Managing Director," with a telephone number and email address. Alex extracted a pen from his sporran, took the card back from her hand, and scribbled an additional number. "Here's my mobile," he said, adding, "in case you ever come to Scotland. I always have it with me."

Without replying, she tucked the card into the small, red leather case where she kept her cellular phone, her credit cards, and a bit of cash. She lingered for a second longer and then said almost as if to herself, "Come to Scotland? Well…I suppose you never know."

"That's right," he said, brown eyes riveted on hers. "One never *does* know what the future holds."

She was certain he could see the sadness and disappointment in her expression that she didn't have the energy to hide. In that moment, she felt so strongly drawn to him that she almost threw her arms around his neck simply to feel that sense of being *home* she'd experienced a few moments earlier when the boat lurched. It had been the same pull, too, when she'd glided into the Strathspey as if they'd danced together all their lives.

She turned abruptly to walk down the gangway, but Alex firmly seized her by the upper arm, turned her to face him, then bent down and swiftly bestowed a kiss of benediction on each cheek. For a long moment, he just looked at her as if imprinting what he saw in his memory bank, his own expression full of undisguised regret.

"Perhaps one day, Ms. Fiona Maxwell Fraser, I will show you the River Tweed, just as you have shown me the Hudson today."

An unnerving wash of tears suddenly filled her eyes. Before the moisture could slid down her cheeks and humiliate them both, Fiona bolted from his grasp and melted into the masses pushing their way through the summer's heat on Pier 83.

CHAPTER 1

Five Years Later

The phone rang beside Fiona's bed on an early Monday morning before she'd even dragged herself upright to prepare for another grueling week at Bernard Sterling. Letting it ring, she gazed sleepily across her tiny bedroom at the sultry light sliding through the slats of the blinds that she'd only pulled half-shut before falling onto her mattress, exhausted from working late on yet another Sunday. Today was bound to be a scorcher, following a week of them. She absolutely *hated* the dog days of summer in New York City, but what choice did she have? Her deadlines never seemed to go away.

It had been as hot all week as that memorable July when a certain Alex Maxwell had burst into Javits Convention Center dressed in a woolen kilt and dazzled everyone.

Dazzled you, you mean...

Fiona immediately chastised herself for even thinking about a man she hadn't laid eyes on—or heard from—in years. He'd kindly informed her that he had a wife and had, no doubt, probably sired a couple of kids by now. End of story. Fiona wondered why the vision of him standing on the deck of the Circle Line Ferry had even crossed her mind?

It's just the heat...I definitely was born for a cooler climate, she thought, considering the two places she'd lived: High Point, North Carolina, and New York.

Two cities with equally disgusting summer weather!

And what had been her reward for hanging tough at Bernard Sterling since that unforgettable day she met M.A.M.— "Married Alex Maxwell," as she'd dubbed him—that is, when she allowed herself to give him a thought at all? What wonderful life had unfolded since accepting the promotion last spring of Home Furnishings Design Director?

A six-or-seven-day workweek, that's what, she thought grimly, even when the boss and his other top lieutenants were vacationing at such luxury spots as the Hamptons and Martha's Vineyard.

But hey, she reminded herself as she turned on her side to face the phone, which mercifully had stopped ringing. She'd made it to her dream job in only half a decade with the company which, given the lousy economy everyone was still digging out of, was an achievement of which she could be justly proud.

Suddenly, the phone started ringing again, jarring her from her desultory musings. Someone was seriously trying to reach her. She lunged for the receiver before the caller went to voice mail again.

"Hello?" she demanded, adding pointedly, "and who the heck has the nerve to call me before seven-thirty a.m.?" She figured it must be Jared Finnegan, ringing to remind her a second time to bring him a white chocolate mocha Frappuccino on her way into work. "With *soy* milk, love bug." He, too, had received a promotion this year: overall supervisor of all the design divisions—sportswear, couture, and home furnishings—and he never let her forget she was one notch below him in the Sterling pecking order.

"Fiona?" said a voice that was definitely not Jared's.

"*Tommy?*"

"Are you awake, now? I wanted to catch you at your apartment. We've gotta talk."

Fiona pulled herself to a sitting position and leaned her back against her bed's padded headboard. In the five-and-a-half years since she'd split with Curt, she'd lived alone in this 73rd Street apartment in a 1908 Beaux Arts building that fronted on West End Avenue. During that time, her twin brother had called her at home exactly twice.

"Hey, whatcha all doin'?" she answered, automatically slipping into her mildly southern drawl while trying to sound casual and wondering what new catastrophe was afoot in High

Point, given the early hour of her brother's call.

Had Grandfather Maxwell Fraser died suddenly? Was their dad sick? More likely, their mother was wreaking some new variety of havoc on the family, like insulting Tommy's wife again. She pressed the phone to one ear and sank her forehead into her other hand, bracing herself.

"Fiona...well...ah..." Tommy paused, then added in a rush, "There's really no easy way to say this, so I'll just say it."

Fiona's heart lurched. "What?" she demanded, closing her eyes to brace herself.

"In six months, I calculate Fraser Furniture's gonna go bust. Since you are nominally a board member, I thought I should tell you."

Fiona's eyes shot open.

"Oh, my God! How can that be? Even *The Wall Street Journal* says the housing and furnishing sectors are slowly turning around."

She'd long assumed that her brother Tommy had pulled the family business out of the nosedive that other manufacturers in High Point's furniture hub had been suffering. Not that he ever told her anything or requested her presence at the occasional board meeting. The only role she'd been invited to play was to have her name on the company stationary and her dividends plowed back into the company each year.

"So, what kind of dire straits are we talking about?" she asked.

"Bad," he said flatly, adding, "as in terminal."

Fiona heaved a sigh. Everything to Tommy and her mother was a drama, which is why they all fought like hound dogs sometimes.

"Okay, Tommy, just give me the facts."

A wave of frustration about the way in which her family dealt with crises washed over her. A few years before the recession hit full force, their grandfather, Maxwell Simon Fraser, had been sidelined due to his severe arthritis. Much to their mother Peachy's on-going disdain and bitterness regarding her husband of nearly forty-one-years, Thomas Fraser, IV had loudly and officially refused to take on his expected role of running the family enterprise in favor of the life of a failed artist. His and Peachy's eldest son, Parker, dutifully stepped up to take the reins, avoiding a complete disaster.

If only Parker hadn't died...

But Fiona knew that such thoughts were pointless. Her twin brother, Thomas Fraser, V "and *final* son", as Peachy Fraser had declared with her usual lilting, but nasty edge, had been forced to quit his fledgling law practice to take over Fraser Furniture, the top job in the family firm that Parker had held for less than two years before he died so unexpectedly.

Tommy's next statement pulled Fiona's thoughts back to the present.

"We've just had the auditors in here examining our second quarter and we can probably keep things going until the end of the year."

"But that's only six months!" Fiona exclaimed, shocked that the situation had deteriorated to such an extent before she was told a single thing.

"Nine at the most," Tommy said, then added defensively, "But the Chinese imports, Fiona, to say nothing of WalMart and Ikea, are eating our lunch at a faster and faster rate."

"This is not exactly news, Tommy," she replied, and then wondered if she were sounding a bit like her mother. "When Bernard Sterling saw the economy was in free-fall, we scaled back to sell only the items our customers kept buying—and ditched the duds."

"Too bad you couldn't give *us* some of that wisdom," Tommy replied sourly.

"Oh, you mean at the get-togethers you called for executive committee members *only*, which, of course, would rule *me* out?" she snapped. It had galled her no end that the company had a "tradition" of excluding the female family members from "closed door" meetings.

"You know how chaotic it was when—" Tommy's voice broke, and Fiona could tell her brother was fighting for control over his emotions. "Well, it's no secret that we had a rocky transition from the moment Grandfather Maxwell stepped down."

So Tommy is in trouble. So what? He's never asked my opinion about anything having to do with the business.

And then she felt ashamed, remembering how she had always done her best to shield her twin brother from the onslaught of their mother's sugar-coated barbs aimed, most often, at the second son who sat in the large leather office chair where her favorite offspring, Parker, was supposed to be.

Gertrude "Peachy" Parker Fraser's unrelenting expressions of grief over the loss of her favorite child and the ongoing dissatisfaction that she felt for having impetuously married beneath the Atlanta Parkers grew worse each year. Fiona's mother had made no secret of the fact she despised the family enterprise and thought "a life peddling spit-and-glue furniture" was far beneath her dignity.

"Why you want to go to that dirty old factory all the time, Fiona, is beyond understandin'!" she'd snap whenever her young daughter had disappeared with Grandfather Maxwell into the dark interiors of a place that smelled deliciously of linseed oil and wood shavings. "I swear you'll never get a boy to even *look* at you with that red hair—that you inherited from your father's side, don't y'all forget—if dust is always clingin' to it!"

"*Fiona?*" Tommy cut into her thoughts. "Are you listening to me? Your twenty percent stake in this business will go down the drain unless you help me! I was never cut out for this job and if you want to know God's honest truth: I don't know what in hell to do right now—and I can't *stand* the idea it's all going to collapse on my watch."

"Does Dad know how bad things really are?" she asked, knowing what a futile question that was.

"Fiona, don't be dumb. You expect our *faux artiste* to be of any use in a situation like this? Tom Quattro wouldn't be caught dead setting a foot in a WalMart or Ikea to see what we've been up against, nor is he in the slightest bit interested in anything other than a perfectly-made whiskey sour served on the veranda at four or five o'clock."

Fiona's mind was racing. She knew from her own experience at Sterling that wooden case goods that could be disassembled, boxed in pieces, and then shipped anywhere in the world to be reassembled were being made at a tenth the cost overseas compared to what was manufactured in American factories paying a living wage.

"Are you saying Dad hasn't heard about the use of virtual slave labor in many of the Far East countries?" she asked, ignoring that her brother had just called her "dumb."

"Nope. Or if he has, he ignores it, as does Peachy."

"Is there anything Fraser Furniture makes that *is* selling?" she asked.

Nobody in the United States made as fine eighteenth century reproductions as their firm. The company had craftsmen whose grandfathers had fashioned highboys and sideboards for some of the grandest homes in America, including the White House.

"Upholstered furniture is about it," Tommy pronounced glumly. "The heavy leather and fabric-covered goods are shrink-wrapped and shipped by truck all across the country at a much cheaper rate than any heavy stuff like that coming by sea from the Far East and *then* shipped by truck. We still do a decent business with upholstered goods, but it's not enough, Fiona, to pay for the staff we have on board, given all the cabinetmakers we employ!" he insisted. "Half of America's retail furniture stores have gone under since 2008, and the other half want the cheap stuff."

"To say nothing of the people who only buy online. I know," Fiona replied soberly. "My boss calls it 'the high cost of low prices.'"

Silence fell between them and Fiona could almost picture her brother swiveling in his high-backed leather chair to gaze out of the square, metal-framed factory windows.

Then Tommy said suddenly, "Fiona, could you come back home and help?"

"*What?*"

"Work with me on how to pare down our costs. Maybe

design a few new, high-end upholstered items for us like the ones you do for Sterling? Maybe—as you suggest—if we concentrate on the things that *have* been selling, and I furlough some of the older workers…"

His voice drifted off and she strongly sensed that the brother fortunate enough to be born male and with brown hair—not red like hers—was definitely near his breaking point. The fraternal twin with whom she'd shared a womb and who always let her know he was of the superior gender and better in all ways, was all but begging. Miracle of miracles, she thought, he had finally acknowledged that she was talented in a way that he was not, and had asked her to rescue him at the eleventh hour.

Fiona frowned at the phone receiver. Where were his petitions for advice and counsel when they made him the company President *and* CEO?

Finally she said, "Move back to High Point? *Now?*"

A wall of resentment and anger began to bubble in the pit of her stomach. She inhaled deeply and pressed back harder against her headboard, conscious that she should be in the shower by now if she wanted to get to Sterling's before Jared arrived.

"Yes. I need you to—"

"Rea-lly?" she interrupted, sounding like the hardened New Yorker she had almost become. "*Now* you ask me for help?"

"Look, I realize you should have been part of the management team from the start," he said, his voice pleading. "But this is now, and I need to know what *you* know about this business. I need you, Fiona. Maybe we can save this thing together. This is your field. This has always been your passion. Maxwell should never have made me CEO. I don't know what in hell I'm doing here. I want to run for High Point District Attorney next year, which I might have before if I hadn't been trapped into this…by this…*albatross!*"

Fiona's laugh was short and full of bitterness.

"Well, after Parker died, you could have recommended *me* for the job, or at least offered to share it with you, but you didn't, did you? You took the title and the salary and the honor of running a hundred-and-twenty-five-year-old business you didn't even *like*—and told me, in so many words, to get out of your way, so I did!"

"You were pretty preoccupied diggin' out of the mess with poor, ol' Chip, if you care to remember. You were tellin' everybody that all you wanted was to go to Parsons and get out of High Point!" he said, sounding exasperated.

Fiona felt as if her twin had just run over her with a forklift.

"What else was I supposed to do when I got wind Grandfather Maxwell was going to anoint you and not even *talk* to me about taking on a significant role?" she demanded, trying to refrain from yelling into the phone. "And besides, Chip was—well, you know what Chip was, and what our future held ten years ago, and as you must remember, even his *parents* agreed with what I did." Then she felt her voice rising as the anger and anguish of that time came rushing back. "Parker was the one person in the family who actually cared about my welfare and suddenly he was *dead!* There was nothing left for me in High Point—"

"You know what, Sis?" Tommy retorted, cutting her off as the fury in his own voice reached through the phone receiver and slapped her ear. "I thought if I were a good boy and took on the family business, maybe y'all would eventually forgive me for what happened with Parker. I thought, at least, my twin sister would!"

Fiona's remorse for her last words was swift.

"Oh, Tommy...I—Please don't—"

His harsh laugh cut her short.

"But y'know? You're right about somethin'. I *should* have told them to make you the CEO of this nightmare. You could have replaced Peachy in the role of dominatrix around here and then my life might not be such a pile of shit!"

In the next second, the line went dead.

Shaken more than she wanted to admit by the exchange of recriminations with her brother, Fiona's heart was still racing as she stood in line at her local coffee bar waiting for her order to be filled: Jared's white chocolate mocha Frappuccino and her iced decaf. Her mood was black as Starbuck's house blend, considering her twin had slammed down the phone and would probably not speak to her for another year or two. The reality had started to hit her that Fraser Furniture, after a proud century and a quarter in existence, might just be another statistic in the carnage that was the aftermath of the melt down people like Curt Vandervort had caused in the global financial system.

Yet, how could she simply forget the way she had been treated all her life with that insulting brand of southern, misogynistic "courtesy" and told not to trouble her pretty little red head about the family business.

From Day One, Tommy deliberately shut me out of Fraser Furniture and now he's come crawling for help...

But he *had* asked her to help and apologized for the way he'd behaved since Parker died—and what had she done? Dished up her mother's usual criticism, which wasn't how she felt at all when it came to her passion about carrying on the Fraser family tradition of beauty and craftsmanship.

As she watched the barista brew Jared's five-hundred-calorie coffee drink, she was forced to acknowledge to herself that she'd acted like a complete sarcastic bitch toward her brother—and now she was thoroughly ashamed of herself.

Even so, she thought, reaching for her wallet to pay for the drinks, knowing full well Jared would, yet again, "forget" to reimburse her for the pricey Frappuccino, there was no way she would agree to Tommy's eleventh hour request to give up her life and her job in New York and play rescue ranger to a family that was constantly at each other's throats. Even if her twin wanted her help, now, and she were willing to give it, she was unlikely to get much enthusiasm from "the boys on the floor" where the furniture was actually constructed, or from her mostly-male fellow board members. And the Lord only knew what her grandfather would do if she assumed a management role in the company he had run in its glory days. He'd always shown her love as his granddaughter—but as CEO or Design Director of

Fraser Furniture? It might put him in his grave.

Of course, if Fraser Furniture went bust on Tommy's watch, that would probably kill the old man, too, she thought, as a mantle of remorse for the way she'd behaved on the phone settled onto her shoulders. Fiona knew she needed to apologize to her brother and see if there was any way she could help—but from a distance.

No more drinking from the poison well.

Wasn't that what her shrink had said that first year when she fled to New York? She had given her client excellent advice—which Fiona had followed to the letter—about "best practices" dealing with her family after Parker had died and she and Chip had—

Don't think about all that! Just drink where the water is sweet...

And where would that be, she wondered, as she carefully took hold of the sides of the cardboard coffee carrier and made her way up another block on Madison Avenue. What human being currently in her life could she trust, let alone even dream of trusting her heart to?

No one. There's no sweet water anywhere in sight, Fiona, my friend...

Johnny, the liveried greeter, who doubled as a security guard, waved her through the elegant front door of the Bernard Sterling emporium of fashion and, on the top floors, the world of home furnishings that Fiona now supervised. She smiled a perfunctory "Good Morning" to sales associates gearing up for a new week of work as her stiletto heels clicked across the black-and-white marbled floor. She pushed the elevator button to take her to the executive offices at the top of the mansard-roofed building that had once been home to some member of the Blue Ribbon 400 in nineteenth century New York.

As the birdcage car lifted off the ground floor, she found herself unaccountably wondering if Alexander Maxwell and his wife lived in some Scottish baronial showplace like this building had once been? The intensifying summer's heat was forgotten as visions of Scotland's rolling green Border Country dotted with stone castles and romantic manor houses flitted across her imagination—scenes that had embedded themselves into her memory after long hours skimming through Google Images of that region of the United Kingdom on her computer.

An idea was beginning to swirl around in her head and suddenly she couldn't wait to arrive upstairs to start exploring the possibilities.

CHAPTER 2

A week to the day of her brother's phone call, Fiona stood at the head of the table in Bernard Sterling's luxurious conference room and glanced at the circle of faces turned in her direction. Some were eager and expectant—excited, she imagined, to hear her proposal for the next line in the Bernard Sterling home furnishings "Lifestyle" collections. Other attendees were obviously apprehensive that her ideas might triumph over theirs. And some present at the meeting weren't even looking at her at all but, like Bernard Sterling himself, were busy swiping their iPads, texting on their cellular phones, or multi-tasking in some other fashion in a show of subtle disrespect.

When she dared to think about it—which she had tried not to do all week—her stomach clenched at the audacity of having called "an important design division meeting" in mid-August. She'd even sent both an email and a priority "invitation" to the boss man, himself—and to her shock, here he was sitting at the conference table, waiting for her to sink or swim.

Fiona took a few even breaths to try to calm her nerves and flicked on the switch of the LCD projector. After a minute's warm-up, up came her PowerPoint presentation's first slide that illuminated a retractable screen at the far end of the room in full view of her audience. It was a color image of a large, turreted, cream-colored manor house with high, wrought iron gates and a long graceful gravel driveway. A 1925 Bugatti motoring car was parked in front of the mammoth oaken door. Her boss, who owned several classic Bugattis himself, looked up briefly—took note—and then back at his iPad.

"This is Traquair House, outside the charming village of Innerleithen," she began. "It's the oldest inhabited home in all of

Scotland…currently occupied by the Twenty-First Lady of Traquair, Catherine Constable Maxwell Stuart…and its resident family have lived in the Scottish Border country for *six hundred years*."

Mentioning the distinguished Constable Maxwell Stuarts—no known connection to her Maxwell Frasers, as far as Fiona was aware—had even recaptured Bernard Sterling's attention. She had long realized that this formerly poor Jewish kid from the Bronx, like his nemesis Ralph Lauren, would have sold his soul for an American family pedigree like hers, or for entrée to a place like Traquair whose existence she had discovered by a series of in depth searches on the Internet. She advanced the slide and detected a sharp intake of breath from the newest intern sitting to her right.

"And this stunning interior is called the 'High Drawing Room' at Traquair."

She gestured toward a beautifully appointed chamber, its walls painted a lustrous pearl gray with white moulding that framed a fire glowing in the marble fireplace. Museum-quality, gold-framed seventeenth and eighteenth century family portraits graced the walls, and on the floor, a finely woven garnet-red Persian carpet cushioned priceless Chinese Chippendale chairs and a harpsichord made by Andreas Ruckers of Antwerp.

She quickly changed the slides to one featuring an elegant "man cave" study sporting hunting-green tartan wallpaper, chocolate brown, close-woven wool carpeting, a magnificent mahogany desk with a large, high-backed chair completely upholstered in a tapestry made of gold-colored needlepoint with a lion rampant decorating its back—and an enormous Irish Wolfhound lounging nearby. It was a room from a castle in the Scottish Highlands she'd also found on the Internet, thanks to Google Images, and she knew Bernard Sterling would summon his interior designer, as soon as this meeting concluded, to recreate its every detail at his house in Westchester.

The fourth slide showed close-ups of swatches of classic tartans as well as other plaid fabrics in more muted shades of brick, beige and taupe. It was followed by an image of luscious balls of colorful cashmere yarns piled high in a rustic wheelbarrow positioned in a rolling green field, dotted with sheep.

She nodded to the intern who began distributing around the conference table a half a dozen large, square, shallow wire trays filled with small samples of the same, luxurious fabrics and a few balls of cashmere yarn, along with wallpaper, silk tassels, a gilded hand mirror with small cherubs decorating its circumference, as well as a black velvet presentation box studded with oval, gold-framed porcelain miniature portraits of men and women looking straight out of a BBC dramatization of Sir Walter Scott's *Rob Roy*.

Looking directly at her boss, she announced, "There are thirteen million citizens of Scottish descent in the U.S. and Canada, alone, and probably another three million outside Scotland, worldwide. There are millions more in North America and elsewhere with *some* claim to Scottish heritage, and even more who *wished* they had Scottish DNA."

A few of her colleagues nodded proudly, and a ripple of laughter spread across the conference room. Fiona breathed a bit more easily and continued, speaking, again, directly to her boss.

"At least twenty-three presidents, including Barack Obama—you may be surprised to learn—have Scots, or Scots-Irish ancestry, to say nothing of American movie stars like the late John Wayne and Charlton Heston, along with Tina Fey and Julianne Moore. Whether a person is Scottish or not, Americans resonate to the allure of this part of the world…its history, its culture, its beauty."

Fiona took a deep breath and plunged ahead.

"I propose that our next Bernard Sterling Home Furnishing Lifestyle effort be called 'The Scottish Home Collection,' and that we bring to Americans and our other clients around the world the very best designs and products and—above all—the *quality* that you see here at Traquair House, and in other iconic homes in the United Kingdom."

She quickly advanced her PowerPoint to a montage of classic, stately homes in Great Britain: Floors Castle, Paxton House, Balmoral, Holyrood Palace. And finally she flipped to an exterior shot of a home nearly everyone in the meeting *would* recognize: Highclere Castle, which had doubled as Downton Abbey in the television series that had taken both America and the United Kingdom by storm.

She gestured toward the screen.

"I say Bernard Sterling declares to its clients 'of course, we represent quality; but we also represent the best home furnishing products that America and the United Kingdom—and especially the woolen weavers of Scotland—have to offer.' *Forget* cheap, inferior furnishings made by slave labor in China or other hellholes in the Far East! Britain and the United States are emerging from one of the worst recessions since the Crash of '29 and make everything we need within their shores!"

"Hear, hear!" chimed in Jared, and Fiona sent him a brief smile of gratitude.

Continuing the pitch she had practiced into the wee hours at her apartment, she said, "Let's show a little patriotism and respect for our own Anglo-American traditions. Let's support the furniture makers in our *own* country who have, for generations, been making the highest quality eighteenth century reproductions…like our North Carolina furniture companies…like *my own family's* one-hundred-and-twenty-five-year-old business in High Point, North Carolina, that has made sideboards and highboys for the White House!"

She had been worried about such blatant self-promotion, but the magic words "White House" had apparently allowed it to slip by. She *had* to get Fraser Furniture on the list of potential suppliers for the new line if her family company was to survive.

Fiona inhaled another deep breath and noticed that Bernard had put his iPad aside and was listening intently. She pointed to the wire trays filled with the various swatches of tartan fabric and skeins of cashmere yarn.

"I believe that mounting a Scottish Home Collection for the millions of Americans and Canadians whose families once hailed from Europe, and for successful immigrants who greatly admire the beauty and craft of products made in Scotland and in our own country is exactly what we *should* do—and it's exactly what the marketplace is calling for right now!"

Aware that, by this time, she had everybody's rapt attention, she added, "And who knows! Bernard Sterling's new direction in home furnishing may even appeal to Saudi princes and Russian billionaires who long to identify with the best the Western world has to offer. Our producing the *best*-of-the-best in our field could have *global* impact!"

By this time, Fiona was nearly out of breath. A part of her brain noted that she had no idea whether Fraser Furniture would still be in business and able to supply pieces for her proposed project. Fortunately, a quick Internet check assured her that Maxwell Mills and a diminishing number of Scottish textile manufacturers remained operational, but she hadn't a clue if they could produce enough fabric for her company's needs at a price that would make economic sense. But despite her doubts and worries, she declared to those staring at her with expressions that ranged from admiration to incredulity, "We can *do* this! Bernard Sterling must *continue* to stand for the very best the world has to offer and still support our own—and Great Britain's—textile and furniture manufacturers!"

She'd planned that sentence as her last line after reading a nasty crack in *Women's Wear Daily* earlier that week carping that the Bernard Sterling merchandise sold in the outlet stores was manufactured in the Far East specifically as sale items and had never seen the inside of a regular Bernard Sterling store—and certainly not at the flagship emporium where the meeting was being held today.

There was dead silence in the conference room. Obviously, no one would venture an opinion about her proposal until Bernie offered his. All eyes shifted to the man himself, his lanky form nattily attired in a tieless baby blue cambric shirt that retailed for $598, and a southern gentleman's white linen suit—a nod to the hot weather and having to drive in from his country place in the Hamptons for the pitch meeting.

There was a long pause and Fiona sensed everyone was holding a collective breath, including her.

"This is *genius*!" Sterling said, a response that nearly knocked

Fiona off her Prada pumps. "It's genuine. It's authentic. It's everything I stand for. Quality. Beauty. Craftsmanship. It tells a story. It speaks to your roots, Fiona Fraser, and it speaks to our company's roots: striving for excellence in all things." He slammed the palm of his hand on the conference table's polished glass surface. "And you're right. We *can* do this!"

He swiveled his head in the direction of Jared and his comptroller. "I want you to give Fiona every ounce of cooperation, you hear me?" as if he knew what a nest of vipers his team could be if they thought someone had become the boss's new pet. He glanced around the table with close to a glare, "And I want you, lot, to jump to, and do whatever she asks. Sketches, schematics, prototypes, color ways, pattern making— whatever she wants. We want to get the wheels rolling on The Bernard Sterling Scottish Home Collection *immediately* so we can debut it at the spring and summer home and textile shows next year."

He stood up, indicating to all that the meeting was over, and turned to address the Woman of the Hour.

"You absolutely nailed it, Fiona. This outfit needs more class. More…*patriotism*. That's why I like your idea of going to American manufacturers for classic furniture designs. We can do a sideboard, a sofa table, side tables, and chests of drawers like those in your pictures…all that sort of thing…as part of this collection. Go big! I've been saying for months that we need to do a lot more than just cushions and shit."

Fiona noticed that the comptroller was fidgety and Jared had an odd, pained expression. By this time, Bernie was at the door. He turned back and addressed Fiona.

"Get me some schematics from your family's firm on the furniture stuff I just mentioned, okay? And give Jared a list of Scottish suppliers." He halted. "Better yet, *you* go over to Scotland yourself, Fiona, and see what are the best deals you can get for us on textiles…and while you're there, poke around some of those big mansions you showed us. Take pictures when nobody's looking. Go visit a bunch of out-of-the-way antique shops," he added. "And *costs*. Find out what everything costs. Do the breakdowns 'cause we might even end up making some of this stuff ourselves." He flashed her a rare, winsome grin. "We gotta have the *specifics*, you know? Dimensions, wood types, whether the good cashmere is two-ply or four when you're making throws and pillows. We gotta know the reliability engineering specs so when we ship it, the breakable crap arrives in one piece, you got it?"

Stunned, all Fiona could do was nod.

And then her balding boss pulled open the glass door, stood at the threshold, and paused for effect. His last words to her were: "You done good, girl."

No doubt about it, Fiona thought, suppressing a wry smile while silently quoting her boss, *this outfit definitely needs more class.*

And now to make a very important phone call to Maxwell Mills…

Alexander Maxwell hit the red button on his mobile phone, watched the screen go black, and leaned back in his chair, staring at the instrument with a dazed expression on his face.

Beneath his office on the second floor of the large, stone building housing Maxwell Mills, he could faintly feel as well as hear the vibrations of various textile looms humming away. There was something soothing about the thought of yards of tartan fabric inching forward that would soon be taken loose to the finishers where the colorful goods would eventually be wrapped around flat boards for storage until cut into lengths for the kilt-makers who had ordered a particular pattern. Other looms were at rest, waiting for operators to thread 2-ply cashmere wool wrapped on cone-shaped spindles that would feed into the mill's two computer-operated sock-making machines that could now weave not only the length of a man's sock, but the toe and heel as well.

Alex's thoughts careened from amazement to other feelings, long suppressed, as he stared out the window at the bank of tree tops, heavy with leaves tinged with the beginning of autumn colors, blowing in the early September breeze.

The first marvel was that Fiona Fraser had kept his business card all these years. Rerunning a movie he'd stored in his head for half a decade, he recalled that enchanted day in steamy New York when the stunning woman with wine-colored hair suddenly appeared from behind the posh Bernard Sterling booth at the Textile Expo and spontaneously beckoned him to join her in the gliding steps of the Strathspey.

She was not only a lovely, slender, accomplished Scottish country dancer, he remembered her sense of fun and adventure as she'd pointed out the sights from the deck of the Circle Line Ferry, along with the open way she had, letting him know how disappointed she'd been to learn he was a married man. Even so, she'd kept her dignity, and he'd admired that to no end.

And she'd kept his card.

Within a split second of saying hello on his mobile phone, he'd instantly recognized her voice with its unusual, musical inflections that bore witness to her southern origins. He'd thought of her more times that he would admit to anyone—especially to Addy—though now he needn't feel as guilty as he had over the years.

Fiona Fraser had told him the happy news that she was currently the director of home design of one of the best-known brands in the world, and was coming to Scotland!

In less than a fortnight!

A ridiculous grin had spread across his face at that revelation and he was glad there was no one else in his office when his mobile phone had signaled from his jacket pocket that someone was calling him. She'd swiftly asked if she could come see him "to pick your brain, a bit," and he could hear in her voice that she'd been a bit nervous to have made the call.

Why, he wondered? Had she remembered that moment when they'd both had their elbows resting on the boat railing and he'd almost bent forward to kiss her? Speaking to her just now, he'd recalled the wave of dejection he'd felt as he watched her slim figure being swallowed up by the sea of humanity making its way from Pier 83 to the sweltering pavement of Eighth Avenue.

Other than Fiona's slight hesitation on the phone when

she'd first begun to explain why she was calling after all this time, she'd conducted their brief conversation in a completely businesslike fashion, explaining that she was on a research mission for her celebrated employer.

"May I also visit your mill?" she'd asked. "You can have some underling show me around if you're too busy," she'd added quickly, "and perhaps you could arrange for me to meet your principal designer and to see one or two other mills in Selkirk and Hawick."

"I see you've done your homework." Alex had found himself smiling into his phone receiver. "Most of it sounds like an easy drive from Maxwell Mills. May I ask the specific purpose of your visit?"

Fiona had paused and Alex thought he heard her taking a deep breath.

"I'm in stealth mode, but I can tell you more when I see you."

"I'll do better than that. I'll escort you myself to the best mills in our region: Johnstons, Lochcarron, and D.C. Dalgliesh here in the Tweed Valley, if you like. After all, we worry about you Yanks driving on the wrong side of the road while you're here."

"Now, Alex," she had chided him in a teasing voice, "I'm not a Yankee...I'm a wayward southern belle, remember?"

Wayward? How delightful that sounded.

She had said the words with a depreciative laugh, erasing any embarrassment he might have felt for having forgotten about the American Civil War and southerners' likely detestation of their Yankee conquerors. But to anyone in the U.K., "Yanks" were American soldiers who had come to Britain during World War II and had left lasting impressions, both good and bad.

Alex recalled that Fiona Fraser was an adopted New Yorker, and now she held an important position in an up-market home furnishings firm that he surmised was thinking about creating products with materials made in the United Kingdom.

Could this *finally* be the break Maxwell Mills had been desperately seeking for such a long time? And on top of that intriguing possibility, the lady herself, would be traveling from London on the night train to Edinburgh, arriving on Tuesday morning.

Alex rested his chin in his hand, speculating with a sudden stab of worry whether Fiona had gone back to the arrogant, two-timing mortgage securities broker she told him about the day he met her. Five years ago, she'd revealed the unhappy ending of her apparently short-lived relationship with Curt.... what was the chap's last name, Alex tried to recall? He wondered if there had been others in her life since then? Surely, someone as attractive as she had plenty of suitors?

An unsettling thought sliced through his speculations: maybe she was spoken for *now*. Or worse yet, married! Didn't American women often retain their maiden names?

That sultry day on the ferry, dressed in all his kilted finery, Alex had been very close to revealing the sorry state of his own marriage, to say nothing of informing Ms. Fraser about a possible ancestral connection between the Scottish Maxwells and Clan Fraser. In fact, after Alex had returned to Scotland, he'd even initiated a day or two of online research into that snippet of family lore, which had only served to embed the memory of Fiona even more deeply in his mind.

Truth was, he hadn't gotten terribly far tracing a possible—and quite amazing—family connection between the Maxwells and the Frasers in eighteenth century Scotland before his father had fallen ill, eliminating any free time he might have given to a conceivable Maxwell-Fraser historical linkage. And from that day to this, Alex had been caught up in a series of life events that occupied his every waking moment—until now.

Alex glanced at his desk awash in paperwork and spreadsheets and a computer screen filled with Quicken software that told the story of the precarious state of his company's financial position since 2008's global financial meltdown. As if to blot it all from his consciousness, he moused over to the "Save" button and then "Close," and watched his screen chronicling his afternoon's work disappear and his screensaver of the Maxwell red and green tartan take its place.

Just at that moment, his second-in-command, Hugh Erskine, popped his head in the door.

"Heading out for a late bite, Alex. Can I get you something?"

Alex looked around his computer screen and nodded. "That would be grand, Hugh. A ploughman's lunch would suit. And a coffee with cream, if you will."

"Can't persuade you to come with us? It's just the loom manager and me."

"Aye, I'd love to, but...well, I have some legal matters to read and thought this might be a good time to do it."

There were no secrets between Hugh Erskine and Alex. His most valued employee and former mate at Edinburgh University, along with his Internet advisor, Lachlan MacNeil, Hugh had gained his confidence in the last decade working his way from a loom operator of the computerized equipment to his right-hand deputy. Alex had rewarded Erskine with increased responsibility and a bit more in his pay packet whenever he could. Hugh was the sort of chap cheerfully willing to do whatever he was asked, which was a rare commodity these days, reflected Alex. He even eagerly played the bagpipes at all company functions and kept their aging computers running as well. All considered, Alex thought, waving Hugh farewell, he was bloody lucky to have such a capable Number Two, especially considering—

"Ah, well," Alex said aloud, cutting short thoughts about his younger brother's lacking work ethic when it came to the family business and instead, reaching for the piles of paper on his desk.

He studied the first file he opened. Alex figured that the major impediment, besides the 2008 worldwide recession, had been the slow motion implosion of the textile manufacturing business throughout Great Britain in the wake of the rise of the Far East manufacturing dragons.

Interrupting these gloomy musings, the door to Alex's office swung open. In walked his brother who, as was his habit, entered without knocking.

Speak of the devil...

A woven-willow fishing creel was slung over Harry

Maxwell's shoulder and his green, rubber Wellington boots left moist impressions on the Persian carpet as he approached Alex's large, mahogany desk. A younger sibling by two years, the sandy-haired thirty-three-year-old dug into a front pocket of his soiled moleskin trousers and pulled out a crumpled piece of paper.

"Here..." he mumbled, "I forgot to give you this. Can you make out a check?"

Alex glanced down and absorbed the figure that Harry had circled on the bottom of his makeshift expense report.

"You must be joking!" Alex exclaimed, unable to disguise his exasperation. "Charging Maxwell Mills for twenty-five new Hardy fishing reels and the gear that goes with them is just not on, Harry. Pay for these yourself! Or get your mate Edward to come up with a few quid this time around."

Harry shrugged. "He doesn't have the funds and neither do I. They're already on order and are probably shipped by now. But not to worry," he assured Alex breezily. "Take it out of next month's salary that's coming to me."

Alex shifted in his seat and pointed in the direction of his computer screen. "Come 'round and have a look at this." He reopened the Quick Books file and tapped the bottom of the page. "I wanted to talk to you about exactly this subject."

Harry spun on his heel and headed for the door. "Sorry, lad. Don't have the time right now."

"Well, you'd better make the time, as there will be *no* salary for either you or me this month. And I suggest you sit down and listen to the reasons *why*."

CHAPTER 3

Harry halted at the office door, his hand resting on the knob. He turned around slowly. Alex continued to speak as his brother retraced his steps toward the edge of the desk.

"Our quarterly losses since the beginning of the year are grim, Harry. The totals, here, don't lie, and one of the big drains has been the long list of items you've been regularly charging to your so-called expense account for a couple of *years*, now."

"What do you mean, 'so-called expense account.' I'm an officer in this company—younger brother though I may be."

"That is correct," Alex replied evenly, "but Father's putting you on as a Director doesn't give you the right to siphon off unjustified company funds. I've had a complete audit done of the books and put them all on Quicken since he died last autumn. What's right here on this page is that you've been using monies for your own purposes and calling it 'Business Development' when, in fact, all you've been doing is developing your fly-fishing enterprise with your friend Edward McVicker. It has to stop, Harry. Maxwell Mills is barely holding on as it is."

"Well maybe that's because of *your* hair-brained scheme to sink money into 'All Things Scottish dot com!'" he retorted, his voice developing a punishing edge. "Don't deny that you spent a pile of lucre going to New York…and what came of it? Nothing!"

Alex shot back, "I spent fifteen hundred pounds on that effort, which is nowhere *near* the money you've frittered away." Stung by his brother's denigrating his efforts to seek a way to diversify and grow their struggling concern, Alex knew that whatever he said would sound defensive, but he couldn't help himself. "And perhaps you've forgotten there was a world-wide recession on. And maybe it's slipped your mind that our father was dying of emphysema when you decided to head further up Tweed Valley and fish for a solid *year* at Edward's derelict country house. And I expect you've buried the truth that you pretended to everyone that you sold what you caught to posh restaurants—which didn't turn out to be exactly accurate, since half the time you two were too pissed or lazy to don your waders and *fish!*"

Harry shook his head, a sardonic smile playing at his lips. "Well, now, you'll be pleased to learn we've decided to let *others* do the fishing, and pay us a thousand quid a week for the privilege of putting in a line on Edward's beat along the Tweed!"

Alex could well imagine the decrepit state of Edward McVicker's more-shabby-than-chic country house that he'd inherited from a bachelor cousin and which the partners had christened a "luxury fishing lodge." The truth was, it would take piles of cash to make the place even remotely habitable for the likes of the upscale clientele they sought.

Alex took a deep breath, realizing that Harry and his arguments echoed disagreements they'd had their entire lives. Harry's get-rich schemes always sounded promising, but not one had ever come to fruition, due to his love of the drink and his desire to find easy money, rather than toiling for it.

Meanwhile, Alex had always plodded along, the obedient first-born, trying to keep the family flag aloft while continuing to make high-quality tartan fabric for Scotland's kilt-making industry. He'd fought the rising tide of Chinese and South Koreans buying up old family firms in the Scottish Borders and transferring the libraries of plaid patterns and know-how to an army of workers who labored for virtually nothing in their home countries. Trying to make Harry grasp the implications of the world market was pointless and required energy Alex didn't possess any longer.

He pointed to his computer screen. "You are, of course, free to use your time however you please, Harry, since you've chosen to have no real role here at the factory." He tried to catch his brother's glance. "But hear this: the company will no longer pay these kinds of charges, nor grant you a salary for doing virtually naught all. Let's just declare what *is*," he said, again pointing to the screen. "You have been diverting the firm's money for several years now into this partnership you've formed with McVicker. Well, the best of luck to you catering to those wealthy international sportsmen…but henceforth, you'll have to finance this project out of personal funds."

"But…you…you *can't* just cut me off like that! Sell The Firs! Give me my half!"

Alex gazed at his brother's truculent expression as a heavy sense of weariness came over him. He'd been working nights and weekends for months, trying to figure out a way for the mill to survive and to preserve the jobs of the many loyal, hardworking citizens in Selkirk. The lovely Maxwell family manor house surrounded by stately trees, known for a hundred years as The Firs, was the only real asset left in Alex's arsenal to stave off bankruptcy, should it come to that. He wasn't about to sell it so his brother could squander the last farthing of their patrimony.

"I'm Father's executor and The Firs is part of the assets of the company, and not left to us, personally…so I'm not going to be selling it," he said firmly. "What you need to understand, Harry, is that we have no capital available to keep things going at the mill *and* develop any new businesses—including my idea for selling Scottish goods online, or your fly-fishing venture."

"Bloody hell you don't have the money!" Harry exploded, pounding his fist on his brother's desk. "I'll…I'll—"

"You'll *what?*" Alex challenged, holding on to his temper, but barely. He pointed to Harry's faked expense account. "If you weren't my brother, any other Managing Director of Maxwell Mills would call you an embezzler. He would have presented the false financial statements to the Board, summoned a constable to escort you off the premises, and filed serious criminal charges. My reading of the books shows you've drained nearly a hundred thousand quid in phony expenses out of our business over the last five years. Father apparently looked the other way, but I can't afford to."

Harry's fist slid off the desk and dangled beside his trousers. His shoulders slumped and he closed his eyes briefly, acknowledging defeat, it seemed—at least for the moment.

Alex took the expense report, crumpled it between his hands, and tossed it in a wire wastepaper basket on the floor next to his desk. Hearing the sound, Harry opened his eyes, met Alex's glance momentarily, and then looked sideways into the distance.

"I want to be free of this millstone, Alex," he said in a low voice. "I want out. I hate being cooped up in this failing factory. I want to be on the river…in the sunshine, whenever it deigns to appear. I was never cut out for this life, but Father and you wouldn't tolerate that. I'll sell you my shares at a bargain. Name your price and let's be done with all this."

Alex remained silent as his mind swiftly sorted through the financial figures he'd just surveyed on his computer. Perhaps this was the answer? Find a way to buy Harry out from the business entirely. His thoughts shifted to his recent phone call from Fiona Fraser. If Bernard Sterling placed a big order in the next month or two, Alex would have the wherewithal to keep his company's juggling act going for a little while longer as well as purchase Harry's shares. It was a big "if," since Fiona had declined to tell him the full details of why she was coming to Scotland, but he could only surmise her company was seriously interested in products that the textile manufacturers in the region had to offer. Perhaps her arrival would provide Alex the means to let his brother go his own way. It was a chance that might never present itself again.

"I don't have enough company cash on hand to buy you out all at once, as you well know," Alex began, "but let's shake on a gentleman's agreement that I'll cover the fishing rods you've just purchased, and will pay you in quarterly amounts for your share of the business and at a price determined by an outside evaluator. Does that sound fair?"

Harry's jaw twitched a few times as if he were grinding his teeth. Alex could practically see the wheels turning around in his brother's head. Harry thrust his dirty hand, smelling mildly of salmon scales, across the desk, and then suddenly withdrew it as if he'd changed his mind about their understanding.

"An outside auditor that *I* choose to evaluate the shares, yes?" he demanded.

So much for Harry's being willing to sell his shares at a bargain.

Alex smiled grimly. "How about *two* chartered company appraisers, one representing each of our interests? We'll then settle on the average worth of the shares and draw up a contract for Maxwell Mills to pay you a specified amount each quarter till you've received the total of what's due you."

Harry didn't hesitate for an instant.

"Done!" he declared, seizing Alex's hand and giving it a hard shake. "Can you write me a check for the twenty-five fishing reels, then, please?"

Alex nodded and reached for the large ledger resting on the shelf to his right. On the check and on the ledger itself, he made the monies out to the Hardy firm, directly, and then penned twice in a bold hand on the bottom memo line and in his check ledger, "First installment: buy-out of Harry Maxwell's shares in Maxwell Mills agreed upon this day…" and dated both statements.

"There you go," Alex said.

Without further comment, Harry snatched the check from his older brother's hand and strode toward the office door.

Alex called after him, "I'll see you later at home, yes? Mrs. Nolan will have supper ready for us at six-thirty." The elderly housekeeper had become a volunteer cook since Addy had decamped.

"Sorry," Harry replied shortly. "I'm due to meet Edward at the pub. Tell Mrs. Nolan to leave mine in the 'fridge."

Fiona caught her second wind after an all-night flight to London and a day spent with a former Parson's classmate who took her on a whirlwind tour of the Chelsea Harbor Design Center where she familiarized herself with current home furnishing trends in Britain.

After supper with her friend, she was directed to the Underground that took her to Euston Station where she was due to board the night train to Edinburgh.

It was barely ten-thirty in London this early September evening, but fortunately, the sleek, blue train with "Caledonian Sleeper" stamped in large, white letters on its cars was already waiting on Track 9. Nearby, steel wheels of arriving trains screeched and announcements over the public address system echoed off the glass roof and iron girders above Fiona's head as she swiftly hauled her 21-inch wheeled suitcase down the ScotRail platform, consulting her ticket for the correct coach to which she was assigned.

She paused in front of Coach C, and a uniformed young woman inquired her name, and then made a check beside a list of passengers assigned to that car.

"Tea or coffee in the morning, love?" she asked cheerily, "and what time? The train pulls into Edinburgh at 7:22 a.m."

"Tea please, with milk, no sugar. 6:30 delivery would be fine."

"And a bit of Scottish shortbread, aye, Ms. Fraser?" she said with a wink.

"That would be lovely."

Fiona then entered the narrow passageway that lead to her stateroom where, fortunately, she'd been able to reserve a single bunk. The train wasn't due to pull out of the station until ten minutes to midnight, so she used the time to change into a pair of black, cotton jersey pajamas that would look respectable when she sought out the bathroom at the end of the car. She retrieved her iPad and, cocooned in her bunk, began to map out her strategy for the month of September.

Her electronic list included:

1. *Visit major tartan mills: Maxwell, Johnston's, Lochcarron, D.C. Dalgliesh, etc. and interview textile designers—both fabric and knit—as well as owners.*
2. *Scout high-end interior design showrooms in Edinburgh. Selkirk? Hawick? Get images & price points of their most luxurious projects.*
3. *Visit Holyrood Palace, Floors Castle, Paxton House,*

> *Traquair House, and other stately homes for inspiration. Possible merchandizing deals on selected objects?*
> 4. *Ask Alex Maxwell about best antique and resale shops in Edinburgh and the Borders. Antique Fairs? Vintage car shows?*

She stared at Alex's name glowing on the last line of her yellow electronic "Notes" app. She was embarrassed to admit that before she'd left New York, she had put "Alexander Maxwell, Selkirk, Scotland" into every search engine she knew of and had been astounded when one of them turned up an entry high in the results that included a short legal notice printed in a local newspaper. In the stilted language of the Scottish court system, it stated that an Alexander Maxwell and Adelina Dalgetty Maxwell—both of Selkirk—had filed for divorce the previous spring.

Fiona had been so shocked by this that she'd read the paragraph three times. Then she'd immediately and severely chastised herself for being such a snoop, and wondered if she'd already made a huge mistake even calling Alex. Yes, he was her best contact in the textile business in Scotland, but there were plenty of other firms she could have rung up. If she were truly honest with herself, she had to admit that she'd also called his mobile number simply to satisfy some sick curiosity about a memory of a man that remained in her thoughts after all this time.

Then she'd recalled one of her girlfriends, consistently unlucky in love, warning their circle of friends at dinner one night, "You *never* want to be the 'bridge' out of somebody else's failed relationship. Trust me, you want to be the woman *after* the women a guy hooks up with as soon as his divorce is final!"

They may not even be divorced yet—or they've reconciled by now!

This was the most important business trip in her career, she reminded herself sternly.

Don't be an idiot and get distracted!

Fiona punched her ScotRail feather pillow a few times and wedged it behind her back, leaning against the wall nearest the stateroom door. She stared at the window blind pulled closed against the view of late-arriving passengers racing to climb on board. Her mission during the next three weeks in Scotland, she lectured herself, was two-fold and required her entire concentration: search for wonderful textile products and *objets d'art* to convince Bernard Sterling that the Scottish Home Collection was going to be a big seller as his next "Lifestyle" project. Her second assignment was to select the kind of furnishings she was bound to see in Scotland's stately homes that could be reproduced in High Point with enough of a profit margin that would make her boss happy—and save Fraser Furniture from collapse.

Fiona reached for a Kit Kat chocolate bar she'd bought at the newsstand in the train station and opened its bright red wrapper. She and her friend had grabbed a quick bite after their tour of London's design district, but there had been no time for dessert before she jumped on the tube to Euston Station. Taking a bite, she began to relax for the first time in weeks. She found herself smiling as she recalled Tommy's astonishment when she rang him up to make peace and then announced the news of her latest project for Bernard Sterling. Before the end of the conversation, she'd asked for schematics of his best-selling furniture pieces.

"We don't release those to anyone, Fiona," he replied cautiously, but she could detect a certain excitement in his voice.

"I know, I know," she agreed, "but how about sending really good photos and just some sketches of each piece with a listing of what you'd charge Sterling, based on whether you'd get an order from us for a hundred of each—or five hundred—or a thousand?"

"Do you think your company would actually ever place that big an order? A hundred of each of, say our upholstered ottoman or a sofa table? That's what it's gonna take to dig Fraser Furniture out of this hole."

"Tommy," she said, trying to contain her own excitement, "when times are good, we'd easily sell a thousand units of each. We're in hundreds of stores, darlin'!" she teased, her spirits rising for the first time in many moons. "I have no idea how the economy will be when we launch this—if everything turns out as we're hoping—but can you work up the numbers and send them to me?"

"Are you talking to other manufactures?" he asked, his voice suddenly hardening.

"I'm not," she said. "At least, not yet. You get the first shot. Sterling has only asked me to get information from Fraser Furniture and a bunch of textile mills in the Scottish Borders. We may have them supply the upholstery, drapery, and cushion fabrics."

She'd paused during that conversation, thinking to herself of all the twists and turns an item labeled "Bernard Sterling" could take before it hit the salesroom floor. "Look, Tommy…I'm only a worker bee around here. I can't guarantee anything, but at this point—for both of us—it's better than a poke in the eye with a sharp stick, right?"

"Well, what you've described so far does sounds promising," Tommy allowed. After a long moment for which Fiona duly waited, her twin added, "Thank you, Sis, for putting our hat in the ring."

Peace had been declared.

"Fingers crossed all around," she'd replied. "Bye now. See you when I get back from Scotland." She remained silent for a beat, and then mumbled, "Love you, Bro."

The day before Fiona was due to leave on her research trip, a large portfolio arrived, Express Mail, to Sterling's on Madison Avenue. In it were beautiful photographs of Tommy's wares, along with fairly detailed sketches of each piece, and cost breakdowns. They weren't the official schematics Bernard had asked for, but close to them. Tommy had selected well—a mix of smaller, more intricate wood items like eighteenth century-style bedroom side tables, scaled-down chests of drawers, and narrow tables with curving, cabriole legs to go at the back of a sofa, as well as larger upholstered items: a love seat, tufted ottoman, and a club chair done in leather with a dark green tartan fabric seat cushion.

Riffling through the packet's impressive contents, she chortled, *"Yes!"* Then she slipped Tommy's materials back into the portfolio and headed upstairs to the executive offices.

She had delivered the packet to Sterling's new assistant, Stella Langdon, who'd solemnly promised she'd make sure their boss would get Tommy's missive right away. Fiona pointed to the word "Confidential" printed on both sides.

"This part's very important, Stella," she'd said, hoping her firm tone would impress the rather fey, willowy blond. Bernie had a penchant for hiring decorative young women to run his office that weren't necessarily trained for anything more complicated than fetching him coffee and looking good in his line of clothing. "Remember, now," she emphasized, "this is for Mr. Sterling's eyes only. Absolutely *no one* else is to see this information before he does. This is very proprietary stuff that my brother sent in strictest confidence, and he's giving this to Sterling *only* because it was me asking for it."

"I understand," Stella replied, patting the large padded container with the block letters FRASER FURNITURE. "I'll messenger this out to Bernie in the Hamptons before I go to lunch."

Bernie, is it? Fiona noted silently. Stella had only been in her job less than a month. No one called Sterling "Bernie"—even behind his back—till they'd been around awhile. She put this exchange into her mental file marked "Might be having an affair with the boss." There were several, similar memos in that folder.

Jolting Fiona back to the present, the Caledonian Sleeper train made a small lurch, and her car began to move. Excitedly, she turned off the lights in her stateroom and scrambled out of her bunk to ease up the blackout shade. She lay on her stomach to watch the train glide past other travelers on the platforms in Euston Station, just outside her window.

She was on her way to Scotland! A little trill skittered down her spine.

Scotland…the land that was once home to her family's first Thomas Fraser!

This northern region of the United Kingdom was the place

from which her forebears had come, but all she knew about her ancestor Thomas was that his parents had both died in the Highlands after the failure of Bonnie Prince Charlie to regain the throne in 1746. Family lore maintained that the orphan had been raised as the ward of distant relatives before immigrating to America. After that.... she knew little else about her Scottish ancestor.

Another shiver went down Fiona's spine as she considered that Scotland also was the place where she would see Alex Maxwell again after five years' time.

But first, she reminded herself, pulling the covers under her chin as the train gently rocked to and fro, she would spend a week in Edinburgh on her mission to see the best that Scottish interior designers had to offer. After that, she'd hire a car, brave driving on the left, and follow the road south to the Scottish Border country...and Maxwell Mills.

CHAPTER 4

A knock on Fiona's compartment door startled her awake after the most deliciously sound sleep she'd had in months.

"Six-thirty, mum," chirped the cheerful attendant she'd met when she boarded the train the night before. "Here with your morning tea!"

Fiona reached across the minuscule space between her bunk and the door and turned the knob. She pulled herself to a sitting position and took hold of the paper carry-bag she was being handed by the attendant who had at least six others draped up her arm that were apparently slated for Fiona's fellow passengers in staterooms in the same sleeping car.

"We're right on schedule," noted the attendant, "so we'll pull into Waverley Station just at 7:22. Enjoy your tea, mum!" And she was gone.

Fiona closed the door and gazed at the lush, green rolling hills flying by her stateroom window. Sheep dotted the hillsides and her heart speeded up at the sight of a turreted, stone structure perched on a distant hill framed by puffy white clouds and a cerulean sky.

"An honest-to-God *castle*!" she breathed aloud.

As the train drew parallel to the hill, she noted that the main part of the building was roofless and cows appeared to be walking through an archway that was minus a door. The Scottish Border country, south of Edinburgh and north of the top of England was renowned for centuries of skirmishes not only between the two regions, but also among various clans claiming the right to disputed lands and cattle. Fiona read in her *DK Eyewitness Travel* guide for Scotland that unnumbered "border wars" dating from the late thirteenth century had been fought. From it she'd also learned that abandoned castles were just one of the unhappy results of the endless conflicts.

Fiona sipped her good, strong tea laced with milk and nibbled a square of shortbread as she continued to gaze out of her window in an almost dreamy state. Slowly, the landscape began to change, and she saw a grittier scene of storage sheds and the backs of sooty factories as they streamed by her window. Scrambling out of bed, she swiftly slipped into her "travel uniform" consisting of trim, black trousers, a hundred-dollar white T-shirt, a black cashmere cardigan that reached to the top of her thighs, her simple gold necklace and tiny gold hoop earrings, and comfortable flats that had enough support to tramp around a city. She donned her lightweight, rainproof three-quarter-length, hooded jacket and a red, black and beige Yves St. Laurent chenille scarf she'd bought for thirty bucks in a posh resale shop on Madison Avenue.

She was all set and ready for any weather Scotland had to offer as her excitement increased with every mile she drew closer to the country's capitol.

Fiona had not even stepped off the train onto the platform when she heard the skirl of a bagpipe echoing off the enormous station's glass ceiling. As it always did, her heart swelled at the sound and she had an almost eerie feeling of homecoming, as if Edinburgh was a familiar destination, and Scotland a place where she might feel as if she belonged.

She easily lifted her small, wheeled suitcase onto solid ground and headed in the direction with the other passengers that were walking into the main part of the station dominated by a huge overhead electronic board announcing the track numbers of departing and arriving trains. As she advanced through the throng, the sound of the pipes grew louder still. She delighted to see several fellow passengers dressed in kilts, also hauling their suitcases behind them. Soon, she drew beside the enormous engine that had pulled the Caledonian Sleeper train all the way from London and received a smile and a wave from the engineer sitting in the cab with his window open.

When she returned her gaze to the main section of the mammoth station, there, obviously waiting for *her*, was none other than a tall, dark-haired figure clad in the distinctive red and green Clan Maxwell tartan kilt, flanked by a shorter fellow, likewise attired—except for the set of bagpipes he was enthusiastically squeezing. The taller man placed his large hand on the other's shoulder and the bagpiper's skirling tune suddenly segued into the familiar waltz time of *The Skye Boat Song.*

Fiona froze in her tracks as the words of the song floated through her head.

Speed, bonnie boat, like a bird on the wing…

The crowds behind her made sharp detours to avoid colliding with her backside.

"*Alex?* Alex Maxwell?" she said, stunned. Her spoken words were lost beneath the loud but lilting music, though Alex must have understood her because he made a courtly bow, a grin on his face.

Passersby watched, amused, as the tall, arrestingly handsome man dressed in full, Scottish regalia strode to the side of the arriving passenger. He reached out to clasp each of her shoulders, and leaned down to kiss her, European style, on both cheeks.

"Welcome to Scotland, Fiona Maxwell Fraser," Alex said with an emphatic Scottish burr, his gaze riveted on hers. "We are well and truly pleased to have you return to the land of your ancestors, lass."

He bent to grasp the handle of her suitcase with one hand and then put a friendly arm around her shoulders, urging her forward through the knots of people rushing in the opposite direction to catch their trains.

"Meet Hugh Erskine, the Maxwell Mills company piper who doubles as my second-in-command at the mill," Alex announced loudly as the piper continued to play.

Hugh nodded politely and then strode on ahead to fetch the car from some mysterious parking place that only a native could have secured in the bustling, crowded streets that surrounded the Victorian-era Waverley Station, built in the center of Edinburgh.

"How was your trip?" Alex asked rather formally as the sounds of the pipes faded. They were waiting on the curb for Hugh to pull the car around. "Did you sleep all right on the train?"

"Like a baby," Fiona said. She darted a sideways glance at her handsome escort, sensing a kind of delicious tension connecting them like a silver thread. "And by the way, I've never had a welcome like that in my *life*. That was…amazing," For some reason, she felt a lump in her throat. "Thank you, Alex. I can't actually believe I'm here!"

"Neither can I."

He tucked her arm in his and she immediately began to wonder how she would handle *this* sort of development if, indeed, Alex Maxwell was experiencing the same rush of excitement about their rendezvous that she was. Yet, before she could even allow herself to revel in the magic of what had just happened in the train station, niggling thoughts that were blooming into full-blown worry were already beginning to plague her. With a man like Alex to upset her equilibrium, how was she to maintain her professional distance and accomplish what was of primary importance to her brother and her: creating a Scottish Home Collection that Bernard Sterling would endorse, thereby helping to rescue Fraser Furniture from bankruptcy?

Keep your eye on the prize, Fiona, my girl! No distractions allowed…

Obviously, Alex's surprise appearance at the train station welcoming her to Scotland was far above and beyond the call of duty, to say nothing of his dressing in "full kit," as he once described to her, and bringing along his personal piper! If his intention was to dazzle her, he had done just that…but what were his *other* intentions, she worried?

Just then, Hugh wheeled up in a dark blue, vintage four-door Jaguar sedan and leapt out to take command of her one piece of luggage.

"Is this all you have with you?" Alex asked with a look of surprise.

"That's it," Fiona replied.

"Amazing."

She laughed. "I always end up wearing the same five things on business trips and can't stand waiting for my luggage to arrive in the baggage claim area, so I pretty much pack in an envelope, as you see."

"I learned that same lesson of how *not* to travel when I had to put this kilt and all the bulky accessories in its own suitcase when I came to New York," he agreed with a chuckle. He stood to one side as Hugh, now serving as their chauffeur, opened the car's back door. "All right, then," Alex said, offering her a hand. "Let's get you settled at your hotel and try to keep you awake all day until at least ten o'clock tonight to avoid the worst aspects of jet lag."

"You mean waking up at 2 a.m. thinking it's lunch time?"

Fiona slid across the classic automobile's well-worn black leather seat while digging into her handbag for her hotel's reservation confirmation slip.

Alex climbed in after her and leaned toward Hugh sitting at the car's right-handed wheel. "The Royal Scots Club, if you will," he directed. "29 Abercromby Place."

"Aye, right you are," confirmed Hugh, who put the car in gear and smoothly pulled away from the curb *on the wrong side of the street.* Fiona's breath caught and she nearly made a comment before realizing that, yes, she was in the United Kingdom where driving on the left side of the thoroughfare was the law of the land.

A week before her trip, Alex had emailed a suggestion that she book into a hotel convenient to the design showrooms and some specific shops that she'd mentioned she wanted to visit while in Edinburgh. He explained that The Royal Scots Club now took paying guests in order to subsidize a bastion of former Scottish military members whose clubhouse—once private and all male—was now open to the paying public.

Fiona suddenly wondered if Alex, too, had booked into her hotel or would merely drop her off and head back to Selkirk and his mill, an hour's journey south of Edinburgh?

As if reading her thoughts, he said, "I'm going to make sure they'll let you have your room early so you can freshen up, and then I'll come back at lunch time and fetch you on foot from our company flat, if that suits. It's just down the road at Royal Circus in New Town—which by the way, was built below Edinburgh Castle about two hundred and fifty years ago, so—in fact—it's rather old by American standards. The area around Royal Circus is the closest thing we have in Scotland to a design district."

"You don't actually mean 'circus' literally, then," she asked, pokerfaced, "with popcorn and elephants and so forth?"

Alex's responding smile signaled he'd gotten her joke.

"No…nary an animal act. Just an area with some lovely terraced houses and, nearby, lots of shops selling home furnishings to decorate the neighborhood's rather elegant dwellings…but I can see we'll have many moments over the next week where we'll have to translate our English for each other."

The next week? Fiona repeated silently. It would appear that Alex intended to serve as her personal guide in Edinburgh as well as when she traveled south of the city to the Scottish Border country to visit Maxwell Mills and the other textile manufacturers on her list. Thus far, he had seen to everything, which was lovely, but how could a man running a busy woolen mill spare the time to spend an entire week in Edinburgh with a woman he'd met once, five years previously?

Alex gestured out the window as the car moved beyond the congestion surrounding the train station and proceeded along streets that faced open green spaces—some square and others round—enclosed by wrought-iron fences. "Here, a 'circus' means an area of a city that's planned to encircle a round park set in its middle, with attached, three-and-four-story terraced houses all around its circumference."

"Ah…we'd call them 'townhouses,' I think…and 'circus' as circus rings. Understood," she nodded and settled into the Jaguar's comfortable back seat. Her companion pointed to the amazing vista of the old city, perched high above an enormous stretch of lawn, trees, and blooming flowerbeds he identified as Princes Street Gardens.

"The ancient city sits on a huge, volcanic up-thrust, with the castle on one end of the Royal Mile and Holyrood Palace on the other…but more on that in a day or two."

Alex appeared to have her time in Scotland all mapped out, Fiona realized, a fact that only served to give her pause.

Is he showering me with all this attention only because he thinks he's stalking a potentially big sale to Bernard Sterling?

From the time she'd been promoted to Home Furnishings Design Director, she'd experienced a few potential suitors working in related fields that had wined and dined her just to make a deal. Or, perhaps, she thought, Alex's attentiveness was simply a case of an extraordinarily good-looking man, accustomed to attracting women in droves, who had decided to mix business with pleasure during the short time she was in Scotland.

At that moment, Fiona determined that it might be prudent to take a small stand to assert her independence.

"I think I *am* going to have to have a little nap," she warned, glancing across the seat to observe how he'd take this news. "I flew all night from New York to London and didn't shut my eyes for a second."

"Excited about coming to Scotland, were you?"

"Excited, yes, and sitting a row away from a crying infant all night, followed by eight hours tramping around the Chelsea Harbor Design Center yesterday before getting on the night train. I'm one of those people who don't recover quickly from jet lag despite a single night of decent sleep."

"Poor you," he replied sympathetically. "Will our meeting at noon allow for enough rest?"

Fiona glanced at her watch. "It's just five after eight in the morning, your time, right?" she asked.

"Exactly. You'll get a few hours kip, and then how about if I come to fetch you just after twelve and we can walk to Café Royal and have some lunch. Otherwise, if you're like me, sleep all day and you'll be off your mark for an entire week."

"Deal," agreed Fiona, relieved he was so amenable to the change in schedule. Just then, their car pulled up to the curb at a curve in the road flanked by an arched expanse of three-story granite row houses, each gated with similar wrought-iron fences and facing a lovely park across the cobbled street.

Hugh sprinted out of the driver's side of the Jaguar to open their door, offering a hand to Fiona and then pulling her suitcase from the car's trunk, or "boot" as he called it.

Alex carried her bag up a few stone steps and entered a door with an impressive brass plaque that read "The Royal Scots War Memorial Club: Visitors' Entrance."

The young woman at the front desk greeted Alex like an old friend and gazed at Fiona with undisguised curiosity. Alex made the introductions.

"Ms. Fraser?" repeated the clerk, consulting her computer screen. "Yes, Mr. Maxwell called ahead to make sure your room was made up. Number 3?" she asked Alex.

"That's the one," Alex confirmed, and Fiona suddenly wondered how often he had escorted young women to this exclusive establishment.

She turned and swiftly thrust out her hand toward her would-be guide.

"Thanks so much, Alex, for all the arrangements," she said with a bright smile. "I can take it from here. I'll meet you in front of the hotel at noon, sharp. I'd like to knock off visiting at least one or two interior design shops this afternoon after lunch, since I'm scheduled so tightly on this business trip," she added for the benefit of the inquisitive desk clerk, who appeared to be all ears. "I've got a map, so don't feel you have to—"

"Sounds like an excellent plan," Alex intervened before she could finish her sentence. He nodded agreeably and gave Fiona a measured look as if he noted her sudden crisp, professional demeanor. "Now be sure to set your alarm."

"Will do," she said, and then turned to the desk clerk. "Through those doors?"

"Yes…take the lift to the third floor and follow the signs to Room Three. It's on the front, overlooking Queen Street Gardens."

With a wave to Alex and the desk clerk, Fiona seized the handle of her wheeled suitcase, pushed open the beveled glass-paned door, and headed for the elevator. She sorely needed some privacy to think through what she should do next.

Fiona swam to consciousness at the sound of a harp playing softly, its soothing cascade of notes echoing through the darkened room with its royal blue brocaded curtains drawn tight against the day. Disoriented, she peered through the dimness that surrounded her and saw her cell phone on the bedside table. Its glowing face indicated that her mellifluous alarm had gone off and that she'd slept solidly for three and a half hours. Still mildly befuddled, she stared at the device from her elegantly canopied bed draped in the same, rich blue and gold brocade as the curtains, and noted it was eleven-thirty in the morning, Scotland time.

Alex must have arranged for the Honeymoon Suite, she thought groggily, given that her accommodations were far grander than any she'd ever enjoyed before on a business trip. She turned off the alarm, swung her bare feet onto the plush carpet and padded into the bathroom. There, an enormous tub, large enough for one of the Queen's Guards to stretch out in, was matched by a giant-sized porcelain sink with vintage chrome handles, set upon a gray-and-white Carrera marble floor. If her host hadn't informed her already, she could have guessed that the building had originally been constructed to suit very large males of Alex's own size who demanded a high standard of luxury.

Fiona made a mental note to enjoy a long, warm bubble bath before going to sleep later that night. Meanwhile, she took a quick shower, luxuriating in the forceful stream of hot water that resulted when she turned the handle to an upright position. With a glance at her watch on the counter, she swiftly dried off and donned her camel-colored turtleneck to compliment her tailored wool trousers the shade of cognac, along with her usual, plain gold jewelry. It was early September, but she'd noted a chill in the air, and was glad she'd brought clothes she could layer, depending on the weather.

Alex was waiting for her outside the hotel, having changed

into a pair of pressed jeans, a grey, glen plaid vest and matching sports jacket, every inch an advertisement for the beautiful woolens she assumed were manufactured at Maxwell Mills. There was no sign of the Jaguar.

"What happened to your piper-chauffeur-second-in-command?"

"Oh, he's headed back to Selkirk by bus to resume his job running the mill in my stead," Alex said with a grin. "Our small management staff has to be multi-talented, as you can see. And besides, you and I will need the car to tour the Borders."

Despite arming herself to appear composed and businesslike, she couldn't help but respond to Alex's warm smile and the quick hug he gave her on the sidewalk before taking her arm and guiding her alongside the elegant arch of row houses. She was beginning to think that this would be a research trip like no other.

"Feeling more rested after your nap?" he inquired, and then stopped their forward progress to turn and survey her from head to toe. "You look marvelous, Fiona. I can't tell you how much I've been looking forward to your arrival."

Taken totally by surprise, Fiona looked up at him wordlessly, incapable, somehow, of making small talk. Her few hours of rest had done nothing to quell the fluttering in her chest when she came within ten yards of Alexander Maxwell.

Why am I so drawn to this man? We don't really know each other at all, yet I—

Fighting against an inexplicable desire to throw her arms around his broad shoulders and tuck her head under his chin—an impulse, she fully realized was pure madness—she knew with sudden certainty that she must immediately come clean about Fraser Furniture's dire straits and the primary reasons she'd called him in the first place. She simply could not allow anything to distract her principal mission in Scotland, which was her promise to her brother Tommy to do what she could to rescue her family's firm.

Finally she began, "Alex…I…well, I…" She swallowed and then continued hastily, "I need to tell you a little bit more about why I'm here, and to get assurances from you that everything I say will remain strictly confidential."

Alex gazed at her with a puzzled expression and then nodded. "Of course. And I have a few disclosures of my own I'd like to make."

For a long moment, they remained standing in the middle of the block with black taxis and other wheeled traffic whizzing by. He seized her hand and drew it to his chest as if to demonstrate to her the rapid beating of his heart. A steady buzz of electricity seemed to be surging up and down her arm.

"Look…" she said in a rush, "on a wildly different subject, but because you've just now seized my hand like this…I know that you're…that you're in the middle of a divorce." She was deeply embarrassed, both by her abrupt switch of topics, as well as her candor. Alex made no attempt to disguise his surprise at hearing her words, but didn't respond other than to offer a confirming nod. Fiona could feel her face flush and cursed her red hair and fair complexion for the thousandth time. "I looked you up on the Internet and the legal notice turned up," she confessed, staring at their joined hands still pressed against Alex's grey woolen vest.

"Did you discover the signed documents are due to be delivered any day, now?"

Fiona shot him a stricken look. "No! Of course not! It was so bad of me, I know…"

He squeezed the hand still held against his chest. "Not to worry. I did the same thing about you. I put your name into the search box and learned you'd been promoted at your job and that, as far as the Internet knew, you had not changed your last name—which I know in America may not signify you hadn't married—but that bit of knowledge kept me sane."

She stared up at him, dumbfounded. "Married? *Me*? No." Then barely above a whisper, she said, "I-I'm sorry. This is all so crazy."

"You mean feeling the same connection we felt five years ago?" he asked quietly.

"We have to *ignore* it, Alex!" she said with a fierceness that surprised even her. "You need to know the details about my coming here. You need to understand—"

"Fiona...it's all *right*," he assured her and pulled her flattened hand more tightly against his chest. "Why don't you tell me everything over lunch? And after that, *I'll* seize the talking stick."

CHAPTER 5

For the next ten minutes, they walked side by side in silence up North St. Andrew Street past the Royal Bank of Scotland with its front façade of striking Corinthian columns. When they entered a narrow passageway called Register Place, Alex assumed the role of the conscientious tour guide and pointed out the building housing the national archives.

"And in this block, one of my favorite spots in Edinburgh," he announced as they came to a corner building with tall arched windows, large black doors with elegant moulding painted gold, and a large sign overhead proclaiming an eatery called Café Royal. Next to the sign were hanging flower baskets, bursting with colorful blooms, attached with wrought-iron chains high up on the stone walls.

"This looks absolutely wonderful!" Fiona exclaimed as Alex held the inner door for her to pass through. She was relieved that the two of them appeared to have recovered a sense of normalcy after their strange, intense, rather intimate exchange walking along Abercromby Place.

The interior of the restaurant was resplendent with high ceilings painted cream and burnt umber, tall columns framing the huge windows enriched by cascading red velvet drapes that Fiona estimated had to be twenty feet long and made with at least thirty yards of fabric for each panel. Booths upholstered in dark burgundy leather encircled the room that also featured an elaborate cherry wood bar at its center with hundreds of bottles of spirits reflected in the enormous mirrors behind them. Brass chandeliers with glowing glass globes made Fiona think of Belle Époque Paris, though she guessed that Edinburgh had experienced a belle époque of its own at the turn of the twentieth century. The lights overhead cast a golden radiance within the restaurant and Fiona suddenly felt as if she had entered another world.

"Welcome, Mr. Maxwell," greeted the hostess who immediately showed them to a quiet booth. "Nice to see you again."

Fiona slid along the burnished leather seat and gazed at Alex across the table.

"You're a regular, I see," she said, again plagued by the thought that she might be embarking on "The Alex Maxwell Standard Tour for Female Visitors From Abroad."

"I eat here all the time when I'm in the city with clients, which is a couple of times a month." The hostess took their drink orders and left luncheon menus for them to peruse.

"Oh," Fiona said, nodding, relieved to think this was Alex's 'local' and not something else.

"I've always loved Edinburgh," he disclosed. "I've come here more often, now that Addy and I have been living apart for six months." He paused, and then continued. "Adelina and I...well, even five years ago, when I was in New York that time, we both knew, it turns out, that our marriage wasn't...well...it wasn't what either of us wanted."

"But you certainly were a loyal spouse that day I met you," Fiona murmured, marveling at how quickly they had launched into an even more intimate discussion than they'd had on the street walking to the restaurant. "At least you kindly revealed you were married, though if we'd gone out to dinner together I've often wondered if..."

She allowed her sentence to drift.

Alex arched an eyebrow and nodded. "Yes I was a loyal dog that day—at least during our trip around Manhattan—and it wasn't easy, believe me." He laughed. "And once I'd told you I was married, you ran away like a hare on the moor. Whoosh, down the gangplank with you and into New York's teaming masses."

"I probably saved both our reputations by doing that," she said with a short laugh. Then she asked, "Do you mind telling me how your marriage finally ended?"

"With rather a bang," Alex replied, studiously consulting the menu.

Fiona, too, kept her eyes lowered, thinking that his wife probably caught her handsome husband in some compromising situation, but before she could voice her assumptions, Alex looked up.

"About a year ago," he said, "she reconnected with a former lover from her University days and hopes to marry him, eventually. Our divorce is due to come through virtually any day now."

"She left *you?*" Fiona said, unable to disguise her astonishment.

"I'm taking your incredulity as a compliment," he replied dryly.

Just then the waitress arrived with their drinks: a Guinness for Alex and a virgin ginger beer, as recommended by him for Fiona who had voiced her fear that alcohol would put her under the table, given the hours she'd kept in the last two days of travel.

Once the server departed from their table, Alex continued. "Addy moved out of our home in Selkirk half a year ago, but not before I confronted her with the petrol bills showing she'd made repeated trips for more than a year back and forth to Peebles where this chap was now living."

"But why would she be open to another relationship like that? What had gone sour between you?"

Alex shifted in his seat, and Fiona knew that whatever answer he gave would be a gauge on how honest he was with himself—and with her.

"Addy and I were young—only twenty-two when we wed. We'd allowed others to dictate to us who should be considered a 'suitable' partner. Our families had been business associates for years; the Dalgetty Bank had kept the mill solvent during various economic downturns. For my part, I *liked* Addy. In fact, we were actually friends. Looking back, I think what happened was that we rather did what was expected of us. Huge mistake."

"Did you ever see the movie *When Harry Met Sally*?" Fiona interjected.

Alex reared back against the leather banquette.

"Yes," he replied, nodding vigorously. "Addy and I were exactly like that! That is to say, our friendship wasn't quite as intense as Harry and Sally's, but we'd known each other since we were in nappies. In some unhealthy fashion, I felt that I *owed* it to my father to marry this pretty, extremely sweet young girl whose father owned a bank to whom *my* father's company was indebted—and who clearly was in love with the idea of being married and having children."

"And you? What did *you* want out of marriage?"

Alex tapped a forefinger several times on the polished surface of their table before he answered.

"At that tender age, I mostly had hoped for a like-minded companion. A happy home, and I imagined I'd have children one day. In fact, I wanted children, but it soon became clear to me it was a case of…right concept…wrong woman."

"Wrong?" Fiona asked more sharply than she intended. "Addy sounds nice."

"She *was*! She *is* a perfectly dear person," he insisted. "But from the start of our marriage, she couldn't understand why I couldn't be home for dinner promptly by six o'clock even when one of our looms broke, or that I had to attend textile expos all over Europe, or that I wanted to launch the Internet start-up when, as she pointed out constantly, I had the mill to run. And her biggest disappointment was why…why I kept putting off committing to having a baby. It hurt her terribly, I know. So much so that two years ago we simply became roommates. No discussion about it, really."

"And you decided you didn't want to have children because…?"

Alex looked down at his menu and said, "I knew that if I had a child, I would never be able to bring myself to end the marriage." He looked across the table at Fiona. "Understandably, when Addy found someone who had loved her since they'd been in school together and wanted what she wanted, she summoned more courage than *I* had shown and...well, she left our home in Selkirk and moved in with Peter."

"That must have caused quite a stir in your social circle."

Alex cast her a rueful smile. "Oh, yes indeed."

Fiona remained silent, taking in all that Alex had disclosed. Then she asked, "What was her father's reaction? He's a shareholder in Maxwell Mills, I take it?"

Alex winced slightly. "No, but his bank loaned us money and he's a member of our board of directors. As you can imagine, he wasn't at all pleased his daughter had run off to be with the same, lowly chartered accountant whom he'd forbidden her to marry when they were students."

"Oh. I'll just bet he wasn't pleased," Fiona said, thinking of her own family's reaction when she and Chip—

"And, of course," continued Alex, "I dared not tell him how please *I* was that I didn't have to play the villain in this drama. But I still had a problem, of course."

"Dalgetty Bank?"

Alex nodded. "Quite a tangle, it's turned out to be, once our divorce was filed. Now, her father's furious at her on several levels."

"Family businesses!" Fiona exclaimed. "Wait till I tell you what's going on with Fraser Furniture."

Just then, a waiter approached and took their orders for venison on braised red cabbage with plum sauce for Alex, while Fiona chose the Café Royal's grilled Loch Duart salmon, a house specialty, the waiter assured her.

When they were again alone, Fiona put her chin in one hand and asked, "Before I tell you my sad tale about my family's firm, fill me in on what happened to your All Things Scottish website? Didn't any of those New York hot shots you were going to meet the day after our ferry ride come across with the funds?"

"They did, actually—or at least they made an offer—but their conditions were pretty much as you predicted they'd be...plus they wanted me, as the founder and managing director, to relocate to New York or Silicon Valley in California. Given my rocky marriage, my responsibilities at the mill, as well as problems I was already having trying to get my brother, Harry, to pull his oar, plus the fact my father, by then, was ailing—it was a completely impossible proposal."

"What a dumb idea to locate a business called "All Things Scottish" outside of Scotland," she noted, shaking her head.

"I suppose I'm lucky that the people I proposed the idea to didn't appropriate my scheme and do it themselves, though a few others with a version of the same idea have popped up since."

Fiona took a sip of her ginger beer and said over the rim of the glass, "I'm so sorry it didn't work out, Alex."

Alex shrugged. "Thanks. And who knows? Maybe there's hope for All Things Scottish, yet, if I take the idea totally up-market and feature only the best-of-the-best Scotland has to offer. Meanwhile, I just have to get through a few things like buying my brother out of the mill and paying off the Dalgetty bank."

"And your father? What did he think of the Internet idea?"

"My father had emphysema. Smoked all his life, plus inhaled the lint and bad air that used to be in the mill before we cleaned up the plant. He was getting worse around the time I went to New York, so I didn't even tell him the real reason for my trip. The disease got him, finally. He died last autumn."

Fiona reached across the table and briefly put a sympathetic hand on Alex's wrist. "You've had quite a tough couple of years, haven't you?"

Alex gave another slight shrug. "I've had better, that's certainly true." He remained silent for a moment, and then, as if he'd made a decision, disclosed, "I've recently discovered that my younger brother has been using his expense account for years to finance a venture that has nothing to do with weaving woolens. I've cut off Harry's money spigot, removed him from the Board of Directors, and have struck a deal to buy his shares, eventually. Now that my father's gone, he has no protector anymore."

"Aren't family businesses a joy?" she asked with a slight lift of her brow.

Alex continued to gaze soberly at Fiona. Then he said,

"You asked for confidentiality earlier. Can I expect the same from you?"

"Of course. We are encased in a Cone of Silence here," she replied, casting him an ironic smile.

"Well, what I'm about to say next might change your thinking about recommending Maxwell Mills to your employer," he warned, "but I want to make everything absolutely transparent from my side of things."

Fiona's glass was suspended between her hand and her mouth. "Tell me," she said quietly.

"Thanks to my brother Harry's misdeeds, along with a number of other reasons…Maxwell Mills is actually on the edge of a financial abyss, Fiona. We have to increase our business very soon or go *out* of business in nine months to a year. After a hundred-and-fifty-years in the weaving trade—and generations of loyal, highly skilled employees—we're on the brink of insolvency."

Fiona slumped against the booth's leather upholstery. "I can't believe this," she murmured.

"Well it's true," Alex said. "I thought you should be told this before you came to see our factory. And just so you know, I'm happy to introduce you to our competitors, should you not want to deal with us."

"No! No! I mean, I can't quite believe you and I are facing the exact, same, equivalently-*dire* straits!"

"Bernard Sterling is in financial peril?" he asked with a look of incredulity, followed by an expression of dismay.

Just that moment, their lunches arrived and the pair waited in silence until their meal was served and the waiter retreated.

"No, absolutely not," she assured him swiftly, taking up her fork. "The Sterling brand managed to survive pretty well since 2008. We stayed very up-market and despite nice, middle-class people like you and me losing our shirts in the recession, there still are a lot of rich people at the top of the pyramid who, apparently, love to see the Bernard Sterling label on everything from their 600-thread organic cotton sheets to their dog's rain slicker." She paused to consider that the secret she was about to reveal was the sort that, if her employer ever caught wind of it, would most likely destroy her chances to save her family firm.

She inhaled deeply, took a bite of her salmon resting on a bed of braised fennel, and then divulged the entire sorry tale of her own family's business problems and the dire financial straits they were in following her brother Parker's death.

"Your brother was killed? I'm so sorry. When?"

"A couple of years before I met you. It was a boating accident. Tommy, the younger son—who's also my twin brother—was at the wheel of our Ski Nautique on our lake when Parker's water ski hit a big log that then smashed into his head." Fiona's throat constricted and she stared down at her plate of salmon. "I was in the boat, too, in the stern, and I saw the log whiz by, but...well, none of us could prevent what happened."

"What a wrenching loss...for your entire family."

"Thank you," she murmured. She toyed with her fork. "My mother never really forgave the two of us, especially poor Tommy. My grandfather, Maxwell—" She looked up and saw that Alex was gazing at her with a peculiar expression. "Yes, not only is my middle name Maxwell, as I mentioned five years ago, I think. I also have a grandfather named Maxwell...Maxwell Simon Fraser, the Third..."

"Maxwell *Simon* Fraser?" he said, with a look of total amazement. Then he spoke in a more normal tone of voice, "Ah, yes...our 'cousin connection.'"

"Grandfather Maxwell has been too ill to work these last years and poor Tommy has hated being saddled with running the company."

"Why weren't *you* involved in your family's firm?" Alex asked. "You obviously know the business."

Fiona gave a quick, negative shake of her head and then narrowed her eyes. "Would you have wanted your sister telling you what to do?" she demanded.

"If she was as intelligent, well-trained, experienced, and as *knowledgeable* as you? I'd have begged her to help me shoulder the burden," he replied.

Fiona studied her half-eaten salmon on her plate and

allowed his words to sink in.

"I do believe you would have." She paused, and then disclosed in a rush, "I pitched our family company to Bernard Sterling as a hard goods manufacturer that could make some of the smaller items of classic furniture designs we'd put in the new home collection. Things like side tables, ottomans, small club chairs, footstools—items upholstered with tartan made by the likes of Maxwell Mills. It could *save* us."

"Was Sterling all right with its being your family's firm?"

"Amazingly, he thought it was a big plus. 'Made in America' by a hundred-and-twenty-five-year-old family-owned firm, and all that. He also said he liked the idea of using indigenous Scottish companies as well. 'Real authentic' was the phrase he used."

Fiona and Alex exchanged amused glances.

"I've read over the years Mr. Sterling is a fervent Anglophile."

"That he is, and very soon, I hope to convert him into a Scot-o-maniac!"

Alex put his head back and roared with laughter.

Fiona merely shrugged and took a last bite of her salmon, adding, "Maybe the Bernard Sterling Scottish Home Collection can save from disaster *two* old-line family companies for the price of one?"

"From your lips to God's ears."

For the rest of their meal, the pair kept to planning the next few days of Fiona's schedule in Edinburgh. It was almost as if they mutually understood how raw the emotions were around the disclosures they had each made and the pair simply wanted, for the moment, to enjoy each other's company and finish their delectable lunch.

Twenty minutes later, Fiona put down her coffee cup and glanced at her watch.

"Oh, wow! Can you believe it? This has been the proverbial three-hour lunch, but it was totally delicious!"

Alex took a last sip of coffee. "Glad you enjoyed your meal." He reached across the table and touched her right hand resting on the base of her water glass. "It's so amazing to me, Fiona, that you're actually here. That we're sitting across from each other in Edinburgh, Scotland, at the Royal Café."

"I know," she replied quietly. "It's amazing to me, too."

Fiona almost felt as if the two of them were beginning to spin on the edges of some vast vortex that threatened to pull them down, down, to unknown depths.

"Alex…" She pulled her hand away from his and then, for some inexplicable reason, she couldn't stop herself from leaning forward again and encasing his two hands with her own. "This…this *feeling* is so crazy…" she whispered.

"No, it's not," he countered, lacing the fingers of one hand through hers. "In fact, when I tell you how I believe we're allied beyond the fact we're both trying to rescue our family firms, *then* you'll think it's crazy. Or that *I* am."

The noisy chatter surrounding them receded and all Fiona saw was Alex, sitting directly across from her, looking grave.

"What do you mean 'allied?'" she asked cautiously.

"I've discovered, recently, a rather long, complicated tale that may involve the two of us in quite an incredible coincidence. What say you that we walk up the Royal Mile from Holyrood Palace to the Castle, since I'm fairly sure that's where it all began."

CHAPTER 6

Outside the Royal Café, Alex hailed one of the boxy, black, London-style taxis and held the door for Fiona to climb into the back. She slid across to leave room for him on the bright red and blue tartan wool throw that had been used to cover the seat, rendering their conveyance definitely "Scottish."

"The front entrance to Holyrood Palace, please, driver," Alex directed.

"I thought our first stop was Carlisle Interiors?" Fiona protested, already feeling guilty about the long duration of their lunch and the huge number of To Do's she had listed on her iPad tucked into her tote bag that rested on the floor of the cab.

"I promise you, Fiona," Alex assured her, "we'll have plenty of time to visit everything you need for your report to Sterling, but before anything else, I want to tell you what I discovered about some pretty amazing historical links you and I may share." Before Fiona could demur, her companion pointed out the window. "Don't miss this, lass...your first, real view of The Mound and the Royal Mile."

Fiona's eyes widened with amazement as the cab rounded a corner and there, stretched before her, was a close-up view of the ancient city perched, stone on stone, like a crown on top of a mile-long volcanic promontory of basalt.

"It's a short but steep journey to where we're going," Alex said as their car toiled up the hill, "so hold on till we get to the top."

A few minutes later the taxi halted in front of the grand stone facade of the Palace of Holyroodhouse.

"This also serves as the British royal family's official residence when they're in Scotland," he informed her, pointing to the turreted structure. "It was built in the fifteenth century on the grounds of an Abbey, and after a serious fire, it was remodeled in the seventeenth century for Charles the Second."

"He was a Stuart, right?" Fiona inquired, "A full-fledged Scot?"

"That's right, and related to the ill-fated Bonnie Prince Charlie."

She gazed above their heads at the palace's enormous arched entrance.

"Bonnie Prince Charlie's loss at the Battle of Culloden Moor in the mid-eighteenth century is about where my knowledge of Scottish history begins and ends," she admitted a bit sheepishly. "My grandfather told me that the Stuart failure to regain the throne after Henry the Eighth excluded his older sister's Scottish line from his will started the huge exodus of Scots to America and Canada, though our Frasers supposedly came over at bit later, at the tail end of the eighteenth century."

"Exactly. Henry's daughter, Elizabeth the First, saw her cousin, Mary Queen of Scots, as a dangerous rival." He pointed to a turret at the corner of the mammoth building. "It's said that when Mary was six months pregnant, she witnessed the murder of her private secretary up there, authorized by her jealous husband, Lord Darley. Given the political turmoil of that time, it's rather a miracle that Mary's son eventually became James the Sixth of Scotland and also James the First of England."

"And Elizabeth was the one who ordered Mary's beheading, if I remember," Fiona murmured, staring up at a small window near the tower's conical roof, thinking what anguish those stone walls must have witnessed. "Not very family-friendly."

"So history says."

"And you wanted me to see the palace before any design houses because...?" she asked skeptically.

"Because, just up the Royal Mile a few paces lived *my* eighteenth century ancestress, the beautiful, extraordinary, quite amazing Jane Maxwell of Monreith, who married a duke and became the Fourth Duchess of Gordon."

"Ah..." teased Fiona. "So would a DNA test prove the Maxwell name in *my* family line means that I'm descended from her as well? How nice to think perhaps I've the blood of a genuine duchess running through my veins. Bernard Sterling will be so pleased," she added with a mild smirk. Meanwhile, she was thinking that if she, too, was linked to this branch of the Maxwells, then Alex and she *could* be cousins, though many times removed.

Alex shook his head. "No, from what I've recently discovered, I don't think you've a blood relationship with either the duchess or me."

"Oh. I'm a bit disappointed to hear that, actually. The duchess part, especially."

Alex cocked an eyebrow. "From what I've learned, we may have an even *closer* connection than *that*. Come along, lassie. Let me show you something I've only just found out."

Mystified by his intriguing words, Fiona allowed Alex to guide her up the left hand side of the Royal Mile. She found she had some difficulty keeping pace with his long strides, and before they reached the end of the first block she asked a bit breathlessly, "Tell me more about this Jane Maxwell person."

"Well, she was the second daughter of Sir William Maxwell, the Third Baronet of Monreith."

"Second daughter...third baronet!" Fiona cut in. "How do y'all keep this stuff straight?"

"Years of practice," Alex replied. "At any rate, the Third Baronet's daughter, the said Jane Maxwell, became a duchess when she married Alexander Gordon, the Fourth Duke, in 1767."

"So that was even before our American War of Independence! 1776 and all that."

"Right you are, and that also plays into this tale," Alex disclosed. "As a result of her marriage to the Duke of Gordon, Jane Maxwell gained serious political standing as the wife of the largest landowner in Scotland, and thus became a kind of back-room advisor to King George the Third, due to her friendship with Queen Charlotte, especially during the war in the American Colonies and the so-called Madness Crisis."

"Oh, I remember reading about that," declared Fiona. "The

king went around the palace gardens talking to himself."

Alex suppressed a smile, replying. "Something like that." He continued leading the way up the Royal Mile, threading a path through the crowds of tourists, also out for a stroll along the stone buildings flanking both sides of the cobbled thoroughfare. "Jane was the one who recommended to the royal couple a doctor who was willing to pull off the leeches from the king's body and order a halt to the infernal blood-letting his other doctors had employed."

"I saw the movie with Nigel Hawthorne and Helen Mirren!" Fiona exclaimed, suddenly recalling the plot of the film. "The treatments prescribed by his original physicians would have driven *anybody* crazy, don't you think?"

Alex laughed and nodded agreement. "George the Third actually recovered for a time, probably due in no small measure to Jane's intervention, though she's gotten little credit in the history books for the role she played."

"Typical," Fiona noted dryly.

Alex cast her a sideways glance and added, "During this period, she also became a favorite of Prime Minister Pitt, the Younger, the Tory politician. He was a bachelor and she hosted salons for him. As a consequence, she became a major rival to the Whig supporter, Georgiana, Duchess of Devonshire. They even campaigned publicly for their opposing parties."

"Her serving as Pitt's hostess must have caused talk," Fiona commented as they passed a shop window featuring a large variety of stained glass items decorated with complicated Celtic and Gaelic designs. Fiona made a mental note to stop by later in the week and see if she could buy a few pieces for future reference.

"There was *always* gossip about the Duchess of Gordon, prompted in no small way by the Duchess of Devonshire's camp. This was even more true when Jane became the patroness of her fellow countryman, the devilishly handsome poet, Robert Burns."

Fiona surveyed her escort's own good looks, her eyes narrowing.

"You're not going to tell me that you are an illegitimate descendant of Jane Maxwell and Robert Burns, *are* you?"

Alex laughed. "No, indeed, not. But you're closer than you think."

"Are you truly a descendant of the duchess, then? I *am* impressed."

Alex seized her hand and guided her through a throng of tourists raptly listening to a kilted guide describing the "ghosts along the Royal Mile." Fiona marveled that the ancient street still appeared as it was in medieval times, but for the vehicles attempting to thread past the rubbernecking crowds.

"I'll explain in a moment why you shouldn't be too impressed with my lineage," he said, pointing out the Museum of Edinburgh across the street and its ancient tower atop the Old Tollbooth featuring a two-faced clock. "That stone building over there at one time contained the law courts, a jail, and now serves as a museum chronicling the lives of ordinary citizens from the late eighteenth century, onwards. The docent there told me that Jane Maxwell and her sisters were famous for riding on the backs of rather large pigs and racing them in a course that ran from this very spot to Fountain Well, a bit further up the road."

"Quite a character, your duchess must have been," chortled Fiona. "Pig races!"

"And as for my connection to that hoyden…are you ready?"

Fiona halted mid-step. "Yes…I guess so. Tell me."

"It is assumed that I am a blood descendant of the Duchess, but from the *wrong* side of the blanket, as it were. Apparently, a descendant of Jane's brother, the Fourth Baronet of Monreith, was a naughty boy. This great—or great, *great*—grandson or grand nephew—of a member of the household of a nineteenth century Baronet of Monreith had his way with a housemaid around 1910, producing a son—my grandfather—after whom I'm named: Alexander Maxwell.

"And you expect me to keep all this straight?" she teased.

"Well," Alex replied, a smile tugging at the corner of his lips, "no one is exactly sure *who* is the responsible party for launching my branch of the Maxwells, for it was all kept very hush-hush in those days, but a male in the titled family—father, son, or nephew—links me by blood to the Duchess of Gordon. And since the current Tenth Baronet is in his seventies, unmarried, presumably childless—my DNA would, indeed, show that I am one of the youngest living descendants of Jane Maxwell, my ancestress."

"Wowser…" Fiona murmured. "So what do you know about your wayward great-grandmother, then?"

"Ah! This part we *do* know. She was an upstairs maid at Monreith House named Maisie McHenry who was working in the aristocratic household in the early twentieth century. She had her out-of-wedlock baby fostered to a childless couple in Selkirk just before the First World War. The story goes that shortly after that era's Baronet died, a rather generous but anonymous bequest was given to this now-grown child, granting him the choice of taking the surname of Maxwell. The inheritance allowed my fortunate grandfather to buy a partnership in the weaving firm where he'd worked all his life as a loom master. Eventually, *his* son, my father, was able to purchase the remaining shares and renamed the firm Maxwell Mills after the Second World War."

"That's amazing! 'Wrong side of the blanket,' are you?" she quoted him. "And I had figured you definitely had all the markings of the Duke of Gordon's descendant."

"Sorry to disappoint," he replied, grinning. He gestured toward a stone passageway with a metal marker over its entrance reading: Hyndford's Close. "Come see where Jane Maxwell, the future duchess, had her rather humble beginnings, given that her father, a titled gentleman from the Scottish Borders of Monreith, abandoned his estranged wife and three daughters to near poverty, right here, while he remained with his sons on his country estate southwest of Edinburgh."

They entered a narrow, stone alley and shortly emerged into a courtyard lined with grey pavers and a similarly-hued stone stairway, its iron railing leading up to the first floor entrance of a five-story granite building that sported three-over-four paned glass windows marching up its façade in tidy rows.

"A lot of these closes—which just means 'passageway,' incidentally—have been tarted up in recent years, and even sold for commonholds, which I think you call condominiums," Alex explained. "But in the eighteenth century, this area was a rabbit warren. The buildings were side-by-jowl and lacked a proper water supply, daylight, and had virtually no ventilation. Terrible diseases like cholera and smallpox would run rampant. It's amazing that Jane and her two sisters, Catherine and Eglantine, survived to adulthood. When she lived here, the structures were little better than tenements, really, where the inhabitants would toss out the contents of human waste from the upper windows, crying, *Gardyloo!* Which was a Scots corruption of the French *Gardez l'Eau,* meaning 'Watch out for the water.'"

"Oh, ick!" replied Fiona, wrinkling her nose at this disgusting snippet of history. "Poor Jane. How in the world did she attract the attention of a duke?" she demanded, staring up at the well-kept stone building that now appeared quite charming, with flowerbeds dotting the courtyard.

Alex said, "Here's where I think you and the Frasers come into the tale." He seized her hand once again, and they retraced their steps back to the broad High Street, as the Royal Mile was also known. He pointed to his right. "So, you see that the palace is at one end of the street, and up there in the opposite direction, just a mile away, is Edinburgh Castle, which stands upon the highest section of that extinct volcano I mentioned."

Fiona craned her neck to the left, past the rows of quaint buildings lining the ancient road, and could just see the tops of the castle's slate roof. Alex waved vaguely in the direction of the buildings across the street from where they stood.

"I only recently located an old map of this area, drawn in the eighteenth century. The various buildings were labeled with the more renowned occupants of the time. Over there, in one of those other tenements, was the home of Simon Fraser, Master of Lovat."

Fiona's breath caught.

"No! You can't be serious! My Grandfather, Maxwell *Simon*

Fraser, claimed he was a descendant of another Maxwell Fraser who was born in Maryland, somewhere, in the early 1790s, I think he said, but whose *father*, Thomas Fraser, was our family's emigrant from Scotland. Do you supposed my Thomas Fraser was related to *that* Simon Fraser across the street?"

Alex slowly nodded his head in agreement. "Perhaps. The story *I* unearthed claims that Jane Maxwell's first love was a young boy named Thomas Fraser of Struy, born in a small village in the Highlands. As an infant, he was orphaned in what's known as The Starving that followed the failure of Bonnie Prince Charlie to regain the throne after the Battle of Culloden Moor. It turns out that the infant Thomas Fraser, because of family and military ties, became the ward of…get ready, Fiona." He paused and then continued. "Thomas Fraser of Struy was brought south from the Highlands and became the ward of Simon Fraser, Master of Lovat—and lived right *there*," he pointed, "directly across the street from the Maxwell sisters."

"You are making this up!"

Alex smiled and emphatically shook his head.

"It's all in the records. Not only did Thomas live across the High Street when a little boy, the accounts say Jane Maxwell fell in love with a 'near neighbor' when they were both mere teenagers."

Fiona was dumbfounded by this news. "But I take it that they never were together…after all, she later married the Duke of Gordon, didn't she, now? Perhaps it was merely puppy love on their parts."

Alex shook his head again. "Hardly. The various accounts I've been reading said that the boy's godfather, Simon Fraser, Master of Lovat, sent Thomas Fraser of Struy away to the army. The senior Fraser wanted his handsome young ward to make a more financially advantageous match than to an impoverished baronet's daughter. Against the wishes of the adults, Jane and Thomas reportedly promised to remain true to each other until he returned from fighting with his Black Watch regiment in the American Colonies."

Fiona could feel a small pulse in her neck begin to throb.

"So this Thomas Fraser of—where did you say?"

"Struy…it's a little village in the Highlands, not too far from Loch Ness."

"So Thomas Fraser of Struy *did* travel to America…as part of the Black Watch regiment?"

"Yes," Alex replied. "And news came back that he was killed by Indians."

"Killed? Oh, poor Jane!" Fiona exclaimed. Then she frowned. "So how could I be related to *that* Thomas Fraser, if he died?"

"Hold on a sec. Right after she heard that the great love of her life had been slaughtered by Indians in America, Jane met the Duke of Gordon here in Edinburgh."

"So when Jane met the Duke of Gordon, she was…basically…on the rebound?"

"No," Alex countered. "From what I read, she was still in deep mourning, but her mother, who was delighted by the idea of being so closely related to a duchess, virtually forced her to marry him. Jane was so devastated by the loss of Thomas that she virtually didn't care what happened to her."

"How horribly sad!" Fiona exclaimed, thinking, suddenly, of Peachy's relentless campaign to promote a relationship between her daughter and one Chip Reynolds.

Alex brought Fiona's unhappy thoughts back with a jolt, revealing, "It's hard to believe, but the 'Lost Lieutenant' Thomas Fraser—as he came to be known—*wasn't* dead!"

Fiona froze in her tracks and allowed tourists to make their way around the stone pavers where she and Alex were standing.

"*What?* This sounds like the plot to a Hollywood movie!"

"Precisely so. One couldn't make this bit up! Lieutenant Fraser apparently received a head injury and was nursed back to health in a cabin on the frontier outside Fort Pitt—which I think you call Pittsburgh, now—and eventually he was able to catch up with his regiment, that was, by then, posted to Ireland."

"Oh no!" Fiona said, breathless with curiosity. "Did Thomas and Jane ever meet again?"

Alex took her arm and continued to guide her up the

crowded street. "Well, what I *do* know is that I read several versions of the story that claimed she received a letter from Thomas, postmarked Dublin, that finally caught up with her at her sister Catherine's house in the village of Ayton on her honeymoon—"

"Where's Ayton?" interrupted Fiona.

"Southeast of Edinburgh, near the mouth of the River Eye."

"Oh, the Eye River is right near Paxton House and not too far from Floors Castle—two of the stately homes on my list to visit," Fiona declared excitedly. "I saw the river noted in my guide book."

"Well, we definitely can visit Ayton on our way to see those houses, if you wish," Alex offered. "Reportedly, the lieutenant's missive said he was coming back to Scotland to make her his bride, but alas, his letter had arrived too late."

"How did you learn about all this?"

"I researched various written accounts of the day," Alex replied. "One version said Jane ran sobbing out of Ayton House toward the river that flowed close by, and collapsed. When her new groom saw her there with the sheets of Fraser's letter 'drifting like leaves in autumn upon the mossy banks of the River Eye,' he read what Thomas had written, realized his bride still loved another man, and got into his carriage, abandoning her for months while he brooded in Gordon Castle."

"What a terrible start for a marriage! Think how things would have been different if there'd just been cell phones back then and Thomas could have texted her from Pennsylvania, 'I'm alive!'"

Alex laughed. "Yes, mobiles would have changed the entire course of history, I suspect." Then his expression grew grave. "Perhaps even *our* history."

Fiona took a moment to digest Alex's words. "So that's it, then," she said regretfully, "Jane Maxwell was married to the Duke of Gordon, so bye-bye Thomas Fraser, and off to America with him."

"Not quite," Alex countered. "Apparently there was strong

evidence that Thomas and Jane Maxwell met a few times in the Highlands *after* she'd become the Duchess of Gordon."

Once again, Fiona turned to stare at her escort.

"But wait a sec! This is getting like a roller coaster ride. If *that* Thomas Fraser came back to Scotland, then I don't think he could be *my* ancestor," she declared, "because we know our Thomas Fraser settled in Maryland, first, and had a son named Maxwell by a woman named Arabella O'Brien Delaney Boyd."

"Hmm," mused Alex. "But don't you wonder why this child of *your* Thomas Fraser was named Maxwell, if you have no kin or associations by that name?"

"Goodness only knows," Fiona replied with a shrug. "Apparently, Arabella had two husbands before Thomas Fraser married her. Or maybe *she* had Maxwell as a family name?" She racked her memory, trying to recall the stories Grandfather Maxwell had told her over the years—to which she'd barely listened. "But you're right, Alex…it is pretty curious that every generation in my family—including the first Thomas Fraser in Maryland—named their progeny either Thomas or Maxwell. It seems like a kind of moral imperative, even after the family moved to North Carolina."

"Well, here's something important I haven't told you," Alex confided. "One account I read said that the Lost Lieutenant eventually *returned* to America and was never heard from again."

Fiona allowed Alex's words to sink in. "So the Duchess's Thomas Fraser and *my* Thomas Fraser both ended up in America?" She shook her head. "What you're telling me is all so bizarre…that you and I might be related by blood to Thomas and Jane—but not to each other."

Alex gently put his hands on both shoulders and the two of them became oblivious of the crowds streaming by. "What if," he said with a wry smile, "you are a female descendant of Thomas Fraser and I am a male descendant of Jane Maxwell, making us heirs to the legend of their star-crossed love affair?"

"Oh…" Fiona said on a long breath. "Oh, my."

"I know it sounds daft, but from the minute we met, I had this strange sense of *knowing* you," he declared, his glance unwavering. "It's what originally prompted me to look into our…our possible connection, since I felt a compelling, rather inexplicable—"

"We *can't* really describe it, can we?" she murmured. "I felt it, too, that day I danced the Strathspey with you at the Convention Center. It was as if someone I'd always known had suddenly reappeared in my life…and it wasn't like reincarnation, or anything…just a *knowing* that we both felt this…bond." She heaved a sigh. "But we don't know if any of this is true, and even if it is, just because Jane and Thomas loved and lost doesn't necessarily mean we—"

She stopped short of finishing her sentence when Alex encased one of her hands between his two. Unnerving her even more, she immediately felt the same, strange pulsing sensation whenever he'd touched her the few times they'd been together.

"If we told anyone about this…this strange feeling we both have," she said softly, "they'd just scoff."

"Well, believe me, at first I was extremely skeptical about what I had experienced in New York, but something made me duty-bound to keep digging, especially since the Internet makes tracing one's ancestry so much easier now. What if we're experiencing some sort of *shared* recollection of two people who loved each other deeply and then were wrenched apart by such tragedy? And now that you and I have miraculously met—"

"Alex?" she interrupted. She pointed to a nearby café. "Do you think we could sit down? Maybe have a coffee? I need a minute to take all this in—and a serious dose of caffeine might help."

CHAPTER 7

Alex and Fiona found themselves at the rather touristy Rabbie Burns "Café Bar" a few doors down from a series of kilt and Celtic craft shops. Alex swiftly found a table outdoors, and since the weather was mild, the pair gratefully sank onto bentwood chairs covered in practical fashion with plastic seats.

"Two coffees, please?" he told the waiter.

"With milk on the side," added Fiona.

"Enough milk for two," Alex amended.

For a long moment, they merely exchanged looks. Finally Fiona said, "How long have you known all this stuff?"

She mentally cautioned herself to remember that the discovery of this possible linkage might be wishful thinking on both their parts, merely a way to justify a normal desire for two, red-blooded people who were obviously attracted to each other, to—

Fiona stopped herself from finishing this thought. She had a job to do and had already lost a day of work, given their long lunch and their unscheduled tour of the Royal Mile. And besides, her amateur guide was still, technically, married. And even *more* significant: could any of this speculation be *proved?*

"How do we know this isn't all some sort of myth that grew around a flamboyant duchess?" she challenged. "After all, you said she was in the public eye because of her relationship with Pitt and Robert Burns and the King and Queen. I bet the newspapers of the day were just as scandal-mongering as they are now."

"I don't know. Maybe," Alex allowed. "No one has ever found Thomas Fraser's letter telling of his abiding love for Jane and that he was coming back to Scotland to marry her. I'm fairly sure it's not contained in any public file, because I've done a pretty thorough search. But the deuced thing is: the story of this letter is in nearly every account of her life."

"You mean more than online?" Fiona asked, amazed at Alex's apparent persistence in seeking out the facts about their possible ancestors.

"A lot of her personal papers and those of family members and people associated with the Dukedom of Gordon are here in Edinburgh, in the National Library or at Register House, which we passed on the way to the Royal Café. Or they're up in Aberdeen, Gordon territory. Last week, when I was in the city on mill business, I spent an entire day at Register House," he admitted, adding with a grimace, "but don't tell Hugh Erskine if you please."

Fiona laughed. "I won't, I promise." She set her coffee cup on its saucer with a clink. "Well, we could both have our DNA tested to see if Thomas Fraser's child Maxwell—whose mother was supposedly Arabella O'Brien and born in Maryland—was, instead, born to *Jane*, whisked to America, and has handed down DNA in your Maxwell as well as my Fraser line," she suggested with a smile.

"We could, but all the accounts say the Duchess and Thomas had a *daughter* together named Louisa, not a son, which would mean that only that female child would have the Fraser genes, not those of Jane's other children, from which *my* male Maxwells descend. And it also indicates that Thomas probably *did* sire the first Maxwell Fraser with Arabella in Maryland— meaning that you have *only* Fraser blood, despite every generation naming their progeny Maxwell in some fashion or another."

Fiona gave a sigh of frustration. "But why the naming, then? This is all so *weird,* Alex. And I guess the only way to prove you and I represent the star-crossed lovers, as you called them, is to *find* Thomas's letter, or at least discover the circumstances surrounding the accounts of Jane Maxwell's receiving it." Fiona frowned, turning over Alex's series of disclosures in her mind. At length, she continued, "And we'd also have to prove that Jane's lover, Thomas Fraser of Struy, and *my* ancestor, Thomas Fraser of Maryland, are positively one and the *same person*."

"That's exactly right," Alex said, reaching into his pocket and paying the waiter for their two coffees. "Proving the Thomases are the same person is probably easier than finding the letter. Even if the pages were rescued from the banks of the River Eye, it's the kind of thing families destroy after a relative dies. Dirty family laundry, and all that."

Fiona slumped back in her chair. "Ferreting all this out sounds like a tall order…trying to chase down a letter that may never have existed and figuring out if the Thomases are the same—especially given all the other things I have to accomplish during the short time I'm in Scotland."

Alex nodded his agreement. "Too bad we can't have the DNA tested of Jane's *daughter*, supposedly sired by Thomas Fraser of Struy. It might tell us if her genes have similar markers to yours. All accounts say Louisa was raised as a Gordon, but there were always rumors about her parentage."

"That must have been horrible for the poor little thing," Fiona said. She touched a strand of her hair. "My father has red hair, and so do half my relatives, so I've never had to deal with wondering where I came from…and how I got stuck with this!"

Alex gently seized the strand between his own fingers, "I love your hair, lass. I'll never forget when I first saw you dancing toward me that day."

Fiona felt a telltale blush invade her cheeks. "I never liked being a redhead much, especially when my fraternal twin Tommy's hair was a nice, boring brown that never garnered attention."

Alex lightly ran the back of his fingers along her jaw line, sending shivers down her spine. He then took a final sip from his coffee cup and set it down.

"Well, the mystery of what really happened to the ill-fated Thomas and Jane has been around for two hundred and fifty-odd years. I suppose we can take our time playing sleuth and get on with the business of your creating a Scottish Home Collection that could possibly save our two worlds."

Fiona smiled then, cheered by Alex's calm approach to

something that had stunned and amazed her. "We should definitely get on with the schedule, but tell me quickly, do we know when Jane died?"

"I know the year: 1812. She was in her fifties, but I don't know much else about those years. I ran out of time. I did ask my father about any connection between the Maxwells and the Frasers."

"Had he ever heard anything about this?"

"Father said he'd been told by *his* grandfather about our being 'blood kin' to the celebrated Match-making Duchess—" Alex paused and then explained, "Jane Maxwell was called that by the cynical press of her day because she married off three of her five daughters to dukes; the fourth child to a Marquis, and the fifth to a mere baronet."

"If you count her husband, and son—a future duke—it sounds like she basically cornered the market on dukes!"

Alex grinned at her joke.

"My father had *also* heard the story that his celebrated ancestress had loved someone else before she married the Duke of Gordon. He hadn't heard the name Fraser mentioned, though. Soon after I'd learned those snippets about Jane's life, my own got very complicated and I didn't look into any more of this until you called me saying you were coming to Scotland. Hearing your voice...well, it reminded me of the powerful sense I had in New York that we were...that somehow it felt as if there was unfinished business between us."

"Oh, Alex," she said softly.

He gazed at her as a lover might and she could barely hold his glance. "I was drawn to you, Fiona Fraser, in a way I'd never experienced with anyone in my life before."

She reached for her handbag resting on the pavement beside her chair to give herself time to calm the powerful fluttering in her chest.

"Drawn?" she repeated with a shaky laugh. "For me, it was more like being pulled into some mystical force field, or something." She resolutely stood up from her chair with a sense that she would lose her grip entirely if she confessed her feeling of abject desolation when she'd left Alex standing on the deck of the Circle Line ferry five years earlier. "Meanwhile, Mr. Tour Guide, how about taking me to visit Carlisle Interiors so I can legitimately claim to have done *some* work on my first day in Scotland?"

She could see Alex had caught her obvious signal that she was choosing to return to the business at hand. He guided her a few more blocks up the Royal Mile to George IV Bridge where he hailed a passing taxi. Within minutes, they were speeding down The Mound that led them through the center of Princes Street Gardens and back into New Town, heading toward the area known as the Royal Circus.

Over the next few days as the pair surveyed several well-known interior design shops and Fiona interviewed their owners, neither spoke much about the strange coincidences that appeared to be adding up to the extraordinary possibility that centuries before, their ancestors had loved and lost each other.

As for Fiona, she took her mind off that unsettling notion by concentrating on the task at hand, and found what she was seeing in the way of "Scottish-ness" had, so far, been rather lackluster.

"It seems amazing to me, Alex, that most modern designers around here seem to have ignored the best this country has to offer," she complained one afternoon at a teashop on Frederick Street not far from the cluster of design and antique shops they'd been surveying in the New Town neighborhood. "An awful lot in these home-ware shops feature grey, black, and chrome, period. It's so *boring*! It's like they're all aping Silicon Valley's sleek-but-soulless high tech design!"

In addition to a pot of good, strong tea that Fiona learned from the waitress was labeled "Awesome Assam," she and Alex were sharing a late lunch of honey roasted ham and Scottish cheddar sandwiches. "Why aren't they making use of the beautiful tartans and tweeds this country produces?"

"That's what their grannies had in their houses out in the

country," Alex replied. "Plaid fabrics and cloth like chintz, herringbone, and Tattersall have been around hundreds of years. Young designers apparently think *them* boring. They want to seem hip...cutting edge."

"Bleached burlap sofas? Well, for the most part, it's ugg-ly or uncomfortable—or both!" Fiona pronounced, "and the styles I've seen thus far will never fly with Bernard Sterling." Fiona sank back in her chair and groaned, "Oh, blast! What am I going to actually take back from this trip? A few pieces of Celtic silver?"

"Well, don't lose heart yet," replied Alex. "The highest-end designers are the ones we've yet to visit tomorrow. They're the restoration experts called in to refurbish Scottish castles and manor houses being bought up by the billionaires from Saudi Arabia and Russia—and those are the customers who generally want the traditionally Scottish 'look.'"

"How totally ironic! I guess it takes outsiders, like I am, to see the timeless beauty of the traditional crafts made here...but I wonder how long Scottish manufacturers can hold out if most of the top designers ignore their goods?"

Alex cast her a grim look. "I wonder that, too. And speaking of Maxwell Mills, after our appointments tomorrow, are you ready to head for the Borders the day after? We can stop at those stately homes you mentioned, and some wonderful antique places en route to the various mills in the Tweed Valley—including mine?"

Fiona consulted her list. "Well, last on my list is Jeffreys Interiors, on North West Circus Place, it says here."

"Jeff Laing and Alison Vance at Jeffreys are actually old friends of mine," Alex volunteered. "Tomorrow morning we can tour the oldest mill in Edinburgh and then visit Jeffreys Interiors after lunch. The shop is just down the road from my company's flat. I think you'll like what you see there."

Fiona was left to wonder if Alex was referring to the design emporium they would visit late in the day tomorrow—or the apartment where Alex Maxwell slept when in Edinburgh?

Alex and Fiona ate an early supper upstairs in the small dining room at the Royal Scots Club and afterward, shared demitasse in the lounge.

"Despite the caffeine, I can see your eyes drooping," he said. "Not completely over jet lag, are you?"

Fiona acknowledged as much. Alex rose, pulled her to her feet, and walked her to the elevator.

When the door opened, she said, "Thank you so much for everything…including the tour on the Royal Mile."

He leaned forward and placed a light kiss on the top of her head.

"My pleasure. Sleep well."

"You, too."

She stepped into the car, put the flat of her fingertips to her lips, and then turned them toward him as the doors slid closed. As she rode the lift to her floor, she mused that Alex had been far more candid with her about what had transpired during the years before and since they'd met than she'd been with him.

Given the busy days ahead, perhaps that was as it should be…

Promptly at nine o'clock the following morning Alex called for Fiona in a taxi at the Royal Scots Club so they could arrive at the Edinburgh Tartan Weaving Mill on Castle Hill when it opened.

"This is a pretty touristy enterprise whose real purpose is to sell rather less expensive kilts, novelty tea mugs, and T-shirts that say 'Granny loves Scotland,'" Alex explained as the taxi toiled up Kings Stable Road to approach Edinburgh Castle from the rear. "But the looms are fairly vintage, and it might be a nice introduction to traditional Scottish weaving. Since we'll be there as they open their doors, there shouldn't be too many people and you can get a good look at the actual process by which complicated tartan designs are produced."

Alex had been correct as to how few visitors were up that early, now that the daylight hours of autumn were growing shorter and the tourist season was winding down. They soon were ushered through the gift shop in the direction of a cacophony of sound where machines were at work manufacturing woolen fabrics.

The entrance to the mill itself led to a balcony viewing area where Fiona peered down twenty feet over a railing at a half dozen looms below, clattering away. She marveled at a large metal drum at least fifteen feet in diameter around which various multi-colored threads were wound that would later feed in stately order into the noisy automated looms dotting the cement floor below. An operator stood by each loom to monitor the warp—which were the threads running lengthwise—as the yarn emerged at the junction where a shuttle with various colors of wool shot through, side to side, creating the weft and producing fabric in the desired tartan pattern.

"This is so amazing!" she exclaimed into Alex's ear over the deafening sound of the clanking looms. "And look at those rows and rows of finished goods." She pointed to a wall, some thirty feet long, where bolts of tartan cloth representing more Scottish clans than she ever thought imaginable were stacked high on a bank of floor-to-ceiling shelves.

"Wait till you see Maxwell Mills," Alex shouted back at her over the clatter. "This is actually a pretty small operation, aimed at selling what you saw in the gift shop as we came in." He gestured to the layout below. "Seen enough?"

Fiona nodded and they retraced their steps, emerging into the relative quiet of the gift shop once more.

As they found their way to the exit, she pointed to a mug made of fine bone china that rested on a nearby display shelf. Embossed around its circumference was the dark brown Hunting Fraser tartan.

"I'm sorry," she said with an embarrassed laugh as she seized it from among a gaggle of mugs stamped with the tartans of Stewart, Campbell, MacLeod, MacRae, and several of the better-known clans. "I guess I'm just a tourist, too. Forgive me, but I can't resist!"

Alex gently took it from her hand and said with mock

gallantry, "We Scots are most happy you feel inclined to select this item, Madam. I insist you allow me to purchase this for you as a token of our appreciation having you here on our shores!"

Laughing, Fiona made only a mild protest, secretly touched by his generosity in everything he'd done to help her navigate her way in a country she'd never visited before. Drinking tea from the mug would always be a pleasant reminder of the trip—and the time she'd spent with this man who was becoming less of a stranger by the minute.

Once Alex completed the purchase, he led Fiona directly across the cobbled street and down a narrow stone passageway into a restaurant called The Witchery.

"Another tourist destination, but quite a nice one," he commented as they walked through the entrance to the ancient building that stood diagonally from the impressive gates of Edinburgh Castle. "This doorway is sixteenth century, but this dining spot actually sits on a former derelict schoolyard."

"Amazing," Fiona marveled as they entered the stone archway and proceeded down a few slate steps into the building.

Within the entrance they were immediately surrounded by intricately carved wooden panels and an exquisitely painted ceiling overhead. Due to the restaurant's positioning on the side of Castle Hill, the interior featured a series of levels with seating areas that consisted of a mix of rich, red leather banquettes alternating with separate tables covered in snowy white linen, a forest of wine glasses, and stunning silver flatware and tableware. On one wall, a bank of arched, paned windows provided a spectacular view of the top end of the Royal Mile.

"So nice to see you, Mr. Maxwell!" enthused an effusive maître d'. "Been busy down in the Borders, have you?"

"Aye," Alex said, nodding. "But I couldn't allow my visitor from America, Ms. Fraser, here, to come to Edinburgh and not have a meal in this august establishment."

"By all means, sir. Come right along. Perhaps you'd enjoy the terrace garden room today?" The maître d' smiled at Fiona conspiratorially. "We call it the Secret Garden, as we tend to reserve it for our best patrons."

Alex replied. "That's very kind of you. I think we'd enjoy that."

They were ushered past a line of tourists already queuing up for an early lunch at the famous eatery and were whisked down yet another level into one of the most beautiful rooms Fiona had ever seen. The back wall was paneled in what could only be repurposed medieval church choir stalls, ornately decorated with dark gothic wooden moulding and intricate marquetry. In this intimate dining room, straight-backed, sable-brown leather chairs surrounded small tables set for two-to-four patrons. Several tall brass candlesticks dotting the room prompted Fiona to wonder if they'd possibly been raided from a cathedral to stand sentry over diners who, today, enjoyed shafts of warm, fall sunshine streaming from the skylight overhead. Garlands of dried fruits—oranges, pomegranates, and apples—were strung against the walls in dramatic ropes in a stately cascade down the stairwell.

They were led to a table for two in the corner where the wall nearest Fiona's chair was covered with a tapestry that she estimated had to be at least two-hundred-years old.

"Will this suit?" asked the maître d' with a knowing smile in Alex's direction.

"Perfectly," he replied, adding, "Thanks so much Alistair."

"You should be dining on your own for a little while," he replied. "The tourists all want the view of the city," and then he scurried up the staircase, leaving them to the ministrations of a very quiet, efficient waiter Alex identified as Ian.

Fiona waited until the server took their order and discreetly disappeared.

"Are you an *investor* in this place?" Fiona whispered, "or just a very good customer?"

"The latter," Alex replied, having a quick sniff of a glass of burgundy he'd ordered. Apparently finding it to his taste, he took a first sip and said, "I bring visiting business acquaintances here quite often, but I thought, since we were directly across the street at the mill and we're on a bit of a tight schedule, it might be amusing for you to have a meal in such a unique spot."

"I love being a tourist today," she replied with a smile,

patting the package containing her new mug that sat on an empty chair between them.

After a bowl of cock-a-leekie soup that was a delicious blend of pureed potatoes and onions, Alex recommended a light meal of open-faced sandwiches made of brown bread, butter, and slivers of smoked salmon sprinkled with fresh dill.

As they finished their coffee and waited for the bill, Alex asked, "Well, what's next on the agenda?"

Fiona dug into her tote, pulled out her iPad. She read off three names from an electronic list she'd created before she'd left New York, including Jeffreys Interiors.

Alex nodded. "Then let's be off. All three establishments are located quite close to each other."

By two-thirty, they'd visited the first two on Fiona's list. Alex then directed their taxi driver to head for the area of Queen Street Gardens near her hotel. However, instead of stopping, Alex asked the driver to turn onto Howe Street toward the magnificent Royal Circus, it's round park encircled by the gray stone terraced houses that, by this time, were becoming familiar landmarks to Fiona.

"I'm not surprised Jeffreys made your list," he said. "They're quite respected in their field. As I mentioned, they're also good friends of mine who actually might be quite helpful to you."

Despite Fiona's protests and attempts to hand him a few pounds, he leaned forward to pay the driver and then held the taxi door for her to climb out after him.

They had arrived at a chalkboard gray building with icy white trim at Number 8 West North Circus Place. A sandwich board painted shiny black with a large, gunmetal gray "J" announced the home design establishment that Fiona had researched on the Internet—and Alex knew as well.

"Now, *this* is what I've been looking for!" Fiona exclaimed the minute they walked into its dramatic front room. The interior design shops they'd just visited after lunch had boosted her spirits somewhat, but she knew, instantly, that Jeffreys was exactly what she had hoped she would find on this scouting trip to Edinburgh.

Peering around the first showroom—a living room setting with a royal blue tufted wool twill sofa sporting rows of brass studs marching down its rolled arms, she gave a contented sigh. The rest of the decor featured an eclectic collection of deer antlers, dark metal statues of hunting dogs, along with carved wooden wall sconces, and a large, square coffee table made of highly polished mahogany.

Curled up on the Persian carpet was a small Border Terrier. At their entrance, he had raised his wheat-colored head and then settled back into blissful sleep.

A shop dog, thought Fiona, and mused how enjoyable a place this probably was to work.

To one side of the room sat a matched pair of chocolate-brown leather club chairs, along with a standing lamp positioned between them whose tall base was made of a slender trunk of a birch tree topped with a shade crafted in amber mica. A short stack of tartan cushions piled decorously on a side table were not in the primary colors of Scottish clans, but instead, featured muted hues of umber, sage, brick red, and winter white—and sported tags that read, "Made expressly for Jeffreys Interiors by Maxwell Mills."

"Stunning!" Fiona pronounced, advancing into a second room—a bedroom setting—whose walls were covered in red and cream toile wallpaper decorated with a series of gilt framed mirrors. A large, brown velvet padded headboard with a footboard in the shape of a wooden sleigh looked as if Ralph Lauren might have slept there.

Then she paused. "Oh, no!" she said under her breathe.

"What's amiss?" Alex asked, who had been examining a handsome brass compass sitting on a stack of vintage leather-bound books perched on a side table.

"Look…over there!"

She pointed to a low chest of drawers where a fan of smart, glossy brochures featured a cover image of an antique car, an enormous, shaggy Scottish Deerhound, and rolls of rich, woolen fabrics draped over a leather chair identical to the ones she'd just seen in the previous showroom. Emblazoned across the top of the handout were the words RALPH LAUREN.

"Jeff and Alison are the exclusive distributors of Ralph Lauren here in Edinburgh," Alex explained, giving Fiona a puzzled glance. "They feature many other products besides his, but it's given them quite a lot of cachet among their high-end clients."

"Well, no wonder all this appeals to me," Fiona said with a rueful smile. "Bernard Sterling and Ralph Lauren are always mentioned in the same breath in the States."

"Is this a problem?"

"Not if it isn't for Jeffreys," Fiona replied, but immediately began to worry that it might be. "Having me visit, I mean. If the tables were turned, Bernard Sterling would think we were spies. Sterling considers Lauren an arch-rival in everything."

Fiona quickly explained how the august Mr. Sterling had been forever going toe-to-toe with his nemesis, famously flying giraffes to Montana for a magazine layout when he'd heard Lauren had flown a zebra to Hawaii. And like Ralph Lauren, Sterling had acquired unnumbered old Jeeps, dozens of huge, battered, decaled leather trunks from the Golden Age of ocean travel, and maintained a warehouse full of classic picnic hampers and antique brass compasses.

"And just like Ralph Lauren, my boss now owns several vintage Bugatti motor cars, a gaggle of pre-World War I Rolls Royces, and even a stuffed swan—which made me want to burst out crying when I first saw it in the company's warehouse on 34th Street."

"Well, let me go look for Jeff," Alex volunteered, "and we'll sort this out."

"Wait just a sec," she said quickly, putting a hand on his sleeve. "The owners, here, are the ones you told me that are hired to refurbish derelict castles and such?"

"And manor houses…hunting lodges, yes. They're really great chums of mine."

"Well, they have exquisite taste, but it's probably best to keep my idea for a Scottish Home Collection by Bernard Sterling to yourself, okay? My boss would fire me on the spot if—because of me—RL's people got wind through Jeffreys of what we're trying to do for a new collection next spring."

"Cone of silence," Alex assured her, but then frowned. "But don't you think you'll have to mention why you're in Edinburgh, Fiona? If we ask them to maintain strictest confidentiality, I promise you, you can trust that they won't breathe a word."

CHAPTER 8

Alex headed off down a hallway while Fiona fretted over the issue of the Edinburgh firm's connection with Sterling's principal competitor. But before she could obsess any further, Jeffrey Laing and Alison Vance appeared in the wide doorway with Alex standing behind them, and both gave Fiona a warm welcome.

"We understand from Alex that you are in 'stealth mode,'" Alison said, smiling after shaking hands. She had a cap of dark hair with an arresting streak of white and her burnt-red jacket and black slacks were minimalist and very chic, Fiona thought. "I know the Bernard Sterling line and it's lovely. Jeff and I promise we won't say a word to anybody that you've been here, given you're merely in the exploratory stages of your project, am I right?"

Fiona nodded, her concerns abating a bit.

"We understand perfectly," chimed in Jeff Laing, who had close cropped hair and sported blue jeans and a tweed jacket, reminiscent of what Alex apparently preferred to wear when not attired in his kilt. "And likewise, we never discuss our private dealings with the Lauren company with anyone—even Alex," he concluded with a wink in his direction.

Relieved to have some of her apprehensions put to rest, Fiona murmured her thanks and began to ask questions about their interior design business: what trends they were noting and what their customers asked for most frequently when they came into the shop.

She soon learned that the couple, in their early fifties, had met at a trade show—he the businessman; she a well-respected designer—and eventually they combined forces personally and professionally.

"I came to work at Jeffreys, which had been in Jeff's family for five generations, and ended up moving in with the boss," Alison joked.

Jeff added, "My family started out in 1842 in the port city of Leith, which is quite close to here, as a kind of nineteenth century department store, selling carpets and floor cloths and the like. By the nineteen-thirties, the company had moved into drapery fabric and other items to furnish the home."

"But when Jeff took over," Alison chimed in, "he made the company's focus up-market, custom interior design. He saw by then that we had to go up-market to survive, especially after the global financial crisis a few years ago."

"Was that shift successful?" Fiona asked, thinking she could pass along some of this information to her brother as he struggled to keep Fraser Furniture afloat.

"Well, thanks, we believe, to this change in focus, we landed a few impressive manor houses to do over, thereby earning the right to be chosen for the Ralph Lauren distributorship—which certainly helps bring people in the front door," Alison frankly acknowledged. "Fortunately, an increasing number of the people who still had money during the worst of the recession came to us for a cushion and ended up having us refurbish their entire home."

Fiona nodded, thinking that one day, perhaps, if her ideas took hold at home and abroad, Bernard Sterling would have such worldwide recognition. RL had already done highly successful lines of home furnishings that featured British goods, including numerous items that hailed from Scotland, but Fiona's idea had always been to do a more extensive collection for the home *exclusively* associated with goods created in the land of the Celts and Gaels.

As Sterling himself had always hammered into his staff, "There's gotta be a *differentiator* to earn the Bernard Sterling label! I have a vision of style...of grace.... of the things in my surroundings that make me *feel* good. I come at everything with a sense of how *I* would want to live! You gotta make me *want to own* the goods you think we should sell!"

Well, as far as Fiona was concerned, she wanted to own nearly every item in Jeffreys Interiors: their elegant selections of furniture, bedding, rugs, china and glassware, lighting accessories, wall coverings and paint colors. Who wouldn't very much like to live in the kind of world that Jeff and Alison had created from all the lovely things Scottish manufacturing had to offer?

Her favorite word *thoroughbred* came to mind. That's what Bronx-born Bernard Sterling longed to be, and Fiona would bet much of new and old moneyed America would agree with him. What she was seeing in the shop before her was a pure Scottish interpretation of what she had been raised around, and she felt more confident than ever that she had started tapping into the kind of 'look' that would result in a Bernard Sterling Scottish Home Collection that merited the name.

Her spirits definitely on the upswing, the following two hours Fiona spent at Jeffreys also convinced her that the couple was among the nicest and most generous people she had ever met. The design team willingly showed her around not only their numerous and stunning room settings, but also their back workrooms packed with rolls of expensive wallpaper, stacks of paint samples, and swatches of rich fabrics from manufacturers like Italy's Fortuny and England's Colfax and Fowler, along with several books of small squares of tartan samples labeled Maxwell Mills, Lochcarron of Scotland, Johnstons of Elgin, and D.C. Dalgliesh.

Fiona's eyes lit up at the sight of a series of Alison's sketches pinned to a cork board that illustrated the complete refurbishment of a dilapidated hunting lodge in the Highlands, as well as an eleventh century castle perched on top of a windswept moor.

"And do you often get requests for Scottish textiles as opposed to Italian Fortuny, and so forth?" she asked, trying to appear only mildly interested in the answer, "...you know, fabric like Alex makes...or the other local firms produce?"

"Interesting that you should ask that," Jeff said with a glance at his partner. "I think the people with the *new* money—the Saudi princes and Russian oil billionaires—are beginning to seek classic furnishings like tartan and leather upholstered furniture because of their desire to appear refined, much like the former owners of these magnificent old houses they're buying up at an astonishing rate."

"Hmmmm…that makes sense," Fiona replied, thinking to herself that the desire of strivers like Wall Street tycoons of Curt Vandervort's stripe and the dot comers in California, who yearned to *appear* to have a family pedigree and good taste, was what had fueled Ralph Lauren's success. That longing to be a member of the A List socially was also at the core of Bernard Sterling's enthusiasm for her Scottish Home Collection concept. Jeff and Alison had just confirmed this supposition and she felt both relieved and increasingly buoyed that she was definitely on the right path—at last.

She glanced, again, at another copy of the Ralph Lauren brochure that rested on a small side table flanking the azure sofa. "I really love what you've done in here," she said sincerely, "in fact, what you've done in *all* of the rooms in your shop. I wish I could just move *in* here!" she added with a smile.

"Why thank you," Alison replied, exchanging a pleased look with her partner. "We use a few pieces of Ralph Lauren here and there, but in our showrooms and our custom work we tend to feature mostly our own finds. We create these inspirational settings at our shop to encourage people to buy more than what they came into the store for."

"Well, from the looks of things, it appears you've found the magic formula. Thank you so much for your time. It's much appreciated and I love everything I saw."

As Fiona and Alex descended the short flight of stone steps leading to the street, Alison called after them, "Do let us know what your company line comes up with next spring as a result to your trip to Scotland. We'd be really interested in having a first look, Fiona. I think we're all on the same page about what sort of interiors we fancy. I *hate* chrome, myself!" she said with a laugh.

Fiona waved the business card Jeff had handed her as they'd left.

"What a darling couple," she declared as she and Alex were

about to head in the direction of the circular park in Royal Circus Place.

"They're stellar," Alex agreed. "They have the kind of personal and professional partnership I've only dreamed about." He gave her arm a gentle squeeze. "Well, now, feel like a spot of supper? My local favorite, Café Fish, is quite near here."

Which could only mean that the Maxwell Mills' company flat was very close by.

Two hours later on the second floor of Alex's terraced house on Royal Circus, Fiona sank onto her host's saddle leather sofa whose seat cushions were upholstered in the forest green and burgundy-red Maxwell tartan.

"Those braised sea scallops were spectacular," Fiona declared, leaning against one of the loose, square pillows covered in paisley fabric and taking a moment to admire the vintage needlepoint footstool nearby. On the floor in front of a white marble fireplace was a large example of the seemingly ubiquitous Persian carpets she'd noted everywhere in Edinburgh interiors.

Alex handed her a crystal tumbler with an inch of single malt whiskey.

"Have a taste of Glenfiddich. It's one of my Highland favorites from the Spey Valley...as in Strathspey," he added with a slight quirk to the corners of his mouth.

"Cheers," she said, raising her glass.

"*Slàinte*," he repeated in Gaelic, gently tapping his glass filled with a similarly modest amount of the amber liquid for which Scotland distilleries were justly famous. "Café Fish does its specialties rather well, I think."

Before dinner, Alex had changed into a pair of khaki-colored wool worsted trousers and now had shed his tweed sports coat and tie. With his Oxford blue shirtsleeves rolled up to his forearms, he settled into a black upholstered wing chair sporting brass studs on both arms.

Fiona glanced around Alex's apartment that occupied two floors of one of the row houses she'd been admiring since her arrival. It was one of the scores of terraced houses that ringed the round park, lush and verdant with foliage that was just beginning to show a hint of fall colors.

"Your place is so lovely, Alex," she said, gesturing with her glass. "I can see why you love coming up to Edinburgh as often as you can."

"I feel…very at home, here," he said, leaning his dark head against the chair's tall back. "And why wouldn't I, with Alison and Jeff advising me on nearly every item that's in here? The only way I could afford them doing up this flat was to give them excellent price points on the tartan fabric for those throw cushions you so admired in their shop."

Fiona raised an appreciative eyebrow. "They definitely get the Good Taste Award, and so do you, for going along with their suggestions. I love what y'all have done to this place."

Alex took a sip of his whiskey and gazed at her over its rim. "And I love the way you speak."

Fiona looked at him, puzzled.

"'Y'all,'" he repeated. "It just slips into your speech unexpectedly and in the most charming fashion. It makes me want to visit your part of the world."

"High Point, North Carolina, isn't really part of my world anymore," she said, gazing down into her glass.

"No? And why is that?"

Fiona hesitated. In light of how honest and open Alex had been from the first moment they'd met, there was so much she yearned to confide to him, so many things about which she longed to hear his opinion. Even more compellingly, there were things she wished to state clearly at the outset in order for this obviously budding relationship to begin cleanly, with no secrets held.

For she had no doubt that during these days they'd spent together in Edinburgh they had begun to build something significant, though where it would take them—given his personal situation, their challenging, dual-continent geography, and her own set of personal hurdles to get over—she had no idea.

She inhaled deeply to work up her nerve. Then she said,

"Because of that 'y'all' accent you find charming, I carry a certain amount of baggage accumulated during my two decades in North Carolina. I still have a ways to go unloading it—but I'm happy to report that I *am* getting there."

"I think that's probably true of nearly everyone I know who has passed the threshold of their thirties. At thirty-five, and with one failed marriage to my credit, I surely fall into the category."

"Well, I come from the American South, Alex, where our childhoods tend to be a bit more Gothic than a lot of other places," she said, flashing him a wry look while noting silently that the whiskey's warmth was beginning to seep into her veins. The excellent spirits were also putting her more at ease in Alex's stunning lair that, she guessed, had seen its fair share of willing maidens.

She inclined her head and asked the question uppermost in her mind since she'd arrived at the Waverley train station.

"And what about your life, Alex…or at least your life since Addy left? Have you been a monk since your wife moved to Peebles?" She almost hoped he'd tell her that there had been some woman serving as his bridge out of Miseryland, remembering her friend's caution never to be the "first girlfriend after a divorce."

"A monk?" he repeated. "Rather an apt description, actually."

"Really?" She couldn't keep the skepticism out of her voice.

"Really," he replied firmly.

Fiona didn't know whether to believe him or not, but before she could question him further he countered with, "But you're changing the subject. We were talking about *your* life these past five years. Did your mortgage securities man, Curt Somebody, ever circle back into your life?"

"Are you kidding me?" Fiona exclaimed, vigorously shaking her head. "Curt and his wife Christiane—" She interrupted herself. "Those two are technically *still* married, mind you, but now he's living with a runway model named Anastasia Volmensky whom I know slightly because occasionally she works for Sterling's apparel division."

"Anastasia," Alex repeated. "She sounds very tall."

"And very Rus-sian!" Fiona said with an attempt at a Slavic accent.

"Doesn't Curt's legal wife object?"

"Christiane? I don't think so. Remember how I figured they'd married so they couldn't be forced to testify against each other about what was going on in their company's derivative business?" Alex nodded. "Well now," continued Fiona, "given that Christiane Amsler apparently doesn't seem to mind that her husband has taken up with Anastasia—I'm convinced they'd just had an office fling and that their marriage was a sham all along."

"All this in only five years?" Alex noted. "Didn't I say to you on the ferry that you were well out of it regarding that lad?"

"And you were so right. Funnily enough, I get emails from Curt occasionally. Wants to remain friends and all that. It's fine."

"And since then?"

Alex allowed the words to hang between them.

"Since then? All I ever do is work."

"Sounds like me. No serious boyfriends?"

Once again, Fiona felt a flush creep up her cheeks.

"This is pretty embarrassing to admit, but no, not a one. I'm a thirty-two-year-old woman who might as well have joined a nunnery," she admitted with a short laugh.

You could never call yourself a nun, Fiona Fraser. Not if you count Chip…

At that moment, Fiona almost gave into an impulse to tell Alex about Chip Reynolds, the rowdy frat boy who—

She heaved a sigh, refusing to let her thoughts drift in that direction. No one outside of High Point, North Carolina knew what had happened between Chip and her, or the decisions that were ultimately made. And as far as Fiona was concerned, she'd disclosed quite enough about herself and her family to Alexander Maxwell for one day.

She dug into her black and brown Michael Kors travel tote bag whose roominess nearly granted it the status of carry-on luggage.

"Shall we look at my *Michelin* map and plot our course for

the next few days?" she asked with forced cheer, steering their conversation back to business. She unfolded the map to its full size and spread it on the large, square coffee table positioned between them. "I've circled Paxton House and Floors Castle that I told you in my email that I want to see. They're not too far distant from each other, are they?"

"No, they're quite close and can be visited on the same day."

She studied the map more closely and then pointed to a town near the Tweed River. "And here's Traquair House, outside the town of Innerleithen, that I also wrote you about a few weeks ago. I definitely want to visit it and—"

"It's already been arranged," Alex declared with a satisfied grin, "plus I've secured you an interview with Catherine Constable Maxwell Stuart, the Twenty-First Lady of Traquair, who can tell you all about what she did to convert part of her lovely manor house into a first-class bed and breakfast. I think the furnishings there will give you a genuine sense of what true Scottish taste has been in elegant family homes for centuries."

"Oh, Alex, that's wonderful!" Fiona said excitedly, "and so kind of you."

"Oh, I also have an ulterior motive for your visiting there."

"Yes? And what is that?" Fiona asked, feeling a little unexplained thrill of anticipation despite her recent vow to keep to business.

"I've asked Catherine to explain her connections to my ancestress, Jane Maxwell, as well as Catherine's links to the royal Stuart line."

"No!" Fiona replied with delight. "Bernie Sterling is going to *love* all this! In fact, Alex, would you be horribly put out if I wrote him a quick email and sent some of the cell phone shots I made around Edinburgh today? It's mid-afternoon in New York and I'll whet his appetite and let him know what we've lined up for the next few days. That way, he and my immediate boss, Jared Finnegan, will be less likely to tell *me* what to do."

"Works perfectly for me," he said, rising from the chair. "In fact, I need to check in with Hugh at the mill by phone, so I'll just go in my study and leave you to it." He paused and asked, "But do you want to use my computer, first?"

"Thanks, but if you give me your Wi-Fi code, I can just write a quick note from my iPad and attach some images I think my bosses will salivate over."

A few minutes later, Fiona quickly set to work communicating her excitement about her discoveries during her first days in Edinburgh, with special emphasis on the area's castle and manor house owners that had become clients of Jeffreys Interiors. She concluded with a mention of her upcoming interview with the 21st Lady of Traquair whose ancient family home was considered a showplace among country bed and breakfast establishments.

In the next room, Alex was deep in conversation with his second in command, Hugh Erskine. She tried not to eavesdrop, but couldn't help but pick up on the myriad problems he apparently faced regarding his struggling mill, to say nothing of dealing with his difficult younger brother, and sorting through the issues of his impending divorce.

On that subject, she was surprised to hear him exclaim, "*No*! That's amazing, Hugh! She's *already* signed and returned a copy of the court documents? Excellent. Yes, do open it and read me her note." There was a long pause, and then he said, "Well…so it's final, at last. And bloody nice of her to say all that, actually. She's a decent woman, that Adelina Dalgetty. I'll email her tonight that all is in order on my end, too, and thank her for her kind words."

Fiona busied herself folding her outsized Michelin map before she proofread her email to her bosses once more. She was about to push the send button, but paused because she couldn't help paying attention to Alex's next words.

"Yes…Addy has the number here. Fine, if she wants to call. Tell her I'll be here until mid-morning, tomorrow. After that, I'll be on my mobile a few days while I'm traveling. Yes, and tell her that I have one or two things to advise her regarding her father. Good, then. I'll call you along the way at some point, or you ring me if anything important comes up. Goodnight, Hugh. And thanks for all your help. You're stellar, laddie."

Fiona felt as if she should have moved out of earshot, but couldn't help but sense a little jolt of electricity to have overheard that Alex was apparently no longer a married man. There was dead silence emanating from the other room during the moments it took Fiona to quickly skim her email for a final time to catch any spelling errors. She sent it on to Bernard, with a copy to Jared Finnegan, who had sharply reminded her on the eve of her departure to keep him "in the loop at every stage when you communicate with the Boss Man."

She rose from the sofa and walked to the door of the small study where Alex sat staring vacantly at the surface of a glass-topped desk set upon ornately carved wooden pedestals.

"Alex? Everything all right?" she asked, concerned by the look of sadness she noted had invaded his expression.

"Ah...Fiona," he said, looking up as if pulling his thoughts from a million miles away. "Forgive me. I'm so sorry to have abandoned you like this."

"No worries," Fiona hastened to assure him, leaning against the door-jam. "Listen, you probably need some time on your own. Why don't I just grab a cab back to the hotel and—"

Alex shook his head. "No! No, please don't leave just yet." He rose from his chair. "Apparently I officially became a single man two days ago, while you and I were walking the Royal Mile," he said, his tone of voice reflecting both melancholy and a vague sense of amazement. "Addy promptly signed the same documents I had, and wrote a very sweet note, wishing me well." Alex searched Fiona's face for a sign she understood what he was about to say next. "And I truly wish the same for her. The local magistrate has declared our divorce final."

"I've never heard of a divorce like this," Fiona responded with a hint of a smile, "but I am glad for both of you, if it's what you two wanted."

"It was the only answer to a mistake for which everyone involved bore some responsibility. I am extremely grateful Addy and I emerged pretty much unscathed, mostly due I imagine, to our finally speaking the truth to each other about how we felt and what we truly wanted." He strode to where Fiona stood at the threshold to his study. "That's what *I* want from here on out with the people I care for," he said, seeking her glance, "the truth, gently spoken. It seems to me to be the only road to any kind of happiness in this life."

Fiona nodded her agreement but in the back of her thoughts, her immediate reaction to his words was when—or if—she should tell him about what happened with Chip?

Before she could marshal her thoughts and begin what she knew would be a difficult conversation, Alex put his arm around her shoulders and retraced their steps to the front room. It was a large, generous space with impressively tall windows that overlooked the park and its circle of wrought iron fencing. Alex reached toward the coffee table and seized their two unfinished glasses of whiskey.

"It's not that I exactly feel like dancing in the streets in celebration over the news I'm no longer married to Addy," he declared, handing her the tumbler that had been hers, "but I do somehow feel at this moment like raising a toast to the future, whatever it may be. *Slàinte*," he said for the second time that evening.

"That's Scottish for 'Cheers…or to your good health, right?"

Nodding, Alex gently touched his glass to hers.

Unable to pull her gaze away from his, she murmured, "To the unknowable future…and the mysterious past of Jane Maxwell and Thomas Fraser."

"To Jane and Thomas…and to whatever is the meaning of their lives to you and me."

Fiona paused, considering the portentousness of what Alex had just stated. Then she said, "Though we really don't know for certain, it's nice to think we might be their representatives in the modern world."

"I *know* we are," he replied with conviction. "All the research I've done points to that fact and I just *feel* that it's true, somehow. And who knows? Given enough time, we might learn if they shared anything more than an intense love in their youth—and apparently the child Louisa that was raised as the Duke's." He glanced down at the coffee table, cleared of Fiona's map and research notes. "Where's the *Guide Michelin*? I want you to point out to me all the other places you have on your list that you'd like to see, so we can make a plan of action for the next few days."

Fiona dug into her tote, pulled out the map again, and the two took seats on the sofa and began studying the area of Scotland south of Edinburgh. After a few minutes of comparing her list of places she'd hope to visit with the distances between them, as shown on the map, she tapped a tattoo with her pen on the coffee table.

"You know, Alex," she said slowly, "If you have a lot weighing on you at the mill…and elsewhere…I'm more than happy to rent a car and do a lot of this on my own. We could meet up later somewhere, if you want."

Fiona couldn't tell if Alex's expression reflected that he was annoyed or offended by her suggestion.

He regarded her steadily and then asked with a challenging look. "Is the fact that I am no longer a married man unnerving you somehow, Fiona?"

A long silence stretched between them. Then she admitted, "Yes, a little. From the very beginning—and even more so since we've spent these days in Edinburgh together—it all feels…very…*intense* between us, somehow, and that's what scares me a bit. It's…it's just *odd*…and a bit spooky, if you don't mind my saying so."

"It rather struck me a bit the same way," he agreed.

"And also, Alex," she added, staring into her glass of half-consumed Scotch Whiskey, "There's no ignoring how much you have on your plate, much as I do, and this added layer of…well, I guess I'm feeling the pressure of everything. And besides, the ink is barely dry on your divorce and—"

"Those are a lot of different thoughts," Alex intervened, "though I can understand how you might be having so many, because so am I." He set his glass on the table again and removed hers from her hand and placed the tumblers side-by-side. "But my single state isn't really a new one for me, Fiona. I want you to know that Addy and I have not been lovers for two years and we haven't lived under the same roof for many months." He seemed to intuit Fiona's unspoken question. "And there haven't been any other women during my marriage before I met you—or since. Not one."

"Oh, Alex..." she said, barely above a whisper.

"What?" he demanded softly. "You must tell me what else is putting that worried look in your eye?"

If she were truly honest with herself, there was something else that had made her want to step back a few paces from the amazing rush of feelings she'd been experiencing from the second she'd seen Alex in his kilt, standing in Waverly Station.

Finally she blurted, "I suppose it would be stupid of me to try to hide the fact that I am also very drawn to you, Alex Maxwell, and in such a powerful, rather other-worldly way. I don't even understand it myself very well. But one thing I *do* know is...I don't want to be your *rebound* lady!"

Alex didn't reply to her outburst and Fiona could tell he was waiting for her to explain her feelings further.

"I don't want to be the woman serving as the bridge out of the relationship with your former wife, regardless of how friendly your parting appears to have been," she added with less heat. "I guess I have to say...I don't trust this. I don't trust myself *in* this."

"Fiona Fraser," he said, slowly shaking his head, "you couldn't possibly be my 'rebound lady,' as you call it." Without warning he took her into his arms and scattered quick kisses on the top of her head and then leaned back to gaze at her full in the face. "You are *the* lady...the woman I have longed to hold again like this ever since that Strathspey we danced together ended five years ago. And yes, we each have a lot to contend with right now on both a personal and professional level...and the possible connection you and I have to our respective ancestors is undoubtedly a bit bizarre. But we are *finally* here together, in a place that I love," he said, glancing around the elegant room with the fireplace embers glowing softly, warming the cool, autumn air outside the tall windows, "...and in a city I love—"

"I already love it too," Fiona interrupted, reaching up to brush a lock of Alex's dark hair off his forehead.

"And since—at long last—I have you next to me, I'm afraid that I really can't waste a second more..."

But it was Fiona who framed Alex's face within her hands and kissed him fully on the lips. How strange it all was, she thought in some part of her brain not reveling in the feel of his mouth against hers. His seeking lips began triggering electrifying sensations that coursed through her limbs. This felt so *right*...so *familiar*...as if they had kissed many times before with the passionate intensity of desperation and a fear that they would be discovered.

But we are both now unmarried adults! We—

Alex's arms tightened around her shoulders, driving away all rational thought as he swiftly took command of their ardent embrace. He showered her cheeks, her eyes, even her nose with fevered kisses, as if *he* thought she was an apparition that might disappear. At length, like two swimmers surfacing for air, Fiona leaned back in his arms and smiled, eyes misty. "Well, so much for renting a car of my own."

"Oh, God, Fiona," he murmured, pulling her close once more. "I think I should tell you that I've actually had some very erotic dreams about you over the years and now, here you are, and I only want to—"

Just then, in the next room, the telephone emitted a series of insistent pips. Alex and Fiona's glances locked as the demanding sound reverberated throughout the flat.

"Bloody hell!" He glanced at his watch. "It's late, so the only person that probably could be is Addy. She asked Hugh if it were all right to call me here and I said yes."

"Of course," Fiona responded, but she despised her own reaction of colossal disappointment. "Better run and get it."

CHAPTER 9

Alex rose from the sofa and swiftly strode into his study to catch the phone on the sixth ring. Hearing him say hello into the receiver, Fiona folded her map with a sense of resignation, storing the rest of her things into her tote bag as well. There was no way to ignore that, despite Alex's being officially a free man, he had plenty of unfinished business to attend to with his former wife. Alex began a conversation in lowered tones and Fiona felt massively uncomfortable being in his flat while he dealt with whatever Adelina Dalgetty — formerly Maxwell — deemed important enough to call at this late hour.

Then she heard him say, "It's all right, Addy. Yes. No, you haven't awakened me. And thank you for your very kind note, by the way. Your sentiments are returned, completely. What's on your mind?"

A long silence ensued and then Fiona heard Alex murmur a series of yeses and quiet assurances that he would figure out a way to resolve an issue that sounded as if it required his urgent attention.

As the minutes rolled by, Fiona felt acutely out of place. She grabbed paper and pen from the depths of her tote and scribbled a note, then quietly slipped out the front door.

The route back to the Royal Scots Club was an easy three-block walk down Howe Street to Heriot Row where she stopped briefly to admire a plaque noting that author Robert Louis Stevenson once lived at Number 17. Crossing Dundas Street, her hotel's front light welcomed her on Abercromby Place. As the tiny elevator whisked her up to her room, a crushing sense of fatigue bore down on her. It was the last remnants of jet lag, she supposed, added to their busy day running all over Edinburgh, plus the emotional rollercoaster that her evening with Alex had turned out to be. All she could think of was sinking into a hot bath and falling into bed.

"Do you think Father would actually *do* something as horrid as this?" cried Adelina Dalgetty. Her high-pitched tone of voice clearly reflected the stress she had been under for months.

"Call in the loan to the mill?" Alex asked. He tried his utmost to concentrate on Addy's distress in the wake of hearing the sound of his front door closing as Fiona quietly took her leave without saying goodbye.

"Yes, call in the loan!" Addy replied heatedly, sounding as if she were about to burst into tears, "to say nothing of swearing to ruin your business in every other way he can think of *if* I don't agree to reconcile our marriage. Alex, you know that I don't want to do anything to hurt you or your company, but I can't…I *won't* let my father control my life anymore!"

"I absolutely agree with you," he hastened to say, trying his best to reassure a woman who had only in recent years stiffened her spine with regard to her relationship with her tyrannical father. "And I appreciate your warning about his threat to call in the bank loan. At least I won't be blindsided by his trying to do something so rash, and I'm sure my board can make him see he's only hurting himself *and* the bank."

Addy continued as if she hadn't heard her former husband's reassurances.

"I can't *imagine* what he'll do if he learns our divorce is already final," she exclaimed, her voice breaking. "Fortunately, he still sees you as the terribly wounded party. Since he won't listen to me, maybe you can make him see he's acting like a madman!"

"That's exactly the line of reason I and our solicitor will take with him," Alex said, hoping to soothe her alarm in the wake of her father's latest threats. "I honestly think a lot of this is pure bluster."

Alex rested his forehead in his left hand, holding the receiver with his right. He didn't blame Fiona for making a hasty exit, but he wasn't happy to think she was walking home alone in the dark in a strange city. He struggled to bring his thoughts back to Addy's voice on the phone.

While he wouldn't say it to his former spouse, he knew perfectly well she was correct to worry. Humphrey Dalgetty's efforts to intimidate those around him were always to be taken seriously. He was the patriarch of a prominent Catholic family in the region, often bragging that his family had "never been tainted by the sin of divorce." Addy's seven sisters and brothers danced to his tune without daring to protest. Dalgetty was a leading member of his church's lay council and the sudden, scandalous departure of his eldest daughter from her marriage the previous year, and her decision to live openly with Peter Murray in Peebles had been the talk of Selkirk when the news first broke.

Alex's now-former father-in-law was not a man accustomed to losing face and Alex guessed that someone feeling so publicly humiliated, as Dalgetty apparently did, would stoop to almost anything to force his daughter back into her marriage.

"Marriage!" Alex declared suddenly. "That's *it*!"

"*What?*" Addy said tearfully. "What are you talking about?"

"Look," Alex said, wanting to end the conversation as quickly as possible and call Fiona's cell to make sure she arrived safely at The Royal Scots Club, "I've got another important phone call I must make to an American colleague visiting Scotland on business, but I'll arrive in Peebles by eleven o'clock tomorrow and will explain to you and Peter my idea for putting a stop to all this nonsense caused by your father."

"I won't sleep a wink, Alex, if you don't tell me *now* what we're going to *do*," she cried, and Alex could hear Peter in the background trying to comfort his fiancée.

Alex briefly described his plan of action, adding quickly, "You're not to worry too much, Addy. I think this will put it all to rights, but I have a few more phone calls to make it happen."

Before she could comment further, he rang off and picked up his mobile phone that had remained on the glass-topped desk. Dialing Fiona's number, his heart sank when, after five rings, his call went to voice mail. His next attempt to reach her was ringing the front desk at the Royal Scots Club where he was relieved to be told, yes, Ms. Fraser recently came through the visitor's entrance and went directly up to her room.

"Shall I ring her there for you, sir?" asked the receptionist.

"Very kind of you, yes, please," he replied.

Again, the hotel phone rang numerous times, but no one picked up. Before the front desk clerk could come back on the line to see if he'd like to leave a message Alex clicked the off button on his mobile phone.

A deepening sense of dejection settled over him. How many more things in his life could go awry, he wondered gloomily? He pushed his leather chair back on its rolling casters and stood with the palms of his hands propped against the desktop, deep in thought. A few moments later, he returned to the front room, wondering whether Fiona's abrupt departure from the flat and her radio silence via phone meant she'd decided that things were too complicated between them and would simply hire a car tomorrow to continue her researches for Bernard Sterling on her own.

Bloody bad timing...all of it! he cursed silently.

Then he noticed there was a handwritten note propped against one of the paisley pillows on the sofa. He seized it quickly and read:

Dear Alex:
I'm totally fading, so I'm happy to walk the two and half blocks to the hotel and let you have some much-needed privacy.

If it still fits with your schedule, I'll be ready by nine tomorrow to head for the Borders. However, if something has come up for you, I can easily rent a car and we can catch up with each other wherever it suits—if it suits.

When you get a sec, send me a text to let me know what works for you as I intend to have a long, hot soak tonight in that amazing tub at the hotel, put in my ear plugs, and then have a good night's sleep.

All best,
Fiona

An almost childish joy coursed through him. He stared at Fiona's clear, readable hand, the penmanship of one trained to sketch and print legibly at design school for the many presentations she undoubtedly made to earn her degree. And her message was clear as well, he considered, as he took a sip from her abandoned glass of whiskey. She'd let him know by her note that, yes, she had personal boundaries and intended to stay on task regarding the reasons she'd come to Scotland, but he could tell…oh, yes, he could tell that she wanted to see him again!

Rereading her missive more slowly, his spirits rose a few more notches at this clear evidence that she hadn't thrown up her hands because of the current complications in his life. He could only hope that Fiona wanted to further explore the extraordinary—and, as she'd stated earlier in her toast—mysterious bond he knew, now, she felt as strongly as he did.

Alex practically sprinted back to his study and grabbed his mobile phone. Within seconds he'd sent her a text message.

At 9am your chariot awaits downstairs…

He then made a quick call to a second-cousin-once-removed who, at first, laughed heartily at the nature of Alex's petition to meet in Peebles and then agreed to help with his relative's rather unorthodox plan regarding his former wife.

And for the first night in months, Alexander Maxwell slept like a stone.

Fiona exited The Royal Scots Club entrance and wheeled her small suitcase toward the Jaguar parked at the curb. Alex greeted her, "Well, good morning. Did you sleep well?"

"I hardly remember putting my head on the pillow," she replied, handing him her suitcase to put in the boot of his car.

She noted that her escort for the trip to Traquair House and the other destinations in the Scottish Border country they had mapped out the day before was dressed in blue jeans once again, with a khaki colored shirt and a different tweed sports coat tossed into the back seat. He was cleanly shaven and she caught a faint whiff of a spicy after-shave that was fresh as the slight autumn nip in the air.

She realized, suddenly, that she was nervous about seeing Alex looking so unbelievably handsome when the first thing she'd remembered upon awakening this morning was his taking her in his arms the previous night.

Ignoring the slight flutter in her chest she said cheerily, "Thanks for your text, by the way. I saw it as soon as I woke up." She searched his face for any signs he was feeling remorse—either about his commitment to escort her around the Scottish Border country, or about the official end of his marriage. "And what about you? Everything all right?"

Alex didn't answer immediately, his approving glance briefly scanning her tan corduroy slacks and the beige, three-quarter-length cashmere cardigan she wore over a matching turtleneck shell.

Finally he said, "Everything appears moderately under control at the moment." He smiled as he added, "And I very much appreciated the note you left last night. Shall we be one our way?"

As he held the passenger side door for her, he bent forward and gently seized her chin, bestowing a soft kiss on both cheeks. "You look absolutely marvelous, by the way."

"Well, thank you, but you have just observed the full extent of my traveling wardrobe."

"It's not what you're wearing. You should see how the sun this morning turns your hair the color of a very fine French burgundy."

"At least you didn't say carrot juice," she joked, and then flushed with pleasure at his complimentary words, embarrassed, as always, how her coloring gave away nearly every thought in her head. She quickly ducked and slid into the seat and Alex shut the car door.

The dark blue Jaguar threaded its way through the morning traffic past the soaring neo-gothic monument to Sir Walter Scott that stood on Princes Street at the edge of the grand gardens bisecting the city. Her thoughts, however, were full of the previous evening and Alex's kiss, just now. And she knew full well that the hour-plus drive to Traquair House from Edinburgh would provide the perfect opportunity to bring up the subject she knew she must disclose before very long. Given the inevitability of how things were unfolding with Alex, she needed to tell him the reasons she had so abruptly departed High Point, North Carolina a decade earlier.

However, from the moment the vintage vehicle made its way out of the city via the A7 through the rolling Lammermuir Hills, Alex kept up a steady, fascinating narrative about the region's history and geography. Soothed by the sound of his voice and the hum of the speeding car, her only wish was to sink back in the comfort of the automobile's leather seats and absorb the stunning autumn scenery rushing by.

She'd think about what she wanted to say on that sticky subject another time, she told herself. Right now, all she wanted to do was enjoy the beautiful drive and the peace and security of Alex's comforting presence—a sensation she couldn't rightly understand, given the short time they'd known each other and the complications that were currently plaguing his life.

Just past the small town of Heriot, Alex pointed the car southwest on the B709, a narrow, two-way roadway with pines and browning fields blanketing the adjacent countryside. Over the soft purr of a well-tuned engine, he began describing the historic background regarding Traquair House.

"It almost looks like a French chateau, with its various turrets and cream-colored stuccoed exterior, but the place has always been associated with Scottish royalty," he explained. "The first structure was already in existence as far back as the twelfth century and was used by a long line of Scottish Stuart kings as a base from which they could hunt and also establish their authority over the surrounding countryside."

"Ah yes, the Border Wars…hence the name Scottish Borders. I read that in the guidebook coming up on the train."

Alex nodded. "For centuries, these rolling hills you're seeing were a highly contested area between clans—and later, between

England and Scotland itself."

"Isn't Traquair House pretty remote?" Fiona asked.

"From any big city? Aye," Alex nodded, keeping his eyes on the road. "Traquair originally not only housed a traveling court for when the Stuart kings were in the Borders, but was also used as a lodge for the favorite royal pastimes of fishing, hunting, and hawking in the Ettrick Forest. Those trees you can see over there," he added, pointing to the windshield, "surround the house near the River Tweed."

"How did the Maxwells come into all this?" she wondered aloud as she absorbed the beautiful sight of the river meandering on one side of the car while a series of signposts pointed toward Innerleithen, near their final destination.

"Catherine can correct me if I'm wrong, but James III, a royal Stuart, gave Traquair to a series of noble favorites until the king's uncle, the Earl of Buchan, bought it for his second son, who became the first Laird of Traquair in the late 1400's, I think it was."

"So Catherine Constable Maxwell Stuart is related to the *royal* Stuarts?"

"Distantly, yes. A female descendant of one of the Earls of Traquair married William, Lord Maxwell, who was related to the Maxwells of Monreith—but you'd have to see a genealogy chart to sort it all out. And given the shady origins of my Maxwells also being related by blood to the Maxwells of Monreith, I believe all that makes Catherine and me back-door cousins."

Fiona quickly made the calculation. "That means I got it right when I told my design group that Catherine's family has owned Traquair House more than six *hundred* years!"

"Give or take a few decades," Alex said with a smile, turning into a tree-lined gravel drive with a stone gatekeeper's cottage on their left. "Late in the nineteenth century, the males all died out, along with the earldom, and the house and estate passed to the nearest male relative, the Honorable Henry Constable Maxwell who also was the great-grandson of another Catherine Stuart, the daughter of the fourth Earl of Traquair."

"Whoa there! You lost me," Fiona laughed, "except I got

that Henry was a Maxwell."

"And he was the one who added the name Stuart to his own to become Henry Constable Maxwell Stuart. And then there's Catherine's *possible* connection to the novelist, Sir Walter Scott, through the convoluted Constable Maxwell-Scott baronetcy."

Fiona clapped her hands and shook her head. "I love it! You Maxwells are related to just about everybody I've ever heard of in Scotland: the Stuart kings, Sir Walter Scott, and maybe even to John Constable, the famous landscape painter!"

"I can't speak to that, but in my case, may I remind you once again," he said dryly, "I am included in this august company thanks *only* to a housemaid named Maisie."

By this time, Alex had piloted the car about a quarter of a mile down the long drive bordered by tall trees on one side and a huge expanse of lawn on the other. Up ahead were enormous, wrought iron gates at least twenty feet high, topped by the royal fleur-de-lis. The gates themselves were held in place by two, tall stone pillars, each crowed by graceful urns that Fiona guessed were another five feet tall. The gravel drive cut a wide swath in front of the imposing four-story cream-colored manor house and around a grassy circle planted with a riot of pansies adorning its center.

"Oh, look! Two black-and-tan Cavalier King Charles Spaniels!" she exclaimed, pointing through the window at two small dogs lolling near the flowerbed in the warm, September sunshine.

"You know the breed?"

"Didn't you ever watch *Sex and the City* when Charlotte York had one she named 'Elizabeth Taylor?'"

"Missed that season," Alex deadpanned. "But they're wonderful animals, don't you think?"

Fiona nodded and then said, "For a castle keep, folks appear pretty casual around here. Look! The entrance is wide open."

The massive wooden front door, studded with heavy metal nails an inch in diameter, stood ajar as if the household was awaiting their arrival.

"Catherine is expecting us, but she said she might be out on the school run when we arrived and to come right in."

"Catherine? Not 'Lady' Catherine? And she drives car pool?" she asked doubtfully.

"She's the Twenty-First Lady of Traquair, but not a titled lady, as I mentioned that the Earldom of Traquair died out in the nineteenth century. However, the property continued to be handed down through the family and she's the twenty-first lady of the household."

"No wonder we Americans decided not to have a titled aristocracy…it's too complicated!"

Alex smiled, and grew somber.

"Catherine and Mark Muller, her husband, have three young children and are great chums of mine. I also knew her first husband who died, tragically, the same year Catherine's father passed away."

"Oh, how horrible!" Fiona exclaimed. She looked out the car window at the enormous manor, her gaze taking in a large wing on its left side that Alex had told her earlier was the site of the small, handcrafted brewery producing Traquair House Ale. "How in the world did she and her mother keep this whole place afloat?"

"With a huge amount of effort," Alex replied soberly. "Traquair continues as a family home, but also offers, as I mentioned earlier, a few rather upscale bed and breakfast accommodations. The family began holding local fairs on the grounds, and set up the gift shop and now holds important business conferences, meetings, and retreats here. They virtually did everything they could think of to keep the estate and its five farms from being sold to pay the death duties. As you will see, Catherine is quite an amazing woman and it was wonderful when Mark came on the scene and they fell in love. Catherine's mother also met a late-life love and only spends half the year on the estate. Come!" he said, opening his car door. "Let me get your luggage."

Fiona looked at her watch. It was just past ten a.m.

"Shouldn't you be off if you want to get to Peebles by eleven?" Alex had explained to her he had an appointment with Addy and Peter Murray, her fiancé that he had to keep. "I was studying the map as you drove. It's about ten miles from here, am I right?"

Alex's expression clouded. "A little less." He set down her bag and lightly rested his hands on her shoulders. "I wish I didn't have to simply drop you here, but—"

"Alex…" Fiona cut in to reassure him, "I understand completely. You've gone way beyond the call of duty with everything you've done to smooth my way. Please! Go! Do what you have to do." She glanced up at the walls of Traquair soaring above her head. "I can't *wait* to see what this place looks like inside!" Then she frowned. "Do you think my hostess will allow me to take photographs?"

"Just ask her, but I'm sure she will. I've explained to her your mission for Bernard Sterling. And worse comes to worse, there's also a very glossy brochure they hand out to guests—and as you've probably seen—there are lots of pictures on their website. Come. I'll just get your bags up to the Pink Room."

"You know the *color* of the room I'm staying in?" she asked, startled.

"Each guest room is known by its color. Over the years, Catherine and Mark and I have become better friends through her efforts to redecorate and take on paying guests. I've often stayed here myself, so I requested the Pink Room for you. It's quite nice."

Without further comment, Fiona followed Alex through the front entrance, ashamed for wondering if Alex and Addy had ever stayed in the Pink Room. Meanwhile, the two resident dogs followed along behind, tails wagging a continuing welcome. She watched as he picked up a set of keys lying on a chest in the stone foyer. There was one large and very ancient metal key that she assumed fit the front door, along with two smaller versions that she guessed would prove to be the way into the upstairs quarters where she'd be staying.

With Alex carrying her suitcase, they mounted a spiral, stone stairway in one of the turrets, but soon heard someone coming down the steps toward them.

"Hello...is that you, Alex?" came a voice from the stairwell. "I saw the car come through the gates."

"Sarah!" Alex exclaimed to the young woman who suddenly appeared as they rounded the flight that led to a landing. He swiftly made introductions. "Meet Sarah MacDonald, Catherine's stellar assistant. Sarah, this is Fiona Fraser from Bernard Sterling's firm in America, here to admire everything you've done to this place."

"Oh, flatterer," she said, smiling warmly at Alex. Then the woman in a jeans skirt and gray sweater set turned to Fiona. "Welcome, Ms. Fraser! We're delighted to have you staying with us. Come, let me show you your room," she said, seizing Fiona's bag.

Fiona turned on the landing and bid Alex a hasty farewell, wondering just when, and under what circumstances, she would see him again.

CHAPTER 10

The Pink Room more than lived up to Alex's description as "quite nice." Sarah, with the two Cavaliers trailing along behind, opened a broad, white door with a shining brass knob to reveal a large bedroom that overlooked the front of the manor house. Out the wavy glass windows was a magnificent view down the stretch of lawn that extended all the way down the drive to the front entrance where Alex's car was just disappearing.

"We hope you'll be comfortable during your stay," Sarah said, gesturing toward a graceful half-tester canopy bed that was draped overhead in flowered chintz with colorful peacocks woven into its design set against walls the color of ballet slippers. The same chintz fabric cascaded down the wall in lieu of a headboard. A matching padded footboard and bed skirt blended beautifully with the pale green carpet, pink slipper chairs in front of the wide fireplace, and antique furniture scattered around the room. All in all, Fiona thought, her gaze sweeping her lovely surroundings, the Pink Room made her truly feel like a princess in a castle. Ideas for interpreting it as part of the soft furnishings in her presentation to her bosses were already swirling in her head.

Turning slowly around the room she said with a wry smile, "Oh, I imagine I'll be *very* comfortable here." Bernard Sterling, himself, wouldn't be able to contain himself if he were standing in her place.

"I'll just let you get settled in for a bit, and then shall I come back to show you the rest of the house?" Sarah inquired politely. "Catherine would love for you to join her later for a light luncheon, if that would suit."

"Oh, yes, definitely. I'd love that. Can you give me twenty minutes?"

Sarah nodded and handed Fiona a slip of paper with the code for the house Wi-Fi. "We've had it installed for our visitors," she said with a laugh. "They can't get along without their mobiles." She clapped her hands and called, "Come, Delilah! Come Daphne!" An instant later, the dogs and Sarah MacDonald had disappeared through the door, leaving Fiona to wander around the room making a closer inspection of her amazingly luxurious surroundings.

"It's like living in a *museum*," she murmured out loud.

She slid her fingers across the surface of a highly polished chest of drawers that was pushed against one wall to the left of the canopied bed. The wooden furniture's craftsmanship probably dated back three hundred years. She could only imagine how her brother Tommy would react to touching not only the lovely wood that the dresser was made of, but also observing the fine marquetry displayed on a pair of low tables positioned next to the chairs in front of the fireplace. There was a door to the left of the hearth—locked—which Fiona guessed probably connected to an adjoining room for family groups that booked into this posh establishment. In front of one window stood a handsome desk—Chippendale? She wondered—that served as a dressing table.

Having completed her inspection and jotting down a few notes, Fiona swiftly unpacked her small suitcase, storing it in a large, walk-in closet that featured a shelf installed with an electric kettle and all the accouterments to make tea in her room.

The bathroom was a separate space entirely, situated across a small foyer that officially turned the Pink Room into a suite. As at The Royal Scots Club, the bathtub was enormous and the pedestal sink came to above her waist. Scotsman generations earlier, thanks to some Viking ancestors, must have been, on average, a lot taller than their English counterparts, she mused. Staring at the large expanse of white porcelain, she found herself considering what it would be like to fill the tub with bubbles and for two people to—

Just then, there was a discreet knock on the door leading to the landing. Fiona opened it and declared unabashedly to Sarah standing at the threshold, "I'm in heaven!"

"Everything's all right, then?" Sarah replied with a smile. "Ready for our tour?" Delilah and Daphne were at her feet, tails wagging madly. "Do you mind if the dogs go with us? Cavaliers can't stand not to be where their people are."

Fiona bent down and gave each animal a swift scratch behind the ear. "They are most welcome to join us. I'll just get my notebook—and is it all right to take photographs?"

"For your use only and not for publication?"

Fiona nodded, holding up her cell phone. "I'll use this just for research purposes and to prod my memory when I get back to New York."

"No problem, then," Sarah assured her.

The pair spent the next hour touring what Sarah called The High Drawing Room on the same floor as the Pink Room, with its seventeenth century harpsichord at one end and a black marble fireplace at the other, along with silk-covered furniture upholstered in creams and pale blues that invited visitors to lounge comfortably among a tasteful scattering of elegant clocks, gilt-framed paintings, and silver trays. Fiona quickly held up her cell phone and snapped the room from several angles, figuring that her bosses would swoon over her close-up views of some of the plush furnishings they'd seen in her original presentation in New York.

Sarah led the way along a corridor where they gazed into numerous elegant bedrooms, including one called The King's Room where, explained Sarah, "Mary Queen of Scots stayed when she visited Traquair in 1566, along with her baby son." Fiona's guide pointed to an ornately carved cradle. "Queen Mary's husband, Lord Darnley, was with her on this visit. Her son, of course—after his mother's beheading on the order of Queen Elizabeth the First—eventually became James the Sixth of Scotland and James the First of England, so the Stuarts won that round."

It was obvious to Fiona by now that the Scots had never forgiven the English for the centuries-long spat among cousins.

The rest of the house provided a chance for Fiona to fill her notebook with all sorts of ideas for her Home Collection: wall tapestries, two book-lined libraries, a small museum filled with everyday items used by the Maxwell Stuarts through the years, along with a dressing room demonstrating domestic life in former times and featuring a portable bathtub, bidet, washstand, slop basin, as well as a mannequin of a woman clothed in an exquisite, eighteenth-century black lace dressing gown who stared somberly out the window.

Fiona suddenly had a weighty sense of the generations of Maxwell Stuarts that lived within these walls.

Just as we Maxwell Frasers spent our lives down through two centuries in Maryland and then North Carolina. Here are deep family roots, for certain...

She wondered if her hostess could shed light on why the Frasers in America might have incorporated the name Maxwell, just as the Stuarts had.

It's just so weird, when we don't know the reason!

Fiona took a few final photographs of the Lower Drawing Room on the first floor that was smaller and far cozier than the one upstairs. Here there were inviting matching pale blue velvet sofas flanking a fireplace and a low, embroidered footstool upholstered in crimson stitchery placed before the hearth. Sarah MacDonald concluded the tour of Traquair's interiors in the grand dining room where the walls were decorated in stunning gold and cream, hand-blocked French wallpaper that Sarah revealed was a hundred and fifty years old and still perfectly intact. She then led her guest to a chamber that was once a housekeeper's room and currently known as The Still Room where breakfast and lunch were served.

"Just make yourself comfortable, won't you? Catherine will join you shortly."

Daphne and Delilah immediately scampered under the table set for two that was covered with a white, damask tablecloth, blue and white chinaware and polished silver. "Do you mind, awfully, if I leave the dogs with you?" Sarah asked. "They'll just keep scratching at the door with you in here and will start barking wildly the minute Catherine arrives."

"I'd love them to keep me company, wouldn't I, girls?" she called to them, but they were already curled up, eyes drooping from scampering up and downstairs all morning.

Sarah apologized, "I'm sorry to leave you like this, but the first bus tour is due to pull up very soon now. We're nearing the end of the season, so we're happy that visitors are still coming to see the house."

"Of course," Fiona assured her, aware that Traquair was not only a family home, it was a business, now, too. "You've been a terrific guide. Thanks so much. I'll be fine."

The door closed on the Still Room whose walls were painted a restful pale blue and featured classic moulding on all four walls. In each corner flanking the fireplace was a built-in cupboard filled with priceless examples of blue transfer ware and magnificent gold-rimmed, formal china that Fiona wagered Bernard Sterling would sell his aged mother to possess. She snapped at least ten photos before she heard voices outside the door that soon opened.

"You must be Fiona," said the slender, blond figure standing on the threshold. "I do apologize for not being here to greet you. Have you settled in all right?" As Fiona stood to greet her hostess, the dogs rushed out from beneath the table. "Oh, dear? Have they been bothering you?"

"Oh, not at all. I love them! They're welcome to sleep on my bed, if it comes to that!"

Fiona realized that she had never expected her hostess to be so near her own age. The lady of the house advanced into the room dressed in casual trousers, a printed blouse and a long, navy blue cardigan that was far less elegant than the cashmere Fiona had on. She wore her hair to her shoulders with a fringe of bangs and appeared every inch a busy, working mom.

"Shall we sit down?" asked the 21st Lady of Traquair. "I'm quite peckish after doing the school run and mucking out a stable this morning. The children have just returned to their classes in the village and now I have to take up some of their chores."

"Sarah has taken wonderful care of everything and I've just had a tour of the house, which I find totally inspiring," Fiona hastened to reply. "I can't thank you enough for your warm hospitality. And I especially love the dogs being part of the Welcoming Committee!"

Her hostess swiftly uncovered several dishes holding a variety of cold salads to which they each served themselves. "We've probably had seven generations of Cavaliers during my lifetime. I love them, too."

Fiona was amazed by the way in which her hostess put her at her ease. She speculated that someone with Catherine's background had been trained since birth in such an art, but nevertheless, she appreciated how natural and friendly she was. Not wanting to waste any time, Fiona swiftly began asking a list of questions about the house, its furnishings, and the possibility there might be for collaboration.

"I love your use of fabrics…the silks, tartans, and cashmere throws. It's such a grand house, and yet it's homey and welcoming to visitors like me."

Catherine looked pleased. "Well, we consciously chose materials that reflected our weaving heritage here in Scotland and also our love of French and Italian silks and wallpaper. It *is* our home, after all."

Fiona hesitated, and then ventured, "What would you think of our calling a group of cushions or throws after Traquair House, if I am able to launch a Scottish Home Collection for Bernard Sterling? We would choose ones we could replicate either here or in America. By our licensing the designs from you, you'd earn a royalty and also get some publicity through our website and stores, which, in turn, might garner more visitors from abroad."

Catherine nodded slowly, and then added in a purely businesslike tone of voice, "That would be wonderful…but do you also think your employer would then give us a substantial price break if we featured these items for sale in our gift shop?"

Fiona smiled broadly. "I would personally guarantee it!"

After agreeing upon a few more details, it seemed the time to ask a few questions about Catherine's branch of the Maxwell clan. Fiona quickly explained the strange habit of her American

Frasers to include the name "Maxwell" in every generation of their own family tree since the late eighteenth century.

Catherine regarded Fiona with heightened interest.

"Alex mentioned that he thinks your Frasers have no blood ties to the Maxwells, though, am I right?"

"Not that he's found in the research he's done. But we think there is another sort of tie…one between Jane Maxwell, the Fourth Duchess of Gordon and—"

"Ah…the Lost Lieutenant, Thomas Fraser?" Catherine declared. "That story about the Match-Making Jane Maxwell having first been in love with a handsome young officer sent off to fight in America, yes? He was the one falsely reported to have died in the Colonies and then returned—too late—to claim Jane Maxwell as his bride because she'd just married the Duke of Gordon."

"That's the one," Fiona said with a smile.

"Well, the tale is well-known throughout the various branches of the Maxwell clan." Catherine flashed a grin. "Even the off-shoot Alex springs from." She smiled even more broadly. "I love to tease him about his dodgy origins, but actually, Mark and I consider him one of the best representatives of our clan. She regarded Fiona closely, as if trying to gauge her relationship to her friend. "He's a wonderful man, that Alex Maxwell, and he certainly knows what it's like to struggle to keep a legacy afloat."

Fiona merely nodded, and then replied, "He and I have a lot in common in that department. Our family furniture firm in North Carolina that makes beautiful eighteenth century reproduction pieces has had a devil of a time staying solvent since the financial crisis." Then she hastened to add, "My interest in the business of the Maxwell and the Fraser connection has just been an interesting sideline of this research trip the Bernard Sterling firm sent me on."

Catherine grew thoughtful and then said, "The saga Alex told me was that, when young Fraser couldn't claim Jane as his bride, he eventually returned to America. Do you think he was *your* ancestor?"

Fiona shrugged. "I don't really know for sure, but he could

be. All I can tell you is that in our Fraser family Bible that dates from the late eighteenth century in America, the succeeding generations were always given the names Thomas or Maxwell."

Catherine took another bite of her cold potato salad.

"Well," she mused, "I can testify to the fact that practically all our Maxwell children get named after their forebears. There must be six or seven Catherines in my own family line. It would have been an even stronger tradition in Thomas Fraser's day to choose a name that had deep meaning for him, and to carry on the tradition in the future."

"Maybe *that* would account for the sort of an unexplained naming fetish in our family, even after they moved from Maryland to North Carolina. Yet I've never heard of anyone in our family ever *marrying* a Maxwell!"

"And have you heard about the Duchess' daughter supposedly sired by Jane's first love?" asked Catherine. "It was always whispered about among the Gordons. *Louisa.* Wasn't that her name?"

"Yes," Fiona murmured. "Lady Louisa Gordon, who was raised as the Duke's child, by all accounts. Alex and I hope to squeeze in a side trip to Ayton to see if there were any clues that the story was true of Jane's receiving a letter while at her sister's house from Thomas Fraser saying he had miraculously survived and intended to marry her. I'd like to know—if the story of the letter is even accurate—did all this actually happened *at* Ayton."

"Well," mused her hostess, "you might try to find out if Jane Maxwell did, in fact, have a strong connection with her sister in Ayton and see if various other aspects of the scene when she supposedly received Thomas' letter there check out."

Outside the Still Room, Fiona heard the sound of many feet tramping by the closed door. Earlier, she'd seen a bus pulling into the car park a hundred yards from the gates.

She placed her linen napkin on the table next to her plate and said, "I think the hordes are descending. Between tracing these bizarre family links and all I've learned from visiting your beautiful home, I've taken up too much of your time."

Catherine shook her head. "Not at all! This is very

interesting and I couldn't be more pleased that you chose Traquair to do your research for the Bernard Sterling brand. We've done our best to continue as the stewards of the place while also allowing the public to enjoy it as well."

"But I'll bet you'll be glad to have your house to yourselves by Christmastime."

Catherine smiled and raised an eyebrow.

"Possibly."

Fiona quickly made her farewells and mounted the circular stone stairs to her guest quarters while the 21st Lady of Traquair headed for the gift shop where the visitors would eventually end their tour. Once inside the sanctity of the Pink Room, Fiona checked her cell phone for any messages from Alex, but there were none. Then her heart skipped a beat when she saw she had a text from Jared Finnegan saying, "Better read your email…. and standby for news!"

She swiftly fired up her iPad and scanned her Inbox. Sure enough, there was a communication from Sterling's assistant, Stella, with a copy to Jared Finnegan.

Hi there, Fiona:

Bernie wanted me to tell you that he's quite pleased with your progress scoping things out in Scotland. Please continue to keep him informed of your itinerary as well as sources and projected costs of the various items you think you'll be including in your final presentation to the Team when you return.

Also, believe it or not, there is an international rally of "Bugatti fanciers" in a few days in a place in Scotland with the funny name of Peebles. I've just arranged for Bernie's 1927 car to be flown to the competition being held at the Hotel Hydro, some old fashioned spa, I gather. I don't know if Boss Man himself will attend, but consider this a heads up that you may be summoned there to report any further developments in person.

Cheeries,
Stella

Fiona stared at her glowing screen, her heart sinking. That's all she needed: the pressure of the big boss looking over her shoulder as she scouted potential goods for inclusion in her final recommendations to the home furnishings team. All she could pray was that Sterling either couldn't break away from business in New York to attend the Bugatti show, or if he came to Scotland, he'd be too busy with his rich car pals to make time to see her. One thing was for certain, however: she'd better get her ducks in a row in case Bernard Sterling suddenly appeared in a region of Scotland he'd only consider "the back of the beyond."

Peebles!

How many coincidences could there be on this trip, she wondered, shocked to realize that Peebles was mere miles away from Traquair House and was the town where Alex had gone to visit Addy and her fiancé!

Fiona quickly did an online search and discovered the hotel in Peebles was built in 1881 as a spa and was later used as a hospital for the ill and feeble. Even though it looked to her to be quite large and well-appointed in its modern-day incarnation, it was not exactly the kind of place Sterling was used to and she marveled that it had been selected as a venue for a gathering of the mega-wealthy owners of the exotic Bugatti motor cars. Amazed that her employer might possibly be invading this piece of heaven in which she'd found herself, she began to write up all her notes from her interview with Catherine Maxwell Stuart, along with her ideas and projected costs for adapting several items from Traquair as part of the new Sterling home furnishings collection. She figured it was a smart idea to be ready, just in case Bernard actually turned up at the car rally.

After supper alone downstairs, she returned to her room and continued working. And thus it was she was wide-awake when her cell phone rang at two o'clock in the morning.

"Fiona? It's Alex. I am *so* sorry to be calling you at such a beastly hour, but—"

"You didn't wake me," Fiona interrupted, looking up from her iPad at the darkened windows across from her bed. "Where *are* you? Are you all right?"

"I'm fine. I'm staring up at your window. I saw your light. Why are you still up?"

"I was organizing all the Scottish sources I've gathered in case I had to meet with Bernard Sterling," she said. "Did you know there's an international Bugatti car competition being held soon in Peebles, of all places on this earth? I just got an email that there's a remote possibility my boss might be coming over to Scotland for it."

Meanwhile, her heart performed a mild flip as she scrambled off her canopied bed and padded across the carpet to verify that Alex was, indeed, standing two stories below her room. She could just make out a tall, shadowy figure near the bed of pansies in the middle of the front lawn. Fortunately, Traquair's two dogs had gone home with Sarah, or Fiona was sure the entire household would be awake by now.

Alex, his mobile phone to his ear, chuckled into hers. "I saw a few posters with Bugattis on them around the town. Would your employer actually come all this way to see a few cars parked at the Hotel Hydro?"

"Let us pray not, but he might because he had one of his Bugattis entered in the competition. Hey! What are you doing down there? What happened today?"

"I attended a wedding and drank a lot of rather indifferent champagne."

"A wedding?"

"Yes, and I'm here because I've a reservation for a room," he added, and she wondered, suddenly, exactly how *much* champagne had he consumed. "As for my day—it went brilliantly."

"Well, that's nice," Fiona said, drawing the conclusion that the more Alex spoke, the more his words sounded slightly slurred.

"I don't have a key. It's freezing down here. Would you be so kind as to let me in?"

Fiona glanced at her drawstring, jersey pajama bottoms and braless T-shirt top and felt color rising up her neck and into her cheeks.

Oh, hell, Fiona. Go downstairs and let the poor man find his room in this pile!

"I look a mess, but I'll be right down."

She saw Alex give her a wave, cell phone still pressed to his ear.

"I quite look forward to seeing that, actually."

Fiona shivered in her bare feet and waved back, clicking off her phone. She quickly donned her cashmere cardigan and a pair of flats and padded down the circular stone stairs, fumbling with the enormous metal key before she could swing open the heavy oaken door. Cold air streamed in and she was more aware than ever of her skimpy nightclothes.

"Quick, come on inside. You must be a block of ice by now. I can brew you a cup of hot tea to warm you up if you want."

"Actually, I can think of a number of ways you could warm me up."

Fiona stared at the set of keys in her hand. Alex stood at the threshold clad only in this tweed sports jacket, tie hanging loose, and with a small duffle bag in his hand. He leaned wearily against the door jam.

"I am extremely fortunate that no constable breathalized me tonight," he admitted, "for I fear I've had a wee bit too much whiskey—as well as the champagne—to pass the test."

Fiona lifted her gaze to stare at his tousled hair and haggard expression. She took his arm and put her foot on the first step.

"Can you make it up the stairs? Hold on while I lock the front door."

Alex removed his arm from hers and when she had returned to his side, slung it about her shoulders once again.

"With your help, my love, I'll follow you anywhere."

My love? I assumed he was in Peebles counseling his former wife, but he was at a wedding?

A sudden thought struck her. Perhaps they attended the festivities together?

"Let's go," she said resignedly, the all-too-familiar act of helping a man who had too much to drink upstairs and into his bed filling her with disappointment. That feeling only intensified as the pair mounted the treads with Alex clinging to the center stonework as they slowly made their way up the circular staircase.

"Forgive me, Fiona…but I *had* to celebrate," he mumbled, slurring his last word to sound like "shell-a-brate." He gave a short laugh. "It was my cousin Seamus' fault."

His trip to Peebles was no mere mission of mercy, she concluded, her ire rising with each step.

"Where is your room, do you know?"

"Right next to yours!" Alex replied sounding very pleased with himself.

"*What?*"

"Isn't that convenient?" he demanded with a chuckle. "One of those keys on your ring should fit. It's a double suite!"

"Is it, now?"

Alex's weight was growing heavier on her shoulders by the minute and she was peeved beyond anything she had experienced in a long time. How clever of him to book the adjoining room, she said to herself, beginning to seethe at his assuming that would be fine with her after partying all night.

At least he was in no condition to give her any serious trouble. After all, she was highly practiced pouring a drunk into his own bed. Once they passed through the entrance to The Pink Room and Alex spotted her unmade bed, he took three long steps and collapsed on it as if he'd finally reached the finish line in a marathon.

"Oh, lord, Fiona…this feels so good. It's such a relief to be here."

"Alex! What in the world is going on with you!" she demanded as she watched him put his arms around her pillow and inhaled deeply. "Where *were* you?"

Burrowing his head into the bedclothes, his eyes closed, he said almost as if to himself, "Ah…it's heaven here! I can smell your wonderful perfume."

"Alex!" she said in frustration and then marched over to her walk-in closet and began brewing a cup of scalding instant coffee, thanks to the electric kettle on the shelf. She'd never get him off her bed and into his own if she didn't sober him up, at least marginally.

By the time she'd returned with a mug of the steaming brew, she knew she was too late. The combination of whiskey and champagne had gotten the better of him, and his was sleeping the sleep of the dead.

Fiona took one of the three keys and tried it in the door to the left of the fireplace. It opened easily into another room, equally as luxurious as the pink palace behind her. Within a few minutes, she'd tucked herself into another canopied bed and tried to go to sleep, a million questions and concerns keeping her awake until the wee hours.

CHAPTER 11

"Fiona? Would you like this cup of tea?"

She woke instantly at the sound of Alex's Scottish accent but remained with her eyes closed, pretending to be asleep.

Damn!

She'd been so upset last night that she'd forgotten to use the key to lock the door to the Pink room! She felt his weight on the mattress beside her, then his large hand settled on her shoulder.

"Wake up, love, so you can hear my apology, and sip this nice cuppa I've made for you."

Sighing, Fiona rolled over on her back, opened her eyes, and stared up at Alex's face, his expression full of misgiving. She pulled herself to a sitting position and leaned against an unfamiliar headboard. Silently, she received the teacup from his hands and took a first, bracing sip. It had just the right amount of milk. She heaved another sigh.

"Well?" she said.

"Well," he repeated. "I married Addy off and then attended a rather impromptu reception in a private room at the Hydro Hotel in—"

"You *what?*"

Fiona didn't know whether to be more surprised that Alex's ex-wife of only a few days had remarried so quickly, or that Adelina Dalgetty's former husband had attended a wedding reception at the Hotel Hydro which, until the previous evening, Fiona had never heard of!

"My former father-in-law was threatening to call in a bank loan he'd given Maxwell Mills many moons ago if Addy didn't agree to reconcile with me—a situation neither of us wanted, as you know." Alex ran his fingers through his dark hair and rubbed his forehead as if he was suffering from a headache, which no doubt he was. "I concluded that unless she was well and truly married to Peter—Peter Murray, the man she'd always loved—Humphrey Dalgetty would do something reckless, such as demand his money from my firm to put pressure on her to come back to our home. If he called in the loan, it would be disastrous to our already-precarious financial situation, to say nothing of our personal lives. So...I took matters in hand and—well, it's done! Adelina Dalgetty is now Mrs. Peter Murray."

"Can you offer a few more details?" Fiona demanded, trying to keep from smiling at the comical vision of Alex engineering his former wife's second marriage.

"I called my rascally cousin, Seamus Maxwell, who is one of those bone fide but rather silly Universal Life Church ministers who can marry two muskrats, if called upon."

Fiona couldn't stop herself from laughing. "I must meet this Seamus sometime."

Alex rolled his eyes and continued, "I asked him to come to the registrar's office at the Peebles Council Chambers where the bride and groom filled out the proper marriage notice forms and then I requested Seamus to say the magic words, 'I now pronounced you husband and wife...kiss the bride' at the Hydro Hotel up the road."

"And then you proceeded to dance on the tables?" Fiona inquired, deadpan.

"Something like that, though I'd much have preferred dancing with *you* rather than Seamus, who must weigh fifteen stone by now, and—"

"How heavy is that?" Fiona interrupted.

"Over two hundred pounds, I'm guessing. Seamus kept pouring far too much whiskey into everyone's glasses after our initial champagne toasts. But frankly, Fiona," Alex said, staring at her with a peculiar light in his eye, "it was an important moment in my life. A wrong righted. Humphrey Dalgetty cannot now force his daughter to return to her marriage since she is legally divorced from me and legally married to *Peter*! At this point, calling his loan has no leverage with Addy, and fortunately, he doesn't hold animosity towards me. What's done is done and I'm betting on the fact that it's simply too complicated a situation for the old tyrant to untangle, thank you St. Ninian."

"St. Ninian? The patron saint of shotgun marriages, I assume?"

Alex grinned and then winced, his hangover definitely a factor this morning.

"All parties concerned felt it was a time to celebrate our freedom and happiness. After the first toasts, I kept trying to take my leave, but Seamus continued calling for another toast, and then *another*, and Addy and Peter were *so* joyous, I couldn't bring myself to abandon their celebration until the moment no one noticed I'd left."

"And that was?"

"Peter and Addy suddenly disappeared upstairs to the wedding suite and Seamus was snoring on the banquette."

"And do you really think this scheme of Adelina's *fait accompli* marriage will keep her father from trying to take revenge via Maxwell Mills? It might make him even angrier, you know."

Alex heaved a sigh and gazed off into the distance.

"I sincerely hope not. Now that she's remarried, Addy's no longer living in sin, as far as her father is concerned. I was merely a Catholic convert, which I did to make *him* happy. Peter's a genuinely good Catholic lad who has never been married before. I told Addy to go ahead and apply for an annulment on the grounds I wasn't a practicing Catholic and we had no children, or some such thing."

An annulment? Now, where have I heard that *before?*

But all she said was, "So you think, in time, Addy's father will see the die is cast and make the best of it?"

"Exactly. Especially when they have the child."

"She's pregnant?"

"She surely is, and over the moon about it. So is Peter."

"So it *was* a shotgun marriage!"

Alex grinned. "Quite. And the good news is, Dalgetty and I have had a perfectly cordial relationship, up to now, and he's been pleased with the way I've run the company after my father died. And since he's never been told that I, too, had felt my marriage was a mistake from its beginnings, he sees me as the one to be pitied. When in his right mind, and when all this settles in, I'm wagering that he wouldn't want to hurt our enterprise—or the relationship I'm sure he and Addy's mum will want with their coming grandchild."

"But what about your brother? Would Harry ever tell him you had been as unhappy as Addy in your marriage and blow your story, just for spite?"

"Thankfully, I've never confided in Harry a thing about my marriage and besides, my brother may be a wild man, and irresponsible, at times, but he's not a snitch."

"Well, lucky for that…"

Alex gently brushed the back of his fingers along the side of her cheek, sending a slight tremor down her spine. "You know, Fiona," he said, "I've never told anyone *any* of the things I've just told you. It's part of this strange feeling I've had from the very first. It's as if you know everything there is to know about me, and accept it all."

Fiona waited until he'd taken his hand away.

"There is one thing I cannot accept," she said flatly. "I *hate* drunk men. I don't accept that at *all!*"

Alex paused, and as if absorbing the vehemence of her last words.

"I am terribly sorry for last night," he apologized quietly. "I don't think I've been quite as pissed as that since my University days."

"Pissed, I assume, translates to blotto, wasted, soused, shavazzed?" Fiona set her cup on the bedside table, swung her legs to the other side of the mattress, and stood up. "Well…that you were."

"You're quite angry with me, aren't you?" Alex said, startled.

Fiona raised her chin and gave him a quick nod.

"Look, Alex, I understand completely why you felt you had cause to celebrate," she said, realizing in that moment that she owed him a reasonable explanation for the judgmental tone she'd used. "But there's something important you need to know about me. Inebriated men...they...well, they—"

"Who is 'they,' Fiona?" Alex asked gently.

She offered no answer, but instead, walked over to the bedroom window. She stood with her back to Alex and looked out at the slightly altered view from the one she'd grown used to in The Pink Room.

"Drunks...hurt...*people*," she said over her shoulder. "And they scare me witless." She gazed sightlessly out the window while her thoughts drifted to far away High Point, North Carolina. "Drunks in cars can ruin your life and believe me, I know what I'm talking about."

In the next instant, she felt his presence behind her and stood completely still as his right arm encircled her shoulder. A moment later, he gently pulled her back against his chest and rested his chin on the top of her head.

"Tell me, Fiona. Tell me about the alcoholics in your life."

"Alcoholic. Singular. And it's a story I can't divulge wearing pajamas."

Alex carefully turned her around to face him.

"Yes, you can, because I have the very strong feeling that if you don't tell me now, you might lose your nerve."

Fiona allowed her gaze to meet his and her lips curved in the tiniest smile, signaling she had retreated from a dark memory that had almost felt like some form of PTSD.

"You haven't known me for long, Alex Maxwell, yet you do know me so well." She stood on tiptoe and brushed her lips like a feather against his. "If you make me another cup of tea and come into the other room, which feels like home, now, I'll tell you about a drunken southern boy I married named Charlton 'Chip' Reynolds."

In the end, Alex suggested they both dress and first have their breakfast in The Still Room downstairs where the staff expected them to turn up by eight o'clock.

"Do you think your stomach is up to it?" she asked.

"Coffee and orange juice," he said firmly. "But I do think I'll give a miss to the cooked breakfast of sausage and egg."

A smaller table than the one Catherine and Fiona had sat at the day before was set and waiting for them when they entered the pale blue Still Room. A very sweet young girl popped in and out the door so often—bringing toast and jam and then a cooked breakfast for Fiona, followed by heating up their pot of tea—that Fiona gave up any attempts to launch into the tale she had avoided relating to anyone for ten years.

When they had finished their meal, she said quietly, "They'll want to do up our rooms, so we can't go there to talk." She reached across the table to hold Alex's hand. "I've wanted to tell you about…about my own first marriage for quite a while, but, just like now, there never seemed any place quiet enough, or secluded enough—"

"Have you seen the property at the back of Traquair House itself?" he intervened.

Startled by this abrupt change of topic, she shook her head no, wondering if Alex actually preferred not to hear about a previous marriage."

Alex said, "Go fetch something warm to wear that you can sit on grass in and I'll meet you just outside the front door in ten minutes. And don't run away, promise?"

Once again, she was taken aback by how perceptive he was, for she *had* wondered, just now, if there were still any way to get out of coming clean about her past. What if Alex was revolted by what she would tell him? What if he would not accept what she, herself, had found unacceptable for so long?

Fiona pushed away from the breakfast table and slowly mounted the stairs to The Pink Room where she pulled on her cardigan and draped a light, wool scarf around her neck. Her breakfast lying heavily in her stomach, she suddenly felt quite ill and wondered for a moment if she were going to be sick. She ran into the bathroom, splashed water on her face, used the facilities, and lectured herself that it was, at last, time to be as honest and forthcoming as Alex had been with her from Day One.

As for Alexander Maxwell, he was no serious drinker, she

judged, coming down the circular steps and steeling herself to meet him outside. He had imbibed too much last night, to be sure, but he knew it himself, acknowledged it to her, and made amends with his immediate apology. Compared to Chip Reynolds, Alex's over indulging in alcohol would appear far from habitual with him. And he'd seemed to understand instantly how upset she'd been by being exposed to such drunkenness. She doubted with a strange certainty that he'd never allow that to happen again if they were together.

If they were together...

How in the world could that ever happen, given the distances involved and the complications in both their lives—to say nothing of what she was about to disclose?

When Fiona reached the bottom of the stone stairs, Alex stood a few feet from the massive oaken entrance to Traquair House. In one hand he held a tartan lap robe that he must have fetched from his car, and in the other, two stadium cushions. At his feet was a picnic basket.

"But we've just eaten breakfast!" she protested nodding in the direction of the hamper. "And you're nursing a hangover." Food was the last thing she wanted.

"Ah, but I'm feeling much better, now, after orange juice and coffee. And we might be a while, mightn't we? I want to be prepared for any eventuality."

Fiona thought guiltily that they should be pushing off to the next stop on her To Do list. Somehow, though, she was able to banish all thought of Bernard Sterling and Jared Finnegan because foremost in her mind was a desire to get the next hour over with.

"Where to for my confessional?" she asked.

"A perfect spot, right around the corner, here."

Mystified, Fiona followed Alex, single file, to the left of the front façade, past a door in the side of the building that announced "The Brew House" where, Fiona had learned on her tour with Sarah MacDonald the day before, two, full-time brew masters in the cool, dark recesses below the manor concocted Traquair House Ale, amber bottles of which were now exported all over the world.

As she and Alex rounded the far corner of the house, Fiona stopped to stare at the sight that met her startled gaze. Twenty yards ahead, long lines of intersecting dark green hedges stretched across the lawn. In front of them was a sign that read "The Traquair Maze," a garden feature—so the placard said—planted in 1980 with over fifteen hundred Leylandi Cypress trees interspersed with hardier beech. Colorful yellow and red autumn leaves from the towering trees nearby lay in drifts upon the lawn and had landed on the tops of the tightly clipped hedges that intersected each other at sharp, right angles.

"While you were getting your cardigan, I checked with Sarah. No tour busses are expected until after two this afternoon. So, come," Alex commanded. "Let's see if we can find our way in here."

As they drew nearer the large white sign near the entrance to the maze, Fiona read that completing the convoluted circuit would take about a half hour.

"That is, if you know what you're doing," Fiona noted skeptically. She pointed to a line of copy on the sign. "Look! It says there are four sub-centers you must navigate before you reach the middle."

"Ah...but you see, I've been here before," Alex assured her with a laugh, adding, "My mother was a school friend of Catherine's mum, and I used to play here as a child." He strode to the entrance, crooked a finger, and said with a leer, "Come into my parlor, said the spider to the fly..."

Fiona followed his lead as they turned one corner after another, walking deeper and deeper into the maze. With sure steps, Alex steered a course directly to the center where a lovely square plot of grass awaited, dappled with sun and protected from any autumn breeze that might decide to blow. Spreading the lap robe on the ground, he invited her to take a seat on one of the flat, tartan-covered cushions he'd brought along.

Fiona lifted her face to the sun, closed her eyes, and soaked up its soothing warmth while Alex took a seat on his cushion nearby.

Her eyes still shut, she heard him say softly, "Today, your hair is the color of autumn leaves. Dark red, of course, but now with streaks of gold."

Then, she felt his fingers lightly trace the outline of one cheekbone as he had when he sat on her bed upstairs earlier this morning. His touch was as soothing as the sun's rays and she suddenly felt she could tell him anything.

"So you, too, have had a failed marriage," he stated matter-of-factly.

"A colossally-failed marriage," she corrected him, opening her eyelids to gaze at him somberly. "A failure so stupendous, I haven't spoken about it, except to a shrink, for more than ten years."

"Any marriage that fails feels like that, I suspect."

"Wait till you hear about mine," she warned.

"Tell me."

Alex indicated they should both shift off their cushions and use them to support their elbows as they reclined upon the tartan blanket, arranging their bodies parallel to each other and each holding a hand against one cheek, their eyes level with one another.

"I have a mother named Gertrude Parker Fraser of the 'Atlanta Parkers,'" she began in a faintly mocking tone of voice, "better known as 'Peachy' Parker to her intimates. And her best friend throughout her life was Suzie Ballard Reynolds. The two of them long plotted a union between her son, Charlton, and Peachy's daughter—"

"That would be you, Fiona, correct?" Alex interrupted. "Somehow, I know where this is going."

"And you would be *so* correct," she agreed, "only in my case—unlike you and Addy—Chip and I were never friends. I don't think I even liked him very much as a kid and hardly saw him at all during middle or high school, given that I went to an all-girls private school in High Point and Chip grew up in Atlanta." Fiona paused for breath, then continued. "But then came my coming-out year."

"Debutante, were you?"

"Reluctant debutante, you mean. Coming out parties are all but a thing of the past in the States, now—excepting, of course, in parts of the American South. At that age, all I wanted was to get away from my mother's scheming and go to art school somewhere, *any*where. My father fancied himself an artist. He certainly was no businessman, but he never took my part. I think Thomas Quattro is as afraid of my mother as I was."

"Thomas who?"

"It's that Fraser *naming* thing again," she explained. "If you didn't get saddled with the name Maxwell, and you were a boy, you were likely to be named Thomas. My father was Thomas Fraser, the Fourth—"

"Ah...yes, I see, Quattro. The Fourth, poor laddie."

"Poor laddie indeed," Fiona repeated, knowing that her tone was sour and unattractive, but she no longer cared.

"A bloody nightmare, was he?"

"No. Just a very weak human being. Nothing at all like the Duchess's original, true-blue Thomas Fraser, I'll bet. But Chip, now. *There* was a genuine nightmare, all right." She stared over Alex's shoulder into the depths of the nearest hedge. "Well, at any rate, Suzie Reynolds and Peachy Parker conspired to throw Chip and me together every single party during my coming out year when I was seventeen. Suzie paid Chip's airfare up to North Carolina each time there was a dance. That boy drank a lot of beer at Georgia Tech before he got thrown out. I heard later it was because he was part of a group that gang-raped a girl at his frat house and got off with dismissal rather than jail time."

"Bloody hell," Alex commented quietly.

Fiona gave a quick nod.

"Well, at any rate, by the time *we* were dating—and believe me, I use that term loosely—he hid his boozing fairly well, but I know, now, he was a full-fledged, mean-as-a-snake alcoholic by then. Turns out, my mother knew that all along, because Suzie kept telling her how worried she was about her precious boy, and that if he'd just get married and settle down, everything would be just fine."

Fiona could hear herself slipping more and more into her

southern drawl but she couldn't seem to help herself.

"To make the proverbial short story *short*, I allowed myself to be persuaded that with my red hair and skinny legs…loud, obnoxious, good-ol' boy Chip Reynolds was about as good as I could expect in a husband, which is what I was advised to secure, since, after all, no one was willing to pay for my education. 'Young lady!'" my mother was fond of saying, 'you'd better find a roof to put over that red head of yours—and quickly. You're not getting any younger…or prettier.'"

"Your parents spoke to you like that?" Alex asked, shaking his head. "But you're *beautiful*, Fiona! Didn't you look in a mirror? You believed what your mother said?"

"When you hear it whispered that you certainly didn't look a thing like your stunning, blond mother, you begin to believe you're ugly as a post—especially when she hated having a 'wild, Scottish throwback' for a daughter, as she was fond of saying my whole life. And by the way," Fiona said, her lips quirking slightly, "my looks improved a lot, once I got to New York. Good hairdresser, nice clothes, plus people up north seemed to admire my hair color. I could never understand it myself, frankly, but living in Manhattan made my life a lot more pleasant."

"You are a stunning-looking woman, Fiona," Alex repeated urgently. "Dazzling, in fact. Don't ever think otherwise." The loving look in his eyes gave her the courage to continue with her sorry tale.

"But as to your question about my parents' attitude towards me: Daddy wouldn't say a word to counter all the disparaging things Peachy said to me, and when I asked him why he and Mother would pay for my brother Tommy's schooling, but wouldn't pay for mine, he'd just mumble that I was a girl, blah, blah, blah. I begged my Grandfather Maxwell to give me a job at the mill, since I knew lots more about the business than Tommy did, but he didn't want to 'discourage young Thomas Cinque from being involved in the family firm,' despite the fact that Tommy—my *twin*, mind you—wanted to go to college and get a law degree and despised working for our furniture company."

"And I thought America was far in advance of Scotland on

the subject of education and employment opportunities for women."

"In the *South*?" Fiona scoffed. "Not in the circles I frequented in the mid-nineteen nineties."

She stared at the plaid lap rug and traced one of the fabric's colorful lines with her forefinger as she continued.

"Tommy duly went off to college and I spent a year or so doing my best to avoid getting married to Chip, who'd been made warehouse foreman at our plant to put us in close proximity and to give him something to do since he'd been kicked out of college. Then one night, he came over to 'sit a spell' on our front porch. I didn't realize how drunk he actually was and…well…I was feeling sad and lonely without my twin to spar with, and I, too, had been persuaded by Chip to have a couple of beers, so I was feeling no pain. The next thing I knew, I was sprawled on the porch swing with Chip on top of me, pants around his ankles and mine, likewise. My mother, on cue, came out the front door, saw us, and declared that we were officially engaged."

Fiona looked over at Alex whose expression was unreadable.

"I think it was all planned," she confided, "but even if it was, I was responsible. I could have said no to Chip. I could have said no to my mother, but I was a weakling, like my Daddy."

"You weren't even *nineteen*, love, and—"

As if she hadn't heard Alex's attempt to justify what happened, Fiona murmured, "I felt so guilty, I allowed everything that followed to take place without protest: the engagement, the showers and parties, and, of course, the big wedding when I turned nineteen. I even went to bed with Chip a few times in the lead-up to that extravaganza, pretending we were in love, but he was usually drunk. It was a disaster every time, and of course, I thought that was my fault, too. I thank God, though, I didn't get pregnant."

Fiona felt a familiar flush spreading up her neck and pointed to where she knew color was invading her cheeks.

"This happens, you see, Alex, whenever I think or talk about sex and Chip…but I digress."

She affected a shrug and continued her narrative, wanting to be done with the worst part.

"Of course, our family couldn't really afford such a big wedding, but Peachy insisted and my father gave in. Fraser Furniture was starting to show the cracks in the early nineties, but I was marrying a *Reynolds*! It had been my mother's ambition for years and she'd played up to Chip's parents, who were big socialites in Atlanta, even though she said terrible things about them behind their backs. So there I was, walking down the aisle in a twenty-thousand-dollar bridal gown in a wedding whose cost I shudder even to think about!"

"So how long did the marriage last?"

Fiona turned from staring into the hedge to meet Alex's glance dead on.

"Not long. Not long at all."

"*How* long?"

"Oh…" Fiona considered carefully, "about two hours."

"No." Alex's shock was obvious.

"I jumped out of the car at a stoplight a few miles after we'd left the reception."

"You *what*?"

"By the time we performed that appalling first dance alone on the floor, Chip was beyond drunk. And when the guests pummeled us with rice, he was beyond consciousness, practically. I couldn't believe all those people at the reception allowed him to get behind the wheel. Once we'd pulled away from the curb, I knew *I* would surely die if we drove any further in Suzie's cute little classic red Ford Thunderbird convertible that she'd given him to drive that night. He got so mad when he saw me open the car door and make a break for it at that first stoplight that he floored the accelerator and drove right into a tree about a hundred yards down the road."

"Killed himself on the day of your wedding?" Alex asked, incredulous.

"Oh, no. Chip Reynolds would never have done anything

so chivalrous."

A long-suppressed but familiar feeling of hysteria had crept into her voice.

"He *lived*, Alex, and was put on life support that day and stayed that way for three years! And I felt so guilt-ridden about it all that I assumed the role of tragic bride and remained right by his bedside. Peachy and Suzie immediately figured out that the reason I didn't have a scratch on me was because I'd jumped out of the car, and they blamed me for what happened. Even so, they had their reputations to preserve so they put their heads together and concocted a story for public consumption that it was such a miracle—plain and simple, God's plan—that I'd been thrown clear of the crash and survived. Why, look what a brave girl I was, taking care of Chip in his awful, vegetative state."

Alex reached across the small space separating them and pulled Fiona hard against the length of his body. "My God...this is the worst story I've ever heard. Gothic doesn't begin to describe what happened to you."

"Oh, but wait!" Fiona leaned back, shunning the comfort of Alex's embrace. "Suzie and Hal Reynolds insisted we bring Chip back to their home in Atlanta where I was given the maid's room and served as his day nurse and they hired someone to take care of him at night. After three years of this, I think I became a vegetable myself."

Alex gazed at her soberly and asked, "You aren't married any longer, are you?"

Fiona shook her head in the negative and she could see relief flood his features.

"So what ultimately happened to Chip?"

Fiona inhaled deeply, desperately wanting the tale to be at its end, yet making a pact with herself to provide Alex with every, last, horrific thing she'd done so he could make up his mind whether he'd ever speak to her again or not.

"Even though the Reynolds family was pretty well-off, Chip's being so disabled became a huge financial drain on their bank account. God knows the Frasers didn't have any money to contribute to that boy's care. By then, I was over twenty-one and as Chip's wife, I was officially next-of-kin. Even though his family was footing the bill for this nightmare, *I* was the only one with the legal authority to pull the plug."

"And did you?" Alex asked quietly.

"I did not. In fact, I refused to make that decision a number of times. I felt back then that I'd murdered him anyway, and I didn't want to do it twice."

"So Chip is still alive?"

"No."

Alex waited for her to continue, asking no more questions.

"Finally," Fiona said, taking another deep breath, "all our lives had become such hell, his parents made me an offer which…I did not have the strength to refuse."

And still, Alex remained silent.

"What was that offer, you ask?" she said, bitterness rising in her throat. "'Fiona,' they said, 'since you and Chip—as every judge and minister in town knows—never had a weddin' night, we can easily get an annulment, if you'd agree to it, thereby making *us* his next-of-kin. It will be as if you never married and *we'll* have the power to make medical decisions concerning our own son, which we think is only right, don't you? Especially since you jumped out of the car, probably distracting poor Chip. In return, though, we will pay for you to move to New York and go to any art school you want.'"

"And you accepted." It was a statement, not a question.

"I accepted," she confirmed. "I lied about not sleeping with Chip *before* the marriage. The minute the annulment came through in the great state of Georgia, I flew out of Atlanta and enrolled in Parsons School of Design in New York as soon as they'd let me in. I went home only once after all that…and that was the weekend Parker got killed water skiing. Back in New York, I got a weekend job in the furniture department at Macy's to pay for my shrink, and never set foot in the south again."

"And Chip?"

"A week after I'd left Atlanta, Suzie and Hal Reynolds took him off the respirator. He died within the hour. They told everybody who knew us that Chip became despondent because

I'd abandoned him and he'd lost his will to live."

A long pause ensued before Alex said, "Your psychiatrist *did* tell you, didn't he, that this double tragedy was *not* your fault?"

"She told me that, yes. And I've spent the last ten years or so convincing myself that fact is true."

"Well, it *is!*"

By this time, the sun had moved closer to its zenith, its rays filling the inner square of the maze with warmth and golden light. A breeze above them detached more leaves from the trees and several floated on the air currents and then gently drifted down to settle softly on the grass, one landing on the blanket at their feet.

It was only when Alex gathered her into the circle of his arms that Fiona began to weep deep, wracking sobs for the seventeen-year-old girl with red hair and skinny legs who didn't have an advocate or friend to stand with her against the onslaught of her mother's disappointment for the way Peachy Parker's own life had turned out.

Finally, spent from tears so long unshed, Fiona lay with her moist cheek against Alex's chest, the top of her head tucked under his chin. The strength of his grasp provided a shield, now, against the ghosts she had summoned from her past. She began to feel her body relax and the noonday sun seeped into her bones.

Her heart, which had been pounding in her chest when she confessed that she'd allowed someone else to end Chip's sorry life, slowly resumed its normal rhythm. She had told Alex this terrible secret—and now she waited for him to say something, anything.

As minutes passed by in silence, it occurred to her that no words were necessary because he continued to kiss the top of her head and hold her tenderly…and hadn't let go.

CHAPTER 12

It was nearly two o'clock that afternoon by the time Alex and Fiona had consumed the light lunch stored in the picnic hamper provided them by the Traquair House kitchen. When they'd finished, Alex easily led them out of the maze via small white signs that read "Fools Exit," and the pair quickly gathered their belongings and stowed them in the Jaguar. They made their farewells to the hospitable Catherine Constable Maxwell Stuart, who was expecting the imminent arrival of a large bus full of children studying Scottish history on a school field trip.

"We'll do anything we can to keep the lights on here at Traquair," she noted cheerfully as her spaniels lolled on the front lawn in dappled sunlight. "Have a wonderful time on your visit to Abbotsford, and do give Jason Dyer my best, won't you?"

"Certainly," Alex replied, "and thanks so much for arranging Fiona's special tour with him. Sir Walter Scott's home is the quintessential baronial pile, wouldn't you agree?" He turned to his traveling companion, "Merely seeing the private quarters of that country house should *fill* that notebook of yours with ideas for Bernard Sterling."

Fiona turned toward her hostess. "I can't thank you enough for all you've done, Catherine…and you can count on my telling everyone I know heading for Scotland not to miss a stay at Traquair House. You've been more than wonderful." She bent down to give Daphne and Delilah friendly pats. "And *you* two! I'm going to miss you madly!" She looked from Catherine to Alex. "I'm thinking I must have one of these little fur balls in my life someday."

Within a few minutes they had left the estate grounds, driven through the nearby town of Innerleithen, and were passing through the tiny village of Walkerburn, paralleling the

Tweed River on the A72, heading toward Melrose.

Pointing through the windshield, Alex drew Fiona's attention to a large, abandoned building.

"That used to be the old Ballantyne woolen mill," he said soberly. "It was founded in the mid-eighteen hundreds and at one time made some ten *thousand* yards of tartan a week for soldiers' uniforms in World War I."

Fiona stared at the boarded up windows and weeds growing everywhere.

"Looks like it was a huge operation," she marveled.

"The plant closed in 1987.... one of the early warning signals to the rest of the weaving industry of the consolidation and downsizing that was to come."

"It must have put hundreds of people out of work," she said, looking back over her shoulder as the derelict building receded from view.

"It decimated the town, as you could see." Alex pointed to the road ahead. "In less than fifteen miles we'll be at Abbotsford where, by the way, Jason Dyer, who's the Chief Executive of the Abbotsford Trust, supervised a recent twelve million pound restoration and refurbishment. You'll be viewing it as it was in Scott's time, and in pristine condition."

Fiona couldn't believe how lucky she'd been to see many aspects of Scotland only Alex could have shown her, and now, thanks both to him and to Catherine, she was about to be treated to a private tour of the home built by one of the world's most famous authors who was also an important collector of books, furniture, paintings, and medieval artifacts.

"I think if Americans know anything about Scotland, it's probably because they saw the film versions of *Ivanhoe* or *Rob Roy*," Fiona noted ruefully. "Sir Walter Scott practically invented the historical novel, didn't he?"

Alex laughed. "We like to claim he absolutely *did* do that, to say nothing of popularizing tartan drapery, carpets, family coats-of-arms, and the wearing of the kilt! We woolen merchants owe the man our undying gratitude. Plus," he added grinning, "today you'll learn that one of his family lines—the Constable Maxwell-

Scotts—reach back, in some tortuous fashion, to the Duchess of Gordon's Almighty Maxwells!"

"Bernard Sterling is going to be so jealous of me and my middle name, even if my ancestors chose it for reasons we haven't quite figured out yet," she joked.

She was amazed to feel as light-hearted—buoyant, even—as she did right now, considering her gut-wrenching morning revealing to Alex the ugly details of her first marriage. She darted a glance at his handsome profile and began to speculate on the void in her life there would be when she ultimately returned to New York.

Before she could dwell any further on a subject that was bound to bring her spirits low again, Alex made a turn off the motorway and soon after, another, past a spanking new sign announcing entry into the Abbotsford estate. Fiona soon caught her first glimpses of the fairytale towers of an author's romance with stone and mortar.

"Oh…my," she said, exhaling a long breath. "That building is everything I could imagine a Scottish country house should look like. It's magnificent."

Alex pulled into the visitor's parking lot and turned off the ignition. In the lengthening afternoon light, Abbotsford's variegated stones of pink and buff were washed a silvery-grey, highlighting its distinctive Scottish Baronial style with an uneven, crenelated roofline, small, lancet windows on the upper floors, and graceful mullioned bays opening out from the public rooms on the lower levels. Wide swaths of lawn led up to a front doorway that Alex explained incorporated a relic of Edinburgh's old Tollbooth on the Royal Mile.

Just as arranged, Jason Dyer was waiting for them in shirtsleeves and a loosened silk tie at the modern Visitor Center. After greeting them warmly, he swiftly escorted the couple past meandering tourists to take them to see Sir Walter Scott's famous book-lined study and the private bedrooms and sitting rooms on the upper floor that could now be leased to overnight guests for a mere fourteen thousand dollars a week.

Dyer noted drolly, "The Hope Scott Wing sleeps at *least*

fourteen, mind you, so compared to hotel rooms, it's rather a bargain! I hope you'll consider getting a group of your colleagues from Bernard Sterling to come visit us someday for a company retreat."

Fiona had to chuckle at the notion of Jared and Bernie springing for such a luxurious "field trip," but indulging in banter was forgotten when she was ushered into the grand gallery of life-sized knights in shining armor standing in front of paneled walls festooned with painted and gilded coats-of-arms that the designer in her soul wanted to transfer immediately to needlepoint pillows and rich, elegant upholstery fabrics.

By the time they were ready to leave Abbotsford, shadows had lengthened even further across the broad expanse of lawn and Fiona's notebook was, indeed, filled with myriad notations, just as Alex had predicted.

"I've taken about a thousand photographs," she apologized to their distinguished guide, "and seeing the wonderful exhibitions in the new museum makes me want to reread every one of Scott's novels. You and your team have done an amazing job to make this home as if Scott still lived here. You were so kind to take the time for our special tour," she added sincerely. "I am hugely appreciative. And perhaps the Trust would be open to the possibility of allowing my company to license some of the smaller objects in the collection for reproduction? It could prove a substantial way to add to your coffers, eventually."

"Just let us know which items you're interested in and I'm sure our merchandizing director would be most pleased to consider such a scheme," Dyer replied genially. "Lovely to meet you, Ms. Fraser." He turned to her companion. "And good to see you again, Alex. I think the drapery in the bedrooms came out wonderfully well, don't you? The Trust is most grateful for your donation."

In the car again, Fiona teased, "Seriously. Do you know absolutely *everyone* in southern Scotland?"

Alex steered the vehicle past a sign that pointed ahead "To Dryburgh Abbey."

"Well, let us hope the woman who sits in the Abbey ticket

booth remembers me, as it's nearly closing time, and there's something I very much want you to see before the sun goes down."

A feathery mist that bordered on light rain began to fall as Alex led the way past the small, wooden ticket kiosk and the kindly woman who took his money and advised them to shut the gate when they left, as she was going home to cook her husband his supper.

"Only in Scotland," Fiona said. "In the States, there'd be security guards taking our name, rank, and serial number if we stayed a minute beyond closing time."

"Dryburgh may be roofless, but it also remains a church, open to all," Alex replied, seizing her hand as he led her down a path marked "To the Abbey."

Fiona pulled up the hood of her rain jacket with her other hand. "I suppose we don't look like anyone likely to cause trouble."

They continued along the path tufted with grass and flanked by a wooden fence on their right side and moss-and-lichen-covered gravestones on their left. Trees as tall as the Abbey itself rose from the verdant grasses surrounding the ruin's glass-less rose window embedded in an enormous stone wall standing on its own that Fiona caught sight of as they came around a curve. To her amazement, Scottish Highland cattle with coats similar to the color of her hair grazed nearby, the only other living creatures on the grounds besides the two of them as the last of the day's light peeking through the pewter rain clouds bathed the ancient stones pink and gray.

"What caused it to be a ruin?" she asked.

"The Abbey's location near the border with England made it subject to repeated attacks by English armies, beginning in the fourteenth century."

Fiona's gaze rose to the tops of the ragged walls. "It's hard to believe battles were fought right *here*, where we're walking. It's so incredibly peaceful," she said, awed by the majestic beauty of soaring stone walls lapped at their base by soft, green grass.

But for the faint crunch of their feet upon the path and the distant lowing of the cattle, all was silent as they approached one wing that Alex identified as the North Transept. It was clearly the best-preserved part of the church, where two, smooth granite crypts were nestled under one of the few intact sections of the Abbey's rock walls.

"Scott's grave..." Fiona murmured, reading aloud the clearly carved inscription that marked Sir Walter's passing on the 21st September 1832. "What an honor to have been buried here, within the Abbey's walls."

"He was probably the first English-language author to have truly an international following in his lifetime," responded Alex. "And what other literary figure can you name has his likeness on every piece of currency in his country?"

They stood silently for a few moments, absorbing the utter serenity of their surroundings as the gentle mist kissed their upturned faces, their eyes scanning the stones soaring above Scott's final resting place. Fiona loved the feel of her hand encased in Alex's own.

At length, he said, "Scott loved the outdoors, you know. You could see that from the gardens and woodlands that surround Abbotsford."

Fiona nodded. "Mr. Dyer told me that during the construction of the house, Scott planted most of the trees himself on the estate and created a network of specially-designed walking paths. I wish we had time to take some of them."

"Not many countries hold up an environmentalist and a writer as their most cherished national hero," he said, and Fiona could hear the pride in his voice. Then, Alex put an arm around her shoulder, his gaze returning to the polished granite containing the author's remains. "I would say that a spot where the first stone was sited here a thousand years ago is the perfect resting place for such a man."

After a few minutes' more contemplation, Alex led her in the opposite direction from Scott's grave to stand in front of the South Transept, also roofless. All that remained of this part of the Abbey was a splendid gable with a window composed of five lancets where there once had been divided sections of stained glass that towered over the parishioners.

"It must have been so beautiful," she said, barely above a whisper. A sense of the church's impressive antiquity and its sacredness unexpectedly brought moisture to her eyes.

"There may have been a smaller chapel here," replied Alex, pointing to a series of gothic stone arches nearby.

As if one, they bowed their heads and the warmth of their clasped hands felt to Fiona as if they were being blessed from a time and space beyond their own.

Alex must have felt it as well, for he turned and took her in his arms as the mist swirled around them and the daylight dwindled. Framing her face with his hands, he kissed her on the lips as gently as a groom kisses his bride. The tears in her eyes and the gentle rain falling on her face became intermingled as Fiona pulled Alex closer and kissed him back with a love and tenderness that warned her she would soon weep openly a second time in a single day for the beauty of this moment and the bond she knew had been forged between them just now.

Alex leaned back and gazed at her steadily. "Is it too soon to say it, Fiona?"

"That we're falling in love?" she replied, their faces only inches apart.

She was shocked that she'd said the words out loud—and in a church, no less.

Alex's forefinger gently brushed a drop of rain off her cheek. "I was actually thinking to say that…I love *you*, my redheaded water sprite. And it feels as if I always have."

By this time, tears ran down her cheek where Alex had touched her face. She turned, hooked her arm through his, and said, "Oh, I'm sure, Sir Walter Scott, the great romantic, would agree that it's never too soon to say something as lovely as *that*." She gave him a watery smile. "And he'd also probably say that you and I should come out of the rain."

Alex's family home, The Firs, was located just outside the town of Selkirk, home of Maxwell Mills. It was a close ten miles from Dryburgh Abbey, but it was nearly eight o'clock before their car's headlights shone the way across a bridge spanning the River Tweed, up a steep drive, and through two stone pillars marking the entrance to the three-acre property belonging to the Maxwell Mills Trust.

Fiona had barely closed the door on the passenger side of the car before a gray-haired woman in an apron appeared on the gravel turn-around that fronted a small, gabled manor house constructed of honey-colored stone.

"Mrs. Nolan," Alex greeted his housekeeper with a broad smile. "I hope you heard my phone message earlier this afternoon and that we haven't thrown you into a whirl."

"Aye, that I did, and I have a nice bit of filet, some roasted potatoes, and carrots from the garden for your supper, if you think that will suit," she replied, casting a curious glance in Fiona's direction. With the ease of a servant who had been in the Maxwell household many a moon, Mrs. Nolan said to Fiona, "You must be the designer from America Alex told me was coming to see the mill. And I also understand that you do an excellent Strathspey."

Fiona shot a startled look at Alex and then nearly laughed out loud.

"That would be me, Mrs. Nolan," she confirmed, smiling and extending her hand in greeting, "though how sprightly I am after my travels all over the countryside today, I can't really say." Through the gloom of evening, she made a quick survey of the closely cut grass and attractive landscaping surrounding the house and added, "It's lovely to be here after a very long day, and you are so kind to have held dinner for us."

Alex proposed rather formally, "Why don't we have Mrs. N show you to your room and have a quick wash myself, and then we'll have our supper?" To his housekeeper he asked in such a casual tone of voice, Fiona suspected the answer meant quite a lot to him, "Will Harry be joining us tonight?"

Mrs. Nolan frowned. "Not that your brother's told me, the

scamp! He left here with all his fishing gear about three days ago and there's not been a peep from the lad since. Said he would be busy looking after a lot of Russian sportsmen, he did. Said they'd bought a weeks' worth of angling, though how he plans to feed those poor souls I canna imagine."

Alex shrugged. "I doubt he much cares what he serves them as long as his clients pay to put their line into the river. Come, Fiona, let me take your case."

Less than twenty minutes later, they were seated at right angles at a long, formal dining table in a room whose four walls were covered in beige and white striped wallpaper and "mod" style drapery that looked as if it might have been installed a good forty years earlier.

Alex caught her studying the room's décor.

"Needs a bit of up-dating, wouldn't you say?" he noted wryly. "After my father died last year, I wanted Jeffreys Interiors to have a go, here, but just couldn't commit the time or the cash reserves to such a project. Maybe someday…if we can just dig ourselves out of the hole we're in currently."

"I love the Persian carpet," she said, nodding over her shoulder. "The sapphire and garnet border is beautiful, and look at the way those birds and leaves are worked into the rug's cream white center. You could key off those colors so wonderfully when you redo this room," she suggested.

"I was told my grandfather bought this carpet the minute he came into his mysterious legacy from the Maxwells of Monreith—and before he even purchased his employer's shares at the mill."

"Well, he knew his Persian rugs, for sure." She grinned across the short distance separating their placemats. "Perhaps you'd let me photograph it tomorrow? I think it would be a wonderful addition to the Sterling Home Collection if we could have it reproduced somewhere. We'd pay you a royalty, of course," she added, her smile growing wider.

"You'd probably have to have knock-offs made in India or China," Alex said rather glumly. "That's where just about everything else in the world is produced these days."

"But not tartan!" Fiona said loyally.

"Oh, there are manufacturers in Singapore who make a few plaids for about eighty percent less per yard than we can here in Scotland," Alex complained, "and the South Koreans have just bought one of our largest woolen fabric and cashmere companies, Lochcarron of Scotland located in Selkirk, like we are, a few miles from here, and its sister firm, the knitwear manufacturer, Peter Scott, in Hawick."

"Well, at least they're still employing local people at the plants here, aren't they?" Fiona asked, disheartened to learn this since Lochcarron was on her list as one of the mills she wanted to visit.

"For the moment they appear to be keeping on all staff, yes," Alex said, nodding his thanks to Mrs. Nolan who had entered to clear their dinner plates and bring them coffee. "But who knows if they won't learn what they need to know from the workers here in Scotland—including gathering a library of tartan patterns—and then just move everything back to the Far East and make the woolens with dirt cheap labor and undercut our prices even more?"

Fiona could see their discussion had touched a raw nerve, one that her own brother, Tommy, had expressed to her when last they'd discussed the global challenges at Fraser Furniture.

"We in the west just have to figure a way to *outfox* these people!" she exclaimed. "It's impossible to compete on price, but no one can match British or American *quality*."

"The way some of these manufacturers in the Far East get around that is to say 'Designed in Scotland' or 'Designed in Italy' and then make it with slave labor in their home countries. The consumer, who always wants a bargain, will think it's the genuine article and go for the cheaper price tag, every time."

Fiona put a hand on Alex's sleeve. It was the first time he'd allowed her to see his deep-seated anxiety concerning the future prospects for his company.

"That's why," she said earnestly, "I think your All Things Scottish dot com could be such a winner. No middleman! People buy real, Scottish goods directly from you, and—"

"But first," he interrupted glumly, "I have to survive this year and make enough money to buy out my brother's shares."

Fiona gently squeezed his arm. "Well, let's hope, after I see your mill tomorrow, that I can recommend to Bernard Sterling he should place a big order for drapery and upholstery fabric that would make your bottom line look much improved for the year. I've already seen at Jeffreys Interiors, Abbotsford, and Traquair House the gorgeous quality goods you make. Now, all you have to do is convince me your factory has the capacity to make enough of what we'll need to do our collection," she finished with an encouraging smile.

Alex gazed at her across his cup of coffee and said, "Let us hope you like what you see."

"I'm sure I will."

Alex stood up and offered her his hand.

"Shall we go into the sitting room? I'm sure Mrs. N. has lit the fire. A cognac? A nip of an obscure brand of malt whiskey?" he asked, lightening their mood.

"A little nightcap would be nice," she said, entering the adjoining large room with a bay window matching the one she'd seen in the dining room. Sure enough, a cheerful fire was glowing in the grate and chintz drapes were already closed against the autumnal chill outside. "Just pour me a thimble-full of whatever you're having."

With a bottle labeled Glenfiddich in his hand, Alex gestured toward the green and white curtains and said, "Behold, you see another room that needs doing up," and handed her a small glass of the amber liquid. He took a seat on the sofa facing the fireplace and patted the seat cushion next to him.

"No wallpaper to rip down in here," Fiona teased, sitting down, "so updating this part of the house wouldn't take any time at all."

"I wish you were here to help me plan what must be done around here," he said, suddenly serious. "I wish you were here, period. When do you have to go back to New York?"

Fiona stared into the depth of her glass. "A week, tomorrow. After I see Paxton House and Floors Castle and a couple of other mills, plus a few more antique dealers."

"And I've got to get back to the office after all this time away." He set his glass down on the coffee table and removed hers from her hand. "This isn't what I want," he said fiercely. "I want to go everywhere with you, show you everything—"

"I know," she whispered, allowing him to enfold her in his arms. "I want that, too."

Their kisses grew so heated so quickly, Fiona could almost imagine peeling off his clothing then and there and making love right on the dated chintz-covered couch. It had been so long since any man had touched her and no one—ever—as skillfully or tenderly as Alex. He threaded a hand through her hair, cradling her head as he began to softly nibble her right ear, her neck, and finally her collarbone through the thin cashmere shell she'd worn all day beneath her cardigan.

"Oh, Fiona," he groaned. "I want you with me so much. Ever since I got your call, from New York, I've been dreaming of you in my bed upstairs…"

He slipped his other hand under the ribbing of her pullover, his warm, caressing fingers seeking the edge of her bra. She arched to meet his touch, communicating silently, *yes…yes…hold my breast…stroke…ah…*

Dimly, she heard a door slam and a clatter of various objects landing on the wooden floor in the foyer off the sitting room where they were practically sprawled across the length of the sofa. Startled by the loud sounds, she abruptly pulled away from Alex like a guilty teenager and leaned on a sofa cushion with her two elbows to steady herself. She could feel moisture between her legs and she didn't dare look to see that state of the front of Alex's trousers.

"Oh, bloody hell!" growled Alex, his teeth clenched. "My brother Harry's back."

"But Mrs. Nolan said—"

Alex rose to his feet and pulled Fiona to stand beside him. The two of them did their best to straighten their clothing.

"Hello? Who's in there?" came a shout. "Mrs. N? I'm perishing for something decent to eat after suffering the rotten fare those worthless chalet bunnies served up to those bloody, thieving Russkies. *Mrs. N?* Where the hell *are* you?"

Alex strode angrily toward the sitting room door and yelled before he yanked it open, "Mrs. Nolan has gone to bed, so cease your shouting, Harry!"

Equally as loud, Alex's brother retorted, "Well, you're making a bloody racket yourself, aren't you, now?"

Alex gestured over his shoulder at Fiona, who hoped by this time she looked presentable.

"We have a guest here! A *business* guest."

CHAPTER 13

Standing on the threshold was a shorter version of Alex, though with sandy hair and sporting a few days' growth of beard. Harry Maxwell was attired in clothing Fiona could only imagine that serious Scottish outdoorsmen wore—dark, grease-stained moleskin trousers, a flannel shirt with tattered collar and cuffs, and a thick, knit pullover with contrasting cloth patches on the shoulders and elbows. Over the intruder's arm was a pair of olive green, hip-high waders she'd seen photographs of fly fishermen wearing, and behind him, heaped upon the floor, was a pile of nets, woven creels, and all manner of paraphernalia that belonged in a storage shed somewhere.

Harry may not have had dinner, but he'd clearly had a fair amount to drink before arriving unexpectedly at The Firs. He glanced over Alex's shoulders and grinned knowingly.

"Ah…brother mine. So sorry to intrude, but where the hell's Mrs. N? We pay her enough and I want some supper!"

"*You* don't pay her a farthing," Alex said, tight-lipped, "and it's quarter to eleven. She's locked up the larder and gone to bed…and so should you. And how about ringing us to warn you'll be coming back unexpectedly next time?" He paused as if suddenly recalling that Fiona was standing only a few feet behind him. Turning, he made awkward introductions. "This is Ms. Fiona Fraser, a client from New York, here to survey the woolen industry in Scotland for her company."

"What's left of it, you mean," Harry said, advancing another step into the room and giving Fiona an obvious once over. Pointing to their abandoned whiskey glasses he said with a smirk, "And I'll just *bet* you two were conducting 'business' tonight, now that laddie, here, is officially a free man." To Alex he said, "The news of your divorce being final had the lassies chattering in every pub from Selkirk to Peebles, I'm told," he added with a short laugh. "Humphrey Dalgetty even asked *me* if it were true that his daughter was no longer your wife."

Fiona could tell that Alex was barely keeping control of his temper. What would Harry and Dalgetty say if they knew Adelina had already married Peter Murray, she wondered?

"I thought you were entertaining your Russian clients this week," Alex said pointedly. "How would you or Humphrey know anything about what's a private matter between Addy and me?"

"I was in Dalgetty Bank a few hours ago, making sure the Russkies' bloody check was good, and he asked me if I'd heard the rumors that you'd both signed the papers. And you'll thank me, Alex, because I said I'd heard nothing about all this. I rushed in there from the lodge because the bloody blokes only paid us *half* of that they owed, saying that was all they would do since they didn't catch a single fish."

"Please tell me, Harry," Alex said, "that you did not *promise* them 'fine, fair fishing' when you booked them at the lodge."

Harry looked down at his leather boots that had left a ring of water around each toe.

"They claimed the food was inedible as well, and given those chalet bunnies' appalling lack of talent in the kitchen, I could forgive 'em that…but the bounders packed up on the third day, and by Saint Ninian, they were gone before daybreak. So here I am, a starving lad with a thirst to match. Mind if I help myself?"

Harry brushed by Alex and Fiona, heading straight for the coffee table where he downed what was left of Alex's glass of whiskey.

Fiona quickly volunteered to her host, "I think we left a few pieces of beef on the platter, Alex, and a potato or two." To Harry, she said, "Would that interest you, even if it's served cold?" hoping some food might sober up the man a bit and avoid World War III with his brother, who looked as if he was going to truly lose his temper any minute.

Harry regarded Fiona with an appraising eye. "Why, that

would be a very nice way to end a thoroughly rotten day...Miss Fraser, is it? From America, you say?"

"Fiona," she urged. Then to Alex, she asked, "Shall we take pity on this poor, starving creature and rustle up some leftovers?"

Alex looked grim, then shrugged, and said with resignation, "Come on, then, Harry. We'll set you up in the kitchen and then say goodnight." He cast a grateful glance to Fiona and added, "And you, Fiona, will be wanting to have a good night's rest if you hope to see the mill when we open tomorrow, and then get to your meeting at Paxton House before noon."

"Well, I'll just say my goodnights here, then," she agreed, embarrassed if Harry saw Alex and her mount the staircase together. She disguised her regret for what might have been by adding cheerily, "Mrs. Nolan showed me to my room earlier, so I hope to see you both in the morning."

And without further comment, she turned and swiftly strode up the red, carpeted staircase that led to the second floor.

Upstairs, she donned a plain white T-shirt and pajama bottoms, brushed her teeth in the adjacent bathroom, and padded toward a large bed in an expansive room that she guessed had once belonged to Alex and Harry's parents, his mother having passed away when the boys were teenagers, she'd learned that day.

This room, too, had a bay window matching the one in the dining room on the floor below. The high-ceilinged chamber was painted a pale peach, with a fireplace on the left wall stripped of paint and now an incongruous Danish-modern blond color, as was all the furniture in this bedroom—none of which belonged in a house that probably was built in the 1880's. After she'd switched off her bedside light, the night sounds in the tall trees outside her window were soothing as she listened alertly for signs the two brothers hadn't come to blows. Within twenty minutes, she heard the treads of both Harry and Alex striding to their rooms with curt "Goodnights." Next, came the sounds of two doors shutting firmly at the end of the hallway.

Which door led to Alex's room, she wondered? Wouldn't

that be a comedy if she were the type of woman who brazenly crept down the hall and then managed to enter the wrong bedroom? Smiling at that thought and doing her best to banish the memory of Alex's hot hands on her midriff just before Harry ruined their evening together, she hugged her feather pillow closer to her body and willed herself to go to sleep.

At first she thought she might be dreaming. A warm, naked body was holding her close, her breasts separated from a hard, muscled chest only by her thin, cotton T-shirt. Her legs were touching the length of longer ones, firmly muscled, and Alex's arousal was pressed hard against her pelvis. Enfolded in his arms, she felt surrounded by a protected world where no harm could come to her, yet all her senses were suddenly on high alert.

"Well...hello there," she murmured, and smiled into the kiss he bestowed on her.

"Sleeping beauty awakes."

She waited for Alex to begin making love to her, but he put his cheek next to her own and merely continued to cradle her as if they were a long-married couple that could only have a peaceful night's sleep in the safety of each other's arms.

"Alex?" she whispered, and then couldn't suppress a giggle.

"You're laughing? I feared you might wake up and scream that some madman had crept into your bed."

"I wanted to sneak into *your* room when I heard you come upstairs, but I was afraid I might stumble into Harry's by mistake."

Alex chuckled then and gently seized her chin so he could gaze into her face in the dim light.

"So it's all right with you, my barging in like this?"

"Harry was the one who barged in! I couldn't be happier that you've magically turned up in my bed tonight." By this time, they were lying on their sides, nearly nose-to-nose, and Fiona pushed a lock of Alex's dark hair off his forehead in what was becoming a familiar gesture. "I do have a question, though."

"And what is that?"

Her smile faded and she gazed at him soberly.

"Can we...can we separate this...what's obviously happening between us...from whatever decisions I must make in the interests of my company? And you do the same?"

"Yes," he answered without hesitation. "They're totally separate."

"Because what I'm feeling right now has absolutely nothing to do with business," she explained and planted a brief kiss on his chin.

"As you certainly are aware by now, I would definitely agree." He gently pushed his pelvis against hers, clear evidence he was still in full arousal. "This has *nothing* to do with business."

A small voice in the back of her head warned her it wasn't quite that simple to settle the issue of the personal versus the professional, but at least she'd raised the subject, she told herself to quiet a half-buried sense of unease about what she knew was about to take place. Oh, yes, she admitted silently, she desperately wanted this man to make love to her and at the moment, his pulsing masculine presence was nearly all she could think about. Pushing away residual, nagging worries to the far recesses of her mind, she leaned on one elbow and brought her lips to his, kissing him with all the fervor she felt radiating throughout her entire body.

"You see..." she whispered in his ear, "I haven't been with a man in five years and all I could think about after your brother suddenly appeared in the foyer tonight was how I could return to the moment when you put your hand on my breast."

"Why, you're a bold lassie, aren't you?" Alex teased, pulling away to seek her gaze, his dark eyes almost smoldering in the murky light that filtered through the bay window opposite their bed. He slid his palm, warm from holding her fast, under her T-shirt to the spot where he could mold his hand to her flesh. "You mean, in the sitting room, when I did this?"

Fiona's breath caught. "Yes...just like that."

"And if I did this, you wouldn't object?"

He strafed his thumb across her nipple and smiled as they both felt it grow rigid at his touch.

"And you?" she murmured, slipping her hand between their bodies. "You have no qualms about my doing this?"

Alex closed his eyes and when he opened them, even in the dark she could see the yearning in his steady glance.

"I feared that your unhappy time with Chip...and then that other man you had been with prior to when we first met, might have hurt you so much, you wouldn't wish to—"

"Curt Vandervort?" Fiona gave a small shake of her head, stroking Alex with light, feathery touches. "Curt was a so-and-so in many ways, but you should thank him for getting me past a lot of the trauma in this department. He genuinely likes women and likes to pleasure them, and for that I will always be grateful because now, I am so ready to be made love to by a man like you, Alex Maxwell."

She couldn't tear her eyes away from his as she moved her fingers along his flank and then again seized the object of her intense desire. "May I touch you here? And here...?"

"Oh, *yes*..." he moaned. Then with more control he added with an edge of humor in his voice, "Yes, I give you my full permission."

Alex did her the honor of allowing her to perform her fevered ministrations until, as if he could bear them no longer, he swiftly turned her onto her back. With his left hand and her help, he eased her pajama bottoms down her legs and pushed the soft fabric to the bottom of the bed. Next, he skimmed her white T-shirt over her torso and flung it aside. Positioning his hands on either side of her shoulders, he suspended the length of his body in a low arch over hers, and stared down at her, searching her face as if he was seeking the answer to a mystery neither of them understood.

"It's one of those moments, isn't it, Fiona?"

"Like crossing the Rubicon?"

He nodded, gently lowering his form onto hers, his forearms absorbing the majority of his weight.

"Crossing the Atlantic, in one direction or the other," he corrected her. "If we make love tonight, I'm giving you fair warning, this will be serious business...with significant consequences."

"Oh, believe me, I know." She reached up and brushed a forefinger across his lips. "Just come and get me, laddie mine. I'm yours."

He was careful to keep from crushing her.

"Oh, God, Fiona," he whispered into her ear. "If you only knew how often I've thought of us together like this."

"It's been the same with me," she confessed, "from the day I left you standing on the deck of the Circle Line Ferry. I've had all sorts of fantasies about you." She smiled against his throat as she began to dispense playful little nips. "Do you think your Duchess and my Thomas somehow had a hand in all this?"

Alex nuzzled her ear. "Perhaps—having us meet the way we did—it's their way of playing a joke on the fates that condemned them to their star-crossed lives. But frankly, at this moment, Fiona Maxwell Fraser, I'm through speculating. I only want to—"

He slipped his hand between their bodies to confirm that she was moist and ready. Without the slightest embarrassment, she helped him with the condom he'd brought with him and had left on the table beside the bed. Then, their kisses became prolonged and deep, an echo of a dream they'd held together— and apart. Fiona felt a strange, otherworldly reaffirmation of a long, lost love that had survived the centuries, only to reemerge in their fevered embraces and whispered endearments.

"Fiona...*Fiona*..."

The longing she heard when Alex spoke her name as if calling her from afar reached past their physical selves to a place she'd never been before.

"I'm here, Alex...I'm right here..."

And then, he entered her slowly, almost reverently, allowing her body time to adjust to his size. After a few moments, they began to move in perfect rhythm, as in a remembered Strathspey danced long ago, gently at first, and then with increasing intensity as if the bagpipes were skirling an ancient air and their movements driven by a tune that only they could hear. She arched against him and after a few moments more of exquisite sensation felt an explosion of warmth that triggered a similar burst of heat inside her, blotting out all rational thought.

They clung to each other, their breathing ragged, while tears welled in Fiona's eyes and splashed onto Alex's shoulder.

Why was she crying, she wondered, when it had all been so wonderful?

"Precious…so precious," he murmured against her skin. "It's all right, darling…" he whispered in the night, kissing the moisture rolling down her cheeks.

"Feeling like this is…is so scary," Fiona said, her shoulders still trembling. "I kept thinking, when I *could* think, 'please…please…never take this away from me.' Almost as if—"

"As if we'd be parted someday? That was Jane and Thomas' fate. *We're* in charge of our lives, Fiona," he said urgently. "We don't have to answer to anyone but ourselves."

But Fiona knew she had many masters to answer to in New York, and she couldn't bear the thought of having to leave for Paxton House soon—and without Alex.

Early the next morning, far in advance of Alex's brother Harry rising to "air the day," as Alex joked, the pair tiptoed down the stairs to the kitchen. They each ate a bowl of warmed oatmeal Mrs. Nolan had left on top of the Aga cooker the night before, made a pot of coffee that Alex served in a pair of mugs, and then headed for the mill located a few miles away in Selkirk, proper. As the Jaguar nosed into a parking slot labeled "Mgr. Director," he pointed to a white Fiat 500 with jaunty red upholstery that he'd asked Hugh Erskine to arrange for the next part of her journey.

"My assistant manager is also available to take you on the tour of the plant this morning," Alex said as he turned off the ignition. "It might be the best way for me to keep my hands off you in front of my staff."

Fiona couldn't help laughing as the tension that she'd been feeling since she awoke lessened somewhat in advance of a complete shift away from the unforgettable days they'd spent together since her arrival in Scotland.

"Ah…yes…Hugh. Our wonderful chauffeur and piper at Waverley Station."

"And the Jack-of-All-Trades at Maxwell Mills," Alex confirmed. "I can certainly spare him, if you want him to drive you to Floors Castle and Paxton House."

Being chauffeured down unknown roads on the left hand side of the street would be a true luxury, Fiona thought, but she knew how much Alex relied on his second-in-command.

"No, no," she assured him with as much conviction as she could muster, "I can accomplish everything fine on my own, and besides, if I can't have you, I don't want any anybody else to go with me."

Alex seized her hand and kissed it swiftly, and then returned it to her lap.

"This won't be easy for me either, Fiona. But you'll be back in two days' time, and we'll plot our course from there."

"Yes," she said, hoping her resignation wasn't reflected in her tone of voice. Why was she suddenly feeling so bereft at the thought of leaving Alex for a few days, she wondered?

Because I've fallen in love with this man, and I'll be leaving him in less than a week to go back to New York. And then what?

"Alex—" she hesitated, as she studied his handsome profile across the car's passenger seat. "Last night was…well…it was more than wonderful."

"And?" he asked, a wary look invading his brown eyes.

"And," she said softly, "I just felt I needed to say that."

Alex reached for her hand a second time and held it fast.

"It's the same for me, Fiona. Don't ever doubt it, promise? What's happening between us may be one for the ages," he added with a wry smile that she suspected was an attempt to deflect the strong current of emotion suddenly flowing between them at the thought they were parting, if only for forty-eight hours.

And then, inexplicably, she felt tears well again, as they had the previous night, and wondered if the first Thomas Fraser had experienced this terrible *ache* whenever he left Jane Maxwell all those times during their many partings.

Fiona sought Alex's glance and said, "I have no idea how we're going to cope with two continents and a million other obstacles, but I love you, Alex Maxwell. Just know that, will you please?" Alex's look of tender affection bestowed a kind of reassurance that surpassed any words he could have spoken. Fiona shook her head, wondering aloud, "I don't understand how I could feel this way so quickly, but I do."

He gently chucked her under the chin.

"Well, remember, I was the first to bravely declare myself," he murmured, his lips brushing her ear. "Whenever anything seems uncertain between us, just remember Dryburgh Abbey where I do believe we plighted our troth."

"I do believe we did," replied Fiona with a shaky laugh. She turned to open the car door. "Well, now that *that's* been decided," she added with a hint of self-mockery, "I guess we'd better get going. I want to allow plenty of time for my tour of Maxwell Mills and for your fellow countrymen to get accustomed to my driving on the wrong side of the road around here."

Alex gave her a worried look. She swiftly stretched out with her other hand to give his arm a pat. "Just a joke, Alex. Honestly, I'll be fine."

They exited the car and headed toward the plant. Alex's office and those of the other members of his small management team were located in a stone building that clearly had been built sometime in the nineteenth century as part of the original mill. The main operations were housed in a relatively modern building with scores of automated weaving machines already humming at full speed when Hugh began her hour-long tour of the factory's production area.

Her friendly guide showed her the process of weaving tartan fabric from the CAD images of a particular tartan pattern on a computer screen in the design center, through the set-up of a loom with its designated 2-ply wool threads of warp and weft for cashmere and 4-ply for tartan—and then on to the fabric emerging, inch-by-inch, not unlike the vintage looms she'd seen earlier at the Old Weaving Mill in Edinburgh. Some of the textiles produced at Alex's mill were used to make garments and thoroughly washed, dried, and then steam-pressed to the proper size. The rest ended up as bolts of cloth of various weights that were wound on heavy cardboard tubes or flats like she'd seen in her local fabric store.

"Some of this will be sold for yard goods," Hugh explained, "the heavier weights for upholstery fabrics, and so forth."

Fiona could see by the stores of goods housed in the adjacent warehouse that if called upon, Maxwell Mills appeared capable of supplying the goodly portion of yardage that would be required, should Bernard Sterling okay her various designs for upholstery fabric, drapes, cushions, and soft goods—like ottomans and lap rugs—as part of the proposed Scottish Home Collection.

Of course, that might be a big "if," Fiona thought. Alex would have to provide the cost breakdowns of materials and labor so that she could convince Bernie that the higher quality of Alex's products were worth the higher cost.

Yes, she thought, there were many miles to travel before she could promise Alex that the project would receive a green light from her employer, but the material he manufactured was first rate. However, Maxwell Mills made mostly woven fabric and her boss specifically said he also wanted the collection to reflect the richness of cashmere goods. Her next stop would be just down the road in Selkirk: Lochcarron of Scotland, now owned, as she'd learned last night, by a South Korean firm, along with its cashmere producing affiliate, Peter Scott.

When Fiona poked her head into Alex's office to bid farewell, he was tied up on the telephone in what sounded as if it might be a long conversation. With Hugh Erskine at her side, she summoned a cheery wave and mouthed "Thank You," and soon found herself in the firm's parking lot, walking toward the rented Fiat.

Hugh held the door for her, saying, "It's a wee enough vehicle to navigate the narrow roads in certain sections of our Scottish countryside, and zippy enough to make your way around those lorries on the motorways."

He means those giant-sized trucks? Well, the best o' Scottish luck to me!

Hugh had transferred her suitcase from the Jaguar into the hatchback and proceeded to give her directions for the short distance to where her appointment with designer Leah Robertson was due to start in half an hour. With a cheery wave, he retreated back to the factory while Fiona managed to turn the ignition on and slowly make her way out of Maxwell Mill's car park.

She cautiously turned into traffic, shifting gears remarkably smoothly, considering she hadn't driven a stick shift in years, and managed to find her way without mishap the mile and a half to Dunsdale Road.

To Fiona's pleasure, the "Lochcarron Visitor Centre" in Selkirk also included a small coffee shop in one corner featuring, of all things, Starbucks, as well as its own brew. She dropped into a chair with a sense of relief that her initial foray on her own had been relatively painless, and at least she hadn't grazed another car or caused a major accident on her way to this first appointment of three she had today.

After consuming a delicious, homemade scone and her usual café latte, she glanced around the large showroom, open to the public, that featured luxury goods made for the Lochcarron of Scotland brand as well as some of the world's top fashion houses including the ubiquitous Ralph Lauren, Burberry, Brooks Brothers, and a number of other names Fiona knew all too well were competitors of the Bernard Sterling sportswear lines. The cashmere sweaters and throws were of exquisite quality, as were the jackets and kilts on display.

Exactly at the appointed hour, Ms. Leah Robertson appeared and graciously took Fiona wherever she asked to go, spending the majority of her time in the areas of the woolen cloth manufacturing, but also explaining how the finest cashmere goods were made at the Peter Scott factory on Buccleuch Street in the nearby town of Hawick.

"It's certainly become an international business," Robertson acknowledged when Fiona asked her about the impact of the

South Koreans taking over her company in 2011. "We're very sales driven, now," she admitted, "and our mandate is to appeal to a global market, but even the Chinese want to know that the tartan, tweeds, and cashmere they're buying are from Scotland."

"Are they satisfied with merely knowing an item was *designed* in Scotland?" Fiona asked, regarding her closely. "What if, eventually, the sample product was created in your shop, here, but the retail versions were made—say—in Malaysia?"

Leah Robertson paused and then answered quietly, "We'll have to see just where we go from here, won't we?"

As fellow designers, Fiona and her Scottish counterpart had an enjoyable discussion about the ways in which colors and fibers determine the degree of sophistication in any given product. Leah then showed her what she called her "Mood Boards"—large posters with a variety of items glued to them.

Pointing to one, she said, "See…here we show trending colors, fabrics, themes that we see turning up in ads, and even images from Pinterest boards that the public creates. We watch what people buy in the shop here, what gets applause on the catwalk at the fashion shows in New York and Milan, and of course, we factor in what the Color Marketing Group says about next year's color trends. By doing all this research, we begin to get a sense of where *our* market is going. Then, the designers get busy on the next group of products we'll manufacture for the coming year."

At the end of their hours together, Fiona thanked her guide profusely and set off on what Leah called "The Textile Trail" on the A7, heading for Hawick, a town, like Selkirk, with a number of still-active mills. She grabbed a bite of lunch on the High Street and had a quick, unscheduled look at a museum housed in the Borders Textile Towerhouse where the history of weaving and some ancient looms were on display.

Mindful of the time, she set off for Johnstons, a respected textile firm just down the road from the museum. The firm had been established in Elgin in the Highlands in 1797, and now it's newer factory in Hawick had recently received the Royal Warrant, granted personally by Prince Charles—who apparently was a good customer. The shop next to the factory carried some of the finest cashmere products Fiona had ever seen.

The tour of Johnstons was similar to what she'd seen at Alex's mill, so by mid-afternoon, she was driving down the A698, a narrow, two-way road that led directly to the ancient market town of Kelso, also on the River Tweed. She easily located Floors Castle where the current Duke of Roxburghe—the 10th she was informed—maintained the magnificent, 56,000-acre agricultural and sporting estate. As Fiona piloted her little Fiat up the lengthy drive, she caught sight of the enormous home with its romantic, fairytale roofscape featuring a smorgasbord of turrets, pinnacles and cupolas. The slight incline told her that the impressively large edifice was built on a natural terrace overlooking the River Tweed to the Cheviot Hills.

Since this was a quiet, autumn weekday, she easily purchased her entrance ticket without waiting in line and had few other visitors to block her views of house interiors that took her breath away. She wandered through room after room of extensive collections of French and English furniture, silk coverings and Persian carpets, as well as the astounding collection of Brussels tapestries that a beautiful American-born heiress, May Goelet, brought from the family's mansion in Newport, Rhode Island when she married the 8th duke.

Shades of Downton Abbey, Fiona thought as she gazed up at a stunning portrait hung in the billiard room of Duchess May, clothed in a froth of white silk organza.

Moving on down the hushed corridor, Fiona emerged into an enormous drawing room with sage green walls and gilded moulding refitted in 1930, so her guidebook said, to accommodate the series of the duchess's woven hangings that the knowledgeable docent told her were called "The Triumphs of the Gods."

Examining them at close range, she was quite shocked to learn that the tapestries had been *cut in two* in order to fit into existing recesses on the walls of a room replete with a collection of priceless French furniture upholstered in rich silks and brocades. Given that sacrilege, Fiona had few qualms about snapping close-ups with her iPhone of the needlework when the docent and a guard briefly withdrew to another room.

Over a strong cup of tea in the charming restaurant in what looked to have been a former stable block, she excitedly jotted down ideas for slipcovers, drapery, and a multitude of needlepoint pillow designs inspired by her wonderful afternoon in a glorious establishment where every detail had been maintained to the highest standard.

Fiona finally looked up from her labors at the sound of cups and saucers from departed visitors being gathered into plastic bins by the wait staff and realized she was being given a subtle sign it was closing time.

It was nearly dusk by the time she found the B&B in the tiny village of Paxton. Alex or one of his minions had reserved the hostelry for her and she was amazed to realize that she was still adjacent to the River Tweed, but only a mile from the border with England. Wearily, she pulled into the last space in the small car park of a tidy-looking establishment called Kirkbank House—a private home refitted for traveling visitors—and hauled her suitcase along the gravel path to the front door.

"Ah, Miss Fraser," the proprietor greeted her warmly. "We've been expecting you, so if you'll just sign in, here," he said, pointing to the guestbook. As she penned her name her host added, "There's a wee, welcoming dram of whiskey in the drawing room—and someone here to see you."

CHAPTER 14

Startled by the news she'd been located in this remote part of the world, Fiona inclined her head to look through the door to the next room just as Alex rose from a sofa, turned around, and raised a glass with a sheepish grin on his face.

"Surprise," he called out to her.

Fiona barely restrained herself from catapulting into his arms. Instead, she walked as calmly as she could toward her unexpected visitor, conscious that her host had discreetly withdrawn from the foyer to take her suitcase up to her reserved room.

"How did I not notice your car in the parking lot?" she marveled.

"You were tired from a long day, I suspect. But for me, it's only a forty-mile drive from the mill. I made it here in less than an hour." Then he leaned closer to her ear and added in a low voice, "I couldn't bear the thought of you being so close and of my sleeping alone in Selkirk."

"There was room at the inn?" she asked with a mischievous smile.

"If you say so," he replied, and she could tell that they both knew they felt like dashing upstairs, appearances be damned.

"I say so, *yes*, but the God's honest truth is, Alex, I'm about to drop from hunger. Driving in your country takes every brain cell I possess."

"A very fine pub, I'm told by our host, is literally fifty steps from here. Shall we take a stroll?"

As promised, a short walk from the Kirkbank's front door led to an eating establishment called The Cross Inn that Fiona judged was far grander than a mere pub. It featured a surprisingly modern interior in a vintage structure whose exterior conformed to most of the other aged stone buildings in the tiny village of Paxton.

They were seated at a table-for-two in a cozy, candlelit corner. Fiona felt a ridiculous thrill when the tips of Alex's shoes gently nudged her own as she and her dinner partner sipped some very fine French burgundy that came with their meal.

"Won't your brother Harry be highly suspicious you've left Selkirk again so soon?" Fiona asked, savoring the delicious flavors of thyme and the flaky crust of her homemade chicken potpie.

"He's gone back to his fishing lodge to greet his next party of unsuspecting anglers due in two day's time," Alex answered with a wolfish grin. "He'll not be worrying about my whereabouts for at least a week." Alex gave a shrug. "Harry's actually not a bad sort," he confided, "just was cast in the wrong role as a member of the staff at the mill. I truly hope he'll make a go of his fishing enterprise. He just needs to grow up a bit after his rebellious youth."

"Didn't follow in your footsteps, then?" she teased.

"Oh, no. I was the boring, first-born, dutiful one. Unfortunately, our father paid Harry little heed as a second son, and our mother died when he was so young, he lacked proper guidance in my view. Mrs. Nolan was his savior from absolute ruin, though he treats her with less appreciation than he ought."

"He'll come to see what a dear she is someday," Fiona replied, thinking of the lovely African-American woman, Richardell Davis, who had worked for her family for years. Fiona had always felt that if Richardell had been white, she'd have been a CEO or something. And so *kind* to a little girl who felt she was a misfit growing up, she thought suddenly, wondering if her mother's housekeeper had retired by now. Bringing her thoughts back to their conversation, she ventured, "And any news from the recent bride and groom?"

Alex, in the process of cutting a piece of his steak, looked up. "Addy and Peter? No, but I had an outraged call from my former father-in-law today, greatly sympathetic to me that his daughter had scandalously remarried so swiftly after her divorce."

"Oh…boy," Fiona said, shaking her head.

"In the proper stance of a forgiving soul, I reminded him that Peter Murray was a good Catholic lad and that perhaps it was all for the best, given Addy was pregnant, now. I discreetly added that since I was not a born member of the Faith, Adelina could probably obtain a legal annulment from cooperative me, and be married to Peter in their parish church one day. I honestly think Humphrey Dalgetty had never thought of that, and as Peter is now a very respected chartered accountant, by the end of our conversation, it sounded as if Addy's father was mollified a bit, though I expect it will take a while for him to admit it to anyone."

"So you don't think he'll make good on his threat to call in your bank loan?"

"Crisis averted, I'm guessing. He doesn't know that *I* know what he'd threatened to do."

Fiona beamed across the table. "Well! This *is* a cause for celebration! What a relief, and clever you. I'm so happy for you, Alex. Now if I could just affect as good a result for my poor, beleaguered brother, and all the problems he's facing."

Alex nodded. "Well, if you can get Bernard Sterling to back you on your plans for the collection, shouldn't that help tremendously?"

Fiona took a sip of her wine. "That would definitely improve Tommy Fraser's bottom line. And by the way," she said, suppressing a smile over the lip of her glass, "My absolutely *objective* opinion is that Maxwell Mills would be a terrific supplier of the tartan goods needed for the upholstered furniture I'm going to design. I saw for myself today that you run a beautiful enterprise, Alex, and I think you and Fraser Furniture could make fabulous furnishings together. Let's just hope Mr. Sterling agrees with me."

"Thank you," he replied soberly. "Since my father died, Hugh Erskine and I have had a lot of work to right the ship, so your professional opinion, after touring the mill this morning, is very appreciated. How did the rest of your day go?"

"Oh, I *loved* the cashmere I saw produced in Selkirk and Hawick. I made good contacts at both firms I toured, thanks to the people you connected me with there. And Floors Castle! What a pile!" she exclaimed. "I loved every inch of it, though I rather wished they hadn't cut those gorgeous tapestries in two to fit the walls."

"Quite controversial that was in its day," Alex agreed.

She reached across the table and took his hand. "I realize that I said we should keep our private and professional concerns separate, but I want to say here-and-now that there is absolutely *no* way I could have accomplished so much in such a short time without your helping me every step of the way. I am truly grateful, Alex."

Alex held her hand fast. "Trust me, Ms. Fraser, I have loved doing this for you."

Fiona drank in Alex's loving glance as the waitress removed their plates and brought them coffee. As their meal drew to a close, thrumming excitement having nothing to do with the caffeine they were consuming pulsed through her veins. Arm-in-arm, they walked back through the pink twilight that had nearly turned to night. The windows of Kirkbank House were glowing their greeting as the pair walked up the small hill, and in silence, mounted the stairs to the room with the number that matched Fiona's key. It turned out to be a luxuriously appointed chamber, and like the Cross Inn, surprisingly contemporary in its décor. Fiona's gaze drank in the butter-yellow walls and modern, king-sized bed with a faux chinchilla coverlet and brick-colored silk pillows.

She and Alex stared at its welcoming warmth, then looked at each other and exchanged knowing smiles. Before Fiona knew what had happened, Alex lifted her in his arms like a bride and carried her over the threshold.

"May I make love to you in this bed tonight?" he asked softly, their foreheads touching. "It's all I thought about while driving down the A689."

Fiona felt a well of happiness bubbling in her chest and couldn't stop smiling.

"Oh, yes…*please* let's make love on this furry whatever-it-is."

They tumbled onto the soft, luxurious warmth of the beige and cream fake fur, tugging at each other's garments until all their clothing was strewn around the room.

"We must try to be very quiet," she said, giggling. "After all, we don't want to disturb the other guests."

Alex lightly skimmed one hand along her upper arm, pausing to stroke her breast, and then down to her waistline before pulling her close.

"All I need is for you to whisper to me what you'd like me to do, and I'll take it from there," he said, the huskiness in his voice startling her.

"Oh, not so fast, Alex Maxwell," she challenged him softly, easing a leg over his mid-section. "I'm an assertive American, remember? This time, you must tell *me* what I can do to make you the happiest man in Scotland."

"Really, now?" he said, looking pleased. "Well, as a matter of fact, I can think of a few things, starting with…"

He gently seized her wrist and guided her hand to the softest, most venerable part of his body, asking her to cup him there.

"So soft…" she murmured, and then she moved her hand only slightly. "And so hard, Alex. Such a beautiful a man you are."

"And you, so generous…so sweet." She could see that his dark eyes drank in the sight of her face, her breasts above him, and the tapering of her waist. "And *so* sexy, Fiona Fraser."

She lowered her head in benediction to demonstrate the love she could finally reveal to this man in all its honesty and lack of shyness or pretense. She heard his sharp intake of breath, which pleased her beyond all measure and they both moaned softly with the pleasure and delight they were discovering in each other.

At length, Alex slipped his strong hands under her arms and

gently brought her up to his chest so he could look into her eyes.

"You are the woman I have always wanted, and I thought I knew it when you danced out from behind the counter of the booth in the convention center. But now...*now* that we have been together like this," he said, kissing her between his words, "I feel like kidnapping you like one of my ancestors who took poor, hapless Scottish maidens to Gretna Green to force their hand in marriage."

"Oh, Alex!" she cried softly, "don't scare me with talk of marriage. There are so many hurdles in front of us. Just like Jane and Thomas..." She blinked fast to keep her eyes from tearing up. "I don't think I could stand the heartbreak if—"

"Fiona!" Alex cut in hoarsely. "I'm giving you fair warning. Whatever future problems present themselves, unless you turn your back, someday you *will* be my wife!"

And then there were no more words to exchange because their dance had begun, only this time, it wasn't a gentle, waltzing Strathspey, but a whirling, pounding rhythm of a Celtic drum. With every thrust it felt to Fiona as if Alex were marking her as his own in some deep, primordial rite buried in the hills of the ancient land that lay outside their door.

Fiona groaned at the sound of cascading harp notes flowing from her cellphone alarm.

Alex mumbled, "I told Hugh to mind the store today...so come here, love."

Fiona silenced the alarm and pulled herself upright. "Don't I wish, but no, Alex. I have to be at Paxton House for my tour in an hour."

Somehow the pair left their warm bed and drove in their separate cars to visit the Palladian mansion that Fiona agreed was one of the finest, eighteenth century homes she'd seen thus far. Designed by John Adam and replete with the most important collection of documented furniture by Chippendale on public display in Scotland, she was dazzled by the house's classically columned front façade and the interior's mahogany pieces constructed in a sturdy, plain style.

"Tommy has made Chippendale reproductions before," she said to Alex, having gotten permission to take photographs, "but just look at these gorgeous satinwood half-moon tables positioned between the windows in the drawing room! If we do any furniture other than upholstered pieces, wouldn't these be marvelous?"

Alex nodded his agreement as she quickly took several shots of the drawing room with its robin's egg blue walls, gilt-framed mirrors and family portraits, and a crystal chandelier hanging from a high ceiling with geometrical patterns molded to its surface.

"The rest of the furniture's a little austere for our style," she said in a low voice so the guard wouldn't overhear her, "but seeing the Chippendale was really worth the trip."

They were able to share a ploughman's lunch and glasses of ale in the old stable block where each table was positioned in a former horse's stall. By one o'clock, the pair decided to leave Fiona's car in the Paxton House car park and headed in Alex's Jaguar the eleven miles northeast to the village of Ayton where Alex's research had revealed Jane Maxwell had been married to Alexander, 4th Duke of Gordon, in 1767.

It was also the location, Alex reminded her, where, a month later, after returning from London where the newly-minted duchess had been presented to George III at court, Jane reportedly received the letter from Thomas Fraser announcing he had survived his near-death experience in the Black Watch regiment assigned to the American colonies and was returning home to make her his bride—but tragically, too late.

"I've never been to Ayton, myself, other than to drive through it on my way to Berwick-on-Tweed," he disclosed, slowing down as they passed a low, brick column with the plaque, "Welcome to Ayton," and nearby, a sign announcing Ayton Castle was coming up on their right hand.

As they rounded a corner, they could only see a substantial guardhouse made of red sandstone, its wooden gate, two-stories high, and shut tight. A "For Sale" sign on a metal stanchion swung in the light breeze that ruffled the tall trees towering above the walls that ringed the huge estate's vast perimeter.

"The house where Jane's sister, Catherine Maxwell Fordyce and her husband, John Fordyce, lived burned down 1834, didn't you tell me, and was never rebuilt, right?" Fiona queried. Thinking of their hostess at Traquair House she added, "The name 'Catherine' was mighty popular among the Maxwells, wasn't it?"

"That's right," Alex confirmed. "As for the Fordyce house, the accounts I read said that a huge, baronial pile called Ayton Castle by its new owners was erected in the mid-nineteen hundreds on the very same site as the old Ayton House—but look how overgrown it's all become a century-and-a-half later."

They parked on the side of the road and followed the wall stretching to their right that soon curved around, ending at a small bridge.

"Look!" Fiona said excitedly, pointing to a white enameled sign that read "Eye Water." She strode a few steps across the bridge. "A river! Or at least a branch of the River Eye that the story you told me said ran along the side of the old house."

Alex and she peered over the bridge's railing to glimpse a meandering stream running sluggishly below.

"It looks as if they haven't thinned the trees in twenty years," Alex said, "but see upstream, there? I'd say there are definitely river banks visible on the side that flanks the house—if that's where the castle is, there on the hill—as the sign indicates."

"Well, so far, one part of the story is true. The River Eye runs *near* the hill that the burned- down house supposedly was originally built upon," Fiona said, pointing to the mass of trees bursting with fall red and yellow foliage that marched up a steep incline. "So if Jane received a letter from Thomas Fraser, as all the accounts claim, and ran out of the house and threw herself down on the bank...*here's* where she did it!"

Fiona swiftly walked the rest of the way across the bridge.

"Alex," she called, "there's a church over here! The sign says 'Church of Scotland...Ayton and Burnmouth Parish' and look! There's a cemetery behind it! Maybe we can find some of the Fordyce family graves that would confirm this is actually near the spot where the old Ayton House was located before the fire destroyed it."

They strode past a simple stone church with a spire framed by another grove of tall trees whose leaves were also turning gold and brown. Passing through a waist-high iron gate into an enormous graveyard the size of two football fields, Fiona whistled softly as she absorbed the sight of hundreds of tombs and stone markers—many tilted and some even having collapsed over the centuries of Scottish winters.

The sun was sinking in the west, with long shadows thrown across the un-mowed grass choking gravestones.

Fiona looked at Alex in dismay.

"How in heaven can we locate the plots where the Fordyce family members might have been buried, given the time and how many gravestones there are?"

Alex's glance swept across the vast expanse. He pointed to a large stone enclosure and said, "Well, let's take a half an hour before it gets too dark and examine only the larger crypts and mausoleums which were built, back then, to commemorate the leading families of Ayton."

"Good idea!" Fiona said. "I'll take this half and perhaps you can search over there where the river winds along the bottom of the hill." She took a dozen steps further into the graveyard. "Whoa! Alex! Look up there! There's the *castle*!"

Towering on the hill rose at least half a dozen turrets marking the structure as one designed in the distinctive Scottish baronial style, popular in the mid-nineteenth century.

"It almost out does Abbotsford for romantic fantasy, wouldn't you say?" chuckled Alex.

"Pretty over the top," agreed Fiona.

"It's obviously the best place to build, so I'm sure the old Fordyce place was there, too, once upon a time."

Fiona nodded. "We'd better get busy."

As the light grew dimmer by the minute, Fiona sped from one falling-down enclosure to another, a feeling of desperation grabbing hold. She turned around, uncertain where to look next.

Frustrated and upset that time was running out, she suddenly felt inexplicably drawn to an ivy-covered, roofless family crypt in the middle of an endless series of headstones and walked through a rusted iron gate. Two rather austere gravestones were on her left. She bent forward and pulled a tendril of ivy that clung across the name incised into the granite. Tracing her fingers along the letters, her breath caught and tingling radiated up her arm as she discerned a series of letters that spelled F O R D Y C E. She let out a scream.

"Alex! Alex! I *found* them! John Fordyce! Jane Maxwell's brother-in-law!"

She quickly began ripping long strings of ivy from the other graves lined against the wall perpendicular to where she'd found John Fordyce's stone. "And here's Jane's sister, *Catherine Maxwell Fordyce*!" she screeched. "The death dates are early nineteenth century. This has to be them!"

By this time, Alex had found where she'd entered the enclosure.

"Amazing, woman! Let me see."

Fiona was shaking and nearly in tears as she pulled away another clump of ivy.

Alex pointed to a large stone she'd revealed incised with a series of names and dates.

"Look, Fiona...here they *all* are...or at least a record of Catherine Maxwell Fordyce's descendants. Can you see the way they named their children and grandchildren after *each other!* It was a very eighteenth century practice, by the way. Here's an 'Eglantine'—who must have been named after Jane's other sister."

"Eglantine!" Fiona exclaimed. "The sister who raced her pig against Jane's down the Royal Mile!"

"The very same name!" Alex chortled. "And here's a namesake for their mother 'Magdalene.'" He pulled another string of ivy from the bottom of the stone. "There's a namesake for one of Jane's other daughters, 'Charlotte.' And, another for her daughter, 'Georgiana...'"

"Oh my God, Alex!" Fiona said excitedly, touching the

name 'Jane Gordon' carved into the large family marker. "Here's a Fordyce child or niece born in 1814, named for Jane herself. Didn't you tell me the Duchess died in 1812? Catherine's family named this female child in her honor!"

"And look here, Fiona…" Alex pointed. "Here is the namesake child for Jane's daughter supposedly sired by Thomas Fraser of Struy. It's another 'Louisa.'"

"This is where the Fordyce family lived, on a house on that hill. They're all *here,* just as the legend says they were," Fiona said, barely above a whisper. "They *lived* here, and Catherine hosted Jane's wedding to the Fourth Duke of Gordon—maybe in *that* church," she said, pointing to the spire, "or one that was built on that spot before this one."

"And so, with the river being where we found it to be today," he said quietly, "the other part of the story may very well be true: that returning here from her court presentation and her honeymoon with the Duke, she and her groom stopped at Ayton House on their way to Gordon Castle and she found the letter from Thomas among all the post-nuptial correspondence that had arrived from Edinburgh."

Fiona nodded in awe. "She read it, ran out of Ayton House and down *that* hill, and collapsed on the riverbank. How did the account you read describe the scene?"

"That the 'pages of the Lost Lieutenant's letter were strewn like autumn leaves upon the mossy banks of the River Eye.'"

Fiona could only stare at Alex, knowing without words that they both felt a sense of their ancestors' blood coursing through their veins. Alex continued to hold her glance, and she could almost read his thoughts of Jane, his ancestress, nearly mad with grief for having lost the love of her life, a tragedy that condemned her as part of a heart-breaking love triangle that endured for thirty years. And she could almost feel the anguish her forbearer must have experienced—if Thomas Fraser of Struy was, indeed, her ancestor—when he learned later of Jane's marriage to the duke at her sister's house in Ayton.

Just at that moment, Fiona's cell phone that she'd thrust in her pocket gave a piercing trill. She was so startled, she couldn't manage to fish it out of her trousers before it stopped ringing. When she looked at the message, she groaned.

"What is it?" Alex demanded.

"Our company number in New York. It's either my boss or his assistant. And either one calling me here can't be good."

"Do you want to ring them back from the car?"

"First let me take some quick pictures of the headstones before we totally lose the light," she said glumly. "And then I'll make the call."

CHAPTER 15

"Don't you ever read your email?" Stella Langdon demanded. "I began texting you yesterday about rendezvousing with Boss Man at the Bugatti thing tomorrow."

Tomorrow?

"Mr. Sterling's coming to Scotland, after all?"

"Well, *yes*!" hissed Stella. "Why do you think I've been trying to get a hold of you for the last twelve hours, Fiona? Because you're my BFF? I don't *think* so! He wants to meet with you and hear about everything you've done so far…that is, if you've actually been working over there."

Whoa, thought Fiona, Ms. Stella Langdon was definitely a nasty piece of work. Then, she glanced at the message icon on her cell phone and was chagrined to see the number "5" glared at her in red. No wonder Bernard's assistant sounded put out, Fiona admitted to herself. But why was Bernie demanding a command performance from her when he's on a junket like a classic car rally? Stella had obviously been anxious to reach her during the previous twelve hours while she and Alex had been…

Focus, Fiona! Find out what's going on!

The last light of day was casting long shadows among the scores of gravestones as Fiona took a seat on a wooden bench surrounded by gravestones. She didn't want to join Alex in his car, parked in front of the church, until she knew more about what was happening.

"I'm so sorry, Stella," she apologized. "I was touring a stately home called Paxton House where there wasn't any Wi-Fi for visitors to use, so I didn't see your messages until just now and called you right away."

"Well, I'm glad I *finally* caught you," Stella said accusingly. "Bernie wants you to meet him at the International Bugatti

Meeting by eleven in the morning! He just texted me that he's touched down at Heathrow and is taking a connecting flight to Scotland. He'll sleep at some airport hotel tonight and then I've arranged for a driver to get him to the rally in this weird place called The Hotel Hydro in…" Stella was obviously consulting her notes. "In Peebles—wherever the heck *that* is—by mid-day, tomorrow. I hope to hell you can get there in time or he'll be plenty mad at both of us!"

"No worries, Stella. As a matter of fact, the place I'll be staying tonight is less than an hour away."

Stella's voice reflected her relief.

"Well, thank God for that. Bernie's mechanic called two days ago to say his Bugatti made the finals, so Boss Man decided to come over for the judging."

"That's impressive," Fiona said, but Stella ignored her.

"Just be sure you get there *early*, tomorrow, and bring all your notes. Bernie said he wanted you to give him a full report about everything you've been doing since you got to Scotland. He wants specifics of what items you think should be in the collection, along with unit costs for all the stuff you liked that you saw on your trip. You know," she said with barely-veiled sarcasm, "all that junk I told you about already in my *first* email."

"I'm already prepared with all that," she replied sharply, "but can't this wait till we both get home and I can do a full-on Power Point presentation and give him samples, swatches, and photographs?"

"Apparently, some textile manufacturers are coming to this millionaires' shindig and he wants you to meet with them to talk about the Scottish project."

"Really?" she said, a small *frisson* of alarm shooting down her spine. "Do you know who these people are?"

With the phone still pressed to her ear, she stood up from the cold bench and began to walk out of the graveyard, past the church, and through the iron gate, to stand ten feet from the hood of Alex's car. Dusk had descended in earnest and she held up her forefinger to signal to him that she'd only be another minute or two.

"The guys he wants you to meet are at the Bugatti thing," repeated Stella impatiently. "I couldn't pronounce their names even if I knew them, Fiona. Just some big honchos he's worked with before in the Far East, he said. Major vintage car collectors, too, as it turns out. I imagine he's going to trot you out to demonstrate what a big mover and shaker *he* is."

Fiona detected a distinct tone of bitterness in Stella's remarks. Could Bernard have ended whatever relationship they had going and demoted his administrative assistant to a mere worker bee, like the rest of his employees? In the end, he always went back to his wife.

To Stella she said, "I'm surprised that what I've been doing in Scotland is even on Bernard's radar."

"*Au contraire,*" Stella said with a nasty edge. "He's hot to have these industrialists meet his fancy designer he sent to Scotland to do research for a new home furnishings line, and all that. And by the way," she added, "just so you know…he's been an absolute asshole, lately, so watch out."

Stella and their boss had *definitely* had a falling out, Fiona surmised. She turned her back to the car so Alex couldn't watch her ask Stella, "So…these folks he wants me to meet are textile *manufacturers?*"

And just the kind of people in the Far East who could make everything on the cheap!

"Yeah, yeah, I guess so," Stella replied. Fiona could hear her speaking to someone nearby. "Look," she said abruptly to Fiona, "I gotta go."

Fiona turned around and glanced through the car window at Alex waiting patiently behind the wheel of his vehicle. A leaden feeling had invaded her limbs and she could barely breathe. Stella had said Bernard was anxious for her to meet manufacturers whom she *thought* were "big honchos from the Far East," but did she have that right, Fiona wondered? She tried to smile in Alex's direction but her mind was awhirl with a number of horrifying possibilities. She forced herself to think logically.

Just go to the Hotel Hydro and see what Bernie has in mind.

"Well, thanks, Stella, for the heads up and I'm sorry you had to track me down like this."

Fiona wondered if maybe she was reading too much into all this. Bernard couldn't have already made a deal with the group that made the junk sold in the outlet stores, could he?

Get the facts first before you go off like a rocket and—

She inhaled a deep breath and summoned a cheery tone as she rang off. "Stella, take good care, y'hear? I owe you a nice, cashmere sweater. You're a petite-medium, right?"

"Oooh, goody…yes, that's my size!" cried Sterling's assistant, her disagreeable tone instantly transformed into sweetness and light. Fiona could see that a gift of luxury goods was one way to keep Stella Langdon from complaining too much about her to her boss—although maybe they weren't sharing intimacies anymore, which would be a relief.

"Great, Stella" she replied, "I'll bring you a nice surprise."

"Can you get me something in either cranberry or beige-heather?"

"Will do, sweetie," Fiona cooed. "I'd better go, though. This phone call is costing our boss a fortune. And thanks again for all you've done to prepare me for the meet-up in Peebles. Take care, y'hear? Bye, now."

Fiona briefly closed her eyes and willed her pulse to slow down. Then she approached the passenger side of the car and gazed through the window at Alex who had a concerned, questioning expression. She opened the door and got in.

"Everything all right?" he asked.

"Well, the best laid plans…"

"Who called you just now? Sterling, himself?"

"No, just his assistant," she replied, trying to sound casual.

Fiona then related only the part of the conversation about her being bidden to the Hotel Hydro to rendezvous with her boss the following day during the final competition of the International Bugatti Meeting. She decided to keep her suspicions to herself until she knew for sure something truly sinister was going on.

"He wants to talk to me about the trip," she said, "so, I guess I'd better keep the Fiat another day or two."

Alex's disappointment plainly showed. "We could return it to Berwick on the way back to Selkirk, right now," he proposed, "and still drive back to The Firs together tonight. You could always borrow *my* car to drive over to Peebles tomorrow."

"No, I'd better not. Boss Man would think I'd rented this gorgeous Jaguar on my expense account," she said, trying to sound lighthearted—which was nothing close to what she was feeling. She forced a smile to her lips and said, "Look, if it's all right with you, Alex, let's go back to the Paxton House car park, pick up my rental car, and I'll follow you back to The Firs tonight.

Meanwhile, Fiona's mind was racing. What if Bernard went against his word that he wanted to source the collection with only the highest quality goods from Scotland and the United States? What if he was perfectly happy to put on the label "Designed in Scotland" and then take her ideas—which, technically, she'd *conceived* while in this country and in his employ—and give them to others to manufacture cut-rate versions, out-sourcing *everything*?

Alex, her brother Tommy, and everyone else whose brains she'd picked doing this project had given of their expertise in good faith, and with the implicit promise that if they freely shared their knowledge, Bernard Sterling would become their customer. And the awful reality was, *both* Maxwell Mills and Fraser Furniture—run by people she loved—needed big orders for their products in the worse way to keep the lights on in their respective factories.

What if Bernie decided to betray them? Betray *her?*

She *had* to find out what he was up to before she blew her cool or revealed her suspicions to anyone, even Alex. She settled into the passenger seat and fastened her seatbelt as Alex put his car in gear.

Fiona said apologetically, "What an absolute pain this is. I'll have to head on to Peebles in the Fiat tomorrow morning in time to get there before eleven."

"Well at least his arrival doesn't deprive us of a night together," he said, bending across the passenger seat to kiss her on the nose. Fiona sensed he felt the same melancholy that had invaded her own thoughts. "You'll only be here for a few more days, love, and we can't miss out on even a one."

Resolutely, he backed into the road, and headed toward Paxton House once again.

Fiona heaved a sigh.

"I've already organized a lot of my notes, but I'm afraid a good amount of my time tonight is going to consist of integrating what I've seen on this leg of my trip so I can make a cogent report about the kinds of products I think our new collection should include." Alex lightly rested his left hand on her thigh. She put her own hand on top of his and gave what she hoped felt like a reassuring squeeze. "I hope you don't mind? And I want you to know that the only thing I long to do is to forget about Bernard Sterling and just enjoy every second together before I have to go back to New York."

"I understand," he said with a nod, keeping his eyes on the road. "But in the end, it's all for a good cause if Sterling likes what he hears." Then he added with a grin, "And how can he *not*? You've seen the best that Scotland has to offer. Surely that's enough to convince him?"

Fiona could only pray that Alex was right, and that Bernard Sterling wasn't the Bronx-born, corner-cutting, wheeler-dealer of legend.

The next morning, Alex's directions to Peebles and specifically to the Hotel Hydro on its outskirts easily brought her to her destination before her deadline of eleven o'clock. She made a left turn past two stone stanchions that announced she'd reached her journey's end and wheeled her little white Fiat up a stately drive past car after stunning car that was manufactured long before even her grandfather Maxwell Fraser was born.

When she finally reached the summit, a line-up of vintage Bugattis in absolute pristine condition were parked side-by-side, showroom style, opposite a large, white building that sprawled the length of the hilltop and harked back to the days of a late nineteenth century country house hotel and spa resort built for the wealthy and infirm. Fiona could easily imagine ailing guests wrapped in blankets and seated in white rocking chairs on the enclosed porches, though, this day, she spotted clusters of well-dressed visitors having morning tea and pre-lunch cocktails while peering through the enormous screened windows that overlooked the beehive of activity among the car enthusiasts arriving in successive waves below.

Another long row of vehicles, their front grills and metal work polished to a satin sheen that made them appear almost factory-new, were already neatly lined up in front of the hotel entrance and down the hill to the right of the massive resort, allowing admiring crowds to inspect the rounded, barrel frontends and large wheel bases of some one hundred priceless Bugattis. Fiona could easily envision Twenties flappers driving these museum pieces wearing goggles and duster coats, their scarves flying in the wind.

Miraculously, she found a parking spot behind the hotel where she could just squeeze into a space with her pint-sized Fiat. She walked around the perimeter of the sprawling white edifice and under a columned *porte cochére* that gave way to a grand, red-carpeted staircase leading to the impressive hotel entrance on the floor above. Fiona had read online the previous evening that the resort once welcomed well-heeled clientele to imbibe of the medicinal waters boasting cures for everything from life-threatening illnesses to lumbago.

She was about to mount the stairs to the hotel when she noticed a television crew consisting of a camera operator, sound man, and very tasty-looking female interviewer grouped around a perfectly restored example of one of the most famous brands of luxury cars of the last century.

There, in their midst, was the balding Bernard Sterling, dressed in an impeccable Harris tweed suit, hand-tailored shirt, and old-school striped silk tie, holding forth like the Great Gatsby on the wonders of the driving machine that he and his "team" had spent untold millions putting into flawless condition.

Standing off to one side was a cluster of Asian gentlemen

nodding to each other in a show of admiration for the American, whose shining, open-air, blue and brass vehicle was among the finalists at this year's International Bugatti Meeting. The previous night, Fiona had quickly run a second search on the web, learning that membership at this gathering was a very exclusive club consisting mostly of men who could afford to fly their classic cars all over the world in pursuit of large silver trophies that testified to their aged vehicle's perfection. When Ralph Lauren had paid a reported forty million for his Bugatti, Bernie had gnashed his teeth for a month.

Just then, her employer looked past the shoulder of the attractive blond holding a microphone and caught sight of Fiona. The interview had apparently just ended, so he waved and announced loudly, "Take as much time as you want for your B roll, Angela, but I must say hello to my fabulous designer, Fiona Fraser, who's just arrived after spending ten days in Scotland on a secret mission for me, right Fiona?"

Embarrassed to be singled out as the television crew whirled in her direction, she was dismayed when she saw the camera's red light go on again, signaling they were recording her presence among the group that had been hanging on Sterling's every word. Camera rolling, Fiona couldn't ignore Bernard's proffered hand and shook it for the benefit of the assembled media, as well as on-lookers.

Trust Bernie to get the cameras pointed his way within minutes of his arrival...

Bernard swiftly turned to the gaggle of Asians who were pressing even closer, eager to meet someone whose activities in Scotland he had obviously trumpeted before her arrival.

"Meet Ms. Fraser, gentlemen," he said, all charm and graciousness. "She's one of the best home furnishings designers working in our business and I'm excited for her to tell you all about her latest project for us. Shall we go into lunch?"

As they walked up the red-carpeted staircase and into the hotel, the camera crew followed along behind, recording the "B Roll" footage the reporter would intercut between the voiced sections of her interview. When their group was about to be seated in the restaurant, the maître d' put out a tuxedo-clad arm and prevented the crew from "disrupting the other diners" and sent them on their way. Bernie halted and swiftly invited the good-looking reporter to join the group he was treating to lunch. Her TV crew headed into the bar, apparently accustomed to being denied entry to places like the upscale hotel's formal dining room.

Angela McCauley from BBC Scotland, based in Edinburgh, took a seat next to Fiona and rested a narrow reporter's notebook in her lap, pen in hand.

"So," she said, "Mr. Sterling tells me you've been all over Scotland researching a new line of home furnishings for his firm."

So much for my 'secret mission'…

Fiona nodded, but said merely, "Yes, it was a great assignment."

"Tell everybody about some of the things you've found," Sterling enthused, and then turned to the waiter to order a bottle of Veuve Clicquot champagne for the table, which set off excited chattering among the Chinese guests. "Fiona sent me some fabulous images of some very classy stuff she'd seen over here."

Fiona spoke in the most general terms about the high quality of the products she'd encountered, not wanting to reveal her "finds" to her audience, and especially not to an inquisitive reporter or the other guests at her boss's table.

"Mr. Sterling," asked Angela, taking a sip of her champagne, her pen poised above the notebook resting on her lap, out of Bernard's line of sight, "does this mean you will be buying large quantities of *Scottish* goods for you new line?"

Fiona regarded her employer closely. He darted a quick glance at the chattering Chinese who had either not heard or perhaps not understood Angela's lilting Scottish accent when she asked such a pointed question.

"Oh, we're just in the very preliminary stages of our exploration," he said, gesturing toward Fiona. "Once we hear the details from my designer, here, we'll know whether it's a go-or-no-go with this project, right, Fiona?" He smiled beatifically. "I put my absolute trust in my very talented people. What they *say* is what we *do*."

Fiona stared fixedly at her champagne flute, praying that color wasn't invading her cheeks.

What a total crock...

She heard Angela say, "Well, then...what about it, Ms. Fraser? Based on what you've seen on your trip, do you give the manufacturers in Scotland the thumbs up, as you say in the States?"

Fiona was about to reply most emphatically she did when Sterling interceded. "Now, Angela, you wouldn't want to pry confidential information out of Ms. Fraser, would you, before she's even had a chance to debrief her boss? After all, this lunch is strictly off the record, agreed?"

Angela paused and gave her host a mildly hostile stare. "From this moment on, yes, sir...it's off the record, if you insist." She glanced at her watch, closed her notebook, and then stood up. "I'm afraid I must go collect my crew and get back to Edinburgh to meet the deadline for today's newscast." She looked briefly at the group of Asians sitting across the table and then at Fiona. "I'll be interested to learn, eventually, what your recommendations are to your boss, Ms. Fraser. I understand that one of his guests from Singapore is a well-known manufacturer of knock-offs," she added pointedly, nodding in the direction of the Asians sitting across the table. "We in Scotland, however, are quite proud of the goods that are made *here*, and I expect the firms you've visited hope you and your employer feel the same."

Fiona jumped to her feet, ignoring Sterling's frown.

"With a last name like Fraser," she said, affecting her friendliest smile, "you can imagine how impressed I was with the exquisite quality of woolen products I saw manufactured at mills like Johnston's and Maxwell's."

Angela nodded with renewed interest. "Well, of course...you're a Scottish-American, aren't you? Is this your first visit to the land of your ancestors?" The reporter was smiling, now, and expressing a much friendlier attitude toward her.

"Yes, and I've loved every minute." Fiona leaned forward

and lowered her voice. "And of course, it will be up to Mr. Sterling and his finance team to decide where we go from here."

Angela gave a quick nod and replied under her breath, "That's what I figured."

"Angela!" said Sterling sharply, noting only that there had been a brief exchange with Fiona. "Remember, now, everything said at this table was off the record. I haven't even had a chance to sit down and hear about Fiona's trip over here. You'll be my staff's first call when—or if—there's an announcement to be made."

"Oh, absolutely, Mr. Sterling. And as for our interview today…I've got everything I need on tape," she said sweetly, and Fiona's heart sank. Angela waved at the array of men seated around the table. "Well, off I go." To Sterling she said, "Thanks for the interview and the champagne. If I make it back to Edinburgh in time, the piece should run on the news tonight. Good luck with the final competition. Your Bugatti is brilliant, Mr. Sterling. Almost as nice as Ralph Lauren's. Since he's not here this year, I'm guessing yours might actually win the grand prize, for once. If you do, I'll be back."

All the men at the table laughed at that, with Sterling laughing the loudest, but Fiona could see he was incensed by the reporter's obvious dig.

Angela McCauley then made a beeline for the exit as Fiona nearly collapsed into her chair, her stomach in knots, and worried what the next few hours would bring.

Alex walked through the front door at The Firs, hearing Mrs. Nolan's excited calls from the kitchen.

"That you, Mr. M? Come in here, quick! Look who's on the telly! It's that lovely Miss Fraser…look…*look*! She's at that fancy car show at the Peebles Hydro. She's quite fetching in her Fraser tartan scarf, isn't she, now?"

Alex strode quickly into his housekeeper's domain and stared at the television screen. Sure enough, someone was interviewing a lanky gentleman with a comb-over that didn't quite cover his baldness and whose suit, made of heather blue and navy herringbone tweed, looked more Scottish than any Scot might wear. Off to one side stood a stunning figure with hair the color of Port wine and whose slender form and lovely face made his breath catch at the mere sight of her.

To Mrs. Nolan he explained, "Her employer, Bernard Sterling, is over here from America with his prized Bugatti motorcar. Apparently, he's in the running for the main award this year."

She laughed, pointing to the screen. "Dressed quite fancy, isn't he?"

"A wee bit over the top, wouldn't you say, Mrs. N?" Alex said blandly.

"Aye, you could say so, but Miss Fraser, now…she looks absolutely beautiful on telly, wouldn't you say?"

Alex's gaze was glued not only on Fiona, but the cluster of Asians standing in a semi-circle around the car. The TV image then cut back to the reporter, Angela McCauley, standing, now, at the foot of the hotel's grand staircase, holding a microphone, winding up her report.

"I also learned today that Mr. Sterling—whose clothing and home furnishing lines are often compared to the better known American designer, Ralph Lauren—has had his Scottish-American designer, Fiona Fraser, combing Scotland for ideas for a new collection," she announced to her viewing audience. "Given the rapt attention of fellow Bugatti collector, Andrew Wu—along with several other Chinese manufacturers that I observed paying Sterling court today at the International Bugatti Meeting—one can't help but wonder if Sterling will be just one more example of appropriating Scotland's traditional styles and products…and then outsourcing them to the Far East where the goods can be produced at far less cost, given the low wages paid workers in sweatshops there."

Next came a close-up shot of the comely electronic journalist.

"We can only hope that Bernard Sterling's visit to Scotland won't eventually result in putting our home industries in even further jeopardy. This is Angela McCauley, reporting."

Mrs. Nolan pulled her alarmed gaze away from the small television set sitting on a shelf near the Aga and shook her head.

"You dinna think that nice Miss Fraser was a *spy* for that Sterling person, do you Mr. M?" she asked, sounding upset at such a notion. "Here to see how you do your cloth-making and such, and then tellin' her employer how to take yer ideas and make them for naught in China?"

His mouth set in a thin line, Alex walked over to the TV and switched it off. "Well, when Ms. Fraser returns to Selkirk tonight, we'll just have to ask her, won't we, Mrs. Nolan?"

CHAPTER 16

Bernard led Fiona into the bar and began peppering her with questions even before they sat down at a corner table. In response, she swiftly pulled out her notebook and began to relate her first impressions that the younger Scottish designers had a tendency to embrace a "chrome and a high tech look, but by the end of my trip, I saw a lot of styles that I think would really appeal to our up-market clientele."

"Well, why don't you organize it into a Power Point on your iPad and we can show my friend Andrew Wu and his colleagues after dinner in my suite?"

Alarmed, Fiona responded quickly that she simply hadn't time to crunch the numbers. "All they'd be seeing is a bunch of pictures, not an overall presentation with samples and sketches, along with cost breakdown—which is the only way this project will have impact." She held Bernard's glance and could instantly discern that he was none too pleased with her answer. "Honestly, Bernie, allow me to gather everything together properly—samples, swatches, mood boards, and so on—and give you a full, professional presentation back in New York. I can get it all together in a day or so, once we're home."

Just at that moment, Mr. Wu himself approached their cocktail table. He smiled at Fiona and made a slight bow.

"Forgive me if I am interrupting," he said in perfect English, "but I couldn't help but overhear you just now. I do not want to tax Ms. Fraser, here, about having to work through all the figures and costs per unit of the items she is suggesting for your collection." He laughed softly. "Just be assured that *whatever* number she comes up with, Bernard, *we* will beat it by a long distance."

"Well, here's an even better idea," Sterling said, and Fiona could tell by his tone of voice that he would brook no refusal from her. "What if we invite Fiona, here, to fly back to the States with us on your private jet tomorrow morning, out of Edinburgh Airport, and at least offer us a *preview* of what's she's learned?" he suggested to Mr. Wu.

"Excellent suggestion, Bernie."

To Fiona Sterling said, "That will give you tonight and a good five hours on the plane to organize what you've collected and show the two of us the work you've done on this little Scottish junket before we touch down in Jersey. We take off at noon, right, Andrew?"

Bernie wanted her to leave Scotland eighteen hours from now?

Fiona searched for any excuse she could think of not to go on the private jet, but plans were moving fast.

"Excellent…excellent!" Andrew Wu enthused. "Hopefully, we will be able to toast you, Bernard, at the awards banquet tonight, get a decent night's sleep, and leave here for the airport at nine, if that is satisfactory?" He turned to Fiona. "We'll have room in my car for you too, of course, Ms. Fraser. Are you staying at this hotel, or can my driver fetch you from someplace?"

"Ah…n-no thanks," Fiona said hastily, her heart in her throat. "I have a rental car that I'll have to return, so I'll meet you at Edinburgh airport at…what…ten tomorrow morning for a twelve o'clock departure?"

"Eleven would suffice," agreed Mr. Wu. "The private jet terminal is sign-posted, I believe."

He bowed again and rejoined his coterie that had gathered in a corner of the well-appointed bar. Fiona managed to nod pleasantly, but as soon as he was out of earshot, she turned to her employer.

"Bernie…something's greatly confusing me, here. When you originally green-lighted my going to Scotland, you *specifically* emphasized that you wanted the products in this new line to be of the best quality and truly authentic by having them made either in the States at a factory like Fraser Furniture, or here in Scotland. That 'this was the moment,' I think you said, 'when our upscale clients want the real deal'—and not—*quoting* you, now, at our final meeting in New York before I left for Scotland—'not some cheap Chinese imitation.'"

"Quiet, Fiona!" Bernard said sharply, glancing over his shoulder at the Chinese delegation that was sharing another bottle of champagne. He turned his gaze on her, frowning. "Look! I'll be straight with you, okay? My financial guys are all over me on this deal, advising me not go overboard on all the patriotic stuff, you know what I'm saying? The economy is improving but we still have to take advantage of every angle."

Fiona looked away and stared, instead, at the water glass she'd wrapped her fingers around. After a pause, she raised her eyes to meet his glance.

"So am I understanding that you've already decided to make most of the products in your Scottish Home Collection in the Far East? With Andrew Wu's firm, perhaps?"

"Don't put words in my mouth!" Sterling snapped, sounding petulant. "I'm just saying it all depends on the numbers you come up with, and I'm telling you, Fiona, you'd better come up with them pretty damn soon!"

"Bernard," Fiona replied quietly, "I took you at your word when I contacted all the textile mills I visited to show me their wares and explain their processes of manufacture. I told them, on *your* say-so, that we were committed to producing quality, authentic goods from their countries of origin. In other words, goods for our new Scottish Home Collection that are made in Scotland and respected firms in the States. *Now* you're saying you're seriously considering going with Andrew Wu's firm?"

"I'm *not* saying that!" he replied defensively. "I'm saying that I just need the numbers!"

"You'll get them, of course," she said, keeping her tone even. "But you need to know that everyone I've dealt with— including my own twin brother—has been amazingly open and forthcoming and *generous* with their time and the sharing of their talents and designs because of what I told them you planned to do. If you outsource a Scottish Home Collection with your firm's name on it to a manufacturer that makes cheap imitations, then all the people I've been dealing with will consider themselves...*ripped-off*, is the technical term, I think," she said, keeping her temper barely under control and adding, "And they *will* have been, if the Bernard Sterling company ultimately does what I think you're suggesting here."

"Hey, look," Sterling said, jabbing his well-manicured forefinger into his own silk tie, "like I said when I first thought of this project, I am totally, one hundred percent *personally* committed to sourcing our new stuff through firms like your family's and the places you've found here in Scotland! I just need you to go through the process of telling me the unit costs you've found over here so I can persuade the money boys, *get it?*"

Fiona made a show of jotting down a note.

"I do get it," she replied carefully, "and I'm very glad to hear you haven't already made up your mind before you have a chance to take a look at all the wonderful items I've found on this trip," she said, forcing a smile. She paused, and then added in an even tone, "But be aware: if we don't follow up with orders to some of these folks who have helped me frame what we're trying to do with this collection, *I, personally,* will be labeled as the 'user'—and that would make me extremely unhappy."

Bernard appeared surprised that a minion of his would dare to speak so bluntly to the boss. Her employer's eyes narrowed.

"Well, I guess it's gonna be up to *you* to come up with the numbers that will make sense to my CFO." He heaved a sigh as if he were carrying the world on his shoulders. "How this all turns out is in *your* hands, Fiona."

"Really?"

BS certainly doesn't merely stand for "Bernard Sterling!"

Fiona rose from her seat.

"Well, then, I'd better get to work. As I mentioned, I've got a rental car, so I'll go back to where I'm staying, hunker down to work the numbers, and meet you tomorrow at Edinburgh Airport."

"Aren't you going to stick around and see if my Bugatti places first in the competition tonight?" he asked, sounding as disappointed as a little boy whose mother didn't watch him plunge off the high diving board.

"Oh, I think the odds are in your favor for this particular show," she replied tersely. She reached for her tote bag resting on the floor near her chair, and without allowing any further discussion, she swiftly bid farewell and descended the red-carpeted stairs to the ground level. All the while, she turned over in her mind in precisely *how* many ways Bernard Sterling might possibly double-cross her.

She was leaving Scotland tomorrow!

Fiona could barely keep her mind on her driving from Peebles back to Selkirk and twice realized with a jerk to the steering wheel that she had automatically drifted into the wrong lane. Her thoughts revolved around trying to find a way she could save the project from being handed over to Mr. Wu and his cronies, if that ultimately turned out to be Bernard's plan.

And how much of what had happened today should she tell Alex? To whom did she owe her loyalty, she fretted—the boss who had hired her and paid for her trip, or the man she'd grown to love beyond all reason who had opened every door in Scotland, making the entire enterprise she'd embarked upon *possible*?

She concentrated on the road signs, and breathed a sigh of relief when she confirmed she was on the A72, heading in the correct direction. Meanwhile, she went over every single aspect of her brief time at the hotel. Yes, on the one hand, Bernard Sterling was her employer and paid her salary. Even so, the idea of turning over to Mr. Wu or any other Far East manufacturer everything she'd learned, thanks to all the honest, talented Scots she'd met along the way, made her feel literally ill.

She reflected upon the extraordinary hospitality provided by Catherine Maxwell Stuart, at Traquair House as well as the amazing insights in the textile business that Leah Robertson had provided her at Lochcarron mills—to say nothing of having been given a private tour of Sir Walter Scott's exquisite home by its busy, Executive Director, Jason Dyer, who had strongly indicated that the Sterling firm might gain permission to merchandise some of the wonderful objects on display there—*if* they were high-quality reproductions.

And then there was Alex, himself. Even if she took *away* the fact she was undeniably in love with this generous, forthright man, what remained was someone who had freely given of his contacts in the textile field, opened every door, and escorted her each step of the way on her incredible journey of discovery about what made Scotland truly wonderful.

And then there's our connection to Jane and Thomas…

Fiona felt tears cloud her vision and she had to pull off the road until she could calm an unexpected wave of grief that had suddenly welled in her chest. Were she and Alex destined to be star-crossed lovers like their forbears? She was American and lived across an ocean, which presented problems enough without the kind of dilemma with Bernard Sterling that could easily erupt into issues that would blow Alex and her relationship to smithereens.

Then she remembered Alex saying that no matter what problems confronted them to always remember those sacred moments they'd shared at Dryburgh Abbey and that they would "sort out *together* where we go from here." She took deep, even breaths, trying to calm the sudden stab of fear that had her in its grip.

There was no doubt that Alex felt the same, compelling, uncanny closeness that she knew had developed between them so quickly. If she didn't tell him tonight that she now suspected Bernard Sterling was going to have the new collection manufactured somewhere other than Scotland, Alex might simply think she'd picked his brain and even gone to bed with him, just to get an inside track on ideas and trends. But if she laid out to him what she thought was about to happen and suddenly all his contacts refused to cooperate or—worse yet—sued for unfair competition or something, her employer would accurately judge her as appallingly disloyal to the firm where she'd worked for these last five years. Bernie would also fire her ass, and where would she be? Unable to help Fraser Furniture *or* Maxwell Mills become viable businesses in a global economy.

But what if she didn't speak now and her suspicious later turned out to be right on the money?

How could Alex and her love survive the failure of Maxwell Mills due to *her* being part of a decision that declined to place orders that she had certainly implied from the outset would be forthcoming?

But I acted in good faith because I thought Sterling meant what he initially said…

And how naïve was that, she wondered?

Despite any explanations she might offer Alex, how could he not think she had taken terrible advantage of his good will? For years, she had fought against a debilitating feeling that she had, in the end, been a "user" to have taken the money for schooling that the Reynolds family had given her if she would agree to annul her marriage to Chip. Even at the tender age of eighteen, she knew it had been wrong to give into her mother's pressure to marry a man she didn't love, but she'd done it. And then she'd used what was essentially a bribe from the Reynolds's to escape Atlanta—and all to her own benefit.

Cars whizzed by as the Fiat remained parked by the side of the road. A knot of well-remembered misery and recrimination closed Fiona's throat and her head sank against the car's steering wheel. She'd confided to Alex the deal she'd made with Mr. and Mrs. Reynolds to end her marriage, thereby bequeathing to Chip's parents control over his life—and ultimately his death.

Wasn't she bequeathing to Alex the end of his family's firm if Bernard chose the Chinese to make the goods more cheaply? What would Alex think of her *then?*

But what if Sterling were just *testing* her, she thought suddenly. What if he merely wanted her to come up with the best possible numbers and had every intention of using them to persuade his financial advisors it would be fiscally feasible to produce the Scottish Home Collection in the manner they'd originally planned? Didn't she owe Bernie the opportunity to make his case to the finance guys, as he said he would?

But can you trust anything *this man says?* echoed a voice in her head.

One thing was certain, she decided, slapping her steering wheel with the palm of her hand. She *had* to be on that plane tomorrow in order to confirm—either way—what was going on. If she were armed with every scrap of information she'd gathered, she could try to convince Bernie, even in the presence of one of China's major textile manufacturers, that her boss *must* choose to stay true to their original concept of authenticity for his home furnishing line. And if she couldn't succeed in doing that…?

Would I really have the guts to quit and keep my Scottish discoveries under wraps?

She must not give away her gold, she lectured herself, and she must make the hard call about all this before Andrew Wu's private jet landed on American soil.

And then another voice in her head whispered.

You knew from the outset that succumbing to the charms of a business colleague was risky business, but you went ahead anyway, didn't you Fiona, and this is the result!

Another wave of guilt washed over her. Her head had told her from the beginning that she should resist *acting* on her feelings for Alex while working on the Scottish project, but her heart said his presence in her life was the best thing that had ever happened to her. She remained with her eyes closed, her forehead on the steering wheel.

Finally she raised her head and stared out the windshield.

Once I know what Bernard truly intends, then I'll know what to do next…

She put the car in gear and cautiously entered the left lane of traffic. Ten minutes later, the Fiat rolled to a stop on the gravel driveway in front of The Firs. Fiona remained in her car for several minutes, her mind continuing to weigh all the facts as she knew them.

She looked up to see Alex, standing motionless on the threshold of his home, the warm, welcoming lights glowing in the foyer outlining his six-foot frame in bold silhouette. His expression was grim.

"Mrs. Nolan saved us some supper," Alex said as she approached the front step. "I granted her a night off, so she's gone to visit her family for the weekend. Do you mind eating in the kitchen?"

"No, of course not. But I'm totally bushed. Is it all right with you if I have a bath first?"

"That's fine. Just come down when you're ready."

Alex was being perfectly polite, but Fiona noticed instantly how subdued he seemed and wondered at the reasons for his obvious change in demeanor. She turned on the first step of the staircase to ask him what was wrong, but he had already walked into the sitting room and closed the door.

Forty minutes later, Alex lifted a pot of veal stew off the top of Aga cooker where it had been left to keep warm. Its hearty aroma was the product of carrots, potatoes, leeks, and herbs grown in Mrs. Nolan's kitchen garden at the back of the house. He placed the heavy iron Dutch oven on a trivet next to a green salad that his housekeeper had also left for them on a hand-hewn table set for two that sat under a small window overlooking a side yard where the lawn soon disappeared into a grove of towering firs.

He had asked Mrs. N if she didn't mind leaving early as he wanted an empty house during the difficult conversation he anticipated having with Fiona. He hadn't been able to think about anything all evening other than the sight of Fiona standing next to those Chinese industrialists.

"So," he said, dishing out the stew into a bowl from a set of Pink Tower Spode china his grandmother had purchased half a century ago. "How did things go with Mr. Sterling in Peebles? Did you have time to discuss anything?"

He noticed that Fiona kept her eyes on her food, her fork poised over her meal.

"When I arrived," she replied, skewering a piece of meat, "he was doing a television interview, and then we went in to lunch with a group of fellow Bugatti owners." She finally raised her eyes to meet his. "You should have *seen* some of those cars, Alex...they were beautiful. Flown in from all over the world. It was amazing." She smiled at him, and Alex was very aware that she had clearly steered their conversation in another direction. "And what were you up to, today?" she asked brightly.

Alex related that he'd spent the day at his desk, even though it was a Saturday, but his thoughts continued to revolve around Angela McCauley's televised story that had broadcast a few hours previously. He waited for Fiona to say something, *anything* about the threat to the project he'd counted on to save Maxwell Mills from bankruptcy.

By the time they'd finished dinner and he was pouring coffee from the pot also kept warm on the top of the Aga, Alex couldn't stand waiting for Fiona to tell him the truth: that her employer was keeping company with one of the most influential, successful, ruthless textile manufacturers in all of the Far East.

"So, tell me," he said, finally, "what did you think of Andrew Wu?"

Fiona's shocked expression revealed that his knowledge that the Chinese industrialist had been in Peebles had taken her completely by surprise.

In a clipped tone of voice he couldn't seem to control he said, "I saw Angela McCauley's report earlier on the BBC, Fiona. Wu is notorious among textile manufacturers and I recognized him immediately." He sought her glance. "I must say, seeing you with that group gave me quite a jolt."

"Alex, I—"

Not allowing her to finish her sentence, he interrupted, "And I thought you might have mentioned, by now, that Bernard Sterling's probably conferring with a Chinese firm that could easily supply tartan for his reputedly *Scottish* Home Collection." Unable to keep the sarcasm out of his voice, he added, "Or did the events in Peebles today simply slip your mind?"

How could she have not told him, first thing, that there was trouble ahead—unless she was a part of that trouble...from the beginning?

He observed with some fascination how color was rising

from her neck to her cheeks. Her coffee cup, half way to her lips, landed with a clatter in the saucer on the table, some of its contents spilling over its rim.

"I didn't know *how* to tell you," she said, her amber eyes full of regret. "And I still don't even know how seriously Bernie is considering doing a deal with Andrew Wu."

"Is that so?"

The flush on Fiona's features deepened and she looked at him, eyes flashing.

"Yes, that is so! I was totally blindsided by Andrew Wu turning up at the Bugatti gathering."

"But your employer asked you to meet him there. Are you saying that you had *no* idea that people in the textile industry would be there, too? After all, you spoke with your New York office just *yesterday*," he said, reminding her of the call she took on her mobile phone when they were about to leave the Ayton church graveyard.

Fiona averted his glance for a second time, and stared fixedly at her coffee cup.

So, she *had* had some idea that the Chinese would be in Peebles, he concluded, a feeling of betrayal and having been an utter fool stabbing him in the chest. She had duplicitously gone to Peebles without telling him first there would be a meeting with men like Andrew Wu about Sterling's new project. Without telling him that sourcing a new Bernard Sterling line on the cheap might have been Sterling's plan from the outset.

And what if it had been *her* plan as well? What if everything he thought she'd felt for him and said to him was just a means to accomplish her "research" and go on her merry way?

"Alex," Fiona said, reaching across the table to touch his hand. "I had no idea until Bernie's assistant, Stella, called me that my boss was actually coming to Scotland and wanted me to meet him in Peebles to introduce me to people whose names I wasn't told until I got there."

"What 'people' did you suppose she meant?" demanded Alex. "And why didn't you tell me what you *did* know? Didn't you have suspicions when Sterling was over here on a lark but insisted on seeing you? Why didn't you mention your...your gut feelings after your conversation with his assistant—which I could see visibly upset you yesterday?" Alex pulled his hand away from hers while fighting a growing conviction that she'd committed some form of treachery.

"I didn't say anything before I left for Peebles because I didn't know all the facts!" Fiona retorted. "And because I am feeling pulled in two directions...between you, and my employer!" She tried to hold his glance. "Remember how I told you that I'd have to keep personal and professional issues separate? Well, I was trying to do that until I knew what was actually going on."

"Oh, really...those were the reasons you kept silent?"

"Yes, those were the reasons. And I must say, your present attitude of suspicion implying I've betrayed you isn't helping me feel it's very safe to level with you. You *can't* think I'm part of this?"

"What do you mean by 'this?'" he snapped, and realized how harsh he must sound.

Fiona stared at her hands in her lap. Frustrated by her silence, Alex pushed his chair back and walked over to the kitchen window, gazing out at the last vestiges of light filtering down on the rows of vegetables in the kitchen garden outside the back door.

Fiona also stood up and walked over to stand behind him.

"This is totally my fault," she said in a low voice. "I knew that I should have kept everything separate until my work for my company was complete, regardless of how drawn to you I was. It's just that you were so...so wonderful...so wonderful *to* me, Alex. I guess I simply couldn't..." She paused and said, finally, "I simply couldn't resist you. And now, what's happening is totally my doing, and I am so *sorry*."

"I would have told *you* instantly," he said, keeping his back to her. "My sense of loyalty and my feelings for you would have trumped everything...that's how close I thought we were. Your welfare is my welfare. I would have trusted you as a kindred spirit and I'd have kept nothing from you."

"I know you would," she whispered, slipping her arms around his waist and resting her cheek against the small of his back.

He felt the muscles in his entire body stiffen, resisting the temptation to turn around and enfold her in his arms.

She asked him, "And you feel I didn't trust you to tell you about my suspicions? But that's not it at all! I didn't trust *myself*. I've *never* trusted myself to speak truth to power, so I felt it 'safer' to go along to the Bugatti gathering and try to assess how bad the damage might be…if there truly is going to be damage. I still don't know."

"Well, what do you *think* is going on?" he asked over his shoulder.

She unlocked her arms around his waist and moved to one side.

"I'm horribly worried, now, and you were right about yesterday. I *did* have a bad feeling after speaking with Stella that it might be something really awful, but I wanted to wait and verify all the facts before I said anything to you. To spare you the worry." Then she added, "And to spare myself what's happening right now: a confrontation with someone who holds my happiness in his hands. I wasn't totally forthright because…because I was *scared*."

"Come on, Fiona!" he said, turning to face her. "You're a grown woman. You're free to make any choices you want. You've already proven that."

She walked away from the window. He could sense that her desire to reach out to him had turned to hurt and anger. She whirled back to face him, her fists clenched by her side.

"Oh, come on, Alex! You've committed a few choices that don't reflect so well on *your* honesty! How honest can you say *you* were, not admitting to your father-in-law you wanted out of your marriage to Addy just as much as she did! You worried that Dalgetty had the power to call the loan to Maxwell Mills, so you've gone on pretending you're the wounded party and let Addy take all the blame so you could both get divorced *and* save your company! You played both sides of the street, just as I did—out of fear of the people who held the power."

Alex faced her across the expanse of the kitchen.

"You know, Fiona, you are right about that. And I see that we are both quick to use the ammunition of our shared truth-telling."

"Well, you've accused me of being a user!"

"No, you've just called yourself that. But can you understand what a shock it was to see you on television, standing with a flock of industrialists that use slave wages in their country to nearly crush *my* country's textile industry? Can you *see* how your not saying a word about it called everything I thought we had between us into question?"

"I do," she murmured. "And now, because I didn't come clean with you about my suspicions before I went to Peebles, *everything else* I do or say is now called into question, is that it?"

Alex didn't know how to answer her, so it was his turn to remain silent.

Fiona's eyes flashed and her face was suffused with color.

"So, now you're thinking that maybe I just pretended to be in love with you and slept with you just to get you to help me open doors to the people in your world. Well," she said hotly, "that's the same thing as calling me a user."

"After I saw that television spot, that's what I thought might be true," he admitted, "And now I don't know *what* to think."

"Well, what I think is that I've lost your trust, and from now on, you'll always have doubts. It feels as if there's probably no earning that back, especially when I'll soon be three thousand miles away." Her anger appearing to have drained away, she gazed at him across the room with an expression full of sorrow. "I'm really sad and disappointed that you don't have more faith in me than that."

"Fiona—"

"I've got to go to bed," she stated dully. "I'm exhausted from everything that's happened today and Sterling has demanded that I do a complete presentation on the plane home, tomorrow. I'm due at the airport by eleven, latest. I'll turn in my car there."

Alex felt his own anger replacing the tentative truce he thought he and Fiona were about to forge between them.

"You're *joking*," he said. "You're just going to *leave?*"

"Bernie wants me to fly back with him on Wu's private jet tomorrow."

"Tell him *no!*"

"I can't. It's my job. I've got to go."

CHAPTER 17

Alex could feel a part of him was spinning out of control. Fiona was leaving.

Tomorrow! No…in less than eight hours from now!

He could barely keep his voice below a shout.

"So when life presents hurdles, you agree with whoever is making demands on you—including that bloody bastard Andrew Wu— and just move on, is that it?" he declared, feeling as if the fabric of his life was being ripped in two. "Just like when you left…what was his name? *Chip?*"

Fiona's expression of having just been stabbed in the heart nearly undid him, but Alex could only think about the fact that she had decided to leave, just like that! And on Andrew Wu's private jet! *How* could he have let this woman affect him so deeply, he thought, despising the debilitating rush of sorrow that had him in its grip? What could explain his feeling like an abandoned *child* on the first day of boarding school?

Struggling to regain his equilibrium he said tersely, "So that's it, then. You'd just leave. You'd do Sterling's bidding no matter what it meant to you and me. No matter what the results could be for the mill, or even your own family's furniture factory!"

In the part of his brain that was barely functioning, he wondered how in the world he would manage the fallout of her departure and not having her a part of his life any more after five years of thinking about her each and every day, to say nothing of the glorious time they'd spent together in Scotland or what was now going to happen to his one hundred employees if Maxwell Mills lost orders for goods to Andrew Wu's nefarious operation.

"I'm not just leaving because there are problems between you and me!" she insisted, and he could hear the pain in her voice that matched the feeling in the pit of his stomach. "I've made a commitment to my firm to produce this project—"

"So no commitments to *me* concern you?"

"I feel hugely committed to you, Alex!"

"Oh, really? You don't consider departing abruptly like this *not* to be a form of running away?"

"I explained," she cried, and he could see she was close to tears. "I have to present all the facts and figures on the way to New York so Bernie can make a decision! *Then* I can make a decision what to do next!"

"And you believe it will be a fair decision? One that takes account of what Sterling allowed you to imply to all the people I've introduced you to?"

Her voice rising in anger, she replied, "I operated on what I *thought* to be true, and now…I don't know what he will do, but why can't you understand this from my side of things? It's my *profession*! Don't you see that I feel I have to play this out?"

He sensed the anguish she was feeling as if it were his own, but something strong as steel prevented him from extending the olive branch.

"Well, you'd better decide what team you're playing *on*, Fiona."

He could actually feel himself going cold and shutting down the intense emotions he had for this beautiful creature that had been the woman haunting dreams since the day he'd met her in New York.

It was a reaction he'd often experienced whenever he felt someone he cared for was unfaithful to the rules already agreed upon. Even though he forgave Adelina for having the affair with Peter, he'd never quite recovered from a sense of her duplicity for not telling him for more than six months that she was sleeping with another man…. or how she felt about their misbegotten marriage. And then there was his own father, keeping from him the knowledge that his mother had terminal cancer until a day before she died, and much later, that Harry was siphoning money out of the family business at a time they desperately needed every farthing. There were few people in

Alex's life beyond his friend, Hugh Erskine, that he could *count* on to be absolutely loyal.

Of course, did you tell Addy how empty you thought your relationship was?

He couldn't rehash all that now, he thought! He grabbed the dishes off the table and carried them to the sink. His actions at least accomplished a break in the acrimonious exchange that had sapped energy out of both of them.

Fiona crossed the room to stand next to him at the sink.

"Let me help you with those."

Alex almost turned toward her and enfolded her in his arms, but the water in the sink was running and his hands were wet. And besides, how did he know she was actually telling him everything that had transpired between her, Sterling and Wu in Peebles? There was too much at stake with his hundreds of employees to be an easy mark. He wondered if her imploring expression as she stood beside him was something she'd learned as a southern belle?

"Ever the young lady with good manners, I see," he replied, feeling as if he might slam his fist into a wall behind the faucet. "No thanks. I can manage the dishes."

Fiona remained silent for a long moment, and he could read the bitter disappointment in her eyes. She marched to the kitchen door, and turned to face him.

In a deliberate drawl, she shot back, "Ah do thank yew, Mr. Maxwell, for your hospitality here in the Borders...you judgmental, holier-than-thou, pig-headed *Scotsman*!" Then she said in a normal tone of voice. "How's *that* for good manners!"

She slammed the kitchen door, leaving Alex wrist-high in soapy water and wondering how the hell his life had come to this.

Absolute misery filled Fiona's chest as she locked the door to her bedroom, got out her iPad and wireless keyboard, and worked the numbers on various products she thought the new collection should include until her neck ached painfully and she noticed it was nearly two a.m.

Alex had not knocked at her door, nor had she padded down the hallway to his room to try to make peace. All she could do now, she told herself, was to put one foot in front of the other by preparing her report and returning to New York. She'd figure out after that what in the world her life was going to be like after falling deeply in love with the man sleeping down the hall.

She set the alarm on her cell phone and fell into bed, but it was nearly four a.m. before she finally drifted off to sleep, a desolation seeping into her bones with each passing minute that was unlike anything she'd ever felt, including hearing the news that Chip Reynolds had died.

*I wonder...*she thought, as fatigue was finally sucking her into an undertow of unconsciousness, *if Thomas Fraser felt this miserable when he finally faced the fact that Jane Maxwell could never be his...*

Barely three hours later, the soft notes of a harp playing on her phone's alarm woke her. She quickly donned the same clothes she'd worn when she stepped off the Caledonian Sleeper train at Waverley Station to the lilting strains of *The Skye Boat Song*. Careful to avoid bumping her wheeled bag on the treads of The Firs' grand staircase, she tiptoed out the front door into the crisp, early morning air and dashed for the Fiat that was sprinkled in dew, its roof dappled with fallen orange and red leaves.

She started the car's engine and glanced back at the lovely stone manor house just as the front door opened and Alex stood on the threshold in the very same spot where he'd greeted her the night before. She waited a few moments, but he made no move to walk toward her. With a jerk, she put the car in gear, scarcely able to see through the moisture welling in her eyes. She released the brake and rolled down the drive and past the gateposts. Blinking furiously, she gazed into the rear view mirror and saw the only man she'd ever truly loved shut the front door just as she was poised to make a turn onto the A72 that would lead her to the principal motorway and ultimately, Edinburgh Airport.

Then, she thought about the note she'd left on her pillow in the room upstairs where they had made love for the first time.

Alex:

Please know that I will do everything I can to make a deal happen between BS and Maxwell Mills. If I am successful in doing that, you will hear from Jared Finnegan or the VP of Purchasing who will place an order directly.

Fiona

When Fiona arrived at Edinburgh's private jet terminal, mechanics were swarming over Andrew Wu's sixty-one million dollar Gulfstream jet trying to determine if an indicator light signaled something was wrong—or merely a malfunction of the light itself. A silver trophy fashioned in the shape of a classic Bugatti sat on the floor beside Bernard Sterling's chair where he was glued to his cell phone and barely gave her a wave.

Meanwhile, one of the industrialist's minions fetched food from the plane's galley for a makeshift lunch while they waited several hours before receiving the all clear. After their meal, Fiona spent her time hunched over her iPad, purportedly refining the presentation she was due to give to her boss and their host on the plane before arriving back in the States. In reality, she found herself barely able to think about anything other than the dreadful hours prior to her departure from The Firs.

It was late afternoon before they were cleared for takeoff by the authorities and granted permission to head for the end of the runway. By this time, Fiona felt she was nearing the end of her tether. Once aloft, the steady hum of the newly-certified airplane did nothing to calm her stomach that had suddenly signaled that the chicken dish she had been served earlier that day had undoubtedly sat too long in the small galley before their party had boarded the plane.

Andrew had consumed some exotic concoction of fish from his native Singapore that Fiona could not have identified, even if she weren't feeling so woozy. Bernard had ordered a pastrami sandwich that had miraculously been produced—but without his favorite mustard. They had been airborne for about an hour in rough weather over the Atlantic when Fiona began to seriously feel ill. At first, she ascribed her tender tummy to the turbulence, and the fact her heart as well as her stomach was in a state of turmoil over the way she and Alex had parted.

She gazed out the small window on her right, willing the mounting nausea to subside.

"Well, Fiona…thanks to our mechanical delay, you've obviously had plenty of time to prepare. What do you have to show us?" Bernard asked as the solitary flight attendant removed the men's champagne glasses and retreated to the galley.

Fiona attempted to smile and struggled to her feet to seek her notebook and iPad from her luggage stowed for takeoff in the overhead bin above her seat. Then, helplessly, she clamped her hand over her mouth and bolted for the small bathroom at the rear of the plane, barely having time to shut the door before she was as sick to her stomach as she'd ever been in her life.

When, fifteen minutes later, the flight attendant tapped timidly on the door, Fiona could only moan that she was mortified, but she needed to remain where she was—which she did for the next five hours. For much of the trip she thought she would die, either because the tossing plane would crash into the sea, or she wouldn't survive the food poisoning that had obviously been her fate on this nightmarish trip back to the United States.

When she thought about it later, she realized that getting sick from the Chinese chicken salad served her from the galley of Andrew Wu's private jet turned out to be the luckiest day of her life.

The Gulfstream landed at the private jet terminal at Teterboro Airport in New Jersey many hours later than originally scheduled. An immigration official found Fiona's passport wedged in her handbag and swiftly stamped it—thereby admitting her back into the land of her birth. Thanks to Andrew Wu, an ambulance was waiting at the foot of the tarmac when they pulled up to the gate. Fiona only vaguely remembered being whisked with sirens wailing to Columbia Presbyterian Hospital in upper Manhattan. Five days later, after forty-eight hours in Intensive Care and a steady stream of antibiotics infused into her system through continuous IVs, she was miraculously brought back to a reasonable state of health.

"You had a very nasty strain of salmonella," noted a sympathetic young female intern who stood by her bed while the paperwork for Fiona's release was processed. "It was lucky you were brought here immediately or…"

The young woman in the starched white coat didn't finish her sentence, so Fiona filled in with, "I think it's going to be a long time before I ever eat chicken I haven't bought and cooked thoroughly myself."

The doctor laughed. "I hear ya! I feel that way about potato salad on a hot day."

Fiona thought of Andrew Wu and the exotic fish dish he consumed with impunity on board the Gulfstream.

"Just bad luck on my part, I guess," said Fiona.

"No," pronounced the doctor. "Just bad food handling. We've sent reports everywhere we could think of. I hope that company gets more than a slap on the wrist." She gave Fiona's shoulder a pat. "You be well, now, okay?"

Fiona tried to return her doctor's smile. The reality of her future was finally starting to sink in.

"Please thank everybody around here for saving my life."

And to herself she thought, *Now, I'll have to decide what to do with it…*"

Hugh Erskine poked his head into Alex's office. His friend and employer was staring off as if his thoughts were a thousand miles away. His boss's mobile phone rested in the palm of his hand.

"It's after six o'clock, mate," said Hugh. "How about we

head for the pub?"

As if waking from a dream, Alex set the phone on his desk.

"Thanks, but I still have to prepare for the board meeting tomorrow. Mrs. Nolan said she'd leave me something for supper before she went home tonight."

Hugh stepped past the door and closed it behind him. He gestured to Alex's mobile phone.

"You tried to reach her?"

"Fiona?" Alex nodded glumly. "Yes. On her mobile. I've called numerous times and she hasn't answered even once."

"Today?" queried Hugh.

"And yesterday. And the day before that. She can see who's calling her and she's not picking up."

"Did you leave a message?"

Alex hesitated. "No. It's not anything I could say into a machine."

"What about her phone at her home?"

"She apparently doesn't have one. I did a search. Lots of Americans only use their mobiles now."

"Why don't you text her or send an email?"

Alex was becoming weary of Hugh's cross-examination.

"No!" he replied shortly. Then, realizing his friend was merely showing his concern, he added, "This is too important, Hugh. Written messages get misconstrued. I need to speak to her in person!"

"Well then, call her at work, laddie!" Hugh insisted.

Alex shook his head. "No. If she wants to talk to me, she can answer her mobile. And besides, I've had time to do some in-depth research into Sterling's reputation and it isn't a pretty picture, so I definitely won't call her at work. I want nothing to do with that sod."

"And you still think Fiona Fraser is in league with him?"

"No...but if she's now learning what kind of a man he is, she'll have to sort it out on her own and reach out..."

"But if she doesn't know you *called*?" Hugh said with a hint of exasperation.

"She *knows* from her caller ID who called," he insisted

testily. "She's just not answering."

Fiona had been sent home from the hospital with instructions to eat simple food and take another week of bed rest. Andrew Wu had sent a limousine full of flowers and gifts to fetch her back to her apartment—most probably, Fiona figured cynically, in the hopes that she wouldn't sue Andrew Wu, Limited, or the company that supervised the food service on his private jet. In the chaos of events, her cell phone had gone missing, either when the immigration officer dug into her purse for her passport or when she was loaded into the ambulance at the airport. Fortunately, her iPad and notebooks, packed in her luggage, were waiting for her when she finally arrived home.

Back in her West End Avenue apartment, she slept fitfully most of that first day, unable to stop re-running the nightmarish memory of leaving Alex and then the hideous flight across the Atlantic. Scattered everywhere on her bedspread were tissues from a box of Kleenex she'd been using to staunch her tears of misery every time she pictured Alex standing motionless on the threshold as she drove away. On her second day home, she finally summoned the courage to fire up her iPad to open her email and quickly scanned the scores of messages that had piled up—but none that came from @maxwellmills.co.uk, or anyone else from Scotland, for that matter.

Alex hadn't tried to reach out, or say he was sorry for his wounding words about Chip and the way she'd left Atlanta—just as she felt she couldn't retract flinging her accusations about his former wife taking all the blame for the end of his marriage.

We all were doing the best we could at the time....so why did I say such a hurtful thing to him?

But hadn't he done the same thing, countered a voice in her head, when he equated her leaving Scotland abruptly with abandoning Chip to his fate?

Another wave of misery nearly suffocated her and she buried her head under her pillow with a moan of regret.

"Alex?"

Hugh Erskine stuck his head inside his employer's office door.

"Oh, hello, Hugh. What is it?"

"The Board meeting, remember? Everyone's in the conference room, waiting for you."

"Oh, bloody hell! Is it five o'clock already?" He glanced at his watch, sprang from his chair and grabbed a file folder off his desk. Outside, the lovely autumn days had given in to winds howling through the Tweed Valley, rattling the windows in his office. "Can you just run in there and tell them I was detained on an important call, or something?"

"Yes, of course, but Alex…" Hugh hesitated, and then continued, "you are seriously off your mark these days. When are you going to call Fiona Fraser again and try to patch up whatever went off the track with that woman? Frankly, I've never seen you in such a state and I'm probably the only one around here who'd tell you to your face that not having your full attention is hurting our business."

"Oh, you're not the only one telling me that," Alex noted ruefully. "Mrs. Nolan has given me an earful, too." At first, Alex's loyal housekeeper had thought Fiona might be an industrial spy after she saw her on television at the Bugatti gathering. But when Mrs. Nolan received Fiona's 'thank you' note, along with a beautiful Bernard Sterling jacket that fit her perfectly, the older woman had completely reversed course. "My own housekeeper has decided that I must be either a fool or an ogre not to get back in touch."

"Well, I agree with her," Hugh said. "Fiona Fraser is just a pawn in this entire situation, same as we are. I feel sorry for the lass. It must have been mortifying to have represented one thing and have your employer change his tactics, entirely."

"We don't know that for a certainty, Hugh."

Erskine pointed to his heart. "I know it, here, and if you were honest with yourself, so do you. She's a lovely lass, that one." He glanced at the antique clock on the wall. "Right. I'd better go make it look to the board like you're a very important lad with calls for orders coming in fast and furiously…but will you hurry it up?"

Alex nodded soberly. "I hope I can put a positive spin on our Third Quarter numbers, enough to satisfy Dalgetty and the others."

Hugh gave a short laugh.

"Tell them about the Dublin Pipe Band calling to inquire about possibly ordering enough fabric for a hundred new kilts from us."

"We don't have a signed agreement, yet, but let's hope that query satisfies Humphrey Dalgetty and the others that we're slowly making progress."

"Not to worry about Dalgetty. I've heard that he's telling everyone how his coming grandson will one day take over the bank. I don't think he's going to be such a problem anymore."

Hugh made a fast exit toward the boardroom located a few doors down the hallway. Alex stood to his full height, donned his jacket from the back of his chair, and headed in the wake of his second-in-command, thinking that Fiona's last words, said in anger, had actually been correct. She accused him of using Adelina's transgressions with Peter Murray to obscure his own: that he was a man who had not chosen to wed for love and had never admitted that fact to his ex-father-in-law. Instead, he'd allowed his former wife to shoulder all the blame for their failed marriage.

I've made a total cock-up of just about every relationship in my life…

The question now was: what was he going to do about it? He had a company to run…to *save*, he corrected himself. That had to be his first priority. So many people depended upon him to pull Maxwell Mills back into profitability: his staff and the mill workers and their families, to say nothing of his friend Hugh, his brother's fishing business—which finally appeared to be making strides—and the fiercely loyal Mrs. Nolan.

Until he knew for certain how things fell out at Bernard Sterling and whether the mill could survive past the New Year, his love life would have to be put on hold.

When Fiona finally dragged herself to work after two weeks away from her job, Johnny, the liveried doorman at Bernard Sterling's elegant emporium who doubled as a security guard greeted her effusively, asking how she was feeling and wanting to know when she had been released from intensive care. She received the same concern and interest from the sales people on the first floor who rushed up to her as she waited for the elevator to the executive office.

"Stella said you nearly *died*!" said the woman who sold luggage and handbags.

"We're so happy to have you back," chimed in her assistant.

"Thanks. I was pretty sick," Fiona admitted, shifting her large, unwieldy leather portfolio into her other hand while holding tight to a package containing a beige cashmere sweater she'd bought for herself, but was offering as a sacrifice to Stella Langdon. She might need Bernie's assistant's help in the future—and besides, a promise was a promise.

She smiled her thanks for everyone's expressions of concern and rode the elevator to the top floor alone, suddenly recalling the small lift that had taken her to Room 3, arranged by Alex, at The Royal Scots Club. The bittersweet memories of the days spent with him discovering the joys of the Fraser and Maxwell homelands, along with the pain of those recollections felt almost physical. In her weakened state, she leaned against the elevator's railing to furiously blink back the tears that came, unbidden and often, since she'd returned to New York.

I will get over this...I will get over him...

The door slid open to reveal Jared Finnegan sitting at his desk in his office, the door open to the showroom floor. He appeared intent on a sheaf of papers he was signing individually—and in quick succession.

"Well," he said, looking up. "*Camille* has returned. I heard you were taken home from the hospital in a Town Car and showered with presents from our fearless leader as well as the Chinese potentate who gave you a lift home in his private jet. Nice going, Fee."

Fiona halted in her tracks. Stella was at her desk, pretending not to be listening.

"I was in *intensive care*, Jared," she reminded him sharply, and then wondered why she couldn't just let Jared's jabs roll off her back like she used to before she went to Scotland. She tried to smile to signal she was willing to make light of his remark. "I'll trade you one ride in Wu's jet and a limo over the George Washington Bridge in exchange for *your* having a near-death experience. Trust me, salmonella is no fun."

"Well, your vacation, however you spent it, is now officially over," he said, maintaining the nasty edge to his voice. "And just so you know, in your absence, I've taken some of the images you sent from Traquair House and costed out what it would come to if Andrew Wu made the items you suggested in his Singapore factory."

"You did *what*?"

"Bernie's orders. News flash! He's doing the whole deal with the guy."

"No!" she protested.

"*Yessss*," hissed Jared, and he sounded like her brother Tommy did sometimes, as if he'd one-upped her somehow. "I want you to turn in your other notes to me that you were supposed to give Bernie on the plane before you were…indisposed…so we can get cranking on the rest of this stuff. We want to debut the new collection in six months, Fiona, so stop being such a prima donna and get busy. Fun's over."

Fiona strode over to his desk and threw her portfolio on the floor.

"What is *with* you, Jared? Got your period, or something? And stop ordering me around. I'm not turning in anything until I have a chance to talk to Bernie. He promised we'd make this collection something special…something of true quality and now—"

"And you believe that crap?" Jared threw down his pen. "We're doing what the Chief Financial Officer and the Board want us to do. Making it cheap and selling it as luxury. It's a winning formula—or haven't you heard?"

"You mean making shit and telling everyone it smells like perfume?"

Jared smiled grimly. "Now you're gettin' it, sugar."

"And you don't care?" she demanded, tossing Stella's cashmere sweater on a chair.

"Why should I? I've got the top design job, and you'll be clinging to yours, girlfriend, if you don't hand in the rest of your research with the cost breakdowns, PDQ."

CHAPTER 18

Fiona stared across the desk at Jared. Honking taxis and the steady flow of traffic gliding up Madison Avenue suddenly roared in her ears, and for the first time in her life, the wayward southern belle thought she might faint.

The noises from the busy Manhattan street also blotted out the tinkling of the baby grand piano that a tuxedoed musician had started to play on their floor as ten o'clock rolled around and the doors opened for customers. Fiona's breath caught in her throat, making it hard to breathe—or think.

"Hey, Fiona," Stella chimed in, apropos of nothing. "Is that my present on the chair?"

"What? Oh…right." She picked up the parcel she'd wrapped in tissue, and walked five paces to Stella's desk. The young woman obviously wanted to collect her goodies in case Jared was about to fire his top designer for insubordination. "I could only get beige in Petite Medium…no heather beige," Fiona added distractedly.

"Oh. That's ok, I guess."

Stella took the package from Fiona's hands and ripped it open without a thank-you.

Meanwhile, Fiona turned and focused her gaze on the stack of work orders piled on Jared's desk. Her heart was pounding as if one of the big busses screeching to a halt at the corner had missed hitting her by inches. When she had recovered enough to speak, she was seething.

"What the hell do you think you're doing?" she demanded, pointing to the papers Jared had resumed signing. "I haven't even completed my designs, or given you the swatches and sample or costs of anything!"

"I'm just doing what our beloved Mr. Sterling told me to

do," Jared replied without emotion, pointing to the remaining papers sitting on his handsomely tooled, leather-topped desk. "Since you're so cozy with Bernie that you flew home with him on a private jet...I'd have thought he'd have shared all this with you by now. I was just sending the approved Andrew Wu, Limited work orders for the Dress Stuart tartan goods up to the comptroller when you walked into my office."

Jared Finnegan was *jealous* that she'd flown on a flipping private jet! He should have tasted the food, she thought darkly.

"This is *insane!*" she exploded. "You and Bernie know perfectly well that the designs I dashed off from Traquair House are only preliminary, and the ideas for upholstered furniture I submitted to Bernard Sterling, Inc., are based on the top quality, eighteenth century reproductions made in *my* brother's factory in North Carolina!" she exclaimed. "Every single plaid we can private label for Bernard Sterling are patterns based on the dress and hunting variations of *my* own family's tartans, not the ubiquitous red Stuart! All the accessories I saw at the Scottish estates I visited have *rights* attached to them. You guys can't just rip off everything and manufacture it all in China! The textile firms in Scotland have been weaving top quality cloth for hundreds of *years* and—"

"Oh, give it a rest, Fiona!"

"I will *not* give it a rest, Jared Finnegan!"

The leader of her firm's design teams slammed his clenched fist on top of the work orders he'd been signing. Then he arched a non-existent eyebrow that matched his meticulously shaved and oiled bald head.

"Side tables and ottomans have been made by many furniture companies for hundreds of years!" he retorted. "So have desk clocks and brass bookends. And I imagine those tartans date back to the mists of time. It's a stretch to say you or your brother or the people at the textile mills you visited in Scotland have patented that stuff."

"No, but the tartans have been registered as authentic to Scotland." Fiona tapped a trembling finger at the corner of Jared's stack of papers that represented a betrayal of work done with enthusiasm and in good faith. "My idea for the entire Scottish themed collection for next year was inspired and informed by everything people shared with me in Scotland, along with my old family photographs and the confidential design specs my brother sent up from North Carolina that Stella passed on to Bernard just before I left."

"That's right," Stella volunteered. "I sent them directly to Bernie."

"Shut up, will you Stella?" Jared snapped. "Stay out of this. Go try on your new sweater in the ladies room, will you?"

Stella glared back at Jared. Even so, she grabbed the package Fiona had handed her and sprinted down the hallway.

When she had disappeared, Fiona shook her head and leaned on Jared's desk.

"When Bernard green-lighted this project, he said he was placing a huge order for hundreds of yards of fabric from whatever Scottish firms *I* designated, along with the custom pieces from Fraser Furniture. He said—and these are his *exact* words, Jared—that he would be 'honored to do business with such old, respected American and Scottish family firms!' What happened? Why the about-face?"

Jared shrugged. "'Would be honored' are the operative words here, and while he was saying that to you, later on that same day in August when you made your pitch to all of us, he was asking *me* to crunch the numbers based on parallel information I could get off the Internet. From the very first, my dear Fiona, he wanted me to compare costs of manufacturing everything in Scotland versus Singapore…as well as the wooden pieces at Fraser Furniture versus a factory in Vietnam."

Stunned by such casual treachery she demanded, "Why didn't you tell me this was going on behind my back?"

Jared shrugged again. "Simple. I'd get the boot if I told you and besides, once I did the math, the margins were obvious and I knew there was no fighting the CFO."

"That's because in China, the poor slaves on the assembly lines are paid a dollar a day for skilled labor in factories that collapse on top of them!" Fiona cried. "My family has always paid living wages and honored the craftspeople who do the work. And from everything I saw, Maxwell Mills and D.C. Dalgliesh, Johnstons, and Lochcarron operate with that same kind of integrity. What Bernie's doing—appropriating ideas and other designers' schematics given to him in good faith—is totally unethical."

Jared slammed his hand down hard on his desk. "Which is why Boss Man drives a Bentley with a black chauffeur named Worthington, ships his Bugatti all over the world, and has houses on three continents. It's also why he can call himself Bernard Sterling, instead of Bernie Steiglitz from the Bronx! Grow up, Fiona!"

Her former Parsons classmate lowered his gaze and angrily signed the rest of the work orders while Fiona fought a fierce battle to keep from grabbing every single piece of paper and shredding each one with her bare hands. Meanwhile, she became acutely aware, now, of the hush inside the well-appointed showroom just outside Jared's office, disrupted only by the faint strains of the live pianist's rendition of Vivaldi's *Four Seasons* heard through built-in speakers throughout the store.

She did her level best to convince herself that it would do her no good to continue to throw a total tantrum. She leaned forward, both hands on Jared's desk, deliberately invading his space.

In a lowered voice she said between clenched teeth, "Didn't you guys learn *anything* from the revelations about American cell phone companies operating their East Asian sweat shops? Didn't you *see* the ghastly pictures of that clothing factory that collapsed?" she demanded. "And don't you *remember* all the horrible press Ralph Lauren got for having the uniforms for the *American* team in the London 2012 Olympics manufactured in *China* and how he ate crow and promised every single ski cap would be made in the USA for the Sochi Olympics in 2014? A purveyor of luxury home goods like Bernard Sterling, using slave labor in the Far East to carve a ten thousand dollar mahogany headboard fit for a king sounds *bad,* Jared. Getting caught selling four-dollar-a-yard synthetic tartan fabric for a thousand percent markup could garner this company some pretty acid and terminally bad PR."

"Not if we all keep our mouths *shut* and put 'assembled in the USA' or 'designed in Scotland' labels on our goods, it won't," Jared shot back.

"But that would be twisting the truth into a pretzel!"

"Maybe so, but please don't forget you signed a non-disclosure-of-company-business clause in your employment contract when you came to work here. If we ever proved you blabbed to the media about this, you'll get your ass sued from here to High Point, North Carolina, so don't even *think* about being the source of any leaks to try to sabotage Bernie's Chinese manufacturing deal."

Her eyes narrowing, Fiona regarded her immediate supervisor for a long moment.

"You've recently read over my employment contract, haven't you?" Jared averted his eyes. "You two have strategized this little fraud right down to the last move on the chessboard."

"Pretty much," he said, a smug smile playing at his thin lips. "After all, darlin', you were the one that volunteered the idea of doing a Scottish Home Collection. It's not as if we committed industrial espionage, or anything."

"Oh, cut the crap, Jared!" Fiona exclaimed, attempting to keep her voice from shaking. "The difference between us is that you kiss Bernard's ass in all matters and tell him what he wants to hear, even if you know that he's doing something totally unscrupulous—and by the way, screwing your supposed friend—me—in the process."

"Well, baby cakes, that's why I'm your supervisor and you're my worker bee. You always were the brilliant one, but I live in the real world now and am much more likely than you ever would be to take over this joint…eventually."

"*What?* Is that what this is all about? Jared Finnegan's very own palace revolution?"

Jared leaned back in his chair. "Relax, Fiona, and just go with the flow, will you? You don't understand Bernie the way I do, but I'll always protect your job around here. And why wouldn't I?" he asked rhetorically. "You're always making me look so good! Now, just hand me those textile samples, along with your report and the color charts I know are in that portfolio there, and run along. I've got to get this paperwork upstairs." He flashed a thin smile. "Oh! And just so you know, while you were in Scotland, Bernie asked me to check on the backgrounds of every single business you were scheduled to visit."

"He asked you to do *what?*"

"You heard me. We know Maxwell Mills is on the ropes financially, just like Fraser Furniture, so just remember, if anything negative gets traced back to you, we'll let those little pussycats outta the bag."

"That is such low, slimy, underhanded, unprofessional, *unethical—*"

"And if the friggin' scribes at *Forbes* or the *Journal* check their facts, they'd soon learn that every single thing I've just said is true, won't they?"

Fiona could feel herself begin to tremble with both fear and outrage. She made a swipe at the folder plump with work orders that sat on Jared's desk, scattering some of them to the floor.

"Good God, Jared…what's happened to you? You weren't like this when I first met you at Parsons. So now you're just a company bum boy, are you?"

Jared pursed his lips, his eyes shooting daggers.

"Poor, polite, oh-so-genteelly-brought-up Fiona Fraser, with that arresting head of hair, your thoroughbred good looks, the lilting southern accent, and such *touching* enthusiasm for your family heritage." He stretched out his hand. "Just give me your work product and maybe we can forget this little spat."

Fiona bent down and grabbed her portfolio before Jared could try to snatch it from her.

"This is *my* work!"

Jared raised his hand in warning.

"Need I remind you that you've been *paid* for the work you've done for Bernard Sterling, and all your suggestions and contributions belong to *us*. End of story."

Fiona knew that what Jared said was true but her pent-up

fury finally exploded like a hurricane heading straight for the Barrier Islands off the Carolina coast.

"My *brain* doesn't belong to you, you son-of-a-bitch!" she shouted. She held on to her bulky portfolio with both hands, yelling, "I *quit!*"

Jared reared back in his two-thousand-dollar Aeron chair. "You can't quit."

"Oh, yes I can! My contract says I have to give two week's notice. And during the next fourteen days, I'm afraid I'll be very, very sick with a relapse of the food poisoning I got as a result of eating Chinese chicken salad on Andrew Wu's company jet—a highly dangerous malady that the nice doctor who saved my life at Columbia Presbyterian Hospital will confirm."

Jared jumped up from his chair.

"Give me that portfolio!" he commanded. "I mean it, Fiona, hand it over."

"Want to wrestle me for it, you little worm?" she taunted him, adding, "And tell Bernie I want my brother's furniture schematics returned. *Now!*"

She was perfectly aware that each item of her brother's line that she had generously provided her employer had undoubtedly been photocopied from every angle for future use in the development of Bernard Sterling's next "lifestyle" home furnishings collection—to be made in China.

Jared's thin lips looked glued together, but he hissed, "Leave your laptop and iPad before you exit the building, please."

"They're not here."

Thanking her lucky stars that she'd felt too weak to bring those devices, along with her heavy portfolio, to work today, Fiona speculated how quickly she could transfer her design files to her own computer at her apartment before she wiped the disks, ditched the equipment in a dumpster, and sent a check to the company to replace the electronics.

"Oh, yeah, right!" Jared yelled. "I'm sending security to your house!"

"Go ahead," she bluffed. "My cell phone, and some of my

other electronic stuff I had on the trip must have been lost or stolen when I was transferred by ambulance to the ER at Columbia Presbyterian Hospital." She smiled grimly. "But everything I know about Scotland is right in here," she added, tapping her forehead.

What a total, naïve chump I've been! Loyalty? How quaint a concept is that *around here?*

Fiona couldn't bring herself to think how she was going to break the news to Tommy about what had just transpired—to say nothing of the impact this latest debacle would have on Maxwell Mills. She clutched the poster-sized portfolio to the front of her camel-colored sweater like a shield while Jared glanced nervously around his well-appointed office. Sensing she was about to storm out the door, he grimaced and held up his hands as if declaring a temporary surrender.

"Now, look, Fiona…hold on a sec. I'm really sorry this has all played out like this. Maybe I—"

Fiona backed toward the door, holding fast to her portfolio for dear life.

"You and Bernie Steiglitz are just a pack of thievin', lyin', fuckin' skunks!" she shouted. She had suddenly started dropping her 'g's' as she had as a young girl growing up in High Point. She was inordinately pleased to see that her loud, vulgar language had finally goaded a shocked expression from her former classmate.

Before he could reply to her insults, she whirled on her one set of Prada heels, stormed through his open door, and sprinted toward the magnificent marble stairway that arched down to the next floor. A few more paces, and she drew close to a pin-stripe-suited young man and his golden-haired wife considering an ornately carved mahogany dining room sideboard and accompanying five-foot gilded mirror with a price tag nearing twenty thousand dollars.

"You know, dah-lins'," she confided in a loud, exaggerated southern drawl, "ah'd think twice about purchasin' those items, if I were yew. Y'all can buy that lil' ol' thing online at 'China-Knockoffs dot com' at a *third* the price they charge *here*."

She swiftly descended the two flights of stairs and when she reached the ground floor, she called out to clients and colleagues alike with the loudest lungpower she could muster.

"Now, suckers, y'all have a very won-der-ful day, y'hear?"

"So, what are you going to do now, Fee?" her brother Tommy asked over the phone, and then added, "At least I only sent pictures of the stuff we make, which Sterling could get off the Internet just as easily. Something told me to hold off and send just a list of what we make and a few photos until I had a better sense of who these guys are."

"Well, now we both know who they are," Fiona replied morosely. "Tommy, I am *so* sorry I ever got you involved in this!"

Tears threatened to choke her again, as they had so often since she'd stalked out of the Bernard Sterling executive offices, burning her bridges as far as the eye could see. She'd made it to the ground sales floor before she'd heard Jared, two flights up, leaning over the ornate railing, screaming to the nice guard at the front of the building to stop her and seize her portfolio. In an instant, she'd reversed direction and ducked into a door marked Exit and raced down a back corridor. She'd barely escaped out the rear door into the narrow alleyway that led to 63rd Street, hopping into a cab that had materialized just in the nick of time, before Johnny-the-guard had rounded the corner in hot pursuit.

She explained to Tommy how—for an entire week—she'd been holed up in her apartment, refusing to answer the door. She'd managed to get a new number assigned to the cell phone she'd purchased immediately following her escape from Jared's office. She'd made a quick stop at the Apple store on Broadway on the way back to her West End apartment and arrived home just before Jared's minions began pounding on her door.

"All that day and half into the night, Tommy, I transferred files from my company laptop and iPad to my home computer."

"Did you also have copies in the Cloud or in Dropbox?" he asked worriedly.

"Deleted them all. I thought better of trashing company

equipment in a dumpster, so I put the devices into a padded envelope with a note to Jared and Bernie saying, sadly, nobody had yet turned in my lost cell phone—which nobody has, by the way—and that the airport scanning machines at the private jet terminal in Edinburgh had apparently crashed all my disks, wiping them clean. When no one was in my hall, I left the package outside my door so my local Fed Ex guy could deliver it to Jared's desk."

"You think they'll believe *that*?" scoffed her brother. "I sure wouldn't."

"It was far-fetched, but what are they going to do about it?"

"What about what's on your desktop computer at work?" Tommy asked.

"Whatever is on there can't be helped," she replied, adding, "but fortunately, most of my ideas and source information for the Scottish Collection were on the devices and in the paper notebook I had with me on the trip."

The rest of her time since her grand exit from the Sterling emporium, she explained, had been spent writing carefully worded notes to all the people in Scotland thanking them profusely for their help and apologizing that she no longer worked for Bernard Sterling in the wake of their having parted ways over "creative differences."

"The cheap goods Bernie will produce this coming season will explain better than I can why I quit."

Fiona never mentioned to her brother about her whirlwind love affair with Alex Maxwell, nor that she hadn't communicated with him at all since coming home.

Tommy asked, "Have you heard from anyone at Sterling since they got your equipment returned?"

"Only emails from their lawyers. They've apparently given up on trying to get my work product from the Scotland trip and have, as they said, 'moved on, delighted with their own designs.' However, I got a registered letter today saying that they would be nice enough to grant me severance money *if* I signed an agreement saying I would not discuss with the media any of the terms of our settlement—or 'any other recent events'—*and* I would agree not to work for a competing firm as a designer for two years."

"Two *years*? Those Yankees can do that to you?"

"I suppose I could hire a New York attorney at three-hundred-and-seventy-five-dollars-an-hour to fight it, but I can't afford that."

"But they *owe* you that money, right? It's in your personal services contract?"

"Not anymore. I was the one who quit, remember? What's going on, I think, is that Bernie's lawyers figure that I'll need the money soon, just to live, and offering to pay severance with all those strings attached is a way to hush me up *and* keep me from going to a competitor."

"You were valuable to them and they want to punish you," Tommy declared.

"I guess so. Too bad you're not licensed to practice law in New York."

The bone-deep unhappiness she'd been living with recently was starting to close in again. There was a long pause, and Fiona figured her twin wanted to end this unpleasant conversation and get off the phone.

Tommy's next words were a total surprise.

"Come home, Fiona. Come back to High Point. I'll make you a member of the executive committee and put you on the payroll with a modest salary, for now, so you can sign their deal and you'll have your severance. We won't call you a designer…you're a member of the family firm, and Sterling can't stop you from being *that*."

Fiona felt tears edging her voice. "That is so sweet of you, Tommy…but I can't just sponge off you like that."

"Oh, you won't be sponging. You'll be Fraser Furniture's designer, all right, but we'll just call you Vice President…how's that sound?"

"You'd do that?" she said, emotion clogging her throat.

"It just might save this sinking ship," he replied. "Nothing else seems to be working very well."

"What would Maxwell think?" she said. Her grandfather

had long opposed having women part of the management's inner circle.

"He doesn't have a vote anymore. In fact, he's totally wheelchair bound, Fiona."

"Oh, lord...that's terrible for him."

"Actually, before I asked you to come home the last time, I talked over with him your coming on board down here, and...well...let's just say he's mellowed a bit."

"Really? Mellowed *that* much?" Fiona was dumbfounded and dabbed her eyes with a tissue.

"Yup. And, by the way, he's seen your Sterling stuff these last years. He knows you're good."

"Wow."

"Yeah. Wow," Tommy echoed, a chuckle in his voice.

"And our beloved mother? What do you suppose she'd have to say about my coming home?"

"She doesn't say much of anything these days, Fee. A few years back, we moved her into the memory care unit at Saint Thomas' Retirement Home."

"Holy Sh—I mean, gosh," she amended, "when did she start to show signs of—?"

Tommy cut in, "We've known she had early, garden variety dementia for quite a while, but it suddenly got real quirky. We had her tested and they confirmed it was actually Alzheimer's. It was gettin' get worse and worse, and given how Dad and she don't exactly get on very well under the best of circumstances—"

"Whoa! Why didn't you tell me about this when we talked before?"

"You were about to leave for Scotland and I figured you didn't want to know."

Fiona paused. "I wouldn't have, I guess." She stared out her window at the traffic flowing along West End Avenue three stories below. "You've had so much to deal with, Tommy. It's about time I came down there and gave you a hand."

"You'd do it?" Her brother sounded incredulous. "You'd move back down here?" She could hear the sheer relief in his voice.

"Honestly? It's not my first choice, but I deeply appreciate your job offer and I accept. Where do you think I should live?"

"In our basement? At least when you first get here. Dabney made it into an in-law unit for her mother, who passed away two years ago. It's available, if you want it."

Fiona felt a stab of bitter remorse. Tommy's wife, Dabney Webb, had a mother who had lived and *died* in their family home and Fiona hadn't even known that, either. She couldn't believe how estranged from her family and childhood home she'd become.

"You and Dabney are way more than I deserve," she said quietly. "I accept that offer of a roof, too."

"It's yours as long as you want it."

Before her brother could sign off, she added, "Tommy…please know that I'm hugely grateful to you both. I'll get down there as soon as I can. There's nothing to keep me here."

CHAPTER 19

Alex flinched at the sound of a knock on his office door.

"Come in," he said, not looking away from his desktop computer where he was analyzing the year's first quarterly report and finding little to cheer about. By sheer willpower, Maxwell Mills had barely survived the winter without staff redundancies.

But what of the coming months?

The Dublin Pipe Band order and the usual increase in custom made kilts requested by the major retailers in Edinburgh during the holidays had staved off disaster, but a long spring and summer stretched ahead, and Alex despaired of what the future might hold.

"I can't really believe what just came in my email," Hugh Erskine said, waving a computer printout and placing it on Alex's desk. "Here…have a look."

Alex read the message and leaned back in his leather chair with an expression of amazement.

"Remind me our profit margins on five thousand yards?" he asked.

"About one hundred and thirty-two thousand pounds…and *more* money, as they say in their request, *if* the ottomans, footstools, and padded headboards and storage boxes they'll be manufacturing, using the Maxwell tartan, sell well."

"And who is Arlington Furniture of High Point, North Carolina?" Alex asked, trying to steady his pulse when saying aloud the name of Fiona Fraser's place of birth.

Hugh grinned happily. "I have absolutely no idea, but I ran a check on them *and* their credit rating and they're considered tops in supplying upholstered furniture to the hospitality industry…you know, hotels, restaurants, and the like."

"And why do you suppose they specifically ordered the

Maxwell tartan?" he said, wondering if his company was the beneficiary of someone's guilty conscience.

"Haven't a clue, but it's a grand surprise, wouldn't you say?"

Alex could detect his lieutenant was watching him closely for his reaction.

He had not heard a single word from Fiona in seven months, nor had he tried to get in touch with her by any means since his first, frantic attempts to call her mobile when she never answered. He'd sent no email, no letter, no text. They had both retreated into stiff-necked radio silence, yet he continued to have disturbing dreams, vaguely recalled the next day, of searching for her, or trying to meet up at airports and train stations and always just missing her—or having some calamity prevent his finding her.

Many a time he'd almost pushed the button that would have connected him directly to her mobile phone for another try, but something had always held him back. He'd had no communication or orders for goods from Bernard Sterling, even though his Google Alert setting had pulled up news reports of the big launch of the company's Scottish Home Collection in March. Just a week ago, that same alert system linked to a story that some enterprising reporter revealed that the products touted "Designed in Scotland" and "Designed in the USA" labels had actually been manufactured entirely in China by the notorious Andrew Wu.

Alex stared at Hugh's email. Did Fiona persuade some company associated with the Sterling firm to buy his textiles? Was this her way of saying a very big "I'm sorry?" Or did she now consider her debt to his hospitality and assistance paid-in-full, and so "Over-and-Out?"

"Hugh," he said, as his second-in-command retrieved the communication from Arlington Furniture, "when do they want the fabric shipped?"

"As soon as possible. I've already alerted our production manager. It's full speed ahead, with your approval, of course."

"Of course," he nodded, making a show of returning to his keyboard and appearing absorbed in whatever the hell he'd been doing before Hugh had burst in with news that could save the mill for at least one more quarter.

He waited five seconds following Hugh's shutting his door and seized his mobile phone off his desk. He'd almost deleted Fiona's number only last week. If she was the reason Maxwell Mills received this life-saving order, he should at least thank her, yes?

He scrolled down until he found Fiona's entry and pushed "Call," remembering to add the country code, first.

After a few unfamiliar rings, a recording told him it was no longer a working number. A shock ran through him and with shaking fingers, he put "Bernard Sterling, Inc., New York, New York" into his search box, dialed the number listed and told the person answering he'd like to speak to Ms. Fiona Fraser.

There was a pause on the other end, and the woman said with a mildly flustered tone of voice, "I-I'm sorry, sir, but Ms. Fraser no longer works for the company."

Alex sat back in his chair and asked, "Do you have a number where she can be reached? This is an old friend. It's very important that I get in touch with her."

There was another pause, and then the store operator said in a low tone, as if she didn't want to be overheard, "I can put you through to someone who might have that information."

The next thing he heard was a sultry sounding voice that said, "Bernard Sterling's line, this is Stella Langdon...how may I help you?"

Taken aback to be put through to Fiona's former employer's direct line, he stated the reason for his call. The woman who'd identified herself as "Stella" lowered her voice in the same soft timbre as the store operator.

"I'm sorry, Mr. Maxwell, is it?" she said, "but no one around here has any contact information for Fiona. All I know is she's left New York."

"Left New York *and* Bernard Sterling?" he asked, fearing in his solar plexus that something truly alarming had transpired in the time since he'd seen the back of the little white Fiat disappear down the driveway at The Firs. "Have you any idea why? I'm a…an old friend. From Scotland."

"Oh! I just *love* the cashmere sweater she brought me from there! Are you the one that helped her so much with our Scottish Home Collection?" Stella asked, her voice brightening. Then she added in a hoarse whisper, "Of course, she took with her most of what she'd learned over there when she quit. That's why my bosses gave her such a hard time, you know?"

"No, I didn't realize that."

Stella warmed to the drama of her tale.

"Well, Jared—Jared Finnegan who's now the number two to my boss? He's at lunch, or I wouldn't be talking to you, but since you're her friend…"

"Yes…a *very* good friend. Please tell me what happened, Stella."

"Well," Stella said cheerfully, "Jared tells everyone Fiona was fired for insubordination, but the truth is she found out our boss had *always* intended to manufacture the Scottish collection in China, so she refused to turn over all her notes of contacts and resources and samples and even claimed the hard drives on her company laptop and iPad had been wiped by Scotland's luggage scanners when she quit. Isn't that a riot?"

"Did the bosses believe her?"

Stella laughed. "Not really, but they couldn't prove why the drives were blank when she Fed-Exed all her company equipment back to us, could they? It drove Jared and my boss crazy 'cause they couldn't use her designs or exploit everything she'd learned over there to give to that shyster, Mr. Wu. It was *awesome!* Basically, they had to research everything on the Internet to meet their deadlines."

"And how did that work out?" he asked, knowing already that Sterling had been caught implying his collection was created by Scottish and American manufacturers when, in fact, everything had been made in the Far East.

"The bad PR has been wicked. Sales have been a total bust 'cause a lot of the stuff turned out real cheesy, you know what I'm saying? I think Jared's days are numbered around here." Then Stella croaked, "Oh dear…promise you won't tell anyone I said that?"

"Your secret is safe," he assured her. "So you have no idea where Ms. Fraser could be now?"

"Well, her deal to get her severance last autumn specified she couldn't work as a designer for a competitor for two years, so who knows where she went?" Stella giggled. "*I* think she took the money and went to Bali or someplace to chill for a while. Wouldn't *that* be nice?" She giggled again. "Hey, *you* sound nice. Do you ever come to New York?"

"Haven't been in donkeys years," said Alex dryly. "But thank you very much for your help, Ms. Langdon. All the best, now. Goodbye."

"But, wait! Maybe—"

Alex firmly pushed the "End" button and inhaled deeply, trying to calm the complicated rush of sensations invading his chest.

Fiona not being permitted to work as a designer for *two years* was a high price to pay for her loyalty to her principles.

For her loyalty to you, *you prideful lout!*

Not only was she without a job, she was *prevented* from seeking one in her field. American corporations could be heartless, and he recalled the stories he'd read about how employees of long-standing were ushered out of the building by armed guards when they'd been let go. Only St. Ninian knew what happened after she *quit* her firm and refused to turn over her work product.

Deeply disturbed by what he'd learned from Stella, Alex tidied his desk and prepared to leave for the day. He felt an inexplicable weariness invade his body and all he longed for was to skip dinner and sleep for a month. He remembered how estranged Fiona had been from her family and could only imagine the loneliness she must have endured these last months. If she were hiding out in a remote place like Bali, he'd surely love to be right there with her.

His thoughts kept circling back to two questions: what in the world had Fiona Fraser been doing all these months? And where was she hiding out, licking her wounds?

A fire crackled in its grate in a stone cottage deep in a Highlands glen. Alex found himself wrapped in a dark green and black tartan blanket—Black Watch, wasn't it, his mind wondered groggily? He was sitting cross-legged in front of the glowing hearth, waiting…waiting…

Two small windows in one wall grew dark and then a moon the size of a dinner platter rose over the hills that encircled this unknown shieling. Someone was coming. Someone was expected soon. Alex knew, somehow, he was dreaming, but gave into the shadows around him as they grew dimmer, still, and then heard the metallic sound of a door latch snapping open.

A figure appeared, silhouetted by the doorframe, just as he remembered himself standing at his own threshold at The Firs, watching Fiona drive away.

Where was Fiona, his heart cried out? Were there only ghosts inside this darkened cottage?

And suddenly the scene shifted to a curving bank of a loch where he caught his first clear view of a tiny castle glowing golden in the lingering sunlight. It was nestled on a miniscule island in the middle of the lake. The fortress's single tower was reflected in sharpest detail in the pellucid waters below, along with tenacious vines that clung to the lower walls. A splash of flowering clematis crowned the small, square fortification in a colorful, leafy net. A pair of swans could be seen in the distance paddling among the clusters of canary grass and yellow marsh marigolds that ringed the stone dock near the castle keep.

Alex halted on a path that skirted the small, gray-green body of water, mesmerized by the beautiful scene, his heart pounding at the thought that, at long last, his dearest love awaited him across the loch.

Gazing at the castle walls made of honey-colored stone, his attention was riveted by the sight of a slender figure with hair the color of garnets running through the stone arch and disappearing inside the fortress. He suddenly knew, with a certainty he didn't understand, that the stronghold had once served as the mysterious lair of the Wolf of Badenoch.

His chest suddenly filled with a grief so piercing that Alex could scarcely catch his breath. Where had she gone? Would he ever see her again?

Gasping for air, he heard himself shout in his dream, "No! Blessed

Saint Ninian, no! I canna bear to hold ye close, only to have ye leave me again!"

And then he woke up.

Over the next several months, Alex was haunted by the dream that refused to fade from his thoughts. One night in early August, when he couldn't sleep, he went to his study and put in the words "Wolf of Badenoch" into a search engine. Amazed, up came a Wikipedia entry about a personage he didn't remember ever knowing about: "an historical figure, the notorious third surviving son of King Robert II of Scotland, remembered primarily for his cruelty and rapacity, to say nothing of the destruction of Elgin Cathedral to the north, a roofless ruin since the Wolf lay waste in the 14th century."

I must have read about the ruddy lad in school....

Even more astounding, though, was the Wikipedia entry describing a miniature castle made of honey-colored stone built on a tiny island sitting in a small body of water in the remote Highlands. The description sounded very much like what he remembered of the tiny fortress in his dream with its stone arch that served as an entrance to the castle's tower through which he'd seen a woman with rich, red hair disappear just before he woke up.

But what did the Wolf of Badenoch have to do with anything, he wondered? And the dream had seemed so absolutely *real,* along with the anguish he still felt in his solar plexus whenever he thought of the beautiful lass vanishing from view.

Noon on Thursday, he called Mrs. Nolan from the mill to tell her he'd be in Edinburgh until at least late Sunday night, and for her to consider herself on paid vacation for the reminder of the week. Alex then made another call to the Register House government records bureau and used his influence as "a descendant of Jane Maxwell, 4th Duchess of Gordon" to book an appointment for nine o'clock the following morning initiating a search for information about the later years of Jane's life.

At the mill's closing time, he directed Hugh Erskine to take charge while he was away and hopped into his car. The navy Jaguar sped out of the Maxwell Mills car park and north on the A68 to Edinburgh and the company flat on Royal Circus Place. As soon as he arrived, he made a tin of soup and then went to bed early in order to be on the steps of the Register House the next morning, well rested. He anticipated a long day searching through dusty records he hadn't had time to go through the last time he'd looked into this history of the intertwining relationship between the Frasers, the Maxwells, and the Gordons. He hoped to discover whatever he could about Jane and Thomas prior to their deaths by looking at family, legal, and estate papers and any documents pertaining to Louisa, Lady Gordon, Jane's daughter who reputedly had been sired by the "Lost Lieutenant" Thomas Fraser.

And if he had time, he'd try to find out more information about the Wolf of Badenoch and how in God's world he could dream about a seven-hundred-year-old ruin that actually existed beyond the fantasies of his mind.

A gray-haired reference librarian whose nametag read "Isabelle Larimore" and whose thick, black-rimmed glasses seemed perfect for her profession wheeled a two-tiered cart stacked high with accordion letter folders, leather-bound books, and ledgers into the massive Reading Room at Register House.

"Ah, there you are, Mr. Maxwell," she said in hushed tones. "Let's go over here."

She pointed to the large area dotted with tables and chairs positioned under the Adam Dome, a top-lit rotunda arching at least some eighty feet above their heads. It was a bright day and sunlight poured in, illuminating the second story, book-lined balcony and above that, the plasterwork medallions depicting various civic ceremonies from Greek myths and legends.

The white-coated Mrs. Larimore smiled, pointing to her bounty on the cart and spoke *sotto voce* to avoid disturbing others already installed at various desks scattered around the huge space that Alex reckoned was at least fifty feet in diameter.

"I dinna know what you'll be wanting with all these ledgers and letters, Mr. Maxwell, but no one's had a look at 'em for a hundred years or more!"

"You are so kind to have done such a thorough search."

The woman, dressed more like a lab technician than the scholar she was, lifted a thick, leather portfolio containing legal documents off the cart and reverently set it on the polished wood table to which Alex had been assigned. Then she handed him a pair of white cotton gloves that matched the ones she was wearing and bid him put them on to protect the contents she indicated she was about to show him.

"This will probably interest you," she said, opening to a section she had marked with a slip of acid-free paper. She flashed a faint smile. "It certainly did *me*. You've quite a set of ancestors, it would seem, Mr. Maxwell."

Alex smiled back. "I've been told enough by my father and grandfather over the years to quite agree with you, Mrs. Larimore."

The researcher nodded. "These pages record a terrible legal wrangle that went on between the Fourth Duke of Gordon and his Duchess, Jane Maxwell of Monreith, specifying how much money he would give her for her separate maintenance after what they finally agreed was to be a permanent break in their relationship—but with no divorce, of course." She pointed to several pages beyond the place she'd marked. "From what I gathered reading this just before you arrived this morning, each accused the other of infidelity, and the marriage had finally arrived at a state of complete disrepair."

While Mrs. Larimore watched patiently, Alex quickly skimmed the deposition each party had given in their legal arguments over money.

When he looked up he said, "I'll read it more thoroughly later, but this is absolutely amazing." Reflecting how blessed he was that Addy and he had never gotten into such an acrimonious dispute he then asked, "And…ah…did you find out anything about the Wolf of Badenoch?"

"Oh, yes," the researcher said with a laugh. "That rascally

fellow lived three hundred years before your duke and duchess and was forever reviled for burning down Elgin Cathedral. One of his lairs was in the middle of a loch in the territories later controlled by the Fourth Duke of Gordon. But then you might have known that since you requested more information?"

"No, actually, I didn't. How amazing," Alex murmured, attempting to disguise his shock that the two aspects of his dream were definitely linked. "And where was that loch?"

"Loch-an-Eilean? And by the way," she noted parenthetically, "some maps spell it 'Loch-an-Eilein'—but no matter. It's in the heart of the Highlands, near the home that the Duchess of Gordon built with the money the Duke gave her after their financial settlement was finally agreed upon." She glanced at a note she'd jotted down. "Kinrara, she called her country home. It was where she lived from her middle years to near the end of her life—that is before the Duke cut off her funds entirely and she apparently couldn't afford to keep it going. Loch-an-Eilean is adjacent to the lands of Kinrara and features a small stone fortress built on a tiny island in the middle. It's a quite common image on postcards for tourists, actually."

"And this lair of the Wolf of Badenoch? Do you have one of those postcards in the file?"

"There's a vintage color picture of the place in one of these folders," she said, seizing one labeled "Badenoch." Pulling out an image and handing it to him, she invited him to have a look. "The old Wolf would hide there when his enemies were after him," Mrs. Larimore chortled, pointing to a color rendering of the small stone fortress while Alex stared at it in silence, dumbfounded to recognize it as the castle in his dream.

He now realized, however, that the photograph in Mrs. Larimore's hand was one of Scotland's most famous views—like that of the steep-sided terrain of Glencoe or a shot of Loch Ness with the monster photo-shopped into the scene. He'd seen pictures of Loch-an-Eilean since childhood, but had never visited the place and had forgotten its name and location.

"I imagine the Wolf wasn't very popular if he burned down Elgin Cathedral," Alex noted, trying to mask his astonishment that it was Loch-an-Eilean he'd seen in his dream.

"Rapist and pillager he was, so they say," Mrs. Larimore added with barely restrained gusto. "Torched the cathedral to the ground, he did. His ghost supposedly lurks in the small tower atop the wee castle on Loch-an-Eilean."

Alex raised a skeptical eyebrow, though he was shaken to remember the peculiar details of his dream. In that vision, he had stood by the shore and stared at what he *knew*—in his state of unconsciousness—*was* the lair of the Wolf and now this had later proved to be true, along with its link to the Duchess of Gordon.

Had his subconscious merely recalled what he'd vaguely known about the place in the same way he knew about other remote areas in the Highlands, or could there be such a thing as *genetic memory*, he wondered suddenly? What if sad or tragic or traumatic or even joyous events somehow got etched into one's DNA through a cascade of adrenaline or cortisol or serotonin—the kind of brain chemicals he'd read about that were capable of changing the very structure of brain cells? What if these changes to one's cells could be *handed down*, generation to generation, and the memories stored in them *recalled* under similarly stressful situations that were reminiscent of the original dramatic event?

He had felt an uncharacteristic sensation he could only describe as sheer abandonment when Fiona returned so abruptly to America, just as he imagined Jane must have felt when Thomas left with his Black Watch regiment and was erroneously reported killed by Indians. He also remembered reading once that some scientists had identified the "shy gene." What if there were a "memory gene" and somehow he and Fiona—as possible descendants of two people who had loved and lost in such dramatic fashion—had *inherited the memory* of that loss? Or at least *he* had inherited it. But what in the world did Loch-an-Eilean have to do with Thomas Fraser, he wondered? Had he and Jane been there together?

This is bloody daft!

And yet, so many pieces of the puzzle pointed to exactly *that*, he thought. However, he declined to try out this strain of scientific inquiry on his hired researcher and changed directions in his questions.

"Mrs. Larimore, what did you find about the ducal Gordons' middle daughter, Louisa, Lady Gordon?" After all, he and Fiona had found the gravestones of Louisa's namesake in the Ayton Churchyard plot dedicated to Jane's sister, Catherine Maxwell Fordyce, and her children, grandchildren, nieces, and nephews—nearly all named after various older members of the Maxwell and Gordon families.

Consulting her notes, the researcher replied, "The Duchess's daughter, Lady Louisa Gordon, was betrothed to General Cornwallis's son, Viscount Brome, and later married him after a bit of bother."

"'Bother' you say? How's that?" asked Alex.

"Well, apparently Cornwallis had heard there was madness in the Gordon family, which there *was*," she said, chuckling, "as the Duke's brother, Lord George Gordon, was thought crazy as a loon for instigating the London Gordon Riots in 1780 and calling into question the entire family's loyalty to the Crown—but that's another matter."

"Yes…" Alex said, anxious to keep Mrs. Larimore on track. "So you were saying that General Cornwallis was concerned his son might be marrying into 'bad blood' as it were?"

The historian warmed to the tale and leaned closer to Alex.

"At any rate, Jane Maxwell, the Fourth Duchess, assured General Cornwallis, right before the nuptials were to take place with his son, Viscount Brome, that—according to several witnesses whose statements you will find in the documents I've brought you—'there's not a drop of Gordon blood in dear Louisa's veins.'"

"So the Duchess didn't seem to worry about how insulting this statement would be to the assumed father, the Duke of Gordon?" Alex marveled.

Mrs. Larimore nodded. "By this stage of her marriage, I dinna think she cared much. I'm guessing this is one reason the Duke and his Duchess ended up having to negotiate their separation and all their financial wrangles."

"In other words, Duchess Jane admitted to Cornwallis that

Louisa was *not* sired by her husband and therefore he shouldn't worry about the Gordon madness being inherited by any future grandchildren?"

"It would seem it was more important to the Duchess to insure Louisa's advantageous match with Viscount Brome than to defend the lass' legitimacy. Perhaps the Duchess wanted to see her daughter safely married in case the Duke refused to support the young woman any longer by alleging he was not her father."

Alex nodded. "And of course, Jane Maxwell had already produced a legitimate heir and a spare, so I suppose it was not uncommon in the eighteenth century for unhappily married couples to take lovers after the dynasty was insured. But she certainly was rather bold about it."

Mrs. Larimore nodded in agreement. "I think Jane Maxwell was dubbed 'The Match-Making Duchess' for a very good reason."

"Quite."

"Cornwallis, as it happened, was a keen horse breeder, so he was more interested in having a sane grandchild by Louisa, with whom his son was apparently wildly infatuated, than bothering about a little thing as to whom her father was."

"I guess I've heard *that* before," Alex murmured.

"And look," his professional researcher said, pulling out a color copy of an enlarged miniature. "See what I was able to find? An image of Louisa, Lady Gordon herself! Isn't she a beauty? No wonder the Viscount was dotty over her."

Alex stared at an oval framing the painted image of a lovely young woman with hair the color of fine port wine.

CHAPTER 20

Alex's gaze remained riveted on the image of Jane Maxwell's daughter who very possibly could have been sired by Thomas Fraser of Struy, a man whose other descendant—Maxwell Fraser—spawned Fiona's family in America.

"Louisa's...beautiful..." he said, releasing a long breath. He'd read accounts she had red hair, but here was the proof!

"And the only redheaded progeny born to the Gordons, as far as we can tell from the portraits of the other six children...and of the Duke himself, along with others on his side of the family."

"So maybe the story *is* true...Louisa Gordon was *not* the duke's daughter, but sired by someone with red hair." He paused, wondering who else in Fiona's family besides her father and her might have had hair of a similar shade. Then he added, "And given the rumors about Thomas and Jane, that means, Lady Louisa could be blood kin to the Frasers of Struy."

"Well, look at the date of Louisa's birth," noted Mrs. Larimore, "1776. Just prior to the American War of Independence, Thomas Fraser of Struy—the Lost Lieutenant, as you called him and possible sire to Louisa—was recruited into a company of the 71st Fraser Highland Regiment captained by none other than the Duchess of Gordon's *brother*, Hamilton Maxwell!"

"What a truly small world it was back then. Amazing that we can confirm they all knew each other, but how do you think that's relevant to Louisa's birth?" he asked.

"Well," chuckled Mrs. Larimore, "just look at this other image I found! It's a copy of a portrait of the Duchess herself seen here on horseback, riding in the Highlands with her arm outstretched, offering the King's shilling in 1775 to the locals if they would enlist in her brother's company of Fraser Highlanders, due to assemble at Gordon Castle and eventually be placed under the command of..." She paused for effect. "General Cornwallis!"

"Oh...my...God," murmured Alex. "So Jane Maxwell and Thomas Fraser of Struy were in the same place nine months before Louisa was born and both knew Cornwallis?"

Mrs. Larimore nodded. "Exactly! I confirmed that Hamilton's troops practiced maneuvers on the grounds of Gordon Castle before they shipped out to the American Colonies from Greenoch for service under General Cornwallis in America."

"Which would have been the Lost Lieutenant's second tour of duty there," Alex pointed out.

"That's right. He first served with the Black Watch regiment, as you know, a decade earlier. Imagine crossing the Atlantic all those times back then."

"And so Cornwallis, Jane, and Thomas definitely knew each other as well," Alex concluded, trying to keep his voice down and excitement at bay. "And Jane, Thomas, and the Duke of Gordon were all at Gordon Castle at the same time, at one point—prior to Louisa's birth."

"So one could make the reasonable assumption that Lieutenant Fraser and Jane were in *close* proximity during that year Louisa was conceived. They could have found a trysting place somewhere on Gordon Castle's lands, or the Gordon estate at Kinrara, or at a sympathetic friend's home during those months when the regiment was in training."

Or at the tiny castle in the middle of Loch-an-Eilean...

Alex slowly inhaled as images of his dream of watching a woman disappear inside the castle replayed in his thoughts.

Isabelle Larimore continued, "The circumstantial evidence to support published rumors that someone other than the Duke of Gordon sired Jane's fourth daughter is actually pretty convincing, don't you think, Mr. Maxwell?"

"Especially if the girl's *father* had red hair," he said, trying to keep his voice down.

And if that garnet mane was inherited by Fiona...

"Sadly," the researcher acknowledged, "In the time I had, I could find very little else about Thomas Fraser—other than his military records. No images of him, whatsoever."

"Pity," Alex said. Then he brightened, "But you've given me some great leads on my quest to understand the linkages between my branch of the Maxwells, the Frasers of Struy, and the ducal Gordons. Thank you so much. I'll just get busy with the rest of what you've brought me here."

Alex spent the next six hours, with only a quick break for lunch at nearby Café Royal, reading through the documents Mrs. Larimore had dug out of the bowels of Register House, along with others she'd requisitioned from the National Library, a few blocks away.

He skimmed through an inventory of Kinrara House taken upon the death of the Duchess and discovered she dined off a green-and-gold bordered chinaware, ordered one hundred "lengths of tartan goods" from a mill near Elgin with which to make curtains for her sitting room, specifying to the mill "...made of the Black Watch Regimental pattern with a yellow stripe at proper intervals in the sett."

Blast, but the woman was cheeky, he thought. *She designs the Clan Gordon tartan from her lover's original Black Watch regimentals, merely adding a bit of yellow!*

He next found a receipt requisitioning a very expensive marble tomb carved with the names of Jane Maxwell's seven children and their titled spouses to be "erected at my death upon my grave that I wish placed on the banks of the River Spey, near my home."

Re-reading more carefully the legal depositions chronicling the long-enduring squabble between the Duke and the Duchess in their last years, Alex could almost hear the bitterness of the Duke's words that "she has been no wife, of late, to me," and her retort, verbatim, "Aye, and what of the nine brats who bear your blood now living in the nursery of Gordon Castle? What of *them*?

What of that harlot of yours, our housekeeper's wench, Jean Christie?"

In a later legal document, Jane Maxwell complains of not receiving her "pin money promised from the Duke" and "being forced to live some days in my coach, going from family to friend to family again to lay down my head beneath a welcome roof, and not having the funds to pay for Kinrara, or even the coachman who has been so loyal during this dreadful time."

Nowhere could Alex find any other reference to Thomas until, by chance, he opened the folder at the bottom of the stack of documents marked "personal correspondence of the 4th Duch. of G" that Mrs. Larimore had mentioned she hadn't had time to read, given the short notice of his requests.

Still wearing his white cotton gloves, he leafed through many letters to and from various family members, including several in which Jane fretted about Louisa and Charlotte when they were children being "taken by a dreadful ague"—the eighteen century equivalent, Alex surmised, of influenza or pneumonia. Within a folded letter that happily confirmed the girls had safely recovered from their winter's illnesses, penned in spidery, eighteenth century script to Jane sent from her sister, Catherine Maxwell Fordyce of Ayton House, he found a scrap of paper inscribed by a bold hand he hadn't seen thus far in the collection.

Jenny,

My heart remains in the Highlands. I leave thee my love...and seek a new home.

Thomas Fraser of Struy
2 June 1788

Alex stared at the small missive that he held between two gloved fingers. The short, poignant message was written upon paper that showed signs of having been folded into an even smaller shape like a tiny fan, as if it had been wedged into something. His hand trembled slightly as he reread it.

Here was the proof that Thomas Fraser of Struy eventually departed the Highlands—and perhaps Scotland—near the end of the eighteenth century, pledging his love to Jane, who was also known by her intimates as 'Jenny' in other correspondence Alex had seen. From the note, it was clear that he had been forced to "seek a new home," most probably, Alex concluded, because the lieutenant ultimately accepted the reality that the Duchess could never leave her seven children and run away with him.

Did he go to America this time for good? Had he ever met his daughter, Louisa, before he departed? Was this further proof that *he*, therefore, was definitely Fiona Fraser's progenitor, the man who Fiona knew sired a *son* by Arabella Boyd that had been named Maxwell—but was no blood kin to Clan Maxwell? A boy whose first name, perhaps, bore witness to Thomas' enduring love for Jane Maxwell of Monreith?

Alex leaned back in the leather chair, conscious of the hushed silence permeating Register House's mammoth Reading Room and gazed at the note that had once been held both by Jane Maxwell, as well as the man of mystery who'd written it. The same man whom he and Fiona had wondered about since first they'd met.

There was so much Alex wanted to tell Fiona. So much he now believed connected them by virtue of a long string of heart-wrenching DNA.

Fiona glanced at the clock on the wall opposite the antique partners desk she and Tommy had shared since she'd arrived in High Point and had taken up the role of Vice President in charge of new products.

It was nearly ten o'clock on a muggy August evening and the air-conditioning in both the upstairs office and the factory downstairs was going full tilt. Even so, to protect against the draft pouring down from a vent on the wall behind her, she'd swathed her neck in a lightweight, cream-colored cashmere scarf. Hugh Erskine had made a present of it at the behest of his employer during her tour of Maxwell Mills. Wearing it always made her think of her time in Scotland, and that, of course, led to melancholy thoughts of Alex Maxwell which then sent her mind into a spiral of regret. This was inevitably followed by a mental battle during which she sternly told herself to think about something else. But she always failed, and somehow the scarf gave her comfort in a way she'd never understood so she continued to wear it in the chilly office.

Late that afternoon, she'd urged her brother to go home to supper while she continued to crunch the numbers of the previous month's sales to see if Fraser Furniture might survive through another summer of typical sales doldrums. Autumn was around the corner, and if they could just keep their heads above water until then, the fall buying season might carry them through to the end of the year when her next collection would be launched after the holidays.

A few days earlier, she'd ordered more fabric from Scotland through Arlington Mills down the road, but she had no more faith that Alex would respond to her "message" this time than he had previously. At least, she thought bleakly, the products had sold well.

Her eyes skimmed over the financial figures for the line of upholstered ottomans, headboards, footstools, and storage trunks she'd designed in a crashing hurry that were swathed in Maxwell tartan and smartly studded with brass tacks. Thanks to a picture and a paragraph in *Traditional Home* magazine, orders for the new line had gone through the roof and literally kept the company from bankruptcy. This success—in turn—rendered their creditors more forgiving and allowed her to order even more yardage. At least she'd finally been able to do Alex a good turn while also avoiding any direct contact with him.

For the truth was, he'd never tried to contact *her* before she'd moved from New York—or even after she'd surreptitiously placed the large order with his firm. Despite her lost cell phone number, he could always have called her at Sterling's before she quit, and he hadn't. And surely a second order for Maxwell tartan from a firm in High Point might have given him a clue where she had gone.

When will I accept that our relationship is truly at an end?

Heaving a sigh for what was past, she reached for the phone and dialed a now-familiar local number. After a few rings, her father picked up.

"Dad? Hi. It's Fiona. Hope I haven't called too late."

"No, no...not at all. Where are you? At work, you naughty girl?"

"I know...I know...it's late for that too. I'm just finishing up. I promise I'll go home in a few minutes. I just called to find out how Peachy was doing. Tommy said you were going over there today."

"It made me mighty sad," her father replied, his voice growing husky. "For the first time, ever, Fee she didn't have any idea who I was. Kept asking me and the nurse if Suzie Reynolds had paid a call while she was sleepin'."

"Oh, Dad..."

Whenever Fiona visited her mother in the memory care unit of the health facility in High Point where Peachy lived now, the older woman had absolutely no notion her daughter had come to call. The surprising thing, however, was that Peachy Parker Fraser treated Fiona like royalty, commanding her caregiver to order "Sweet Tea and those darlin' lil' ol' iced cakes for this pretty young thing visitin' me today!"

As Fiona had said to Tommy and Dabney at dinner one night, "It's almost as if her mean gene has been surgically removed from her DNA!"

Her father broke into her wandering thoughts saying, "Now, Fiona, I think it's wonderful how you're helpin' Tommy put the company back on a much firmer footin' and all, but you work too hard, girl! Go on home now, will you please?"

Tommy had reported before she'd moved to High Point that her father had radically cut down on his cocktail consumption in the late afternoons ever since Peachy had been living away from home. Fiona found herself appreciating his artistic talents in ways she never had before, now that he'd been exercising them in a burst of lovely watercolors painted near Stone Mountain where he'd taken her to the Highland Games when she was a little girl.

"I promise you, Dad," she said, smiling into the phone, "I'm shutting down my computer as we speak, and I'll be out of here in less than ten minutes."

"Good girl," he said. "And come by when you get a moment. I'd like to show you a paintin' I've been workin' on for a quite a while, now."

"I'd love to see it. Maybe Sunday? Bye now..."

She had just unwound her cashmere scarf from her neck and packed it into her tote bag in preparation to head out to her car in the sultry evening air when, over the hum of the air-conditioning, the faint sound of bagpipes drifted toward the second floor.

"What in the world...?" she said aloud, thinking she must be hallucinating as the tune to *The Skye Boat Song* grew louder and louder.

She ran to the office window and peered down at two figures dressed in woolen kilts despite the stifling North Carolina temperatures. The pair was weaving a path through the few parked cars owned by the night shift workers, drawing increasingly close to the entrance to her building.

Frozen with amazement, she allowed the strains of the tune to wash over her as the words came back with a rush.

> *Speed, Bonnie Boat, like a bird on the wing*
> *Onwards, the sailors cry...*
> *Carry the lad who was born to be King*
> *Over the sea to Skye...*

"*Alex?*" It was more of a scream than a declaration. "Oh...my...God, it's *you!*"

Fiona tore out of her office and took the metal stairs, two steps at a time, repeating his name as she flew down to the factory's ground floor and sped past a few lumber cutters who looked up, startled, to see one of the Fraser twins going past them at a dead run, heading toward the steel door that led to the parking lot.

Workers on the night shift who had been moving large pieces of quilt-covered furniture on forklifts, along with a few mechanics who tended the factory's various machines, stared in astonishment as Fiona slammed the door wide, giving them a perfect view of her hurtling toward the tallest of the two men dressed in the familiar Maxwell tartan they'd been affixing to furniture all season. Fortunately, the man into whose arms she flung herself was not the fellow playing the pipes and was able to stop her forward motion in time to clasp her to his chest and kiss her soundly in front of several staff who had emerged from the doorway to shout and cheer.

"Alex! Oh, I can't believe you're here! Oh, *Alex*!"

The piper played on as they kissed and kissed some more, until finally, breathless, Alex said, "If I don't get out of this woolen kilt soon, I may just be your *dead* Alex Maxwell. Good God, it's *hot* in this part of the world!"

Fiona laughed, her heart still beating madly in her chest. "Come inside into the air-conditioning while I go back upstairs to get my car keys."

She glanced at the other man dressed in a kilt whose face was as red as the tartan he wore from his exertions on the bagpipes that he'd finally allowed to fall silent.

"Where did you corral this poor person?" she asked with a grin in the direction of Alex's accompanist.

Alex answered for him. "The Grandfather Mountain Games pipe-master, aren't you?" he inquired. The piper nodded, taking out a handkerchief and wiping the sweat off his brow. To Fiona, Alex said, "Isn't the Internet a marvelous invention? I just keyed in 'pipers for hire in High Point, North Carolina' and up he popped."

Alex dug in his sporran and handed his companion a crisp, one hundred dollar bill. "And thanks for picking me up at the airport and driving me here."

The piper grinned back and in a Carolina drawl replied, "I left your suitcase over they-ere," he replied, pointing. "And thank *yew*, Sir...and Miss. And I'm glad mah playin' had such a promisin' result!"

By the time Fiona drove Alex, who'd traveled with only a carry-on bag, to her basement apartment at her brother's house, Thomas Fraser V's home was dark, except for a light on the side of the house that led to the basement apartment she'd been occupying since her arrival.

"So this is where you grew up," Alex said, gazing through the windshield at the white, pillared home with black shutters and a shiny black front door. "The house looks rather what I remember of the film I saw as a boy... *Gone with the Wind?*"

"Tara?" Fiona gave a little laugh. "Just without the cotton fields."

"Tara... right! That was it."

"When Peachy went into the memory care unit, Dad got himself a small condo and insisted Tommy and Dabney move into our family home, which is good because there's a lot more room and my nephew and niece have a nice place to play. Come on inside," she said in a low voice so as not to disturb the household or the neighbor's dog a few hundred feet on the other side of a white fence separating her brother's property from the Folgers, next door. She led him down a short flight of stairs and opened the screened door to the separate entrance to her quarters. "Let's first get you out of that kilt and into something comfortable."

"Oh... blessed air-conditioning," Alex said as she led the way into a cool, belowground room with clerestory windows allowing light to stream in from a streetlamp nearby. "As soon as I'd donned all this, I realized it was going to be even hotter than that New York in July."

He began to undo the silver buttons dotting his Prince Charlie Coatee while Fiona switched on a few lamps, illuminating her small living room.

"North Carolina is not known for its pleasant summer climate, except for the mountain country around Ashville," she noted with a frown. "Frankly, to my mind, it's totally disgusting here, this time of year. Here, let me help you with that."

Fiona took his black, worsted wool jacket and laid it on the back of a barcalounger that had belonged to Dabney's mother when she'd lived in the apartment. As Alex removed his heavy, woolen knee socks and shoes, she glanced around the room, suddenly imagining how the tiny place must look in Alex's eyes. The widowed Mrs. Webb had attempted to squeeze a lifetime of possessions into the thousand square feet of living space during the two years she'd stayed in the flat. A large, mahogany secretary dominated one wall, along with myriad knick-knacks on the shelves and a huge coffee table that belonged in a proper living room.

"How do you like the 'widow décor' I've got going here?" she joked.

"Widow?" Alex asked, puzzled. "Don't you mean 'window?'"

Fiona shook her head and explained in a more serious tone.

"No, I mean *widow*. After Dabney's father died, Mrs. Webb brought too much furniture to this apartment from her former home, poor dear. She only lived a few more years…but you know?" she added, glancing about the room. "I was just grateful for a cool place to stay when I arrived last year. And the price can't be beat."

Alex paused, his hands on his silver belt buckle after already shedding his fur sporran. "May I say something before I do anything else?"

"Of course," Fiona said, suddenly wary.

Alex seized one of her hands, his dark eyes full of regret.

"I can't believe I was so pure mad and bloody daft to let you drive away from The Firs last year. What I said about your disabled first husband and your using his family's money to go to design school…well, that was a despicable thing to have done. I should have apologized immediately, but…well…you slammed out of the kitchen and up to your room—"

"I was feeling pretty attacked," she acknowledged.

"And then, I knew, you had to get to your plane in Edinburgh and wanted to sleep."

"I didn't sleep much."

"Neither did I," he admitted.

"And when I sat in the car, you never made a move toward me."

"I wanted you to come to *me*...and once you'd gone, you never answered my calls—"

"My cell phone got lost—or stolen—at the airport on my way to the hospital."

Alex looked startled.

"The hospital?"

"It's a complicated story. I'll tell you later."

"Well," Alex continued uncertainly, "I suppose my Maxwell pride got in the way and I—"

"You thought I'd used *you*. I left abruptly. On Andrew Wu's private plane. You thought I'd pulled a double-cross," she intervened in a quiet voice. "And I can totally understand what it must have felt like."

"But a voice kept telling me you'd never do that. That what we had between us had *nothing* to do with business. That if you hurt me, you'd be hurting yourself..."

Fiona nodded, her eyes filling with tears.

"That's exactly how I've felt too, all these months. I felt I *was* hurting myself by not contacting you, but somehow, events in New York and here in High Point were so overwhelming, and I kept thinking that if you'd forgiven me or understood what had happened with Bernard Sterling, you'd have gotten in touch with me some way or other...and since you hadn't, I figured that—"

Minus his wide, black belt, Alex strode to her side and framed her face in his large hands.

"But *you* did get in touch, didn't you?" he asked. "You initiated those huge orders of Maxwell tartan through Arlington Furniture here in High Point, am I right?" When a faint shrug of her shoulders confirmed his conclusion, he kissed her lips gently and then pulled her hard against his chest. "Oh, Fiona...how I've missed you, lass! I'm so sorry for doubting you."

"It took you *two* orders of fabric before you finally figured out I'd moved back home?" she mumbled into his broad chest, inhaling the perspiration that still dampened his shirt and thinking it the most erotic scent she'd ever encountered.

"At first I thought you were merely settling a debt out of guilt."

"Alex!"

"But Hugh Erskine and Mrs. Nolan both kept telling me I was barmy…and that you were just a pawn in all this like we were."

"I was hoping you would eventually see that…or at least know how mortified and sorry *I* was not to have immediately shared my suspicions about what was going on within my own company, the rats!"

"Well, I finally held my nose and called Sterling's, only to be told you'd left New York and had probably gone to Bali or some place exotic to live off your severance money."

"*Bali?* All these months you thought I was in *Bali?* Don't I wish!"

Alex's chuckle reverberated against her cheek. But Fiona realized she had one more confession to make.

"Alex…" she began, and wondered if she had the nerve to be as honest with him as he'd been with her. "I need to tell you something."

CHAPTER 21

Alex drew back, encasing Fiona within the circle of his arms, his expression wary for the first time since they'd seen each other this night.

"And what would that be?" he asked.

She seized his hand and pressed it to her cheek.

"This confession is about the unhealthy way I've often made deals with the devil because I was too afraid to confront the powerful people in my life…people who were manipulating me to get me to do what they wanted."

"I hope you don't count me in that camp?" he asked, his gaze searching hers.

Fiona shook her head vehemently. "Absolutely *not!* In fact, the respectful way you always treated me the entire time I was in Scotland—except for that last day—has helped me to figure out why I didn't have the courage to tell you about what was going on with Sterling the minute I suspected it myself."

"And why couldn't you? Had I ever done anything to lose your trust?"

"No!" Fiona cried. "It wasn't anything *you'd* done. It was *me*. That was why I felt so awful about everything, afterward. I've always been an absolute chicken about speaking 'Truth to Power,' as they say—power I vested in people like my mother and the others in my family who had their own expectations for me. I was afraid—and I was *right*—that they *would* withdraw their affection whenever I didn't act or behave or *do* what they wanted me to."

"But we're adults, now," he said gently. "We can make other choices and the sky probably won't fall."

"That's what the shrink kept telling me," she said with a shaky laugh, "but I want you to understand what crazy stuff was going on with me when I was in Scotland. I would make these pacts with the devil, as I said—hoping to ward off Jared or Bernie's anger or rejection by appearing to go along with them—until I didn't—or couldn't stand to—as in the case of jumping out of Chip Reynolds' car following our wedding."

"It's lucky you *did* jump out of that car. When it came to that Chip laddie, you could have been killed."

Fiona nodded, a sad smile tingeing her lips.

"As I grew older, I foolishly thought that I could outfox these people who appeared to hold my fate in their hands, and so I'd go along with their plans until something inside me just…just *rebelled*! Then, I'd run away. What I should have learned to say to the Jareds and Bernies of the world was, 'No. No, that doesn't work for me, but here's what I *will* do' and see if there was a way to find a path out of the morass without giving up my core beliefs."

Alex put a hand on each of her shoulders.

"But look at the way you ultimately stood up to your employer? Somehow, you avoided giving your research notes and samples and wonderful ideas to people who had abused your good faith." At Fiona's startled gaze he added, "When I called Sterling's, trying to track you down, Stella Langdon told me you'd quit the company, taking the majority of what you'd gathered in Scotland with you, she said."

"*Stella* told you that?" she marveled. "Well, I guess that cashmere sweater I brought back to her paid off handsomely." Then she shook her head. "And if you must know, the way I dodged handing over all my research was thanks to a large serving of Chinese chicken salad—*way* past its sell date—given me on Andrew Wu's private jet prior to the flight home."

Fiona gave Alex a brief recitation of the terrible days she'd spent in Columbia Presbyterian Hospital recovering from food poisoning.

"What a bloody nightmare! I am so, *so* sorry for what you've been through, love."

"I was so deathly sick, even Bernard was sympathetic, though the same can't be said for that little weasel, Jared

Finnegan!"

"Well, you might be pleased to learn that, according to Stella, quote: 'Jared's days may be numbered at Sterling' because of the way that the collection they launched without your input cratered so spectacularly."

"You know something?" Fiona asked rhetorically, "I don't even care anymore." She reached up and brushed a lock of Alex's dark hair from his forehead, a gesture that prompted a cascade of memories from their other times together. "All I can think of is that you're *here*. It's such a total miracle…"

"It was that second order for fabric. Ding-dong, I figured where you'd gone," he said pulling her close again and murmuring into her hair. "And now that I've cooled down enough to feel human again, you may have noticed…"

He allowed his sentence to drift off, gently rubbing the front of his kilt against her thigh to demonstrate his rampant state of arousal.

"Why, Mr. Maxwell," she said, "how overheated you *still* would appear to be." Then, she reached for the side fastening of his kilt while he began to ravish her lips, her cheeks, her eyelids, the shell of her ear with a shower of probing kisses.

"Oh, God, Fiona, you taste so good."

"I'm hoping very much that what a traveling Scotsmen wears under his kilt isn't some urban legend," she said with a throaty laugh.

"Would you care to know the answer to that question?" he mumbled, his tongue now lashing her other ear.

"Yes, I would," she said, licking the curve of his shoulder. "Even in America, do you guys actually go commando?"

"Aye, lassie," he murmured, "always and ever…but why don't you see for yourself?"

Nuzzling his neck, she whispered, "I just think I might do that."

By this time, Fiona's frantic fingers had managed to unbuckle Alex's kilt and push it down over his hips, allowing the pleats to form a circle on the carpet around his ankles. His naked, muscled thighs and calves made her heart skip a beat as he stood before her. Slowly, she lifted her eyes to his waistline where his white shirt did little to disguise his unbridled state of desire.

Alex pointed to his shirt's top button. "And this? Shall I make fast work of it?"

Fiona could only nod, watching him strip off his last piece of clothing.

She allowed herself a long moment to absorb the sight of the man who stood less than a foot away from her in the tiny, cluttered apartment. Her eyes roamed from his dark head to his beautiful, well-proportioned body a good foot taller than her own, and then her glance settled on his chiseled cheek bones that reminded her of the Romney painting of Jane Maxwell hanging in the Scottish National Portrait Gallery in Edinburgh.

"Cooler, now?" she asked with an innocent smile.

"Yes…and no," was his reply.

"Oh, lord," she said softly, her gaze moving leisurely, now, from his bare toes to his waist, "you *do* make a fine, figure of a lad."

"And you, my ruby wonder, are the sight I've seen in my dreams."

Alex seized the hem of her cotton knit top, and then slowly and with studied deliberation, drew it over her head, tossing it aside while Fiona swiftly unbuttoned the beige, light-weight slacks that had been her uniform during the long, hot summer. He reached behind her back and in a trice, her bra was on the floor, nestled in the folds of his kilt, along with her trousers and panties that he swiftly skimmed down the length of her legs.

"Could I entice you into taking a shower with me?" he asked. "It's rather imperative, in my case."

"Come, laddie, but hands to ourselves till bedtime," she replied, and led him to a nicely renovated bathroom. "I want tonight to be one for the ages."

"Just watch what quick work I'll make of this," he laughed, and sure enough, they were in and out of the water in record time, toweling off with mounting excitement for what was soon to come.

Before Alex could reach for her, Fiona settled her flattened palms at his waist, and slowly slid her hands along the length of his thighs as she knelt before him on his towel, a supplicant at his feet. She raised her eyes to meet his.

"When I...I actually thought I would die from Chinese chicken salad," she said with a crooked smile, "it was the memory of our time together in Scotland that helped me get through it all." She reached to stoke him with infinite tenderness and gently began scattering little kisses on his flank and groin, murmuring, "And the instant I heard the first notes of *The Skye Boat Song*, I knew that to have tried to forget you...was impossible."

"But have you *forgiven* me?" he demanded, pain and regret reflected in the intensity of his words. "Forgiven me for attacking your character?" He threaded his fingers lightly through her hair. "Do you forgive the fact that it took me so long to come to my senses?"

"We have punished each other too much, already," she answered, holding his glance. "No more...ever again..."

For Alex, her words were like a healing balm poured over the wounds of the previous ten months. He remained absolutely still as she shifted her head to the center of his body, gently nibbling and licking his flesh until he thought he would go mad. His skin had cooled, but a new source of heat had taken possession of him and Alex felt an overwhelming physical need for the woman now pleasuring him that went beyond anything he had ever known.

"Fiona! Please...let me love you! Let me be inside you..."

He felt her little gasp against his skin. He reached for her, pulling her to her feet, their faces only inches apart.

"Do you have any notion how much I want you right now?" he demanded hoarsely. He cupped her derriere between his hands and pulled her against his pelvis, drinking in the light blazing in her eyes. "*Only* love from now on, Fiona Fraser."

"Only love," she whispered back, and he wondered if his heart would leap out of his chest from the heat of her gaze.

Alex knew, now, that the huge gamble he had made with

himself had won him everything he hoped for. For the second time in his life he'd made an impulsive flight across an ocean. This time his actions proved, more than anything else could, that he and Fiona belonged together. He had so much to tell her, but all he could see were her beautiful, amber eyes, and her hair, slightly damp from their shower, glowing like a precious jewel in the lamplight.

"Come," she murmured, opening the bathroom door. "Have you ever heard of a matrimonial double bed?" she asked, leading him down a short hall to the only other room in the flat.

"Sounds delightful," he replied, stepping into the living room to grab his sporran from a side table.

She laughed softly. "We'll see if you agree in the morning. It's an American term for the smallest double bed made in this country. Tommy's mother-in-law slept in it when she lived here, and I'm fairly certain she never had any company—especially, anyone as tall as you are."

"Well, it's a good thing she never saw these," he said, pulling several condoms from the recesses of the sporran and tossing the furry thing to one side.

"I'll just take those." Fiona scooped the silver packets from his open palm and placing them on the postage-stamp bedside table. She pointed to the bed. "I wasn't kidding, Alex. You're six-feet-four. Do you think we can manage this?" she asked, laughing over her shoulder as she pulled the white cotton spread to the foot of the bed.

"We'll make do," he mumbled, capturing her from behind to clasp her by her naked waist.

He cupped a breast in each of his palms and experienced a jolt of intense excitement as he felt hard rose buds bloom under his thumbs. He scattered kisses on her neck, her shoulders, freshly-scented from the soap they'd used, and then buried his face in her hair, inhaling its intoxicating perfume. Slowly, he shunted his pelvis against her rounded backside in a gentle, rhythmic movement calculated to make them both cry out with longing.

She covered his hands, still molded to her breasts, with her own and firmly pushed back against his mid-section, matching his every move and signaling how ready she was for whatever came next.

Finally, she moaned, "Please, Alex...I want you...I want us...*please*!"

He turned her around to face him and then gently pushed her toward the bed, cradling her head as they tumbled onto the crisp sheets.

At first their kisses held a sweetness of rediscovery as their hands touched and stroked and roamed a landscape they'd not explored since Scotland nearly a year ago. Alex soon felt a shift of intensity as Fiona parted her lips and with that movement, urged him to plumb the depths of her own mounting desire.

He slipped one hand between her thighs to make certain she was moist enough to accommodate his unbridled thirst for her and then quickly made use of protection before hovering over her, reveling in her look of longing and impatience. She reached for him and raising her hips, allowed him to sink slowly into her softness with an audible sigh. He exulted in the feel of her flesh surrounding his own, her arms wound tightly around his back, holding him close.

"It's just us now, Fiona," he whispered. "No ghosts...no interlopers. We bless whoever is in charge of our fate for bringing us to this moment."

"Yes," she replied, a single tear escaping from the corner of her eye. "Yes we do..."

At first he merely reveled in the feel of her moving in response to his measured thrusts. His heart quickened as she gasped with pleasure and cried out his name.

"Alex...*Alex*," she whispered, "Please...*please*!"

And then she buried her lips in the hollow base of his neck as they both hurtled toward a longed-for release. When it burst forth, he heard her cry out again, the sound muffled against his shoulder as he, too, was overcome by wave after wave of exquisite sensation that echoed her own.

He heard her murmur her love for him, over and over, as if it were a chant that had been spoken down through the ages by those who had loved for a lifetime...and beyond.

The next morning, over a pot of steaming coffee, Fiona recounted for Alex the entire saga of her legal wrangles with the Sterling organization and her financial imperative to abandon New York, return to High Point, and in the process, help her brother stem the red ink at Fraser Furniture.

"Tommy told Sterling's lawyers to back off trying to keep me from working for my own family's firm or we would counter-sue and a lot of dirty linen would be aired."

"So they've left you alone? They paid you what they owed you?"

"Yes to both questions, but those were pretty dark days," she said soberly. "But you know...hitting bottom like that forced me to take a closer look at what I brought to the party."

"What do you mean?" Alex asked, puzzled.

"As I alluded last night, I've always been afraid to say what I felt if the other person held some sway over me, whether it was my mother or Bernard Sterling or that rat, Jared Finnegan. I knew I had to return to High Point and face my devils." Her smile was faintly rueful. "Once I got here, the devils seemed a lot tamer than I feared. Since my mother has Alzheimer's and has completely lost all memory, she actually is glad to see me whenever I visit, even if she doesn't know who I am. And my father," she said, her smile spreading to the corners of her mouth, "...well, I want you to meet my father if we have time while you're here."

"I'd like that," Alex replied, giving her hand a squeeze. "But tell me, how does such a city lass find the move back to High Point?"

"Definitely not my first choice," she said firmly, "but frankly, it was about my only option. And I *like* being a vice president," she added with a grin.

"And as VP, you ordered all that tartan yardage from

Maxwell Mills." He felt like leaping up from the table and hauling her back to bed to show his gratitude, but instead he simply said, "Thank you for that. You saved *us* from the financial abyss."

"Well, we got lucky with the mention of our footstools and ottomans in a popular shelter magazine here, so Fraser Furniture also managed to live for another day…or at least, for another couple of quarters." She gazed at him across the table-for-two that was squeezed into her equally pint-sized kitchen area. "So how *is* Maxwell Mills faring?"

"About the same as Fraser Furniture," he acknowledged. "Limping along from order to order. It's brutal out there, Fiona, as you well know. If we're going to survive, these sorts of companies have to find a better business model."

"What about All Things Scottish dot com?" she asked. "No progress on that?"

Alex shook his head regretfully. "I've done the numbers. The project needs a million and a half pounds to buy enough runway for us to launch and nourish it for a while. Look how long it took Amazon to be profitable?" he reminded her. "If I want to be the Amazon of Scottish goods, I'm going to need staying power."

"And that takes some mighty deep pockets, I know," Fiona agreed, "which sadly, we middle class folk just don't have these days."

"Well, at least the economy is picking up here and in the U.K., it seems."

"Yeah, and the vast majority of those thieving hedge fund guys and derivative traders have landed right back on their feet and are making millions," groused Fiona. Then, she brightened. "You know something? I've just had an *idea* about that, but first, let's go upstairs so I can introduced you to Tommy, Dabney, and their kids."

Alex looked mildly chagrined.

"I've already met them, actually, and they must think me a mad man."

"Really? You met them last night?"

"Well, Stella told me you'd disappeared from New York, so

I gave up trying to find you for a while. When that second order came in, I did a search for Fraser Furniture and it brought up the article in *Traditional Home* about the Maxwell tartan ottomans made by your firm. I knew, then, those had to be your designs and *my* textiles."

"No warning phone call you were on your way?" she chided gently.

"I was rather afraid you might hang up on me if I called your office land line, here, so I decided to surprise you."

"It was a surprise, all right. And the weird thing was, I had literally been thinking about you just before I heard the skirl of the pipes."

"When I finally figured out that you'd returned to North Carolina, I caught the first plane I could. The piper I found on the Internet knew right where the celebrated Fraser family home was located, so I came here first to try to find you."

"What in the world did Tommy think was going on, I wonder?" she asked, laughing with amazement.

"I rather think he was quite intrigued. Your brother and sister-in-law kindly directed me to the factory where they said you stayed far too late, far too often."

"They're right," said Fiona, pushing her chair back from the table. "Let's go upstairs and allow me to make a *proper* introduction."

Alex paused, and then asked, "As your fiancé?" He rose to his full height to stand beside her, his expression growing grave. "It's what I want for us, Fiona. This is *serious*, as far as I'm concerned. I don't want a girl friend." Fiona stared at him, dumbfounded that he should be so quick to propose marriage. "I want you as my wife. So, will you have me, lass?"

She held out her hands and drew him to her.

"Oh…Alex," she murmured, reaching up to wrap her arms around his neck and kiss him. Pulling back, she sighed. "I don't want a boyfriend either…I want *you*…but given the complications of such a bi-continental alliance, don't you think we should probably give ourselves some time to figure out how we'll manage it, before we tell the world?"

Alex nodded slowly, but his eyes reflected his disappointment.

"Alex, you don't know my family, yet, but trust me, they'll be filled with questions we don't yet know the answers to, and they're bound to peck at me like a flock of chickens, especially my brother, who's terrified right now that our company's going to go bust on his watch. For some reason, after shunning me for years, and despite some battles royal that we've had in the last nine months, he thinks that I'm his salvation."

"He thinks that because you *are* his salvation."

What Alex didn't say aloud was, *You're mine, too, Fiona.*

"Tommy will absolutely panic if he believes I'm abandoning ship at this precarious juncture."

Alex paused, and then nodded his reluctant agreement.

"Yes, I suppose we should go a bit slow until your family knows me better, since we both have the fate of our two firms and the lives of our employees as part of the equation…but I don't *like* waiting."

"I don't like it either," she concurred with another sigh. She stood on tiptoe and landed a kiss on his chin, a chaste reminder of their previous night together. Then she grinned. "But I sure like *you,* laddie mine. What do you say if I introduce you as my *serious* boyfriend?"

"Well, it's a ludicrous term for people at our age, but I guess it'll have to do for a start."

Much to Fiona's amazement, Tommy and Dabney welcomed Alex with genuine southern hospitality, apparently unfazed that the two of them came up the stairs from the basement apartment, hand in hand.

"We knew something significant was going on when your gentleman caller arrived with his own piper," Dabney teased, pouring another round of coffee as the four sat at the kitchen table with the sounds of children's laughter coming from a swing set in the back yard. "I said to Tommy, 'Mark my words, we're gonna hear more about this Scotsman.'"

Alex raised his coffee cup in salute, announcing to his hosts, "I feel I must tell you both that I *seriously* intend to court this woman while we sort out how we can make our lives work on two different continents."

Tommy, a tall, brown-haired male version of his twin sister, warned, "I'm happy to see your intentions toward my sister *and* business partner are honorable, sir."

"They are, indeed...and I think we share a lot in common, actually, given the company struggles all of us have been through these last ten years. But I've been...thinking," he said slowly, as if turning something over in his mind. "I haven't even talked this over with Fiona, yet, but would Fraser Furniture consider trying a small, joint venture between our two firms?"

"If we can find a way to finance it and not go broke, sure," replied Tommy.

"What kind of joint venture?" Fiona asked curiously.

"I'm just thinking out loud as I speak," Alex admitted, "but what if we joined forces...Fraser Furniture and Maxwell Mills...to manufacture a more extensive line of soft furnishings like Fiona created for you this year that are in the Scottish vein?"

"You mean, besides tartan upholstered footstools and ottomans?" she asked. "We'd jointly produce goods like soft-sided benches, love-seats, drapes and cushions and—"

"Upholstered dining room chairs, more padded headboards...anything and everything that could use your furniture know-how and design savvy and my top quality tartans and tweeds."

Fiona said excitedly, "We could do a scaled down version of my original idea for Sterling."

Alex nodded. "You could be the head designer of products on both sides of the Atlantic—and my mill—and the Fraser furniture plant could manufacture whatever we decided to make. The furniture items could bear the Fraser USA label, and the fabrics could say 'Woven by Maxwell Mills, Scotland.'"

"I could create all the products I dreamed of in Scotland, and more!" Fiona exclaimed, thrilled by such a prospect. She looked over at her brother and breathed a sigh of relief when he nodded with a modicum of enthusiasm.

"Given how well our first items sold, I say it's worth the gamble. Let's work out the details—and it's *all* in the details, of course," Tommy warned, "but Fiona told me your goods were the best to be found, and our success this spring proved it beyond a doubt." Tommy thrust out his hand toward Alex to seal the bargain. "I'd be honored if we could make this work—because I'm damned if I know what else to try these days."

"Well, I know it's only eleven o'clock on a Saturday mornin'," chimed in Dabney, "but don't y'all think this calls for a toast?"

"Excellent idea!" Alex exclaimed. "Wait right there!" And before Fiona knew it, he'd disappeared downstairs into her apartment. In less than a minute he reappeared with a bottle of Glenfiddich single malt whiskey and handed it to Dabney. "My house present, Mrs. Fraser," he said, "Direct to you from Scotland's Whiskey Trail."

"You are so sweet! Thank you, but please, call me Dabney! You're practically a relative, now," she said, waving the hand not holding the amber bottle that Alex had just presented her.

Fiona could feel the color rising up her neck and into her cheeks, but she didn't protest as Tommy opened the bottle and poured a half an inch of spirits into each of four shot glasses that Dabney had produced from a kitchen cupboard.

"To our joint venture," said Tommy, raising his glass.

"To our joint venture," they chorused.

In the silence that followed, Fiona gazed across the table at Alex.

"Why couldn't we also think about using our two companies to launch All Things Scottish dot com?" she said, adding, "that is, unless that's something you want to keep as your own project?" She looked embarrassed. "I'm sorry, Alex," she apologized, "I had no right even to suggest that. Your online concept has always been your own. It's just that I think it's such a great idea."

"What in the world is All Things Scottish dot com?" asked Tommy.

Alex quickly offered his hosts the same statistics he'd shared with Fiona about the millions of Scottish diaspora loyally clinging to their ethnic origins around the world.

"As I keep telling Fiona, we'd be the Amazon of Scottish goods, selling high-end items like the products you make, to everything from the best malt whiskeys like what you have in your hand, to cashmere lap rugs, to shortbread and even posh tartan dog beds. For a couple of years, now, it's always been my thought to create an online business selling all manner of top-quality Scottish goods to the millions of customers that I know exist around the globe who are Scot-o-philes."

"Scot-o-maniacs, don't you mean?" Tommy replied dryly. He looked at his wife. "You know, like Dad and Maxwell and the crazy folks who do those battle re-enactments and search for their family roots and sell scones at the Grandfather Mountain Highland Games every year."

"Exactly!" Fiona agreed. "And stop snickering!" she scolded her brother. "Those are the same demographics that bought up all those Maxwell tartan footstools this year and saved our bacon!"

Alex said, "Well, on my side of the pond, these people are the couple of million Scots and Irish who join pipe bands and Scottish country dance troops, hold kilted weddings, and attend Burns Night suppers every year. These customers buy a million yards annually of what we produce at Maxwell Mills. They're fanatics!"

"We *know* there's a powerful niche market out there," Fiona insisted to Tommy, feeling her excitement rise. "Think of the economies of scale we might have if we had operations both in Scotland and the U.S." Before her brother could raise an objection, she said, "And *yes*, Tommy, it always gets down to having the money to *access* that niche."

Before Tommy could offer a rejoinder, Alex chimed in, "I didn't mention this before, Fiona, but I've actually found a few investors in Scotland who'd put up some money for this. Just not enough."

Fiona excitedly waved her shot glass of half-consumed

whiskey. "We can try to raise more over here! This new project could eventually work in tandem with our two companies' regular, core commerce!" She looked at her brother for some sign that he could conceive of such a radical shift in their way of doing business.

"But where," Tommy demanded, his initial enthusiasm clearly waning, "are we going to raise the extra money we're going to need to *sustain* something like this until we see a decent profit from the start-up, Fee? To do it right, we should begin first by automating even more of the plant's production process, which means eliminating humans, and buying additional computer-controlled machinery, and that, my dear, will cost at least a million dollars and plenty of heartburn."

Alex shot Tommy a look of sympathy.

"You know, this is a lot for all of us to absorb, given you just met me last night. And I agree with both of you," he continued, already assuming the role of mediator between the siblings. "I think Fiona's ideas are spot on, but Tommy's also right. Shifting into such a new business paradigm is tricky and we should carefully plot our course—"

"And, again, I ask you, darling Sis," Tommy broke in, a hint of his old habit of trying to assert his authority over his twin, "where are we going to get the funds to give us the wherewithal to do any of this?" He spoke directly to Alex. "Typical female, right? All excited about the products with no idea how we're going to pay to produce them."

CHAPTER 22

Fiona felt she'd just had a mighty wind knocked out of her sails. She gazed from her brother's skeptical expression to Alex's furrowed brow, and then she heaved an exaggerated shrug. Tommy had just insulted her business acumen in front of Alex, but she knew from her past wrangles with her sibling, her best path was to resist taking umbrage at his jab.

"Now, look, Tommy. Don't go all negative on us so quickly," she said lightly. "Keep the faith, will you? Because earlier this morning I had an idea of how to raise some serious investment capital, but it will require a big, tall, muscled, enforcer-type of guy to go with me to the place where the serious money lives: New York City." Ignoring her brother, she looked directly at Alex. "And that would be *you*."

"*Fiona…*" Tommy warned, "you aren't going up there to see who I think you are, are you?"

"And who is that?" she asked innocently.

"The one person you know who has more money than God."

"Bernard Sterling?" Alex said, looking as alarmed as Tommy and Dabney.

"Oh heavens no!" she retorted. "Trust me, y'all…I am *never*, in my entire life, going to speak to B.S.—that S.O.B.!" she declared. "No…I'm going straight to the man with oodles of lovely money these days, who just happens to owe me a favor, big time."

"*Who?*" Tommy asked with undisguised skepticism.

Fiona flashed a smug grin.

"Curt Vandervort."

Alex's jaw dropped. "That Wall Street crook you told me about?"

"He never went to jail, so I don't think we can technically call him a crook."

"Your old...*boyfriend?*" Dabney asked, incredulous.

Fiona nodded.

"I had an email recently from a mutual friend that Curt's landed right on his feet selling mortgages he bundles into high-flying securities and is currently making more moolah than ever."

"Oh, boy," Tommy said, shaking his head, exchanging a worried look with Dabney. "You sure are lucky you have a lawyer for a brother."

Fiona's sister-in-law ventured nervously, "I'm not sure that asking Curt's new company to be one of your investors is such a good idea, Fee."

"I'm not planning on asking him to be an investor. I'm asking him to be our *bank*...and it's a great idea, 'cause I am going up to Yankee Land and speak Truth to Power!"

"Why in the world would he want to give *you* money?" Tommy scoffed. "After all, he dumped you for that cube-mate he married, didn't he?"

Ignoring her brother, she looked across the table at Alex. "You game for this adventure, laddie?"

Alex hesitated only an instant.

"Aye, lassie...I'm game for whatever you've got up your sleeve."

By noon, Fiona and Alex had bought airline tickets for Delta's Sunday night flight from Raleigh-Durham to JFK. Sunday morning, however, Fiona decided to pay a promised visit to her father and introduce him to Alex. They found him at his easel in the second bedroom of his condo that he'd turned into a studio. His russet hair was now a burnished gray, and his back had a noticeable curvature from both his age—nearing sixty— and a lifetime spent leaning over canvas.

After introductions, Thomas Fraser IV put down his paintbrush and regarded Alex silently for a moment.

Then he said, "Name's Maxwell, is it, now?" He shook

Alex's outstretched hand. "Well, given that every damned generation of my family has somebody called Maxwell *in* it, maybe your Maxwells have a connection with our Frasers, way back when." He looked at Fiona, adding, "You'll have to take him to meet Maxwell Simon Fraser while he's here." To Alex, he said, "My father knows all the family history. Maybe he can explain how your clan might have gotten mixed up with our Frasers back in the mists of time."

"Dad, Alex has looked into this and doesn't think there are any blood ties to our American Frasers."

Her father returned his gaze to his visitor.

"That so? Hmmm." Then he said to Fiona, "Even so, you should pay your Grandpa Maxwell a visit soon, darlin'. He's not doing well at all."

"If we have time, we'll drive over after we leave here," she agreed. "He's got the family Bible, doesn't he? Maybe he'd show it to us. There's got to be a reason why the obligation to name someone Maxwell has stuck."

Her father warned Alex, "He'll bore you rigid with all that family heritage stuff."

Fiona gave her full attention to the canvas her father had been working on before their arrival.

"That's Grandfather Mountain, isn't it?" she asked, gazing at a perfect rendition of the mile high peak in the Blue Ridge range as she remembered it from her childhood. "It's wonderful, Dad. I love it! I think it's your best work, ever."

"Why thank you, darlin', because I did it for you."

"You *did?*"

"I was remembering that time I took you to the Highland games up there when you were just a little bit of a thing…four or five, I think…and we had tea and scones and we saw a hundred pipers marching in…remember?"

Fiona looked at Alex and then at her father.

"They were playing *The Skye Boat Song*. I never forgot it," she said softly. "I came right home and demanded Mama enroll me in Scottish country dancing lessons."

He waved his paintbrush. "Such a beautiful tune." Pointing

with the wooden end, he added, "I'm not quite finished with this yet, but when I am, it's yours." Then he looked at Alex. "Do *you* like it?" he demanded suddenly.

"I do, sir," Alex said. "It reminds me of the Scottish Highlands, in fact…those craggy ranges, and the pine forest. No wonder Scottish immigrants to America decided to hold the games there all these years. It could be Glencoe or Glen Affric, or any number of places I know."

Looking pleased, Fiona's father nodded and remarked, "You know, son, my daughter's never brought a young man to meet me since…well, not for a long time."

Well…Dad finally mentions the elephant in the room…

Fiona had been surprised when virtually no one she'd reconnected with in High Point ever brought up her ill-fated marriage to Chip, and her father hadn't mentioned it once in all the months she'd been home.

Thomas Fraser swiveled on his artist's stool to face Alex, still holding his paintbrush, and gestured to him.

"If Fiona brought you here to meet me, it probably means you two likely make a lot of decisions together, and I don't want to foist a painting on you if it's not to your taste."

Fiona knew color was infusing her cheeks. She braved a glance at Alex who was grinning.

"I can think of a number of walls in Fiona's flat, or mine in Edinburgh where I'd be proud for us to hang it, right Fiona?"

She slipped her arm around her father's shoulders. "Yes. Thanks so much Dad."

Her father had a pitcher of sweet tea cooling in the refrigerator that he served them before they bid farewell so they'd have time to drive the few miles to Grandfather Maxwell's retirement home before the two of them had to head for the airport.

As they were leaving, Thomas confided, "I think that the old folks home Maxwell's in is a ghastly place, but he wanted to stay there, even after Mother died." He paused, and then said, "When you see him, tell him his wayward son says 'hello,' will you, Fee?"

Fiona kissed the top of his head. "I will Dad. And I'm excited about the painting. Thank you *so* much. It means a lot."

"To me too, darlin'…to me, too."

Fiona understood why her father hadn't liked the retirement home where Maxwell Simon Fraser currently resided. Her grandfather's one bedroom apartment was at the end of a long corridor that smelled like a hospital ward and was close to just that, as far as the sterile interiors were concerned. Every time she'd paid him a visit since she'd been home, her design sensibilities were appalled at the cheap quality furniture and harsh lighting that prevailed throughout the building. She made a mental note to order a new bedspread and curtains to make his reduced living quarters more cheerful.

"That you, Fiona?" Maxwell said, when she called his name from the doorway. "The light's putting you in silhouette and I can't see you very well. C'mon in, darlin'."

She whispered to Alex, "His eyes and hearing are pretty bad, so we won't stay very long." In a louder voice she said, "I've brought you a visitor I want you to meet."

"What's that?" he asked, leaning forward from a worn, wing-backed upholstered chair that had once resided in the house where Thomas and Dabney now lived. An empty wheelchair was parked against one wall of the small front room.

"Maxwell," she said, full-voiced, "I'd like you to meet *Alex* Maxwell. From Scotland."

"Well, well, isn't this a pleasant surprise!" the octogenarian said heartily. "A Maxwell, are you? Sit down, sit down, sir," he urged, pointing to the only other chair in the room. "What part of Scotland?"

Fiona perched on the arm of her grandfather's chair while Alex took a seat, as bidden, and explained how he was raised in the Borders but spent a good portion of his time in Edinburgh.

"We were wondering, Granddad, if you could show us the Fraser family Bible, so we could see if there is anything interesting about the first Thomas Fraser and the first Maxwell

Fraser."

Maxwell pointed an arthritic finger at a shelf under the window.

"Right over there, Fiona...that thick, leather book. You can't miss it."

Alex retrieved the heavy tome and placed it carefully on their host's knees.

"Now, let's have a look-see," Maxwell said, gingerly opening the worn cover to the front of the book. "Hmmm...where are my glasses, Fee? I can't see the page too well."

She saw a pair on the table beside his chair and handed them to him. Then, peering over one shoulder, with Alex looking over the other, Maxwell pointed to the first entry which read: "Thomas Fraser of" and then a smudge of ink, followed by "married Arabella O'Brien Delaney Boyd, 1791. Of this issue: Maxwell Fraser, b. 1791."

Maxwell chuckled. "It would seem that our Thomas Fraser married Arabella not a moment too soon!"

"Do you have a magnifying glass anywhere close by?" Fiona asked.

"Look in the middle desk drawer," Maxwell directed. "That's it. Should be in there somewhere."

Fiona thrust her hand into the clutter and soon declared, "I found it." She then eased the standing lamp nearer the wing-backed chair closer to the Bible and positioned the magnifier over the page in question.

Alex exhaled softly and said, "You can just make out a 'S...T...R...U—"

"Struy!" Fiona exclaimed. "It must be that! Thomas Fraser of Struy! It's the *Lost Lieutenant!*"

"The who?" demanded Maxwell, and then Alex and Fiona related an abbreviated version of their various efforts to confirm they were, indeed, descendants of the star-crossed lovers who had a female child together, "a lass who was raised as Lady Louisa Gordon and married General Cornwallis's son, Viscount Brome," explained Alex.

"Alex and I think that *our* American Thomas Fraser sired

out-of-wedlock Louisa by Jane Maxwell, the Fourth Duchess of Gordon—*his* ancestor," she declared, pointing at Alex. "And we've theorized that the same Thomas Fraser produced the first Maxwell Fraser by his wife in America...here," she pointed to the Bible, "the widow, Arabella O'Brien Delaney Boyd. In Edinburgh, Alex saw a portrait of Lady Louisa Gordon, who had red hair, by the way."

Maxwell chuckled. "I'll give you your Lady Louisa's red hair, and raise you one! Go back to that middle desk drawer, will you please, Fiona, and feel back to the far, right corner."

Fiona obeyed his instructions and brought forth a small, leather box whose paper hinge had come unglued.

"It's very old, so open the box carefully, Fee," he directed, "and have a look."

Both Fiona and Alex exclaimed aloud as their gazes absorbed the site of an enameled oval miniature of a young man in a crimson military jacket, Scottish blue bonnet, and a full head of wine-red hair.

"If you ever doubted your heritage, my girl, here's the proof of who your Scottish ancestor was. Thomas Fraser, who served both in the Black Watch regiment before we were even a country, and then lived in the Maryland Tidewater after the Revolutionary War where he fought for the British in the 71st Fraser Highlanders," he finished proudly. "And just look at that head of red hair. I'll bet if he'd had a dozen offspring, they'd *all* have red hair, just like your Lady Louisa and *you*!"

"I have shivers running up my spine!" admitted Fiona.

"This is amazing..." Alex murmured under his breath. More loudly he asked, "I could see that Fiona's father once had red hair. Did red hair turn up in your generation?"

"Oh, yes indeed," Maxwell said, nodding. "I only have a black and white picture of your Great Aunt Jane Belle," her grandfather told Fiona, "but she had flamin' red hair as a girl. She was a nurse...died during World War II in a jeep accident in 1944. Terrible year, that was, for the family, and for the country..."

He had a far-away look, as if fondly recalling a past Fiona

knew little about.

She asked gently, "And why do you suppose the name Maxwell was urged on subsequent generations, even though it seems as if there was no blood tie to Clan Maxwell?"

"I don't rightly know," he answered promptly. "All I was ever told is that the first Thomas Fraser made his son promise to make that name part of any generations that followed. Each father told his son or daughter, and so it went. Funny thing was...we just *did* it."

"And you knew all this other stuff about the family?" Fiona asked stunned, and wondering silently why she'd never bothered to ask him about her Fraser history all these years.

"Yes," Maxwell replied, "but nobody in the family ever seemed very interested." He pointed a forefinger to the spidery handwriting chronicling the births, deaths, marriages, and baptisms of generations of Frasers, down to the present day. "My great uncle told me the first Maxwell Fraser went way out west, for a time—as a fur trapper or some such—and then came back to the Tidewater. His descendants eventually moved to the Carolinas because the plantation they lived on went to some other male relative. They ended up here in High Point when they founded the furniture factory, always giving the Bible and that miniature portrait of the first Thomas Fraser to the eldest son for safe-keeping."

"That's amazing..." she murmured, wondering silently if he would ever entrust her father with it, given all the misunderstandings between them over the years.

"See?" he said, his gnarled finger tracing a name on the second page. "I'm Maxwell Simon Fraser, the Third, and you, of course, Fiona, are listed here with your middle name as Maxwell."

Alex spoke for the first time since the Bible had been opened.

"Look at these dates, you two. As you noted, sir," he said the Fiona's grandfather, "the first Maxwell Fraser's mother died in childbirth in 1791, so it would have been up to the father, Thomas Fraser of Struy, to name the child. I think all signs point to his honoring the memory of *my* ancestress, the apparent love of his life, Jane Maxwell, the Fourth Duchess of Gordon."

"Oh…wow…" Fiona breathed, and even her grandfather remained silent. She stared at the enameled miniature of the first Thomas Fraser she cupped in her palm, the light from a nearby window casting a glow on his red mane.

Alex said quietly, "It looks as if the Lost Lieutenant isn't lost any longer, Fiona…"

Her eyes brimming, she reached for her grandfather's hand.

"From the first day Alex and I met…nearly six years ago, now…we've felt this strange, almost other-worldly pull toward each other…"

Maxwell shifted his gaze from his granddaughter to his visitor. "Well, that was pretty obvious to *me* from the moment you two walked through my door!"

They all laughed, then, and Fiona gave his frail shoulders a hug.

"You've helped us solve a big part of the mystery. What we still don't know is if the first Thomas ever met the daughter he had sired with the Duchess. But I'm very glad to understand, now, why the name of Maxwell has been so important to our family."

Her grandfather gently took the box containing the miniature from Fiona's hand and closed it. Then he handed it back to her.

"Here, Fiona. You're the Fraser in your generation with the name Maxwell…and you've got the red hair. By all rights, this should be yours." She noted a twinkle in her grandfather's eye. "Just don't tell Thomas Quattro or Cinque I gave it to you, all right?"

"I promise, and by the way, Quattro said to me today to send you regards from your 'wayward son.'"

Her grandfather looked startled, then smiled faintly, and merely waved them farewell.

The flight to New York was uneventful, arriving at JFK just before eleven that evening. Fiona had booked into the sleek, streamlined Millenium Hilton on Church Street just a few steps from the National 9/11 Memorial in the heart of Manhattan's financial district.

As the taxi pulled up in front of the hotel a few minutes after midnight, the August temperatures felt just as muggy as they had been in North Carolina, due to a blanket of hot weather mantling the entire Eastern seaboard.

"I came to New York to go to Parsons only a few years after September eleventh," she noted to Alex as they rode the elevator up to their room. "This hotel was seriously damaged by the attacks, but solid enough to be rebuilt."

"It's odd, though," Alex said as the car reached the forty-fifth floor, "that they spell 'Millenium' with only one 'n'," he said, pointing to a poster advertising the hotel's restaurant. "We spell it 'Millennium.' Is that a British versus American thing?"

Fiona laughed. "No...we spell the word your way. Must be a marketing thing. We're going to have to learn all that kind of stuff when we launch All Things Scottish, won't we?"

Alex gave her a look. "You sound pretty confident we're going to secure the funds."

"Of course I am," she replied airily, though privately all she could do was hope she could play the one card she held when it came to Curt Vandervort.

The elevator doors opened and the heretofore-silent bellhop showed them to their room with its stunning view of the reconfigured World Trade Center.

"Here you are, folks," he said, pulling open the drapes on the other window in the room with spectacular vista over lower Manhattan. "You're surrounded by the neighborhoods of SoHo, Tribeca and the Village, and close to the Statue of Liberty at the mouth of the Hudson River." He eyed their sparse amount of luggage and added with a barely concealed leer, "Well, folks, even if you don't do much sight-seeing, enjoy yourselves."

Alex tipped him and the pair waited until the door was closed before they both burst out laughing, falling into each others' arms with Alex murmuring into Fiona's hair, "Trust me, laddie, we *do* plan to enjoy ourselves tonight."

The following morning, Fiona sat at the desk overlooking the breathtaking view and tried the last number she'd had for Curt Vandervort. Using the hotel phone, after a few rings all she got was an innocuous, preprogrammed message restating the telephone number and the request to leave word. She hung up quickly without stating her name or business.

"He's probably already at the office," Fiona mumbled. "Those financial guys get into work at the crack of dawn when the London markets open." She punched the buttons again for Curt's new office, a number that she'd tracked down—along with the name of the company he'd founded—through another refugee from Curt's former firm whom Fiona had once known casually.

Again, she heard a recorded message delivered by a well-spoken female saying, "This is Curt Vandervort's line of V and S Mortgages Securities. He is either away from his desk…or in a meeting. Leave word here, and he'll call you when he can."

Before the phone could beep, Fiona again hung up quickly.

"He'll never call me back," she predicted. "He'll probably assume that my getting in touch with him only means trouble, which it does," she added with a short laugh. She remained silent for a moment and pondered what to do next.

Alex remained at the window surveying the view. "Well, I guess the only thing for it is to ambush him at his place of business."

"I like your thinking, partner!"

They swiftly dressed in their most business-like attire and made the short walk the few blocks to Curt's new office. It was housed in one of the rebuilt skyscrapers that had also survived the 9/11 attacks well enough to be revamped into a high-tech, all steel-and-glass silo filled with an army of financial kingpins and their support troops.

The innocuous-sounding V & S Mortgage Securities was

housed on the 57th floor, but when they walked through the revolving glass door into the downstairs lobby, the uniformed guard standing a few feet inside the building immediately approached them.

"You'll need to get a security pass at the concierge desk," he said, pointing to a bank of similarly attired guards who apparently would issue the necessary documentation to pass through a checkpoint at the bottom of a lengthy, slanted escalator that took the anointed to the second floor elevator bank.

Fiona gave a slight shake of her head and said to Alex, "Oh, darn! I forgot my portfolio in the cab! Let's try to catch it!" and they quickly exited through the revolving door they'd just entered. Once back outside where the temperature hinted of another stifling New York day, Fiona was plunged in gloom.

"There's no way he would okay our coming up to his office." Unable to mask her frustration, she asked, "Now what do we do?"

Alex stood beside her on the curb, silent while he appeared focused on the traffic passing by. Then he turned and said, "I suppose I could stand it one more time."

"Stand what, one more time?"

"Wearing my bloody kilt in this bloody, hot weather. And, if you give me a few hours, I'll bet I could locate that piper from five years ago…or somebody like him."

"And do what?" she asked him with a puzzled gaze.

"We've got to get past that electronic shield in there, right? Well, here's my idea how we might, possibly, do it."

When Fiona heard the details of his plan, she threw her head back and laughed so hard, her eyes ran.

When she could finally talk, she said, "This actually might be fun."

Alex could only imagine what people on the street outside Curt Vandervort's latest place of business must have thought of the costumed trio hesitating at the entrance to the towering office building in lower Manhattan this stiflingly hot day.

Fiona's arms were filled with four dozen long-stemmed red roses that looked quite stunning against the bright red Stewart tartan gown she'd rented from a nearby costume shop, complete with long skirt, petticoats, boned bustier, and daring décolletage.

Standing beside her was the raw-boned teenage son of a bagpiper recruited from the local St Andrew's Society. The scrawny youth had a day's growth of beard, a rumpled shirt and wrinkled kilt, and his father's set of bagpipes under his arm. Roger Ferguson was only present by dint of the hundred-dollar bill already tucked into his sporran.

Alex's heavy kilt lay against his perspiring thighs and for the first time in his life, he wished he hadn't gone "commando," and, instead, was wearing a pair of Bermuda shorts to protect his bare torso from the itchy wool.

One by one, they filed through the revolving glass door, garnering curious looks every step of the way as they approached the sleek, marble-topped concierge desk where a new team of guards looked up briefly at the sound of their approach, and then did a double take.

"And how may I help you folks?" asked one, a smile playing at the corners of his lips.

Fiona waved her bundle of roses and a small box tied with a tartan ribbon, replying, "We're from All Things Scottish dot com and are scheduled to deliver these as a surprise for…"

Alex was highly amused by the way his co-conspirator made a show of glancing down at a slip of paper she held in her hand. "For Mr. Curt Vandervort from Ms. Heather McGinnis…"

"All three of you going up?" asked the guard. Fiona nodded. "Well then, I'd better give them a call to let them know you're on your way."

As he reached for the phone Fiona cried, "Oh, don't do that! It's a *surprise!*" She lowered her voice, "Ms. McGinnis is…well…ah…a…*special* friend of Mr. Vandervort and she wants this to be a surprise for his birthday. She hired us to deliver the roses and a gift and we'll catch it, big time, if we screw this up."

"Then I'll have to inspect all that, I'm afraid, if I let you go up, unannounced."

Fiona obediently handed him the roses, along with a small, turquoise box. The guard, whose nameplate read "Jose Querillo," gave a cursory inspection of Roger's bagpipes and Fiona's bouquet of flowers. Next, he untied the tartan ribbon, lifted the box's lid, peered inside, and blushed under his tan. Nestled in the confines of the package was a collection of condoms in silver packets. The guard replaced the lid and handed it back, along with the length of ribbon.

Alex observed Fiona coloring with embarrassment, which he knew could only convince the guards they were legitimate. He could barely suppress a grin when she stammered, "I-I had no idea that's what was in this little box! I thought it was probably—"

"Just go on…go on!" Jose said, also embarrassed. He pointed at the bagpipes. "But do you mind not playing those things until you're *inside* the offices of V & S?"

"Thank you, sir," she said, flashing him her broadest smile. To Alex and their bagpiper she said, "Let's go. I wanna get this over with. I'm about to *die* in this corset!"

CHAPTER 23

The three interlopers remained silent in the elevator heading for Curt Vandervort's floor while the only other passenger studiously regarded the lighted numerals flashing overhead with nary a glance at his uniquely attired fellow riders. Fiona handed her flowers to Alex and swiftly retied the ribbon on the small box the guard had inspected downstairs.

At the 57th floor, Alex lifted his blue bonnet and said, "G'day" to the man in the pin-stripped suit who barely acknowledged his farewell greeting as their party trod onto the lobby's plush carpet of V & S Mortgage Securities. On the wall in front of them, the company name and logo was emblazoned in large, chrome letters behind yet another desk, but this time, the gatekeeper was a very comely blonde in her early twenties.

She took in the sight of the visitors and broke into a smile.

"Well…this is sure different!" She giggled and gave Alex the once over. "What can I do for you?"

On cue, Fiona held up the flowers and beribboned present.

In a hoarse whisper she said, "We're from All Things Scottish dot com…the Birthday Surprise Division and…we're here to deliver a present to Curt Vandervort from his girlfriend."

"Girlfriend?" repeated the receptionist, her tone suddenly chilly. "I thought he was *married.*"

Fiona affected a shrug and consulted the slip of paper she'd referred to downstairs. "That's what it says here: deliver this to Heather McGinnis' boyfriend, Curt Vandervort at V and S Mortgage Securities."

With a roll of her eyes, the receptionist shook her head and pressed a buzzer.

"Go right through," she said, pointing a well-manicured finger toward a glass door to their right. "His is the corner office at the end of the hall."

Once the door closed behind them, the three silently strode along a corridor the length of half a football field. A few office doors were open, revealing both men and women staring at computer screens and talking quietly into their phones.

The door to the corner office was open only a crack. Alex could tell by the deep breath Fiona inhaled that she was suddenly very nervous, but she gamely gave Curt's door a knock and led her confederates into the inner sanctum of "Curt Vandervort, President of V&S Mortgage Securities," as it said on the nameplate. For a long moment their quarry continued to speak on his telephone and finally looked up just as Alex shut the door.

"What's going on here?" Curt demanded brusquely, and then, recognizing Fiona, he said into the phone, "Gotta call you later. Something's come up." The young tycoon, whose polished blond looks gave him the appearance of a tennis pro, shifted his gaze to Alex and the scruffy-looking bagpiper. "Okay, Fiona. Why are you here? Who are these guys? And why are you dressed in that ridiculous getup?"

"No 'hello?' No 'nice to see you?'" she queried sweetly, advancing further into his office. "No, 'how have you been, Fiona, since I two-timed you the entire six months we were together and then skipped out without a word?'"

"I paid you the money I owed you on our apartment lease," he said belligerently, and Alex felt like heaving Curt's trim frame across the room like a caber toss.

"Yes, I did receive your check for your half of the apartment lease. Thank you."

The head of V&S Mortgage Securities blinked, startled, it appeared, by Fiona's calm politesse. Then he recovered his arrogant air and said, "You made it so easy for me when I bailed that I got the impression you were just fine with the way things turned out."

"Actually, I am—now," Fiona replied. "But I didn't give you any trouble then because I was shocked and humiliated by your behavior and didn't have the guts to tell you so."

Curt's gaze wavered and he shuffled a few papers on his desk.

"Well...I had a lot going on in my life in 2008. Sorry."

She cocked her head, looking at him steadily.

"The Feds nearly nailed you, didn't they? Good thing they didn't come talk to *me* after that first time they contacted me since I knew almost as much about what you were doing to churn those derivatives as your saucy little cube-mate, didn't I? I just didn't understand then—as I do *now*—that the work you were doing practically caused the global meltdown all by itself."

Curt remained silent, picking up and putting down on his desk his gold-plated Montblanc fountain pen.

Fiona set the large bundle of roses and the wrapped box of condoms on the floor near Curt's desk and pulled up a chair opposite her prey. Alex remained standing with his arms crossed on his chest and nodded to the piper who he'd instructed to maintain silence and stand close to the door.

"I'll get right to the point," Fiona said, and Alex was relieved to see she didn't seemed rattled by seeing her former flat-mate. "I'm here to ask for a loan."

"You're *what*?"

Before Curt could protest her cheek, Fiona launched into her prepared pitch, practiced many times in their hotel at the Millenium Hilton, finishing, "So, given how low a profile I kept when the Feds were looking into your activities as a derivatives trader, I figured you might be of a mind to do *me* a good turn as a little 'thank you' present."

"Are you blackmailing me?" Curt demanded. "Because, if you are...?"

Fiona looked at him, steely-eyed. "You'll do what? I happen to know that you haven't been living with your alibi-wife for months, but as long as you and that lil' ol' cube-mate are legally wed, you two remain each other's protection. As for me," she said with a faint smile, "you remember my twin brother, the lawyer? He advises me that there are still two years to run before you hit the seven-year-statute-of-limitations-you're-home-free mark. I certainly don't see why we can't find a way to…ah…cooperate with each other, do you?" She grinned. "And besides, our idea is a winner and you have an excellent chance of getting all your money back, along with an above-prime rate of interest that we're prepared to pay you."

"I don't need a good rate," Curt snapped. "I'm rich again—or haven't you heard?"

"So my sources tell me," she replied. "All the more reason you don't want all that lovely money to go away…*again*."

Curt's phone began to ring insistently. He ignored it, while Alex could see he was turning over Fiona's proposition in his mind.

"What if I made an *investment* in this start-up of yours? Took a percentage and sat on the board?"

"We don't want an active investor," Alex spoke up. "We're simply asking for a loan."

Curt turned his attention to Alex who was gratified to note that, in his heavy Scottish brogues, he was at least a head-and-a-half taller than their quarry.

Curt paused, and then asked tersely, "How much money are we talking about here?"

Fiona spoke up first. "Two and a half million dollars."

Alex was amazed when that dollar figure produced no visible reaction from Vandervort.

Chump change to this lad…

From her bustier, Fiona pulled out a rolled-up legal document with a blue cover.

"As I said, I'm sure you remember my talking about my twin before? Thomas Fraser…the *Fifth*?" she said with studied emphasis. "The one who might run for DA, down home? Well, he's prepared these documents for you to sign. You loan us the money from your personal account, and we'll guarantee we'll pay you back in seven years—or the dot com business will be yours."

To Alex's astonishment, Curt silently reached for the document, skimmed it as Fiona waited patiently, and then looked up.

"I could call Security, you know. Get you three tossed out in five minutes."

"But you won't," Fiona replied, pointing to the signature line. "What we're doing here is totally in everybody's best interest, and you know it. Just sign, Curt, and you'll never have to deal with us again…"

"And what's the guarantee of that?"

Fiona sat up straighter in her chair. "Because I'm a women of my word. I don't even betray *former* friends." Curt remained silent and stared at his gold-tipped pen on the desk. Fiona said, "We'll wait while you go online to make the transfers."

Vandervort hesitated only a moment, then picked up his pen that Alex reckoned cost at least five hundred pounds sterling, and signed. He looked up, a puzzled expression on his face.

"You've changed, Fiona. Not so eager to please, now, are you?"

"You noticed."

He nodded in Alex's direction.

"The new boyfriend?"

"The new business partner. And fiancé—in that order."

Alex couldn't have been happier to be so described. His thoughts leapt to the top drawer in his bureau at The Firs where he'd stored his late mother's jewelry, but kept his gaze steady as Curt swiveled in his high-back leather desk chair to give the interloper a closer look.

To Alex's surprise, the bloody bastard said, "Lucky guy," and appeared to mean it.

"That I am," Alex offered. "Luckier than I ever dreamed."

Fiona then retrieved the signed document and handed Curt a slip of paper with the bank routing numbers for Fraser Furniture, Maxwell Mills, plus a third account they'd set up under the name All Things Scottish. Then they waited in silence while he keyed into his online bank accounts on his desktop computer.

"Deposit a million, each, in the first two accounts, and the half million in the dot com," Fiona instructed him, *sotto voce*.

"Hey! I thought this loan was for a start-up, only!"

"It is, but thanks to the financial crisis *you* helped create, small firms like ours need an infusion of cash to keep our two principal businesses going that will then support our efforts for our new online enterprise. It's just the way we've structured this effort so we won't run out of runway before All Things Scottish is on a firm footing."

Curt regarded the two of them with grudging admiration.

"Okay," he said finally, typing in the instructions to his bank. "That plan makes sense. Knowing diligent *you*, Fiona, I might get this money back, after all."

While Curt continued to affect the cash transfers to the three accounts, Alex watched without further comment while Fiona fished her mobile phone out of a pocket in her skirt and keyed in the name and password for her family firm's bank account.

Curt had just logged out of his bank's website when Fiona said, "Bingo! The funds just landed in the Fraser account." Then she quickly checked the two other accounts, smiled to see the figures change, and closed down her portable device, stowing it swiftly in her skirt pocket. "Thank you very much." She leaned down and scooped up the roses and the wrapped present, then stood up from her chair while Alex stepped forward to serve as her escort.

Curt also stood and said, "Well…it's been very…interesting to see you again, Fiona." He looked at the flowers. "Don't I get those?"

Fiona gave a short laugh and pulled one long stem from her pile and laid it on the desk. "It's the least I can do." She thrust out her hand to shake his, symbolically sealing the deal. "You may not believe this, Curt, but you *will* get your money back within the time limit."

Alex felt a strange stab of what he could only assume was unfounded jealousy when she smiled at their Mr. Moneybags with genuine warmth. He almost thought he detected a note of sincere regret when Curt replied, "I know you'll do your best, Fiona. That's why I gave in to this ridiculous ploy of yours. As you said, you did me a good turn by not volunteering what you know to the feds…and you never tried to turn my…my sudden marriage to Christiane into a big drama, given everything that was going on."

"Nor did I call them about your new, best squeeze, Anastasia Volmensky."

Curt reared his head with surprise, but merely said, "Well thank you for that, too."

Fiona nodded, and Alex could tell she was thinking about the unhappiness Curt Vandervort had repeatedly caused her. She said quietly, "Those days were pretty awful so it's decent of you to acknowledge that, actually. Thanks."

Curt seemed to recover his usual cynicism when he said, "Well, business is booming. I guess I can afford to be generous."

"That's a good way to look at it, Curt," Fiona replied with a faintly mocking smile. "And I appreciate it more than you know." She cradled the signed documents around the stems of the roses and turned to leave.

Alex nodded at the piper who had watched the proceedings slack-jawed.

"Okay, Roger…shall we allow Mr. Vandervort a chance to get on with his day? May we have *The Soldier's Retreat,* 4-4 march time, please?"

The piper gave the bag under his arm a firm squeeze, producing a loud, dissonant wail that caused Curt to cover his ears with his hands. After a few more whines from the pipes, Roger began the first notes of the sprightly tune as Alex opened the office door for them and led the way down the office corridor. Curt's startled colleagues began to appear at their doors as the threesome made its way down the long hallway to the small lobby of Curt's company.

When the trio reached the reception desk next to the elevators, Alex summoned a car to their floor. The elevator doors were just sliding open when Fiona suddenly turned to her left and presented the four-dozen roses-minus-one to the young woman who had buzzed them through to Curt's wing of the building.

Over the wail of the pipes she shouted, "Please accept these with our sincerest compliments. Without you, none of this would have happened!"

The receptionist appeared dumbfounded but held out her arms to receive the colorful bounty.

Once in the elevator, the pipes fell silent. The threesome rode down fifty-seven floors while Alex pulled two one-hundred dollar bills out of his sporran.

"This," he said to Roger, "is your bonus for playing the pipes, and this," he continued, "is for taking a Scottish oath you will *never* reveal what you just witnessed, understood?"

Roger's eyes grew wide at the sight of such riches that Alex tucked into the teenager's cheap, leather sporran.

"Thank you, sir," he said. "And I swear on my Grandma McGann's grave I won't ever breathe a word, not even to my dad."

"Good lad," Alex said, clapping him on the shoulder. "And you wouldn't be wanting him to know you played truant from school, today, would you now?"

"*Noooo*, sir!"

Once outside the skyscraper, Roger headed down the entrance to the subway while Fiona put her fingers in her mouth like the seasoned New Yorker she'd become and whistled for a cab heading their way.

Once settled in the back seat heading back to their hotel Alex quickly scanned the signed document Fiona had handed him and asked with a grin. "By the way, what did you do with that little box of condoms?"

Fiona smiled smugly and patted the other pocket in her voluminous skirt. "Why darlin' why in the world would we waste them? Got 'em right in here."

Later, in their room at the Millenium, Alex and Fiona shed their Scottish attire and donned the thick, Turkish robes supplied by the hotel while they shared a twenty-dollar BLT sandwich and a beer, delivered by room service. Alex was jubilant.

"You were amazing...ah-mazing!" he chortled. "You played hardball with that eejit, and used what you knew to take care of yourself and not get ground into little bits by that bloody bastard!"

She bowed her head modestly. "I like that word 'eejit.' It means 'idiot,' right?"

"But in Curt's case, he wasn't a *stupid* sort of eejit, and you were stellar in how you dealt with him."

"'Truth to Power,'" she quoted herself. She paused and rested her chin on her hand. "You know, Alex...I owe you an apology."

"For what?" he asked, appearing mystified at the turn in their conversation.

"I *finally* understand why you pretended to be the wounded party to your former father-in-law. Like what we did today, we needed to take action to protect our interests and save the jobs of the people who work for us. What we decided to do didn't hurt anyone because we fully *do* intend to repay Curt. And, in the case of ending your marriage the way you did, you helped Addy find happiness with Peter, at last. I should never have thrown that in your face. I'm so sorry."

Alex nodded. "You're forgiven. And let's not forget, what I did also served *me* in a good way. It allowed me to leave a marriage that I should never have permitted to take place, and do that with a modicum of grace."

Fiona said bleakly, "I wish I'd known how to say 'no' to my mother when she pressured me into a marriage with Chip..."

"Lessons learned, I guess."

"Better late than never..."

Alex gazed across the table that the waiter had wheeled into their room. "To my mind, there's nothing wrong with looking after ourselves if—as you say, we don't do damage to anyone else. Curt Vandervort's a very wealthy snake, and not one I'd want to be in business with as an investor, but he'll get his money back, if all goes well."

"No harm, no foul," Fiona agreed, taking a sip from their communal beer glass.

Alex nodded. "You had every right to extract some assistance from the bloke after the way he hurt you and left you to clean up the mess he'd made. He gave us a no-strings-attached loan...and as we found out, he could well afford it."

Fiona grinned. "I felt like we were Robin Hood and Maid Marian on steroids, didn't you?"

"A wee bit, and bravo us!" Alex responded, retrieving the beer glass to hold it high in a toast. He handed it back to her for another sip. "You know, though...there's something we haven't talked about, yet."

Fiona shot him a wary look.

"What?"

"That I still owe *you* an apology." In response to her quizzical gaze he said, "As you no doubt remember, I was pretty upset when you told me in the kitchen at The Firs that you were leaving so abruptly to go back to New York with Sterling and you hadn't revealed precisely what was going on with Andrew Wu and company."

"I know," she said regretfully. "Alex, I—"

"Like a blooming infant," he continued, overriding her response, "I wrongly accused you of using me during your time in Scotland and made the unfair parallel to the situation with Chip Reynolds."

"You already apologized for that when you first arrived, remember?"

"Yes, but the truth is, I *did* allow Addy to shoulder all the blame for our divorce and you were right to call me on it after I'd upped the ante by linking what was going on with us to the decisions you made regarding what happened with Chip. I know I mentioned that the first day I saw you again, but it still bothers me that I said that. It wasn't my finest hour."

Fiona remained silent a long moment before she replied.

"Look, Alex. There was actually a grain of truth in what you said about taking the money from Chip's parents, which is why it hurt me so much. And it's weird," she mused, almost as if to herself. "Getting Curt to cough up a two-and-a-half-million-dollar loan today felt totally different from the deal Chip's parents made with me—and that I accepted.

"Well, even so," Alex responded. "My only explanation for

how poorly I handled things that day is that I had this rather irrational feeling that you were...well...abandoning me and I'd never see you again. Not very manly, I must say, but it was a sensation unlike anything I'd ever experienced."

"Oh, Alex, you are the most manly creature I ever—"

Alex interrupted her. "Wait," he said urgently. "I want you to really hear this, and—hopefully—not think me completely mad."

Fiona remained silent and gave a small nod to indicate she was listening.

"After you left and months went by with no communication, either way, I began to have disturbing dreams about you running away from me, but the setting was from a long, long time ago...as in *really* long ago."

"What do you mean...were you dreaming in another century, or something?"

Alex described the part of his dream that took place in the stone cottage and then told her about standing on the banks of a loch watching a redheaded woman disappear into the castle keep.

"When I lost sight of her—of *you*—I was filled with a kind of anguish I've never felt in my life! My thoughts as I swam to consciousness were that all was hopeless...that life was hardly worth living...that I'd lost you."

"Oh, sweetheart..." she murmured, her eyes filled with sympathy.

"And here's the...bizarre part," he said soberly. "Later I confirmed that there *is* such a loch in the Highlands with a tiny island and castle in the middle—and you'll never guess exactly where it's located."

"Where?" Fiona asked, her eyes wide.

"Adjacent to lands owned by the Fourth Duke of Gordon in that day."

"Oh...my...God," she murmured.

Alex nodded. "My reaction, exactly. Think of it! It's as if I fell into some sort of time warp. I dreamt about a place *I'd* never seen except on a postcard when I was a boy and it actually *exists*. And I think those dreams were another reason I hesitated to call you to try to sort all this out. The fear that some terrible cycle of fate had us in its grip in a way I didn't understand and that I'd lost you, forever, like Jane had lost Thomas, so there was no point trying to get you back. It all seemed so real..."

"But you came to High Point," she said, puzzled.

Alex nodded. "Well, on my end, I nearly went crazy. Then it finally dawned on me that the second big order for the Maxwell tartan was *you* sending me a signal that you missed me as much as I missed you. Or at least I gambled on that being true..."

"And oh, how I missed you!" She rose and stood behind him where he'd remained sitting in the chair next to the rolling table brought in by room service. She wrapped her arms around his shoulders, bestowing little kisses on the back of his neck. "And I'm not going anywhere, Alex Maxwell," she murmured against his skin, "except to take a long hot bath in the next room. Want to come with me?"

Alex folded his arms over hers.

"I give you fair warning, I'm not *ever* letting you go, again." Alex could feel her arms, draped around his shoulders, tense slightly. He cocked his head to one side to look at her. "What?" he demanded.

"Tommy—when he has time to think about what's happening with you and me—is not going to be happy. He's going to want me to be in High Point helping him run Fraser Furniture. And I can't quite picture your wanting to live in High Point..."

"Look, it'll take some doing, but we can figure this out."

"But how can I just leave everything and live with you in Scotland?" she protested, releasing her hold of his shoulders and walking toward the window.

"Fiona!" he said more sharply than he intended. "You've forgotten one important factor."

"What?" she asked, keeping her back to him.

"What is it *you* want?"

She turned, her expression filled with worry.

"I-I don't know. I just want *everyone* to be happy."

"Fiona!" he repeated, unable to keep his frustration from

showing. "You are so *un*accustomed to thinking what's in your own interest!"

She walked toward him and held out her hands. "Well one thing I have learned," she said, "is that *you* definitely have my interests at heart."

"That I do," he replied, wondering bleakly if, in the end, he would lose her to the pull of family obligations.

Then, she framed his face with her hands.

"Look, Alex, I don't know exactly how we'll make this work, but we will. C'mon…take a bath with me."

Relieved, he seized her hand and propelled her toward the brightly lit, marble-tiled bathroom. Pausing at the door, he pointed at the bathroom fixtures.

"This isn't the Royal Scots Club or The Firs. I doubt we'll both fit in that tub."

Fiona reached in and turned on the taps to the shower.

"Shall we try this, instead?" she asked with a come-hither smile, and they both knew they were trying to forget the complicated issues that confronted them.

Fiona began to shed her own clothing, and Alex did likewise. He was the first to gingerly step into the shower stall and extended her a hand. She immediately put her mane of red hair under the cascading water.

"Here, let me do that," he said, taking the little bottle of hotel shampoo from her hand and gently rubbing its contents into her hair, producing a rich lather.

"Mmmm…" she murmured, eyes closed. Then she raised her arms to work the soap more deeply into her scalp.

Alex couldn't help himself. He cupped each of her beautifully rounded breasts and gently massaged them as water poured down on them both. For a long moment, there was silence as he continued his explorations while Fiona kept her head under the shower and rinsed the soap out of her hair. Then, laughing, she stepped aside.

"You're turn, laddie mine," she said, allowing him to enjoy the gush of liquid warmth spilling down his frame, and before long, their soapy hands were pleasuring each other until they both were breathless with desire.

Fiona gently seized the evidence of his arousal and repeated the gentle massage he'd given her breasts. She smiled when he groaned and leaned against the white tiles.

"This will let you know you aren't still dreaming, Alex," she said with a throaty laugh. "This is the twenty-first century, may I remind you, and I'm going to prove to you that there is no way I'm going to disappear before I've had my way with you."

Alex's eyes were closed and he only managed a tiny nod of agreement.

Yet in a small recess of his brain, he wondered what choices Fiona would ultimately make? How strong would she have to be to counteract a lifetime of giving in to the demands of the hard-charging, high-energy Thomas Fraser V?

CHAPTER 24

Later, when they were dried off and were luxuriating under the crisp hotel bed sheets, Alex traced his forefinger along the ridge of Fiona's perfectly proportioned nose.

"I've been thinking," he said. "How about coming to Scotland during September to strategize about the furniture collections we'll do as a joint venture? Then, we can take some time together to create the content architecture for our online project?"

Fiona turned and smiled, her delight at his proposal obvious. "Oh…Scotland in September…" she said, exhaling a long breath. "What a fabulous idea!"

"And, as you saw last year, there's nothing lovelier than autumn in Edinburgh."

"But what do we do after that?" she said with a slight frown.

"Perhaps you'll invite me to bask in the warmth of a North Carolina winter?"

She stared at him, her face only inches away. "You'd do that?" she marveled. "You'd spend time in High Point with me?"

"In the winter when there's only about five hours of daylight in Scotland? That I would."

Fiona laughed. "Well, I hope you're not expecting a climate as warm as Florida, but it would be a heck of a lot sunnier than Scotland in the winter. But what about the mill?"

"I've been thinking about making Hugh Erskine a junior partner in the firm," he said, his thoughts still working out an idea he'd just had. "He's perfectly capable of running the place from November through…say…March, with plenty of daily consultation from me via text, email, and Skype."

"Do you honestly think we can *do* this?" she whispered.

"Can we actually pull off this bi-continental hat trick?"

"If that's what you want, Fiona."

"Oh, I do!" Then she sobered. "But we just have to convince Tommy it would work. He's been hinting that he wants to run for District Attorney because he assumes he can now turn Fraser Furniture over to *me* to manage." Then she brightened. "Well, as you have demonstrated time and time again, we just have to find a solution that has something good in it for everyone."

Alex reached for her, pulling her hard against the length of his body and inhaling the sweet fragrance of her freshly washed hair.

"You are the most loving, generous woman on the planet, do you know that?" he whispered into her ear. He felt her chuckle, her lips against his neck.

"A wanton, I expect I'd be called in Jane Maxwell's day."

"And I imagine that Thomas Fraser of Struy would have loved every second of what just happened in the shower," he said, scattering kisses all over her head.

"Alex?"

"Hmmmm…"

"We still don't know exactly how it all ended with Thomas and Jane, do we?" she reminded him. "Once he left Scotland to live permanently in America, was that the end of it, finally? And did he ever know he had a daughter?"

Alex rose to one elbow, leaned forward, and kissed her lips, the loving look in her eyes making his heart turn over.

"I'll tell you on the plane about everything I've learned, lately, but I think another trip to the Register House is in order—only this time, you're coming *with* me. Meanwhile," he whispered, blowing gently against her ear, "come closer, lass…there's something else on my mind right now…"

As Fiona feared, when she called Tommy from New York, her brother was not at all happy to hear his sister had airline reservations to fly to Scotland.

"But I need you *here*, Fiona," he said over the phone. "I have plans to go to the county Democratic caucus next week."

"Well, what would you have done a year ago, before I moved home?" she demanded, relieved that Alex had gone down to the lobby's concierge desk to arrange the airport shuttle to JFK.

There was silence on the other end of the phone. Then he said, "I would only have gone a day or two, instead of staying for the entire thing."

"Well? See? You can manage, and it's important to the overall enterprise that Alex and I plan exactly what fabrics he's going to make to upholster the furniture you and I want to produce this year."

"You could do all that by phone and computer," Tommy charged, and she could almost picture his face in a sulk.

"But I don't want to do it that way. I need to be there…to see the colors of the yarns and to get a feeling for—"

"You just want to 'be there' so you can *be* with that guy."

Fiona could feel her blood pressuring begin to rise.

"Look, Tommy…this is not some 'guy'—this is Alex Maxwell, we're talking about. The man I love and the man I want to be with. Our *business* partner. You're going to have to trust us to do what's best for all of us and cut us some slack while we figure out what that might be."

Silence.

Fiona tried to keep her temper in check, but couldn't resist saying, "Hey! You saw that million dollars fall into the Fraser Furniture account, didn't you? Alex and I haven't done too badly, thus far."

"Money from an *old* boyfriend so you can launch a company with your *new* boyfriend? That must not have been very hard."

Fiona felt her fast intake of breath. This was the punishing Tommy of their youth and she was shocked that he reverted so quickly to that habit when he didn't get his way.

In a low voice she said, "If you want me to stick around and partner with *you* in the furniture company, you've got to stop saying crap like that to me. And I certainly hope you don't speak to our other women employees like that!"

"Fiona, that's not the point!" he retorted.

"That's exactly the point," she replied heatedly, "and if you don't want me to bail on you and High Point, you'd better find a way to treat me with a little bit more respect, do you understand, or you won't get *my* vote if you run for DA. We're not fifteen anymore, Tommy! Just cut it out!"

Again, silence.

Fiona heaved a sigh of frustration and said, "Well, gotta go. I hope you'll think about what I just said. I'll email or text you from Scotland this week so we can get started on the new collection that's gonna dig us out of this hole our company has been wallowing in for years. Bye now, and remember, bro…I love you. Y'all take care, y'hear?"

With a supreme effort not to hang up on him, she gently set the phone receiver in its cradle and wondered how in the world she and Alex could make all this work?

⁂

The British Airways Boeing 747-400 took off from New York in the late evening for Heathrow, with a connecting flight to Edinburgh, with Alex and Fiona onboard in the Economy section.

"At six-feet-four, aren't you in agony in these seats?" Fiona demanded looking at Alex's long legs bent nearly double behind the seat in front of him. "I'm five-eight and I'm finding this not really a lot of fun."

"Oh, yes it is," he whispered, leaning over to kiss the ear nearest him. "Just think how much we're going to appreciate our bed at the Edinburgh flat tonight. And besides, until we begin to show a profit in our various ventures, we'd better keep a close count of our farthings. You must remember, Fiona, you're with a true Scot, now."

"Hmmmm…" she murmured, snuggling her head against his shoulder. "I hope Tommy appreciates our sacrifice."

Fiona had immediately told Alex about her difficult conversation with her brother and had been relieved when it didn't appear to upset him very much.

"Ah...brothers," he'd replied. "Brothers in business. Not always the easiest thing, but we'll work it through."

The plane had leveled off from its climb out of New York airspace when Alex fished a piece of paper from his inside jacket pocket.

"Before you conk out, love, I've been meaning to show you this ever since I got it."

"Hmmm? What?" she asked, and sat up straighter in her uncomfortable seat.

"This might wake you up. It's a copy of the Duchess of Gordon's obituary that appeared in the newspapers in 1812. My wonderful researcher, Isabelle Larimore, found it deep in the bowels of the Register House records and emailed it to me today. It answers many of the questions we've been asking ourselves for a year."

Alex then related what he'd learned from the documents that Alex's hired researcher had found.

"It was tragic really," Alex said, "to read the lawyer's account of the Duke deciding to cut off all his wife's funds toward the last quarter of Jane's life."

"That's terrible he did that! What a jerk!" Fiona retrieved the obituary from Alex's hand. "It sounds as if the duke was determined to punish poor Jane."

Alex nodded. "Perhaps he knew that the redheaded child, Louisa, living in his own household, wasn't sired by him? That *would* be upsetting."

"Well, maybe *Jane* was upset about the housemaid in Gordon Castle serving as the duke's mistress all those years!" she retorted. "Or maybe Jane didn't care any more if her husband knew she'd been sleeping with Thomas before he'd left to fight for the British in the American Revolution."

"Military records show Thomas made it back from that war, so perhaps he and Jane saw each other after that and the duke found out about it."

Fiona nodded, her eyes scanning the copy of Jane Maxwell's obituary once again. She said, "But how heartbreaking for Jane it must have been to find that note from Thomas telling her—after all their meetings and partings—he'd finally given up on their ever being together and would emigrate to America?"

"Well," said Alex, nodding, "without telegraph or phones or mobile phones, of course, there was no other way to communicate. You said it a year ago, remember? If there had been cell phones then, history might have been written differently."

Fiona held Alex's glance. "Don't you think it has been...*now?*"

"Yes," he agreed, suppressing a smile, "now that you have a new mobile number."

He leaned over and kissed her on the lips as a flight attendant walked by, a slight smile edging the corners of her mouth.

Fiona pulled away and asked, "Do you suppose Thomas's note you found in the archives means that was the last they ever saw each other? Probably," she said glumly, answering her own question.

"I also think the fact the Duke of Gordon knew he'd never have Jane's complete love, even if she did care for him as the father of her other six children, played into their ultimate parting of the ways."

"Jane...the duke...Thomas Fraser...this was the classic love triangle, wasn't it?"

"It definitely was," concurred Alex. "And you know, I agree that the duke's refusing to support his duchess must have been some kind of revenge. The Gordon Estate documents Mrs. Larimore found showed that Jane eventually had to close down her beloved Kinrara, due to this lack of funds."

"Kinrara? Oh, that was the country house she'd built in the Highlands before the son-of-a-gun cut off her money?"

"Right. And, of course, it didn't help matters that the duke flaunted his nine illegitimate children."

"*Nine?*" Fiona exclaimed.

"That's what the legal briefs in Register House said."

Fiona grew silent as the steady hum of the jet's engines

filled the crowded cabin. She read the last few paragraphs of the obituary's mournful recitation of Jane's final days when, virtually homeless, it reported, she lived in her coach most of the time between stays at the abodes of her various children.

"Why didn't Jane just move in with one of her children?" Fiona demanded. "Surely of the seven, one would have offered her shelter."

"Pride?" Alex replied with a shrug. "Embarrassed by her financial straits? Not wanting to be a burden or an object of pity?"

Alex pointed to a line of print near Fiona's thumb.

"It says here that she died of a lung infection at a hotel."

"The woman had lived in a *castle,* for pity's sake!" Fiona exclaimed. "What a horrible end to her amazing life."

Alex pointed to a further paragraph.

"But it also says she was 'surrounded by her children at the Poultney Hotel' and that 'her son, the Marquis of Huntly, accompanied the cortege from London to Kinrara where thousands of people came from the hills to see her buried on the banks of the River Spey, near her home,'" he quoted from the obituary.

Fiona murmured, "Our family Bible said that Thomas Fraser died in 1822. I wonder if he ever saw Jane's obituary in 1812? Do you suppose he even knew about her desperate financial situation at the time of her death? And what about Louisa, do you suppose? I can't stop wondering if Thomas ever learned he'd *had* a daughter by the love of his life, or that the girl had married Cornwallis's son, as you say?"

"Mrs. Larimore confirmed that the 71st Fraser Highlanders served under General Cornwallis and were present at the surrender at the Battle of Yorktown. During the American Revolution, Thomas was promoted from lieutenant, to Captain, so it's likely they were at least acquainted at the time of Louisa's marriage."

"Whoa! And can you believe that she ultimately married the son of Thomas's commanding officer?" exclaimed Fiona. "*I* might even be related to Cornwallis by marriage! Maybe we could ask your Mrs. Larimore if there's anything more she can research about the life of Lady Louisa Gordon. You never know. Something new might turn up."

And then she settled her head against Alex's shoulder and soon they both fell asleep as the 747 flew through ink-black skies and over the ice floes of Greenland and on to Great Britain's welcoming shores.

Alex and Fiona's first days back in Edinburgh were filled with the two of them putting in long hours in front of their computers. Alex spent his time in his study, crunching numbers and on the phone with his deputy, Hugh Erskine, initiating tartan orders specified by Fiona for his woolen looms at Maxwell Mills to fulfill various fabric designs to be shipped over to Fraser Furniture for the next line of products in their joint venture. Fiona was both sketching by hand and working on her CAD program to finalize designs and the specifications for draperies, throws, padded storage trunks and ottomans, along with a single style of upholstered wing chair whose manufacture her brother Tommy would supervise in North Carolina.

When she called High Point to confirm that all her emails and jpeg images had arrived in good form, Tommy was a little more agreeable.

Fiona asked directly, "So what do you think about my designs?"

"The stuff you sent looks pretty good," he acknowledged. "I forwarded it downstairs to the production manager for final specifications."

"Great," she replied cautiously. "Oh...and how did it go at the caucus meetings?"

"It's down to two of us," Tommy said, lowering his voice as if he didn't want anyone in his office to hear. "I told the party big wigs that since you've joined the company as vice-president, I'm freed up to run for DA."

"Well...congratulations for making it through the first round," she said, trying to mean it despite the sinking feeling in the pit of her stomach. "Who's your opponent?"

"Some bitchy woman lawyer at my old firm," he said dismissively. "She moved to High Point long after you left here, so you wouldn't know her."

"Oh. Well, let me know how it turns out."

"I called her 'Miss-High-and-Mighty' to the press the other day. Made the front page."

"Miss? Not Ms.?" she said, trying to make light of her brother's typical chauvinism.

"Oh, she's married, but she thinks she's the Joan of Arc of women's rights, for God's sake. It got a good laugh from the boys covering the caucus."

"Any women reporters covering politics in High Point these days?" She wondered what kind of minced meat the BBC's Angela McCauley would make of her brother?

"Oh, there's a few skirts on the campaign trail. The guys hate having 'em around, I can tell you that."

Fiona took a deep breath but only said, "Gotta go, now. I'll send you more stuff in a few days. Love to Dabney and the kids. Bye, now."

"When are you coming back?"

Fiona pretended she didn't hear his last question and quietly hung up.

After a week of intense work, Alex clicked the "off" button on his laptop and walked into the sitting room where Fiona had set up shop for her part of their partnership.

"I think we should take a break," he announced.

"But what about working on the business plan for All Things Scottish? We haven't done a thing in that department," she said with a worried frown.

"Remember, the money's in the bank," Alex reassured her, bending close to kiss her at the base of her neck. "We've been slaving, nonstop, since we got back here. We can afford to take a breather. I've just now made an appointment with Mrs. Larimore for tomorrow at Register House. I've asked her to find every scrap she can about the final years of the Duchess and the life of Lady Louisa Gordon."

"Louisa Fraser, don't you mean?" Fiona said, flashing him a sly smile.

The next morning, in hushed tones suitable for meetings in a library, Alex introduced Fiona to Isabella Larimore as soon as the researcher arrived in the Adams Rotunda, her white coat starched and pressed. She was holding several folders in her arms.

"The few documents I was able to find were various accounts of Lady Louisa Gordon's wedding to Cornwallis's son, Viscount Brome."

"Oh…well…that's nice," Fiona said, trying to keep the disappointment out of her voice.

Mrs. Larimore smiled faintly. "I think one or two things should be of interest. Here," she said, opening the file and handing to Fiona and Alex the requisite pairs of white cotton gloves, "have a look for yourselves."

"These are newspaper accounts from the day, yes?" Alex asked as he and Fiona donned their gloves and gazed at a typed abstract someone had copied from a contemporary news journal.

"Yes. The originals are so fragile, we don't make them accessible to the public anymore, but look here," Mrs. Larimore said, pointing to the third paragraph. "After the writer describes 'the beautiful, flame-haired bride and her dignified groom,' we learn that it was considered a very important wedding since both the Bishop of Coventry and the Bishop of Litchfield officiated."

"But it says here that the wedding was held at the London home of the Duke and Duchess of Gordon in St. James Square," Fiona pointed out. "Not in a church? Why would two bishops attend, then?"

Mrs. Larimore nodded. "This account notes that the ceremony 'was by special license' which was starting to become popular in the eighteenth century among the social set who were becoming less religious and bound by convention. The Gordons were very important people…intimates of King George the Third…so I'm not surprised the bishops were willing to officiate.

Alex said, "And don't forget, if there were a question of Lady Louisa's legitimacy, the Duchess of Gordon might have decided there'd be fewer problems with a service at home rather the demands and requirements of a formal church wedding."

Mrs. Larimore nodded. "Obtaining a license made the marriage just as official." She pointed her cotton-clad forefinger to two columns of names. "This is what I think will interest you both very much."

Fiona scanned down the lists of the attending guests.

Alex noted, "Looks like every lord and lady in the kingdom was invited. General Cornwallis, of course, was there," he said, pointing to the name, "and all the Gordon and Maxwell relatives whose descendants' names we spotted at the Ayton graveyard that day…see, Fiona?"

"Oh!" she declared excitedly, "…there's Jane's younger sister, Eglantine Maxwell, Lady Wallace. And Catherine Maxwell Fordyce—that's Jane's other sister."

"Yes, Eglantine was the eccentric lady playwright, who married a terrible bounder, I think I read somewhere," replied Alex. "And there's Jane's mother, Magdalene Blair Maxwell." He pointed to the Duke of Gordon's name. "At least he didn't boycott the wedding."

Mrs. Larimore ventured dryly, "Well, it was important to close ranks on such public occasions, I suspect."

"Oh…my…*God*!" exclaimed Fiona, and then clamped her gloved hand over her mouth, embarrassed she had spoken so loudly in the silent rotunda. "Look!" she whispered hoarsely, pointing a trembling finger at a name toward the bottom of the second column.

Alex leaned forward and read in hushed tones, "'Captain Thomas Fraser of Struy and son, Maxwell Fraser, now residing in America.'"

Mrs. Larimore noted proudly, "After I spotted that, I checked the regimental records for the 71st Fraser Highlanders and discovered your Lost Lieutenant had eventually been promoted to the rank of Captain during the American War of Independence at the *personal* recommendation of none other than General Cornwallis, himself."

"*No!*" her clients exclaimed in unison.

Mrs. Larimore nodded.

"The endorsement was written in the general's own hand! My guess is that Thomas Fraser came from America to London to see his daughter, Louisa, wed at the express invitation of his former commanding general."

Alex and Fiona stared at each other in amazement.

Then Alex noted, "And let's not forget that Jane Maxwell reportedly declared to Cornwallis 'there's not a drop of Gordon blood in dear Louisa's veins' when the General was concerned over rumors of madness in Clan Gordon."

"Yes," confirmed the researcher. "So perhaps Jane *revealed* to Cornwallis who Louisa's father was, which would have sat very well with Thomas's commanding officer, given that he'd promoted the young lieutenant he obviously respected to the rank of captain during their war years in the Colonies. All accounts are that young Viscount Brome was besotted with the lovely Louisa, so his father probably was willing to overlook the rumors about her parentage, especially if he liked the girl's father."

"So Thomas most likely *did* know he'd had a daughter by Jane," speculated Fiona, "and he brought Louisa's half brother, Maxwell Fraser, to attend the wedding with him!" She looked at Alex. "This is just so amazing...I can hardly take it all in."

Alex wondered out loud, "Do you think that Louisa ever knew that Thomas was her *father*? Or that the little boy at her wedding with Jane Maxwell's birth name was her half brother by the American, Arabella O'Brien?"

Mrs. Larimore shook her head. "There was no evidence I could find in the record that could answer either of those questions."

"You know," Fiona said slowly, "our family Bible proves that Thomas and his son, Maxwell returned to Maryland at some point after that wedding in 1797. We know that Thomas lived for another twenty-five years on a Maryland plantation and died in the spring of 1822. His son Maxwell went west for a time, and then returned east and settled in North Carolina, where I'm from," she explained to Mrs. Larimore.

Nodding, their researcher produced one more folder and opened it.

"I was able to find some of the management records for Kinrara," she said, "dated over the summer of the same year as Louisa's wedding. See?" she said, pointing at the top document. "Look who signed these orders for farming supplies."

She offered Alex a magnifying glass through which he and Fiona peered at the spidery signature scratched at the bottom of the page: "Tho. F."

"This immediately caught my eye, of course, so I went through the rest of the bills for that year and saw that by autumn, another name had replaced 'Tho. F' on the estate invoices. I could find no trace of that signature anywhere else, nor any documents that placed Thomas Fraser of Struy in Scotland any longer."

Alex silently recalled the clarity of his dream about waiting in a remote shielding in the Highlands for someone to come to the cottage door, and then experiencing a haunting feeling of bereavement when he saw the redheaded figure disappear inside the tiny castle on Loch-an-Eilean where the Wolf of Badenoch once hid, hard by the lands of Kinrara that belonged to the Duke of Gordon.

As if thinking out loud, Alex mused, "So after his daughter's wedding in London, Thomas Fraser of Struy spent the summer of 1797 helping Jane manage the Kinrara estate." He looked directly at Fiona. "I *know* that's what happened," he added with a conviction that came somewhere from deep inside.

"And then...by autumn...he had to leave," murmured Fiona barely above a whisper as if she knew the story as well as Alex. "He and little Maxwell, who was no blood kin to Jane, had to leave Scotland forever..."

"And then the Duke, in a rage having discovered, somehow, that his legal wife had been living with her lover in that remote part of the Highlands," Alex concluded softly, "cut Jane off without a farthing. And because of this, she had to leave the home she loved more than any other she'd ever lived in—and basically live in her coach."

The pair stared at each other, moisture edging the corners of their eyes.

"And now, here we are, you and I," Fiona murmured. "We've proven we're Jane and Thomas's descendants. Two hundred and fifty-plus-years later."

Alex reached for her hand across the desk where the folders lay.

"Full circle," he said. "It's all come full circle, hasn't it, Ms. Fiona Maxwell Fraser?"

Mrs. Larimore glanced from one to the other of her clients, her faint smile clear evidence that the researcher understood the import of these last revelations.

"I'll just leave you with these," she said gently, setting the folder of Kinrara House papers on the library table with the others she'd brought. "Feel free to look at the documents as long as you like. Just return them to the archival desk when you're finished, if you will, please."

"Thank you," murmured Fiona.

By this time, Mrs. Larimore was smiling broadly, her eyes luminous behind her thick glasses. "And the best of Scottish luck to you both."

CHAPTER 25

The following week, still reeling from all they'd learned at Register House about the historic links between them, Fiona and Alex worked side-by-side in his Edinburgh study writing and rewriting their business plan for how they believed All Things Scottish should be set up. Alex called in his friend from University days, Lachlan MacNeil, to update the tech expert that the project the men had talked about six years earlier had, at long last, acquired some seed funding.

If Lachlan—who was nearly as tall as Alex, but sandy-haired where his friend was dark—was surprised when he dropped by their flat that his friend's new business partner was a woman, and an American at that, he seemed perfectly at ease with this development.

"It's a masterful job, you've done, pulling the plan together," he said when he finished the fifteen-page proposal. "And that now you have some funds, you'll be wanting someone to create the website's back end, you're saying?"

"That's right," Fiona replied eagerly, relieved Lachlan hadn't found any major flaws in their initial scheme. "We need to build a really robust site, and create a shopping cart and fulfillment system that will accommodate all the diverse products we hope to offer."

"There must be online competition out there by now," Lachlan posed.

Fiona nodded. "Oh, yes…we found several sites offering Scottish goods, but we are aiming to differentiate ourselves by being totally up-market. We want a classic, beautifully-designed website and will feature only the best-of-the-best—whatever products we feature." She grinned at Alex. "We intend this to be a *thoroughbred* operation, right?"

"Are you still interested in this project, Lachlan?" Alex asked. "Do you want to work on this with us…or are you too busy, now?"

"Och, I'm busy, alright, but I've always liked your idea, laddie, and can help you out nights and weekends, if both of you would like me to."

Fiona smiled with pleasure and handed him a slice of smoked salmon on a square of dark, brown bread. "We would like that very much, wouldn't we Alex?"

Over drinks and a few other hors d'oeuvres Fiona had picked up from a shop down the street, the trio toasted the new project and worked out the details of the their new IT Director's job—and how much he'd be paid until they could afford to have him join them, fulltime.

"This is basically a boot-strap operation, as we say in the States," Fiona admitted, "but once we're up-and-running, I think we're all going to be very happy with our little enterprise."

Alex promised, "And, Lachlan, you'll definitely get some shares in the company if we get past the beta stage. We'll put that in your employment contract from the outset."

"'Tis music to my ears," Lachlan said with a laugh. "Working for the bank's IT system is never going to make me a rich lad, that's for certain."

Fiona spent the rest of the week perfecting her furniture designs and doing a final version of the business plan, now that they had Lachlan MacNeil on board. Tommy had drawn up the terms of use and all the other legal documents, but as September drew to a close, news from High Point had been ominously absent.

"Tommy hasn't responded to any of my emails lately," she complained to Alex one evening. "I can't postpone calling him much longer. It's three o'clock in the afternoon in North Carolina. I'd better do it now."

"Do you know what you want to say?" Alex asked.

"I want to tell him we're getting married in the middle of October," she replied with a mischievous smile, "and that we plan to spend November through March in North Carolina, and the other half of the year in Scotland. We'll miss the worst of the winter weather in Scotland, and avoid the horrible heat in North Carolina the rest of the year."

"Brava!"

"But, believe me, Alex, I don't look forward to breaking the news. This is supposed to be a joyous announcement, but all I feel is dread."

"What's the worst he can do? Get angry with you?"

"That, and not speak to me for another ten years, to say nothing of screwing up our three-way partnership."

"You've already proven that he needs you to survive in the business, Fiona. He'll make peace with this eventually."

"Not if he gets the nomination to run for District Attorney—and wins. He'll gladly let Fraser Furniture die an unnatural death and revel in being a big fish in a little pond. It's what he's always wanted to do."

"Well, what happens with all that is out of your realm of influence, and remember, you can't control what *he* does, even though you shared a womb."

"But Dad...and Grandfather Maxwell," Fiona protested. "They *depend* on the furniture company to provide them an income."

"Then they'll have to help you make Tommy see it's in his interest—and theirs—to strike a compromise with us."

"I don't know..." she murmured. She heaved a sigh and resolutely headed for Alex's office to make the dreaded call.

Tommy's private line rang several times and then voice mail picked up, which Fiona found odd, given the time of day.

She rang his home number and was grateful when her sister-in-law, Dabney, answered.

"Hey, there," Fiona said with forced cheer. "Good to hear your voice. I was trying to get hold of Tommy."

"He's gone to Florida."

"Florida? What's he doing there?"

"Licking his wounds deep sea fishin'."

Fiona inhaled and asked, "What's happened, Dabney? Is everything all right?"

"Not with Tommy, I'm afraid. He lost his party's support to run for DA."

"That *woman* won?" Fiona asked, amazed. The South sure must be changing, she thought.

"Right. Alison Cartwright. The woman lawyer who works in his old firm."

Fiona felt a guilty rush of relief, but all she said was, "I bet he was really disappointed."

"Disappointed does not begin to describe it."

"What happened? Why'd he lose?"

"You want to know the real reason?" her brother's wife asked rhetorically. She gave a short laugh. "How did I know you'd ask that question?"

Fiona could hear a television set in the background blaring some football game Dabney's kids must have been watching when she called.

"Can you wait a sec?" Dabney said. "Let me close the door." Moments later her sister-in-law returned to the phone. "Hi...you still there?"

"Yes. I can't believe a woman beat him out in North Carolina!"

"Well, you know how hard it can be for a progressive to get elected—period—in most of the counties in this state. It seems to win in a county where they actually had a chance, the party figured they really had to attract the women's vote."

"Oh."

"Yeah. 'Oh.' I love the man, as you know, Fiona, but he's certainly no feminist. Apparently, Alison collected enough ammunition about Tommy's behavior toward the other women in her firm when he worked there, and also his attitude toward the women at the furniture plant over the years to sink Tommy's chances."

"Wow," was all Fiona could say.

"He just hasn't learned the art of political correctness, to say nothing of showing some respect for a woman's brain in his everyday dealings with our sex."

"What did Alison Cartwright do to bring this all about?"

"She gathered about a hundred signatures on a petition of 'Professional Women of High Point' that she got someone else to submit to the caucus and that was the end of Tommy's chances—at least this time around."

"Oh, boy. That must have been a crusher," Fiona ventured.

"It definitely was, but to tell you the truth—and don't you ever *dare* repeat this to your twin—I'm kinda relieved," Dabney confided. "You know politics. It would have been a huge, nasty, uphill battle, even if you were back here full time to take over the factory. And, by the way, sister-in-law. Are you ever coming back to the land of your birth?"

Fiona filled Dabney in on the plans for a small wedding to be held in the Scottish Borders in mid-October and outlined the schedule she and Alex had worked out for spending the winters in High Point and the rest of the year in Scotland.

"But I want to assure Tommy that when Alex and I are living in Scotland, I'll be doing the same things I'd do if I were in the High Point office," Fiona assured her. "We can stay in daily touch by email and Skype. Thanks to all this technology and the great IT guy we've hired who's going to set up everything, it'll almost be as if we're right there!"

"I hope Tommy can see it that way," Dabney replied, her tone sounding doubtful.

Fiona hastened to add, "And don't worry, when we're living in High Point, we'll rent or buy some place of our own in town and get out from under your feet during the months we're there."

"Well, you're family, Fee," she replied. "You are always welcome to stay in the downstairs apartment." Then Dabney's voice brightened. "Sounds like you two have thought of everything…and it's wonderful news about your getting married! Alex is such a great guy."

Fiona was touched by Dabney's enthusiasm.

"Well you know, Dab, it would mean everything if y'all would come over for the festivities."

"I don't know," she replied, the renewed doubt in her voice sending Fiona's spirits plummeting. "I would love to come—you know that—and the kids would adore gettin' out of school for a week. Your father will be there with bells on, for sure. He really liked Alex."

"But?"

"Well, Your grandfather's probably too frail to make the trip."

"I guess I expected that," Fiona said, waiting to hear what Dabney thought her brother would do. A silence grew before her sister-in-law spoke again.

"Tommy's real upset by what happened about runnin' for office. And without you committed to being here, physically, full time...I know him. He'll be mad and—"

"I wasn't in High Point or involved in Fraser Furniture for a *decade*!" Fiona interrupted with exasperation. "Can't he get behind something that is good for *me* for a change?"

"Well, you know how that boy gets when—"

"When he doesn't get his own way!" Fiona cried, unable to stem the angry tone of her voice. "Well, please tell him I'm very sorry he didn't get the support as his party's nominee, but maybe he should pay attention as to *why*!"

"That's what *I* told him," Dabney replied matter-of-factly, "and he slammed outta here and went to Florida for a week to cool off."

Fiona was immediately apologetic for her heated words.

"Look, I'm sorry, Dab for exploding like that...but he can get me so mad sometimes...like we were still fifteen. Just tell him that Alex and I would dearly love y'all to come to the wedding. I'll send you an official invitation this week, along with a lot of new designs for Fraser Furniture's upholstered division that I think are real winners. We can make this work—he and I—if he'll just grow up a little!"

"Good luck with that!" Dabney said with a short laugh. "You know these southern frat boys...takes a lot to change 'em. Believe me, I've tried."

"Tommy is one lucky guy to have you in his life," Fiona said quietly.

"Well, despite all, I love him, and I just try to accept the good parts."

"You are one, wise woman, Dabney," Fiona said with a laugh. "I think you should go into marriage counseling. Okay, I'd better ring off now, but will you try to persuade Tommy that in the end, it will be less of a burden on him if Fraser Furniture does well? Alex and I will always pull our weight on both sides of the Atlantic—"

"I know you will, darlin'," Dabney intervened. "You've worked wonders for the company already. Don't get your hopes up, but I'll see what I can do. Bye now, and my best to that gorgeous Scotsman of yours."

The gently rolling hills of the Scottish Border country along the A68 were just as Fiona remembered them with the trees turning red and golden, and sheep and castles dotting the landscape as they entered the Tweed Valley. As Alex guided his vintage Jaguar around the corner to head west on the A7 toward Melrose, he turned to Fiona and made an unexpected proposal.

"Since we haven't gotten a yes or no from your brother about coming to our wedding, shall we give *my* brother a go?"

Fiona gamely masked her disappointment that she'd heard nothing from anyone in High Point for more than a week.

"Well, why not? You can't do any worse than I have."

"We're less than ten miles from the country house Harry and his business partner have been doing up as luxury fishing accommodations. I brought along a check so I can give him the final payment of what I owe him for his shares in the mill."

The engaged couple had decided that their joint investments would include clearing the books of moneys owed Harry before their financial futures were joined.

"Shouldn't we call first?" she asked, glancing at her watch. "It's just after four o'clock. We don't want them to think we expect dinner."

"I doubt that Harry Maxwell has ever—in his life—called me or Mrs. Nolan to warn of his arrival," Alex replied. "No, I think surprising him is just the thing."

Within minutes, their car turned off the main highway and along a freshly paved tarmac road with a stand of trees on their left dotting the landscape that glowed a deep magenta with touches of orange and yellow.

"This is such beautiful countryside!" Fiona exclaimed. "And look how nicely the grass is trimmed leading up to that very pretty white stucco house. It looks quite grand, actually."

"It's Georgian...the oldest section built around 1750, I believe Harry said. Looks as if the last payment I gave him was invested in that nice, new slate roof."

"To say nothing of the smooth road we're driving on," Fiona said, smiling. "Maybe your baby brother is actually making a go of this place?"

"Don't get too excited before we see the inside. I haven't been here in years, but it was pretty derelict, as I remember."

The car's wheels crunched to a stop on the gravel area that had been laid out in a circle in front of the manor house, tinged a faint pink in the fading sunlight. The car had barely reached the front door before a tall figure in waders came from around the far corner of the building.

"Alex! Well, hello. What are you doing here?"

Alex got out of the car and went around the front to open the door for Fiona.

"I bring money, brother mine...and some big news."

The brother Fiona had met once before when he was carrying the same pair of chest-high waders over his arm took in the sight of his brother's companion and halted in his tracks.

"Fiona, isn't it?" he grinned. He glanced at Alex. "Well, well...so this is the person Mrs. Nolan said you'd gone off to America to catch in your net. How are you?"

Fiona flushed, but found herself laughing.

"Well, we're here to report your brother landed me, Harry! We're getting married at the end of October and we've stopped by to invite you to the wedding."

Harry's jaw dropped and then his beaming expression took her completely by surprise.

"Well, that's...amazing. Congratulations, you two. This calls for champagne. I probably have half a bottle left from the mad Hungarians who just left. Just take yourself inside the front door, here, while I go 'round the back to the mud room and divest m'self of m'waders. Make yourselves at home in the front sitting room, and light the fire, will you Alex?"

The couple proceeded to go into the house, turning on lights as they located the sitting room. When Alex flipped the switch just inside the door, their gazes took in a charming space with peach painted walls, soft, slipcovered furniture and a polished brass grate with a fire neatly waiting to be lit.

"Glory be, St. Ninian," Alex said, whistling under his breath. "Trust me, Fiona, this is a complete transformation."

"Your quarterly payments for his stock have obviously been put to good use. I love the elegant, but comfortable way this room's been furnished."

"I heard that!" Harry exclaimed, charging through the door, "and since you're about to become my sister-in-law, may I say that I like you already!" He looked briefly at Alex and said, "Let's put out of our mind the memory of the first time I met this lady, shall we?"

Fiona thrust out her hand and said with a grin, "Good idea. How do you do? Harry, is it? You must be my fiancé's brother."

They all laughed and before the trio could even sit down, a lovely-looking brunette appeared carrying a tea tray.

"Meet Kenna McLeod," Harry said. "She was mad enough to answer my advert for a housekeeper/cook and has been working here—what? Two months, is it?"

"Two months and four days," Kenna replied with a nod, adding pertly, "and I've yet to go fly fishing, which is why I originally responded to the advert!" To Alex and Fiona she said, "My father was a ghillie—a famous one in these parts, I might add—guiding people how to cast a line into this river for forty years. I know as much about salmon and trout angling as this laddie, here…but so far, all I've done is scrub and cook and lay fires. Will you have a cup of tea?"

Harry just laughed at the help's saucy retort and invited Kenna to join the party.

"These two are getting married, did you hear?" he said, and then added "But don't you be getting any ideas there, lassie." Kenna looked askance as Harry pointed to his own chest. "This Maxwell's been a hold out thus far, with no plans of changing my status, do you hear that, now?"

"What a high opinion of yourself!" retorted Kenna. To Fiona she asked without taking a breath, "Milk? Lemon?" and then passed around a tray of delicious shortbread.

After a few comments about the change in the season, Alex pulled out an envelope and handed it to his brother.

"You can sign this before we leave. The document says you acknowledge that this is the final payment in full for the rest of what you're owed for your company shares."

Harry ripped open the envelope and, beside the paperwork, pulled out the check and stared at it, his mouth slightly ajar.

"Bloody hell! So you're marrying a rich American, are you, now Alex?"

Before Alex could make a reply, Fiona spoke up quickly.

"Don't I wish I were such a person, Harry…but no, this money can be paid because your brother and I have managed to put both our family firms on a sounder financial footing this year."

Alex chimed in, "We wanted you to have your shares so you could continue here and we could all just be friends, without any outstanding financial issues between us."

Harry merely nodded, still staring at the check. Fiona glanced around the room.

"I didn't see this place before you started," she said, "but I can tell you've made wonderful progress since you gave it your full attention."

Harry beamed under her praise. "Nice words, coming from a designer, aren't you? Well, I think my…attitude…toward many things improved, once I escaped from that blasted mill—pardon my calling it that."

"Well…" Alex replied slowly, "each person has to find a path that suits him, I suppose. It took me a while to learn that, but I'm glad things are going so well for you here, Harry."

Harry gazed at his brother for a long moment.

"Thanks. I appreciate your saying that," adding with a sly grin spreading from the corners of his mouth, "And while you sip your tea, *my* business partner, is picking up our next victims at Edinburgh Airport. Since I now own half of this place, I'll be sure to tell him what you've just said." He paused, and then asked Fiona with a serious expression, "Perhaps you'd be willing to write a positive review for us on TripAdvisor?"

Fiona bit back a smile and winked at Kenna. "Absolutely. I'll write that the Afternoon Tea service is fabulous!"

Alex intervened. "But only on one condition."

"What's that?" Harry asked with a wary expression.

Alex said, "That you serve as my Best Man."

Fiona sat in front of the late Julia McLaren Maxwell's dressing table overlooking the lawn at the back of The Firs property and fought off a feeling of melancholy, despite the fact it was her wedding day. Walter, the black-and-tan Cavalier King Charles Spaniel that Alex had given her for an engagement present sat curled up on the carpet at her feet.

"He's already been given a name, I'm afraid," Alex apologized when be presented the puppy in a fishing creel lined with a length of Maxwell tartan. "It's Walter. I hope that's all right?"

"As in Sir Walter Scott? I *love* it!"

"I had to write in a name when I signed the papers and fetched him at the breeders. Here, have a look at the official documents. He's quite a distinguished wee lad."

She'd opened an envelope containing the registration documents and saw that there was also a small velvet box.

"Alex?" she'd questioned him.

"I had to wait till we returned to The Firs before…"

But by that time, Fiona had opened the box that was lined in burgundy silk and had the name of an Edinburgh jeweler stamped inside—and promptly burst into tears.

"It's your mother's, isn't it?" she'd said, sniffling. "It's absolutely beautiful!"

"*And* my grandmother's. Try it on."

Now that Fiona had grown accustomed to the sight of her beautiful engagement ring on her finger, its square-cut emerald set, Victorian style, in a raised circlet of diamonds, she admired its sparkle for the hundredth time.

She leaned down from her dressing table to scratch one of Walter's ears and then righted herself to stare at the image in the mirror that reflected back to her. Her expression was somber above her simple ivory, bias-cut, long-sleeved, floor length silk gown with a twelve-foot train of dress red Fraser tartan taffeta falling from her shoulders. She wore matching red satin slippers and her hair was arranged in a simple chignon, topped by a small crown of purple heather—and no veil. She tried to smile.

The last word she'd received from High Point was that her father intended to arrive in time to give her away at the nuptials, but as far as she knew, only Thomas Fraser IV would be representing her American family and make the journey across the Atlantic. At least she'd been told that his plane had landed, and Alex had sent Hugh Erskine to fetch him in his car.

"Time to be getting to your weddin', lass," said a soft voice from the doorway. "Alex and Harry have gone on ahead," announced Mrs. Nolan.

"And Seamus?" Fiona asked worriedly for word of Alex's cousin who had all the legal documents in his possession and would serve as Universal Life Minister. She'd reluctantly given into this arrangement, telling Alex she maintained serious doubts as to whether their marriage would actually be legal.

Alex had laughed and assured her that the proper marriage license from the local magistrate was all they needed for him to sign and the local clerk's signature would make it truly legal, having gained permission to hold a late afternoon ceremony after Dryburgh Abbey had closed.

Glancing in the mirror one last time, she pushed a stray strand of red hair under the circlet of purple heather and wondered if they shouldn't have organized the wedding to take place in a regular place of worship. What if it started to rain or a fog rolled in?

"Dinna you be frettin' about Seamus," Mrs. Nolan assured her. "I gave him specific instructions, including the edict that not a *dram* of whiskey was to pass his lips till after you were wed."

"Thank you so much, Mrs. N," she said, feeling, suddenly, as if she would soon begin to weep, given the woman's kindness and consideration during the lead up to today's festivities. "This wedding and reception would never have taken place without everything you've done to make it happen."

Fiona thought of her mother, totally oblivious of anything beyond her world at the memory care unit in High Point, and had to swallow the growing lump in her throat.

Mrs. Nolan, dressed in her Sunday best, drove Fiona in her Ford Escort the short distance from The Firs to the Abbey. Fortunately, the October day was fine, with banks of pure white, puffy, cumulus clouds dotting the horizon and no rain in sight.

As they entered the lane leading to the Abbey parking lot, Fiona recognized Hugh's car, along with Alex's midnight blue Jaguar, and a number of other vehicles that had brought their few invited guests to the ceremony.

The final rays of the day's sunshine filtered through the trees as Fiona caught her first sight of her father, resplendent in his Fraser kilt that she doubted he'd worn since the days he'd taken her to the Grandfather Mountain Games, three decades earlier.

"Dad...you got here," she breathed, and felt her spirits raise a notch when he enfolded her in his arms.

"Just barely," he said. "Our plane was late out of Raleigh-Durham and we almost missed the flight out of Dulles, but here I am."

He stood back and Fiona could feel his appraising glance.

"You are the picture of a perfect Scottish beauty, Fiona Maxwell Fraser," he pronounced and she heard the catch in his voice. Then he added, "I'm sorry Peachy couldn't come, but—"

"I totally understand," she said with a watery smile. "I am just so grateful *you're* here."

Her father pointed to the pouch he wore around his waist. "Alex supplied this furry thing with the beady eyes," he declared, pointing to the small head of an unknown animal that formed the front of his sporran. "I'd misplaced mine, but your future husband said I wouldn't look like a proper Scot without it."

"Well, you wouldn't," she teased him back.

He proffered his arm.

"Ready?" he asked and gave her an anxious look. "Big step, you're taking here."

Fiona had no doubts whatsoever that she wanted to be married to Alex Maxwell. What made her less than an ecstatic bride this October day was the apparent rift between her brother and her. Their ongoing estrangement upset her deeply and called to question their ability to juggle their commitments in Scotland and High Point. Every single member of her family depended on Fraser Furniture to keep the wolf from the door, and yet, if she and her twin couldn't—

This is my wedding day...I can't think about the business...

Her father solemnly led her down the gravel path ten more feet to the spot where Hugh Erskine awaited them, pipes at the ready. From there, they would pass by the grass and gravestones on their left, shaded by tall trees that Alex had told her had been planted in the 1700s. A few, redheaded Highland cattle grazed in the distance.

"I see my chauffeur doubles as a musician," chuckled her father. "Hello again, Hugh, and thank you again for coming to pick me up."

"Happy to do it, sir. And glad we could hire that van for the rest of them."

By this time, Hugh had squeezed the tartan-covered bag under his arm and the pipes emitted their characteristically loud wail, the signal that their procession was about to start.

In her head she heard the words to *The Skye Boat Song* and her heart began to soar at the lilting, waltz-time tune.

Speed, Bonnie Boat, like a bird on the wing...
Onwards, the sailors cry...
Carry the lad who was born to be King...
Over the sea to Skye.

She caught sight of Mrs. Nolan slipping into her seat among a collection of a dozen or so white, wooden folding chairs that Alex had procured for the occasion. When planning the wedding, her husband-to-be had checked that the sun would set precisely at eighteen minutes after six on the twelfth of October. At four-thirty this afternoon, a golden cast bathed the surroundings and the shadows of the gravestones and trees lay like fallen giants on the grass as she slowly advanced down the gravel path beside her father.

From the top of a stone walkway embedded in lawn that stretched toward the ancient Abbey's roofless nave, Fiona could see massive bunches of heather in tall stone urns that flanked the spot where she and Alex had determined the ceremony would take place. Fiona's thoughts drifted to that magical, misty afternoon when, standing here in Dryburgh Abbey, they had almost felt that they were two souls melded into one. She knew, suddenly, that all that really mattered this day was that she had found the one person the fates had determined would be part of her life for as long as she lived.

As the pipes echoed against the Abbey's thousand-year-old walls—now turned a rosy hue as the sun fell deeper in the west—she glanced to her left at the grave of Sir Walter Scott and felt an almost other-worldly sense that she was bound to Alex by a silver thread that would now be made visible to the assembled.

She was dimly aware that the few invited guests had turned in their chairs to witness the bride's entrance along the stone path and then onto the grass where the south transept's magnificent, empty window towered on their right. A reassuring sight greeted her from the friends-of-the-groom side: Catherine Maxwell Stuart of Traquair House and her husband, Mark Muller, along with designers Jeff Laing and Alison Vance of Jeffreys Interiors of Edinburgh. In the next row sat Jason Dyer of Abbotsford, whom Fiona suspected had had a hand in securing Dryburgh Abbey as their wedding venue. She almost grinned to see, sitting at the rear of the more sparsely populated friends-of-the bride side, Harry's "chalet bunny and wanna-be female ghillie," Kenna MacLeod, who gave a discreet little wave, along with Sarah MacDonald, the tour guide at Traquair, and Leah Robertson, the talented designer from the Lochcarron textile firm who had been so helpful and kind on Fiona's initial trip to the Scottish Borders.

Directly ahead of her stood Cousin Seamus Maxwell, an overweight cherub, rotund in his Maxwell kilt that matched those of the two brothers standing side-by-side—all awaiting her arrival.

Then she almost stumbled when she caught sight of Dabney Fraser seated closer to the front on the friends-of-the bride side. Next to her were her two children—everyone completely decked out in Scottish attire. Beside Dabney, in the aisle seat, sat Fiona's twin, Tommy, also in kilt. All four faces were wreathed in smiles, as was Grandfather Maxwell parked in his wheelchair at the end of the row. They were proud, she supposed, that they'd pulled off such an enormous surprise but there was a part of her that felt robbed by the hours of deep sadness leading to this moment where, now, all seemed right with the world.

Gratitude, Fiona! This is your very own miracle right here in Dryburgh Abbey!

She pulled away from her father and threw her arms around Dabney, whispering, "Oh thank you...thank you...*thank you*!"

Then, Tommy reached for her and enfolded her a bear hug. "You don't really think I'd miss this?" he said gruffly. "Tell her, Dabney! Coming to your wedding was *my* idea! And besides, I want to see what the hell kind of outfit I'm partners with!"

Almost out of habit, she started to challenge her twin brother's version of how his family came to be sitting in a thousand-year-old-church in Scotland. Instead, she simply kissed him on both cheeks.

"I love you all for...for...*being* here," was all she could manage before a tear slid down her cheek.

Then she again hooked her arm in her father's and joyfully covered the short distance where Harry stood ready to serve as his brother's best man, and Alex stepped forward to claim her for his own.

EPILOGUE

Mr. and Mrs. Alexander Maxwell's honeymoon didn't officially began until ten days after their wedding when the last of the guests departed for America.

On the drive north of Edinburgh along the road beyond Perth and into the Scottish Highlands, Alex and Fiona confessed to each other that neither could remember many of the words Cousin Seamus uttered over them during the ceremony at Dryburgh Abbey, nor much of the joyous reception Mrs. Nolan produced at The Firs. All that had truly penetrated amidst the excitement and tumult of a house full of friends and relatives from both sides of the Atlantic was the uncanny sense each of them had experienced that the joining of their lives felt so *right*.

In the spirit of that conclusion, they set out at dawn from The Firs and sped north, eventually reaching the A82 that ran along the east side of Loch Ness. The day was crisp and clear and the watery home of the famous monster gave no signs of revealing its secrets, but the scenery, Fiona thought, was sheer magnificence.

"I had no idea Scotland put on such a show this late in October!" Fiona exclaimed as they rounded a corner and glimpsed yet another hillside resplendent in yellows, reds and oranges that rivaled anything she'd ever seen in upstate New York in autumn.

At Fort Augustus, Alex turned the dark blue Jaguar west on a small road that led to the charming down of Invergarry where they had booked in at the Glengarry Castle Hotel. Tired from their long journey, they fell into their modest four-poster and kissed each other goodnight.

"I feel like an old, married couple already, love," Alex said wearily, "but I promise I'll make it up to you when we stay at

Castle Stuart, two days from now."

"Mmmm…?" Fiona said sleepily, whispering, "I love feeling like an old married couple."

Early the next morning, after a hearty breakfast of smoked kippers and strong coffee, the pair set off again on the A82, soon arriving at the fishing village of Drumnadrochit and turned north again on the narrower A831, following signposts for the "Cannich-Struy Road."

Fiona felt her heart begin to speed up as they drove through the small village of Glassburn and she caught sight of the Beauly River, its banks skirted by piles of golden, fallen leaves. She suddenly remembered her grandfather's tales of Beaufort Castle in Beauly, the Highland seat of the once powerful family of Simon, Lord Lovat of Fraser, their clan chieftain.

"This is where *our* Thomas Fraser came from," she said with a sense of wonder as the loveliness of her surroundings brought a lump to her throat. The forests on both sides of the steep-sided glen they had entered grew denser, casting deep shadows across the road. As the morning drew on, the air was damp and silvery, with an alpine tang to it. Fiona sensed they had entered a magical kingdom, ruled by some ancient chieftain, long buried in this primordial soil.

Alex said, "I read somewhere that near here is a cave nestled in the rocks where Bonnie Prince Charlie hid out with seven men prior to the prince's escape to France via the Isle of Skye."

"He was disguised as a maid to a lady named Flora MacDonald, right?" Fiona said with a laugh. "I remember being told the story by Grandfather Maxwell." She remained silent for a moment, deep in thought. "So, *that* must be the origin of *The Skye Boat Song*, isn't it?" she marveled, and burst into, *"Speed, Bonnie Boat, like a bird on the wing…onwards, the sailors cry…"*

Alex joined in a rich baritone, *"Carry the lad that was born to be King…over the sea to Skye."* He nodded as he piloted the car down yet another narrower lane. "Yes, m'lady," he teased, "that's where that tune came from. The story is ancient, but the song didn't appear in a collection until the 1870s."

"Wow..." Fiona said on a long breath. "That's all I have to say: Wow."

They soon came upon a cluster of low-lying stone structures, mostly roofless, except for a few with thatch greatly in need of repair.

Alex said, "These villages were decimated by the Clearances in the early nineteenth century when the raising of sheep by the landlords replaced the crofters' attempts to grow crops."

Fiona replied, "Half the Scots in America and Canada probably descended from people kicked off the land when that happened here."

Alex slowed the car as they caught sight of a hill behind the abandoned village and glimpsed through the colorful trees a falling-down structure they surmised had been Struy House, mostly roofless and with its remaining walls made of rough Moray freestone covered in vines.

"The house looks as unkempt as the village, and as deserted too," he said somberly. "Before the Battle of Culloden Moor, Thomas's family also owned some cottages on Broch Lane, Mrs. Larimore discovered. Probably part of the original estate that they lost to the Crown after Thomas's father took part in the rebellion at Culloden in 1746, so she told me."

Fiona consulted her cell phone's GPS. "Broch Lane is literally about three hundred yards from where we are now, down that rutted road," she said, pointing through the windshield.

Soon they saw ahead of them a rough, stone cottage that was hardly more than a deserted hovel. It sat in a small clearing overgrown with brambles and thorns. A roof no longer protected the cottage's dirt floor—which could be seen through its side entrance. Getting out of the car, Fiona felt an overwhelming stab of sadness fill her chest as she approached the croft's door that was half off its hinges. She and Alex stepped inside the one-room hut, devoid of furniture, with only a blackened iron pot near the cold hearth.

In a voice choking with emotion, she asked Alex, "Do you suppose this is what poor Thomas was reduced to, waiting for

Jane to come to him? Do you think this was where he placed that note for her that you found at Register House saying he left her his love but sought a new home in America?"

"It was written on a scrap of paper and had been folded up," Alex said, glancing around the room, "as if it had been wedged into something...perhaps between that hand-hewn mantel and the fireplace's jagged stones over there," he added, pointing.

"Could Jane have come here, looking for him, but he'd already given up and emigrated to America and the note was all she found? After all, you said you found it among *her* correspondence. Oh, Alex..."

She was comforted when he drew her into his arms and she burrowed her face into his chest, shocked that a sob welled up and she found herself crying for the sorrow of her ancestor's life and Thomas's steadfast love for a woman he could never have as his wife.

They remained standing in that desolate outbuilding with their arms around each other for a long time, as if by merely being together and holding each other close, something in their world had healed.

When, finally, they were on their way once more to the Battlefield of Culloden Moor, Fiona seriously wondered if she could stand to see where Clan Fraser had virtually lost all and the infant Thomas Fraser had been left to starve here in Struy, until rescued by his godfather, Simon, Master of Lovat. She remembered Alex telling her that first day she'd gotten off the night train in Edinburgh that Simon Lovat had taken the orphaned kinsman to Edinburgh where the boy had apparently met the flamboyant nine-year-old Jane Maxwell and her younger sister, Eglantine, riding competing pigs in a race down the center of the Royal Mile. But it had all started *here*.

After stopping for lunch in a pub in Inverness, they reached the battlefield just after one o'clock in the afternoon. Fortunately, the weather was holding and they joined a few other tourists wandering the wide expanse of the field where some 1400 of Bonnie Prince Charlie's troops were slaughtered within forty-five minutes when the King's forces began to fire their muskets at point blank range one cool April day.

"Here's the stone marker commemorating Clan Fraser," Fiona said, pointing a few yards away. All across the field were similar piles of stones—or Cairns, as Alex called them—dedicated to the various clans who had lost so much that day.

Alex read from a list as Fiona tried to spot the nearest monuments. "MacDuff, MacGregor, Drummond, Ogilvy, Farquharson…there's a list of about forty clans, here, including…and I didn't know this," he declared, "some Maxwells who apparently were part of the Atholl Highlanders that joined Prince Charles."

"And who were the ones who fought for the blasted English?"

"Now…Fiona," Alex chided. "You have to keep remembering, this was more than 250 years ago!"

"I know, I know," she said, shading her eyes from the sun as she gazed across the silent moor. "But so many people died here…it's a bit like when you visit Gettysburg…the Civil War battlefield in Pennsylvania. There's such a feeling of…of *tragedy* and waste when you come to these places."

Alex put his arm around her and gave her shoulders a squeeze. "Well, my darling bride, would you like to see a place I'm certain is going to cheer you up?"

Fiona turned and framed his face with her hands, kissing him soundly on his mouth as tourists ambled by, either smiling or averting their glance to avoid such a pubic show of affection.

From Culloden, Alex turned onto the A9, heading south toward signposts that said, "Aviemore" and "The Whiskey Trail."

"Well this definitely looks more cheerful," Fiona said, suddenly filled with a sense of joy and gratitude for sitting beside this man who was now her husband.

"Are you up for a little gate-crashing this afternoon?" Alex asked, keeping his eyes on the road as they picked up speed along this well-maintained motorway.

"Yes, of course. Where are you taking me, you rogue?"

"Just be patient and find 'Kinrara' on the mobile's GPS."

"No! How exciting!" Fiona exclaimed. "Is it open to the public?"

"No," Alex said, "but a friend of a friend has gotten us permission to go on the property."

"Honestly, Alex, you *do* know everyone in Scotland!"

"A lot of people buy tartan in this country," he said, deadpan.

They peeled off the main road to a narrow track and soon parked beside a closed gate. Pines and meadows blanketed the landscape as the pair gingerly scaled the locked wooden fence and walked along a faint path in the browning grass of autumn.

Alex spotted a peak of pale marble before Fiona did and pointed to a stand of low bushes. "There! Do you see it? The Duchess of Gordon's monument! Right there, just as we've read, beside the banks of the River Spey."

They drew closer and soon stood just feet away from a large marble block with another chunk of stone shaped into an impressive pyramid taller than even Alex.

"And look, there are the names of all her children engraved, along with those of their impressive spouses. Three dukes, a marquis and a baronet those girls married," Fiona chortled. "Jane Maxwell truly earned the title of 'The Match-making Duchess.'"

She drew closer and traced the name "Louisa" beside which was the name "Marquis of Cornwallis, Viscount Brome."

"And look…at the bottom, there…at least the Duke of Gordon didn't prevent her being buried here, as she wished."

"No…" Alex concurred, gesturing to words inscribed at the base of the monument. "It says that 'this monument is installed by the express wishes of the Duchess of Gordon' and then he's put his name beneath." Alex gazed around at the monument's lonely surroundings and Fiona could tell he was experiencing the same sort of melancholy she had felt when standing in Thomas's abandoned shieling at Struy.

"Can we see Kinrara House?" she murmured.

"My friend didn't know the owners well enough to get us beyond a peek through the trees, but you can at least get a glimpse of the house from down there," he said, gesturing in the direction of the sloping path. "And then, I have one more surprise for you."

They walked about a hundred yards before they could see a white, stuccoed house rather reminiscent of the Georgian manor that Harry Maxwell was currently turning into a posh fishing lodge.

"I imagine this place started out with a few shielings and a barn, along with a lot of sheep," Alex said, quietly and then told Fiona that what they were seeing seemed very familiar to him, somehow. "When I woke up from that dream I told you about, I started wondering if memories can be handed down, you know? In one's DNA?"

"What a wild idea, but I have to say that at Struy this morning, the feelings of loss were so strong..."

"I know exactly what you're saying," said Alex. "It sounds insanely far-fetched, but in my dream, the shieling in which I was waiting for you to come to me was small...and the property around it was laid out exactly like this land."

"But the person waiting in that cottage would have been *Jane*...expecting Thomas to come...probably before this manor house had even been built," declared Fiona on a swift intake of breath. "The dream or memory would have been Jane Maxwell's."

"That's right," Alex said. "I'm Jane Maxwell's descendant. You're Thomas Fraser's. What if you and I have been pulled together like magnets, across more than two centuries? Genetic memory is the only explanation I can come up with."

Fiona squeezed his hand. "It works for me."

It was nearly four by the time they retraced their steps to their car and found the tiny track that led to the final stop on their day's journey, just a few miles away from Kinrara. Alex brought the car to a halt beside a small lake. He grew silent, his hands resting on the steering wheel, gazing out the windshield with a thousand-yard stare.

Finally he said, "Well, here we are…Loch-an-Eilean…or 'Loch-an-Eilein' on the older maps I've studied." He pointed to a tiny island a football field away. "That's the castle of the Wolf of Badenoch—the fifteenth century wild man who terrorized the neighborhood long before Jane and Thomas lived."

"Wasn't this the second part of your dream? You found yourself at the 'lair of the Wolf of Badenoch'?" She studied Alex's profile. "Does it also look the same as in your dream?"

Alex nodded. "It's beyond strange, but it's exactly as I dreamed it."

"You're kidding me, right?"

"No, Fiona, I swear it. In my dream, I was standing right *there*, at the edge of the water, near that grove of pines, a few feet from us here. I saw a woman with hair exactly your color, but only for an instant and then the figure disappeared through that stone doorway leading to the castle keep."

"What's *really* strange is that you, my husband, felt in that dream all the longings that your female ancestor, Jane Maxwell, felt for the man, Thomas Fraser—a redhead Highlander, from whom *I* descended! Yet your subconscious mind translated it into a regular man-woman thing," she said with a puzzled shake of her head.

"Well, I was missing you terribly after nearly a year apart," Alex said soberly. "The subconscious mind was working it through, I guess, using the metaphor of Jane and Thomas's star crossed love affair to tell me to get over my false sense of having been betrayed and go *find* you!"

"I think we'll get the prize for the most bizarre honeymoon trip on record," Fiona said, seizing Alex's hand and kissing it as he continued to stare out the car window. She allowed him a few more moments of silence and said, "Well, where do we go from here?"

"To the castle, of course," Alex said, as if waking from a dream.

Fifty yards to the right of their parked car, a small boat was tied to a tree that grew beside the water.

"Now, how in the world did you know this dinghy would be here?" she demanded.

Alex laughed. "The Grant family of Grantown-on-Spey, up river, eventually took control of this land next to the Gordon holdings. One of the cousins was a friend of Lachlan MacNeil from Edinburgh University. I called him last week and told him where we were going on our honeymoon, and could he call Johnnie Grant to get permission to row over to view the island—"

"You are amazing," Fiona exclaimed. "Absolutely amazing!"

"Just that friends-of-friends thing," Alex replied modestly. From the back of his car, Alex loaded in a picnic basket and a pile of tartan blankets, products of Maxwell Mills, into the small craft. He handed Fiona into the rowboat and untied the painter line. "You relax and I'll row."

His bride of less than a month settled her back against the pile of woolen lap rugs in the stern and allowed the peace and solitude to envelop her as the little boat made its way the short distance across the placid loch. For several minutes while she closed her eyes, all she could hear was the lap of the water against the oars, and then a sound of "Koh-hoo…koh-hoh" growing louder as they approached the sandstone walls of the small fortress built almost to the edge of its minuscule island.

"Swans," declared Alex, as they grew closer to clusters of canary grass cloaking the island's perimeter. "That's where those birds like to make their nests. Don't ever go near them when they're guarding their cygnets as they can do humans a lot of damage if they feel their young are threatened."

Alex stepped from the boat and secured the bowline to a rusty iron ring embedded at the rim of the stone dock. They could hear rustling in the reeds and soon a large-breasted trumpeter swan, and then his mate, emerged and glided away at high speed.

Fiona carefully handed Alex their collection of woolen blankets and the picnic hamper. Gingerly, she stood up in the boat, clasped his outstretched hand, and hopped onto land. Her sweeping glance took in a close-up view of the Wolf of Badenoch's crumbling fortress with walls several feet thick and tall trees, resplendent in their fall foliage, leaning against the stones as if seeking support. An open passage led into a weed-strewn forecourt.

Alex pointed to a section of the far wall where a gigantic black cauldron was tipped over on its side next to a disintegrating patch of masonry.

Fiona proclaimed, "The kitchen, yes? And over there, the roofless, not-so-great hall?"

"I think you're right," said Alex, his arms filled with the picnic basket, along with the few blankets Fiona wasn't carrying. He nodded in the direction of a winding staircase that apparently led to rooms above the main floor. "Shall we see how safe it is to go up to the tower? Or we could just have our picnic here."

"To the tower, laddie!" she said, heading for the stairs. "We've come this far, we can't let the tales that the Wolf haunts this teeny-weeny castle scare us away."

The stone stairs were worn smooth in their centers by thousands of feet that had trod up and down over as many years. As the pair neared the top, without warning, a bat flapped its wings and made a hasty retreat out a small window sliced into the tower where the Laird of Badenoch most likely shot flaming arrows at his approaching adversaries. Three more stairs, and they reached the top landing where they peered into a tiny round chamber, also constructed entirely of stone. Two windows were cut into the thick walls that allowed for light and plenty of crisp autumn air to make the space inviting, "if a wee bit chilly," Alex noted with a wolfish grin. Above was a barrel-vaulted ceiling and a small fireplace cut into one wall. "Despite a bit of a breeze, I think this will do nicely for our afternoon tea, don't you?"

"You had these provisions packed for us back in Invergarry?" she asked, amazed as she pulled out a thermos, a variety of finger sandwich, a few scones and jam, and a tea cake or two. "You are absolutely brilliant, my husband. I don't know about you, but tramping over Culloden Moor and along the banks of the Spey has made me ravenous!"

They spread several layers of plaid blankets on the stone floor and gazed from the tower windows at the deserted waters below that mirrored a ring crimson and yellow trees, along with green firs dotted amongst their colorful branches. Fiona poured the tea, still hot in its thermos, and added milk from a vial the hotel had provided, while Alex tucked into the sandwiches.

"Here," he mumbled, his mouth full, "you must have one of the cream cheese and salmon ones."

When they had finished their delicious repast and packed away the remains of their meal into the hamper, Alex patted the blanket and bid Fiona snuggle close.

"I'll do better than that," she teased, pulling him down to lay beside her, pressing the length of her body as close to him as she could. They kissed and the taste of tea and vestiges of jam mingled with the knowledge they were utterly alone, answerable to no one but themselves, held in the embrace of this ancient tower and all its history.

As she'd felt in the abandoned cottage in Struy, a sudden surge of emotion swept over her, almost as if she might be holding Alex for the last time. Inexplicably, she felt a well of tears that traveled from her chest to her throat and a small sob escaped her lips.

Expecting Alex to ask her what in the world was wrong, she looked up through streaming eyes and saw that his cheeks, too, were bathed in moisture. He held her fast and they buried their heads against each other's shoulders.

"W-What *is* this?" Fiona said with a gulp? "What's happening?"

She could feel Alex inhale deeply a couple of times. His voice in her ear whispered, "I think Jane and Thomas met here. I think they made love in *this* chamber."

Fiona felt her body go absolutely still.

Then she said with utter conviction. "Louisa was conceived here…she became a spark of life right *here*, within these ancient walls. I just know it, Alex, don't you?"

He rose to his elbow. "Well, Struy and Kinrara were a day's ride apart, but how can anyone know if that's true?"

"But you believe it to be true, don't you?" she said, holding his hand tightly within her own two.

Alex nodded. "I do, my love. I do," he said, leaning forward to kiss her white knuckles. Then he withdrew his hand and ran the back of his fingers along her cheek in a now-familiar gesture. He gazed at her with a love so intense that his brown eyes seemed to kindle fire in the darkening shadows growing around them as the day declined. Gently, he threaded his long fingers through her hair, pulling it loose so its lustrous lengths fanned around her shoulders.

"Make love to me, Alex," she whispered, her gaze taking in every angle of his high cheekbones, his mouth and nose, and his wonderful dark mane. "It would be my heart's joy if we created a life together here."

Alex smiled faintly and began to search for the button on her camel-colored slacks.

"Ah…but naming the poor bairn," he said, using the Scottish word for baby as if he were living in another age. "Now, *that* would be such a hard choice, given all the family names we've learned since we met each other."

"Well, you're jumping quite far ahead of yourself, laddie. Don't you think the first order of business is to…"

Fiona began to do what she could to help Alex divest himself of his clothing while he did the same for her. She pulled her sweater over her head, sitting cross-legged on the tartan throw.

She cocked an eyebrow and announced, "Actually, Alex, I think we can readily agree on names."

"Oh, do you, now?" He reached behind her back and made fast work of her underclothing, as he had his own. "I'm expecting endless negotiations."

Pulling her down into the plushness of the blankets that had been designed by Fiona and manufactured at Maxwell Mills, he swiftly put her on her back and hovered above her like a giant male swan, wings poised for flight.

"We can discuss names later," he mumbled, and began to lick her ear, her neck, and a spot he knew she loved in the hollow of her shoulder. Shards of lightening flashed through her limbs and she wrapped her arms around his neck, begging for him to press his chest against hers.

Instead, Alex sat up and straddled her thighs. He reached for another woolen rug, draping it like a cloak around his shoulders. Then, he positioned himself above her while she gazed up at her new husband with a kind of awe.

"Alex, I never have wanted you as much as I do now," she said, humbled by her love for him.

"You are...so beautiful, Fiona...and—"

He stopped speaking, opening his eyes wide as she lifted her hips to be closer, still.

"Please...Alex...please," and pushed against his thighs with her own. She smiled to see his reaction. "From the minute I saw you marching down the aisle at the expo in New York, I thought *you* quite the most beautiful man I'd ever seen." She raised her hips again and winked. "And just look—in the space of a single year—how you've driven me to such wicked ways."

Alex placed a hand on each side of her shoulders. "Do you have any idea what a hold you have over me?" he demanded. "You danced into my life, invaded my dreams, brought a host of ghosts into our world, and now..."

Fiona lifted one arm and kissed her own forefinger, then pressed it against his lips. "Jane and Thomas can be at rest, now. The circle is closed, Alex. No more star-crossed lovers. We can now transform their tragedy into our *own* story of finding each other and promising to love 'until death do us part...'"

As if charged with that very mission, Alex was both gentle and demanding as he slowly lowered himself, while she urgently begged him to come closer, still. She reveled in the weight of him, the warmth of their joined bodies, and the dearness of this man who was now her own. She began to rock against him, slowly at first, and then with a wildness that was born of their passion and desire and a longing to blot out anything but a tactile awareness of each other. For Fiona, it felt as if they'd been together always, as if they were light as the sylvan, autumn air outside the tower, mere ghosts of memories past, melded with the precious reality of their present. They were one with it all...one with their joined histories...and all was love.

When at last they were silent and lay facing one another, they could only hear the lapping of water against the base of their tower and the soft *Koh...hoh...koh...hoh...* of the swans guarding their castle keep. Fiona heaved a contented sigh.

"We won't have a bit of trouble naming this child," she whispered.

She felt Alex chuckle into her hair. "Is that so?"

"Yes," she said confidently.

"Hmmm. So, if it's a boy," he said, "we'll call him...?"

"Thomas Fraser Maxwell, of course," Fiona answered promptly, and then asked, smiling, "And if it's a girl...we'll call her...?"

"*Louisa.*"

"Louisa *Jane*," Fiona corrected.

And then they said in unison, "Louisa Jane Fraser Maxwell."

And so they did.

Don't miss Ciji Ware's first novel in the Four Seasons Series:
That Summer in Cornwall.
Available now.

That Summer in Cornwall

A different latitude…a different world…

Meredith Champlin unexpectedly finds herself the legal guardian of a child she's never met: Jane Barton Stowe, an unruly eleven-year-old "Beverly Hills brat," whose mother—Meredith's cousin—has died in a private plane crash.

At the urging of the child's Anglo-American aunt, Lady Blythe Barton-Teague, Meredith and her Welsh Corgi decamp from Wyoming to spend the summer at Barton Hall, a shabby-chic castle perched on the remote cliffs of Cornwall, England.

Taming the wild child proves a handful, but Meredith's summer escape gets even more complicated when former British Army Lieutenant Sebastian Pryce, veteran of a bomb-sniffing K-9 squad in Afghanistan, proposes they establish the Barton Hall Canine Obedience Academy and that she join him on the Cornwall Search and Rescue Team. Is their instant attraction an unexpected blessing or the prelude to another heartbreak like the one she left behind in the Rocky Mountains?

Even with assistance from a novice search dog named T-Rex, the odds seem long that three months in the land of Meredith's Cornish ancestors can transform her troubled ward into a happier child, heal the wounds suffered by her soldier-turned-rescuer, and save the Barton-Teague estate from pending insolvency.

As one friend confides, "It all sounds like a stretch, but we never rule out miracles."

Island of the Swans

The award-winning, bestselling biographical novel based on the life of the flamboyant political figure, Jane Maxwell, the 4th Duchess of Gordon (1749-1812)—one of the most influential women of her time. Named "Best Biographical Historical" by *Romantic Times* magazine and bestowed the Dorothy Parker Award of Excellence in the "Classics Division," this beloved novel weaves fact with fiction about the amazing life of the patroness of the poet Robert Burns, advisor to King George III, friend to Queen Charlotte, and the mastermind behind her husband's political success, along with the rival of the equally flamboyant Georgian, the Duchess of Devonshire.

Rich in historical detail, passion and intrigue, the novel brings to life one of the most celebrated beauties of her day whose tempestuous marriage after she thought her childhood sweetheart was killed created a lifelong love triangle that threatened to destroy them all.

If you'd like more information about these or any of my books, please visit my website: **http://www.cijiware.com**.

Author's Note and Acknowledgments

The idea for many a novel comes from asking the question "what if?" In the case of *That Autumn in Edinburgh*, the question "What if humans possess a genetic memory sequence in their DNA that echoes throughout their lives?" was quickly followed by another, prompted by a novel, *Island of the Swans*, that I wrote twenty-five years ago: "Whatever happened— *after* the book ended— to the historical 4th Duchess of Gordon and her lover who came to be known as 'The Lost Lieutenant?'"

The "Whatever happened to Jane and Thomas?" question has been asked of me by readers the world over. Eventually, the two queries came together when I decided to reveal what I'd known about those star-crossed lovers all along, but as a storyteller, had made the editorial decision to end *Island of the Swans* at a point in the lives of these historical figures when they achieved what they yearned for: to live together as if they were man and wife—if only for a summer.

Sadly, their true-to-life end was too tragic for a reader to bear who had followed the saga of these characters' lives for nearly 600 pages, and so I ended the novel at a moment when they could (finally) be together—but with an uncertain future. This conclusion was akin to the ending of *Gone with the Wind* when Rhett Butler walks out of Scarlett O'Hara's life and everyone wondered, "Will they ever get back together?"

Answering these questions in this stand-alone sequel to *Island of the Swans* turned out to be a marvelous adventure in 2013 when I retraced steps I had taken nearly thirty years earlier in preparing to write the first book. There was no full-length biography of this little-known historical figure in 1983 when, then a television news broadcaster, I embarked on the four-year effort to write the story of Jane Maxwell of Monreith. The lore in my family, perpetuated by my great grandmother, Elfie McCullough (whom I knew and who lived to be 97), was the claim that we descended from Jane Maxwell "back in the mists of time." After years of research, I could never prove that fact beyond a reasonable doubt, but the journey introduced me to my Scottish-American heritage and greatly informed that earlier novel, as well as *That Autumn in Edinburgh*—a book that tells the story of a pair of fictional modern descendants, Alexander Maxwell and Fiona Fraser, and their search to find out what happened to their respective eighteenth century ancestors.

In a sense the book you have just read is "the story of the story" of tracing the life of a woman and the great, lost love of her life. All the scenes of Alex and Fiona seeking an understanding of their ancestors' lives after 1797 and until the deaths of Jane and Thomas are based on my own research into documents that go far in establishing what really happened to the pair in their later years.

For anyone willing to spend the time to dig out the piece-by-piece facts, Jane's life is fairly well documented. However, the "Lost Lieutenant," as the young man whom she loved for a lifetime, is a far more shadowy figure. Much of what I wrote about him is based on a reading of what *is* documented through records of the Black Watch and 71st Fraser Highland regiments, combined with intelligent supposition about the facts that are unknown—or unknowable—some 250 years later.

Weaving truth and imagination into a believable whole is the joy of both fiction and historical fiction work, and it is my view that we novelists who bother to do our homework often "get it right" in the sense of understanding the meaning of a life, as well as the mere facts that surround it.

As regards the research for *Island of the Swans,* my obligations to the many people who helped me bring that story to life are legion and are chronicled in the Author's Note at the back of that book. Nevertheless, I must again express my gratitude to the staff at, and institution that is, The Henry E. Huntington Library and Art Gallery in San Marino, California where I held a Readership in Eighteenth-Century British and American History for more than a decade. Any violations of the high standards of historical research embraced by this extraordinary place are clearly my own responsibility.

I also wish to thank the various anonymous librarians throughout Scotland who granted innumerable kindnesses to this American novelist dashing in and out of their quiet lairs over several years. There really was a "white coated researcher" in Edinburgh who pushed a cart full of documents relating to Jane Maxwell into the vast reading room and whispered hoarsely, "I dinna know what you'll be wanting with all these boxes, lass, but nobody's looked at 'em in a hundred years or more!"

On the research trip in 2013 dedicated to *That Autumn in Edinburgh,* I wish to acknowledge the kind hospitality at The Royal Scots Club, a hostelry in that city that I discovered on TripAdvisor.com and is as wonderful as described during the heroine's stay there.

Perhaps the interview during my most recent foray to Scotland where several light bulbs went off in this novelist's head was a meeting in Edinburgh with Dr. Nick Fiddes, founder of **www.scotweb.com**, who shared the anecdote about the time he actually wore his complete Scottish attire to business meetings in America to woo potential investors for his online enterprise! He was also an invaluable source and "fact-checker" about "All Things Scottish," and allowed me to visit his latest acquisition, D.C. Dalgliesh, a legendary tartan mill in Selkirk where his general manager, Christine Payne, kindly showed me both the vintage and more modern equipment at the factory and even gave me a small, exquisite, keepsake swatch of tartan associated with Katherine, the Duchess of Cambridge whose Scottish title is HRH, The Countess of Strathearn.

One morning, after revisiting the haunts of Jane Maxwell of Monreith and the Fraser family across the street on the Royal Mile, I walked from Holyroodhouse Palace on one end, to Edinburgh Castle on the other. Next, I spent that afternoon at Jeffreys Interiors on North West Circus Place in fashionable New Town visiting the bespoke design emporium of Jeff Laing and Alison Vance whom I could not resist casting as themselves when Fiona arrives in Edinburgh for the first time, seeking the "look" she needs for her new Scottish Home Collection. The pair is just as talented and charming in person as I trust I have created them in fiction. Their knowledge of the world of up-market interior design was invaluable as I began to build the storyline for the hero and heroine.

The next leg of my journey to discover what Scotland is like in the twenty-first century was south of Edinburgh to the Borders where I was lucky enough to stay a few days at Traquair House, a stunning country home that figures prominently in the story. I wish to extend sincere thanks to Catherine, the 21st Lady of Traquair, along with Sarah MacDonald of her staff at Traquair, Innerleithen, for the warm welcome and incredible pampering I received at their elegant B&B, as well as a lovely breakfast during which Catherine helped unravel some of the connections between her family names: Constable, Maxwell, and Stuart. (We're still debating how close a connection she has to Sir Walter Scott. I say *yes*!) Incidentally, Cavalier King Charles Spaniels Daphne and Delilah were part of Traquair's official greeting party.

Thanks as well to the staff at Kirkbank House in Paxton, "just down the road," who advised the best food to be had was at The Cross Inn, and to the owners of The Bank House in Hawick—where I also got an excellent education in the history of Scottish weaving at the local Borders Textile Towerhouse Museum. (All these delightful places to stay can be found by putting the names into any online search box...)

In London, we were hosted, as we so often are, by dear friends of long standing, Bill and Fiona Orde and Anthony and Susanna Jennens, to whom my special love and appreciation will always be theirs.

As for gaining a more complete working grasp of modern tartan and cashmere manufacturing, I owe a huge debt of gratitude to "Jill, The Tour Guide" at the Hawick factory of Johnstons of Elgin and their "Cashmere Visitor Centre" where she showed me that amazing operation without a prior appointment. Deepest thanks are also due designer Leah

Robertson of Lochcarron of Scotland in Selkirk, who not only gave me an extensive tour of that state-of-the-art mill, but shared with me her knowledge of what textile, clothing, and home furnishing designers *do* on the job which helped enormously in the creation of the heroine's work world. Leah also knew of a lovely manor house, The Firs, which I drove over the River Tweed to see, that served as Alex Maxwell's home in the Scottish Borders.

I am deeply grateful to Jason Dyer, Executive Director of Abbotsford, the newly-refurbished nineteenth century home of Sir Walter Scott who graciously gave me a private tour of the house and grounds barely two weeks before Queen Elizabeth II was due to arrive for the official re-opening. Painters and carpenters and restoration experts were swarming all over the place, yet Mr. Dyer was warm and welcoming and a font of information about the life of the writer credited with creating the historical novel. Scott also had a connection to both the Maxwell and Stuart clans, which figured in my story, so seeing his home was a must—and if you go to Scotland, don't miss it!

A side trip to nearby Ayton near Berwick-on-Tweed resulted in one of the most amazing afternoons in my life as a writer. Twenty-five years earlier, when I wrote the novel *Island of the Swans* that chronicled the life of Jane Maxwell, I hadn't had the budget nor the opportunity to visit Ayton where a key event in Jane's life had occurred and I'd fretted about the accuracy of my fictional rendering of that pivotal moment ever since. It was at Jane's sister's home in Ayton that Jane, recently married to the Duke of Gordon, received word that the great love of her life had *not* been killed—as reported—in the Black Watch regiment on duty in the Colonies, and in a letter she supposedly received there, he wrote he was returning to Scotland to "make her his own"—but alas, too late.

My mission to Ayton was to see if the circumstances of the great tragedy of Jane Maxwell's life could be established in *fact*.

The accounts I'd read claimed that Jane opened the missive in her guest bedroom at the old Ayton House and ran, distraught, out of the house "to the nearby banks of the River

Eye," crying hysterically and then fainting beside its flowing waters. I had always wondered if that was how it *really* happened? Were the basic elements of the story "provable," given I had never found the lieutenant's letter in the archives, nor visited the region where the event reportedly took place?

The first thing I saw when driving into Ayton in June of 2013 was that a very large castle, then for sale, now stood where Catherine Maxwell Fordyce's home was said to have been before it had burned in the 1834. Fifty feet from the locked entrance gate to Ayton Castle was an enameled sign that indicated how close the property ran to the River Eye, which was my first encouraging sign that I was on the right path.

A few yards beyond the river (which indeed ran at the base of the hill where the long-gone Ayton House had been positioned) was a church surrounded by an enormous graveyard with hundreds of tombs and stone markers. I set about examining only the "mausoleums" built to commemorate the area's leading families.

Now, this may sound more than a bit woo-woo, but after speeding from one falling-down enclosure to another, I felt myself pulled toward a particular ivy-covered, roofless family crypt, and walked through the gate. *Eureka*! I screamed aloud, for I had found the graves of Jane's sister, Catherine Maxwell Fordyce, and brother-in-law, John Fordyce, and scores of graves of family members, many who bore names linking them to Jane and most of her seven children: Charlotte, Georgiana, Jane Gordon (a niece or great-niece named for Jane herself) and—the absolute kicker—a marker for a child named "Louisa"…a Fordyce named in honor of Jane Maxwell's red-headed daughter who—gossips of the day insinuated—had *not* been sired by the duke, but by the "Lost Lieutenant"—the love of Jane's life. Here my "intelligent supposition" as presented in *Island of the Swans* twenty-five years earlier came closer to being verified. And what a joy to be able to weave this part of the tale into "the rest of the story" in *That Autumn in Edinburgh*.

Much appreciation goes to my "beta readers," novelist Cynthia Wright, and a bevy of designers and/or interior architects including friend and fashionista Fiona Orde—who guided me through London's Chelsea Harbor Design Center—as well as Leah Robertson, Alison Vance, Diane Barr, Betsy Brawley, Millie Zinman, and Carol Kavalaris, who read earlier drafts of the manuscript and kept me "out of the weeds" regarding their professions. Susan Wintersteen, a friend and ace internet researcher, often forwarded juicy "fact-lettes" about Scotland she'd encountered, which were gratefully received. My sister, Joy Ware, gave the novel her usual and excellent once-over before it went off to the copyeditor/formatter, the amazing Pam Headrick of A Thirsty Mind Book Design.

And finally, I owe love and gratitude to my husband, Internet marketing consultant, Tony Cook, who is also a former financial journalist for such national publications as *Forbes, Fortune* and *Money Magazine*. He helped chronicle this journey with his wonderful photographs (one of which was used as background on the novel's cover) and made sage observations regarding the global challenges to Western manufacturers from textile factories in the Far East.

And now that I am home from my Scottish travels and have dispatched my latest novel into the world, it's plain to see what an adventure this most recent journey to the land of my own ancestors turned out to be.

Ciji Ware, Sausalito, California

Visit Ciji at:
http://www.cijiware.com

Facebook:
https://www.facebook.com/CijiWareNovelist

Images of the author's researches can be seen at:
http://www.pinterest.com/cijiware/that-autumn-in-edinburgh/

About the Author

Ciji Ware is the *New York Times* and *USA Today* bestselling author of eight novels and two nonfiction works. She is the daughter, niece, and descendant of writers (including William Ware, author of the historical romance *Zenobia*, 1836; Henry Ware, author of *On the Formation of the Christian Character*, 1831), so writing fiction is just part of the "family business." She has been honored with the Dorothy Parker Award of Excellence and a *Romantic Times* Award for Best Fictionalized Biography for *Island of the Swans*, and in 2012, was a finalist in the prestigious WILLA (Cather) Literary Award for *A Race to Splendor*.

An Emmy-award winning television producer, former radio and TV on-air broadcaster for ABC in Los Angeles, as well as print and online journalist, Ware received a BA in History from Harvard University and has the distinction of being the first woman graduate of Harvard College to serve as the President of the Harvard Alumni Association, Worldwide.

As a result of Ware's first novel, *Island of the Swans,* she was made a Fellow of the Society of Antiquaries of Scotland (FSA Scot), an honor she treasures.

The author lives in the San Francisco Bay Area and can be contacted at **http://www.cijiware.com**.

READING GROUP GUIDE

1. A substantial portion of the story concerned the efforts of the heroine and hero to unravel the mystery of what, ultimately, happened to their respective ancestors involved in a 250-year-old star-crossed love affair. Are there ancestors in your family whose fates you've wondered about? Why do you think becoming "ancestor sleuths" was important to Alex and Fiona?

2. Fiona tried to put her past traumas in North Carolina behind her by leaving her hometown and striking out for a career and life in New York City. How might events have transpired differently if she'd never left the circle of her family's influence?

3. Mortgage derivatives trader, Curt Vandervort, Bernard Sterling, and his employees like Fiona's classmate at design school, Jared Finnegan, epitomized hard-shell business types who worship the bottom line. Fiona viewed her work through a different lens. What were those differences?

4. The fictional Bernard Sterling had few qualms about charging high prices for less-than-quality goods made in factories where workers were most likely exploited. What other instances of that same business approach can you name? How have your buying choices been affected by what you read in the news about foreign-versus-domestically manufactured goods?

5. Alexander Maxwell, whose grandfather was the illegitimate offspring of a titled Scottish family and a housemaid, moves easily among all levels of society. What do you think accounts for this and how has he gained the respect of his peers?

6. Fiona, a seasoned professional woman by the time she is sent

to Scotland to research a new home furnishings collection for her American boss, is conflicted by her immediate attraction to Alexander Maxwell versus her duty to fulfill her research assignment. How significant do you think that conflict is in workplaces today and what is your view of the way the heroine and hero navigated these troubled waters?

7. Neither Fiona nor Alex can resist, nor explain, the uncanny attraction they feel for each other from the moment they meet. What is your opinion about the concept of "genetic memory?" Have you ever experienced something that seems almost "other worldly?" Do you think science will one day prove that our genes contain memories handed down from our forebears? Why or why not?

8. The novel explores the cultural links between the United States and Britain with specific reference to Scotland. How do you think our close ties with the "Mother Country" have impacted the U.S. over two-and-a-half centuries? Is that changing now because of new immigration patterns?

9. Alex Maxwell disclosed he was a married man at the end of the ferry ride he and Fiona went on around Manhattan at the beginning of the book. Do you think he would have been that "honorable" if she hadn't asked the question, "Tell me cousin, what lassies' hearts have *you* broken recently?"

10. There are several references in the novel about the importance of communication, especially due to the prevalence of cellular phones. How did Fiona's mobile device getting lost or stolen after her flight home from Scotland influence the subsequent year of her life? How do you think such instantaneous communication will affect the unfolding of both personal and global events in the future?

11. The novel grapples with issues affecting adult siblings. What did Alex come to realize about his wayward brother who

refused to take part in the family firm? Fiona often clashed with her twin, but eventually found a way forward both personally and professionally. What did they learn about coping with these sometimes tumultuous family relationships in terms of their *own* behavior?

12. Fiona must learn to "speak truth to power," as she says. Why is this difficult? What inner strengths do you believe are required to summon the courage to confront uncomfortable situations? Can you think of instances where you failed to speak up when you realized, later, perhaps you should have?

13. *The Skye Boat Song* is woven throughout the novel. Its words are haunting and speak of "what might have been." Why do you think the novelist chose this particular Scottish air?

14. For people who love Scottish pipe music, what do those sounds evoke for the listener? Why do you think people of Scottish descent the world over continue to claim their heritage many generations after leaving their homeland?

15. The hero and heroine must contend with a tumultuous and changing economy and forge a new business model in order to survive in their chosen fields. How common is this in other professions? What does this novel say about "outfoxing" those who would use devious means to wipe out their competition?

Book Groups can contact the author at:
http://www.cijiware.com

Made in the USA
San Bernardino, CA
24 March 2014